Eden

Also by Janet Mary Tomson

Garnet Fair
The Love Tokens
Devil On My Shoulder

Eden

Janet Mary Tomson

PIATKUS

First published in Great Britain in 1998 by
Judy Piatkus (Publishers) Ltd of
5 Windmill Street, London W1

This edition published 1998

*A catalogue record for this book
is available from the British Library*

ISBN 0 7499 0451 8

Set in Times by
Wyvern 21 Ltd, Bristol

Printed and bound in Great Britain by
Mackays of Chatham PLC

For Linda Delandro, and for all Afro-Caribbean Britons
who are a legacy of the Slave Trade.

Also, for the Isle of Wight New Writers' Group,
Who offered such unstinting support during
The Wilderness Years.

"There is a certain type of man who can tolerate any existence, provided he is independent, and his leisure can be relieved by heavy drinking and native women"

A Family of Islands, Alec Waugh

"I am black but I am comely . . . Look not upon me because I am black, because the sun hath looked upon me"

Song of Solomon, I

Foreword

This book was inspired by the adventures of the English Providence Company. In 1621 a group of puritan nobles took possession of three islands in the Caribbean: Providence, St Catalina and Henrietta. Their intention was threefold: to set up a profitable trading enterprise, to create a community based on the highest Christian ideals, and to take advantage of any opportunity to challenge the trading supremacy of the detested Spanish. Not surprisingly these aims were self-defeating.

In this tropical paradise where sin was to be unknown, discord soon broke out between the puritan idealists and the privateers and traders. Crop failures, disease and climate conspired against the settlers from the start.

The cultivation of tobacco and the consequent use of slaves caused moral dissent, but ultimately the desire to prey on the Spanish galleons that crossed the Main loaded with gold and silver proved too great a temptation.

In England, King Charles I gave tacit permission for the company to pursue a private war with Spain. Finally the might of the Spanish navy descended on the colony with devastating consequences.

The islands of Providence, St Catalina and Henrietta are now administered by Colombia.

Part I
The Year of Our Lord
1634

ONE

If Esmee Jackson had learned one lesson in life, it was to keep away from men. She did not need to think about it. It came as naturally to her as breathing. In her view men were quarrelsome, raucous and totally unpredictable – and she had plenty of experience to go on.

In her fifteen years, Esmee had spent less than one year on dry land. The rest of her life she had passed on board her father's ships. More often than not she was the only female on a voyage. Oh yes, she knew all about men.

But for tonight she deliberately sought out the company of old Ezra. He was one of the few exceptions, someone she had known ever since she could remember, even-tempered, patient – and apart from her father, the only other person to know the secret of her past.

Ezra had hinted at her story before, when the drink was upon him and her father safely ashore. Tonight was just such a night. Jeronimo Jackson was enjoying a last evening of freedom at Tilbury before the *Destiny* began her voyage to the Caribbees.

Most of the crew were confined below decks to save them from the temptation to jump ship. In any case, guards patrolled the deck armed with muskets and there was enough gin flowing aboard to paralyse every man's legs. No one would be going far this evening. Only Esmee and Ezra sat out in the darkening February evening. For their different reasons they were immune to the cold.

Ezra drank deep of the harsh Dutch waters. His skin was leathery, tanned the colour of mahogany by the elements. His expression reminded Esmee of a dried apricot as he screwed up his face, the burning liquid assaulting his throat. Earlier she had tried the brew herself. It took away her voice, leaving her gasping for breath. She shook her head as Ezra pushed the jug towards her. She was on the verge of a discovery. She wanted every sense to be honed razor sharp to capture the moment.

When he did not speak, she silently rehearsed what she had learned so far: *I was conceived a few miles out from the Guinea Coast, upon the body of a girl younger than I am now, singled out because my father liked the tilt of her breasts, the curve of her behind.*

Esmee faltered. The words were suspended like wood smoke in her head, hanging immobile in the windless, foggy haze. She could feel the cold blanket of their meaning embrace her – silky, enticing as spiders' webs. In their way they were just as deadly.

For a moment she paused, scratching her armpit. Her cheeks began to burn at the silent use of the phrases. Over the past months she had been secretly weaving her story. The raw materials were as hard to come by as the silk threads used by rich women ashore. Esmee had to wait her chance, be vigilant, store away every scrap of material she might glean.

Ashore, in the mansions where her father's masters lived, the daughters of the houses embroidered silks on to satins to make gowns, created lace for special collars, stitched tapestries so fine they almost seemed to come alive. Esmee was weaving her own private tapestry – the story of her life.

The words she used were not hers but those she had overheard. She knew that the sailors used them without thought, caring little whether she witnessed their uncouth speculations about her father, Jeronimo Jackson, their captain and master of the *Destiny*.

Before they sailed she hoped to add more strands of colour to her history. To herself, she continued: *I was conceived amid screams, in pain, on the flow of a sailor's lust and a black girl's terror.* When the sailors were drunk, their language poured forth like poetry. Esmee had to admit that these lines were even better than the shanties that they intoned on many a lonely watch.

She rested her hand delicately in front of her mouth so that Ezra should not see her lips moving. Silently she repeated the words to capture them. Later she would relate them to her invisible friend who lived inside her head. This might be the only time that the truth of her history was revealed. She must memorise it forever.

Reciting the tale by rote, she hoped that one day she would have a real friend who would listen open-mouthed and amazed to the adventures of the beautiful princess, Esmeralda Jackson.

Ezra had fallen silent.

Esmee said: 'What happened next?'

'Well . . .' The old man took another swig from the jug. He wiped his chin with the back of his hand and leaned against the rope coiled next to the capstan.

'I remember the night you was born.' He paused, giving emphasis to the event. Esmee tensed to receive his momentous description.

'What happened?' It couldn't have been an ordinary birth. Her mother was surely never like the other 'dinahs' that Jeronimo brought to his cabin at night. They were common slaves. At the end of each journey they went ashore, never to be seen again. In one of those moments of insight she realised that her father never knew if his offspring left the ship in their bellies. It was of no interest to him. But surely her mother had been special? Esmee was special. He had kept her alone of all the others. To what purpose? Face to face with the unknown, her thoughts quickly changed course.

Ezra digressed. 'A seaman knows the safest gal is a virgin. That way there's no danger of the pox. You learn that lesson young in life. Anyhows, it's miserable hard to find such a gal ashore, but along the coast of Africky . . .'

'What of my mother?'

'Mmm.' Ezra took another drink. 'Pretty she was, for a darky. That much I do remember. The ship was your father's first command. She was leaky as a bucket but . . .'

'My mother?'

Ezra acceded. 'Even then the Captain knew how to pick the ripest, sweetest fruit for a journey.'

At his words the blackness threatened. Esmee had watched her father often enough. Green eyes glazed with lust, breath fetid with the stink of stale rum, he would survey the new cargo, selecting, choosing . . . Mercifully, Ezra's monologue cut into her accelerating fear.

'It started off like any other voyage. We was carrying mostly bucks, picked up on the Slave Coast. Can't get enough of them, they can't. There's a good market out there in the Indies. Anyhows, the voyage was dogged by unfavourable winds and it took us nigh on six weeks to reach London. Once there we sold off some of the cargo but the majority was bound for the Antilles.'

He drank deep of the strong water. In the damp foggy evening, his grey whiskers glistened like fairy dust. Softly, he said: 'Such a long time ago.'

7

'My mother?'

'Well, afore we could revictual, the ship was hit by fever. Three weeks we was anchored outside the harbour here at Tilbury and no one allowed ashore. By the time we sailed the slaves had been more'n two months on board.'

The imagined stench offended Esmee's nostrils. That and the stink of fish had been with her all her life. Ezra shifted his position, slowly, painfully. Esmee thought how thin and shrivelled he had become. Even as a child she had thought of him as old. Now he was really so, sixty at the least. Soon he might die.

This slow unfolding of her history was tantalising. She wanted to shake him, shout at him. It might be the last chance she had to hear the tale, but she was afraid even now that he might change his mind. Her father would not take kindly to his life being discussed in this way, and on board ship nothing was secret for long.

Finding a more comfortable position Ezra at last continued with his tale and Esmee breathed a sigh of relief, letting out her breath gently so as not to distract him.

'Naturally your pa was anxious to get rid of the slaves as soon as possible, but that voyage was jinxed. When we reached Jamaica the Captain was struck down by fever. He was that sick his skin turned black. Near threw him over the side, we did. Anyhows, after several weeks he pulled through but by then the mate had done the trading and we was back at sea. Somehow yer ma had been over-looked. She was still aboard so she was charged with nursing the Captain back to health.'

Esmee held her breath. Surely there must have been some tenderness? Her mother had nursed her father, cared for him. Had he loved her in return?

'What was she like?' She scrabbled through her mind for a mental image, creating a composite picture of the prettiest women she had ever seen, bundled aboard, chained up, looked over by the officers. Her heart fluttered against her ribs, reaching towards the mystery of her life, grasping for the reality of her mother's experience.

Ezra sighed expansively. 'Can't rightly recall. I never spoke to her. She only had her own lingo. She was comely, though. She had spirit too – she needed it with the Captain. Anyways, when we got back to England yer pa kept her as his privilege slave. He would probably have sold her on the next voyage only, somehow, he didn't. By then her belly was big as a bladder.'

'That was me?'

'It was.' Ezra gave a little chuckle. 'I was the first to see ye. Little scrap you was. A few days later, yer pa was feeling – well, let's just say he wanted a bit of company. I said to un: '' 'Sno good you wanting her, she's just sprung a tiddler. Looks like you an' all.'' He was flabbergasted. I think the drink made him sentimental. He went down to have a look. When he saw you he said: ''Sprog's got green eyes, same as me – proper Esmeralda.'' That's what he called ye. I reckon if it hadn't been for your eyes . . .' Again Ezra hesitated.

'You think he'd have sold me?' Esmee willed him to deny it, to confirm her fragile belief that she was different.

Ezra shrugged. 'Don't rightly know. You never know with the Captain. A law unto himself, he is. Anyway, he kept you both, even though he moaned about the cost, but after a while yer ma grew sick and died, then he gave you into the charge of some black mammy until you was big enough to look to yourself.'

Accubah! Esmee had no trouble in remembering Accubah. Closing her eyes she could feel the warm safety of the black woman's hug, smell her reassuring sweat, hear the infectious laughter that had kept her own childish fears at bay.

Tears prickled for her unknown mother, her substitute mammy. Accubah, big and fleshy, not the sort of woman to inspire lust in Jeronimo. Esmee didn't even know if she had been his comfort slave, but she had stayed with them until her charge was about seven. Then, at the end of one voyage, Esmee could not find her.

'Where's Accubah?' She hardly ever addressed her father directly but she had searched the ship for so long, stumbling over cargo, wading through the putrid water of the bilges, climbing between stores of sugar and tobacco, peering through the gaps in piles of logwood. 'Where's Mammy?'

'Gone.'

'Where?'

'Sold. You're big enough to look to yourself.'

The pain of loss gnawed at her anew. Everything was outside of her control. It always would be. Although she had been with her father for fifteen years, at any moment he might decide to part with her. He had threatened to do so often enough.

To stifle the thought, she said: 'What was my mother called?'

Ezra's eyes jerked open. He had been on the verge of dozing off.

'Called? I don't rightly know. Dinah, that's what we called her. That's what we called 'em all – the Captain's dinahs – bit of a joke it was.'

In the darkness Esmee hugged herself, trying to find comfort. The last dinah had left the ship in Hispaniola. Travelling back from the Indies, Esmee had been the only woman aboard.

A frightening knot began to form just below her ribs. Tomorrow some thirty passengers, all male, would be boarding the *Destiny* – fervent, religious men concerned with the soul's salvation. There would be no place on this voyage for women of pleasure. Again she would be the only female – and men were always men . . .

Below them in the hold, the various calls of cows and sheep, chickens and pigs, echoed against the gentle lap of the water. The livestock had been loaded earlier that day. Some would supplement the diet of dried pork and biscuit on the outward journey but the majority were there for a different purpose.

This voyage was one of exploration. Her father had been charged to sail to the Antilles and there seek out an island not already claimed by the Spaniards and suitable for colonisation. When he found it the animals below, plus the passengers and some of the crew, were to be put ashore to claim it. By this time tomorrow night they would be out of sight of land.

Esmee sucked on the knuckle of her index finger. Her reverie was shattered by a sudden crash and the sound of curses. Like lightning she leaped to her feet and old Ezra scrambled up behind her. Tottering up the gangplank, swaying dangerously, was her father.

'What the . . .' He blinked at them both. 'What in the name of Lucifer are you two doing?'

'Just taking the air.' Esmee glanced at Ezra for confirmation. Covertly she studied her father, trying to assess his mood. Dear God, don't let him be in bad spirits!

Old Ezra stared at the Captain with bleary eyes. 'Looks like you've had a skinful, Captain. D'you need any help?'

Jeronimo shook his head impatiently. To Esmeralda, he said: 'Get below. I've got something for you.'

Quickly she stumbled down the ladder, her heart still beating too fast, her imagination flailing after some safe possibility. The cabin was stacked with bales and boxes, the air rank with rum and stale sweat. Jeronimo's hammock hung across the width of the room. It cast a dark shadow, menacing as the leathery wings of a bat.

Esmee made a dive for the corner where a pile of covers marked out her own bed. Here she slept each night, except when her father had company. Then she was unceremoniously turfed outside to make the best of it, curling up near the door, or if the elements were too rough, risking the narrow corridor that connected the Captain's cabin with the quarter deck. She suspected that none of the crew would dare to touch her, and yet . . .

She noticed that Jeronimo carried a large canvas sack. Swaying dangerously, he began to search about inside it, cursing quietly under his breath. Finally he hauled out what looked like a dark length of cloth.

'Here.'

Uncertainly Esmee reached forward to take it. The material felt smooth beneath her fingers. Holding it up, she realised that it was a woman's gown, deep emerald in colour, the bodice picked out in lace, the cuffs trimmed with fur.

She met his eyes. 'What is it?'

'It's time I got some return for keeping you all these years.'

'I don't know what you mean.'

Jeronimo tilted back his head. His eyes were bloodshot. For a long time he surveyed her in silence and Esmee froze into herself. She had seen him look at the slave women in the same way: assessing, choosing. Her gaze became riveted to his hands, clenched in front of him. At any moment his right fist might fly out at her, send her head crashing back against the wall. Then he would curse her for her stupidity, for the burden she imposed on him, for having been born.

To her amazement, he said: 'It's time we found a man for you.'

'I am to be married?' She almost dropped the gown in her surprise.

'Married?' He snorted. 'There's no gain in marriage, not for the likes of you.' The candle flickered crazily and he twisted his head aside, avoiding the direct light of the flame. Still he watched her, calculating.

His voice thick from the effect of too much rum, he said: 'Put it on.'

Turning her back, Esmee struggled into the gown, fumbling with the laces, dismayed by the tight bodice which emphasised the swell of her breasts. In the folds of her canvas shirt, her body was concealed, protected. She felt panic begin to grip her.

11

Jeronimo clicked his tongue and Esmee moved to left and right, the better for him to see. On land, men clicked so at horses, making them move. The touch of the damask against her skin was smooth as a snake. When she went to take a step, the fabric caught about her ankles, making her stumble. She'd had no idea a gown was so restricting.

'That'll do.' Her father belched and indicated that she should change. With relief she regained the safety of her own clothes, then she folded the gown and placed it in a wooden box beneath the bunk where Jeronimo slept only when he pleasured a woman.

He said: 'Out there, back in the Caribbees, we'll be calling at several islands. There'll be no shortage of opportunities. Every cove, every tavern, is full of lonely men. Rich men. Men with money.' He began to walk around her as if she were a mare he was thinking of buying, weighing up her worth against the cost. Then he stopped, his lips turned down in the semblance of a jaded, cynical smile.

Grasping her arm, he said: 'Don't you fret yourself, Chickadee, I'll see that you're well taken care of. But marriage . . .?'

He laughed.

TWO

The next morning, disobeying her father's instructions to stay inside the cabin, Esmee watched for the arrival of the passengers. By pushing the door open a fraction she had a clear though restricted view of the quayside, still littered with boxes and bales waiting to be loaded. A rickety board was thrown up to act as a gangplank and the crew formed a wavering ribbon as they filed up the incline, backs hunched, struggling under the weight of their burdens.

She was distracted by a sudden squealing. A black piglet which had not been crated up, wriggled free from the seaman who was carrying it aboard. Dropping on to the gangplank it wavered precariously. For a second it seemed certain that it would lose its balance and fall into the narrow strip of water between the *Destiny* and the harbour wall, but miraculously it found its footing and made a hasty if misguided dash for the deck.

For several minutes members of the crew dived to left and right in their efforts to catch it, just missing an ear, grasping for a leg, holding briefly to a tail, but the creature eluded them all. Esmee felt something of its fear, its need for protection. She wanted to rush out and save it, hold it close and defend it. She had never felt such a strange emotion before, an almost overwhelming need to care for something and keep it safe as once, long ago, Mammy had kept her from danger. But even as the thought claimed her she knew that the crew would take the piglet from her – and if Jeronimo were to see her on deck, he would take his whip to her.

Hardening her heart, she closed the door a fraction to distance herself from the creature's terror. Finally, driven towards the centre of the ship by a wall of sailors, the piglet made a last-ditch bid to escape, trying to scrabble up the tightly packed bodies that surrounded it. It was forced backwards and dropped heavily into the hold where its squeals took on a distant, echoing resonance.

Her stomach knotting with anxiety, Esmee turned her attention back to the quayside where a subdued group of men were making their way to the water's edge. These were the passengers. Inconsequentially she remembered her father's complaint: 'For every one of these noble saints, I could house ten slaves.'

The group seemed to form a composite whole, their warm, sober clothing of uniform quality, their mute demeanour binding them together. Only unmarried men had been selected for this voyage and mostly men with skills – carpenters, masons, planters and the like.

One or two stood apart in family groups, saying their farewells. Sons, daughters and parents waited in line for a kiss, a final blessing. A few wept. Others looked on awkwardly as if a display of feeling would be viewed as unseemly, the parting something to be got over with as quickly as possible.

Again Esmee was assailed by a concentrated outpouring of emotion. What must it be like to feel another person's tenderness, that strange, elusive love that the sailors sometimes talked of when they were in their cups and far from home? In her living memory no one had ever kissed her, blessed her with the touch of their lips. The only kindness she could recall was an awkward pat on the shoulder from old Ezra.

A few of the passengers were simply gazing at the ship, their faces tense, perhaps alarmed by what they saw, for the *Destiny* was not new.

Some two hundred tons burthen, she had been several weeks in dock for refitting. In spite of the work her timbers were still rotting, her hull patched with a criss-cross of planks, glaring as a darned stocking. She would not last forever.

The hire of the vessel by a group of English noblemen had come as a welcome surprise. Known puritans, the new masters were men governed by almost impossibly narrow ideals. Although Esmee's father had lied a little, pretended to a religious observance he rarely troubled himself with, he had not expected to gain this badly needed appointment. To everyone's surprise the commission had been granted. Esmee dared not speculate on the grimness of their future had he failed to secure it.

In the past the *Destiny* had many times made the triangular trip from the Thames to the west coast of Africa, then across the Atlantic. This time the route would be more direct: Plymouth, the Azores, then picking up the trade winds to Barbados. After that – where? From habit, she tried not to dwell on the future. It was beyond her control. Wherever they went it made little difference to her. She thought with misgivings that the cargo was not particularly to her father's liking and this would not improve his temper. His preferred voyages involved taking muskets and baubles to trade along the Ivory Coast in return for that most valuable of commodities: slaves. When they reached the New World, no matter that Spain was not a recognised trading partner, the colonists would be avid for this prized source of labour and prices would be high. Once the slaves were unloaded around the islands, the ship would be stocked with dye woods and spices, sugar, tobacco and other valuable cargo to sell in England.

Only then would Jeronimo mellow, show that incongruously sentimental side to his nature which Esmee found even more alarming than his usual, brooding self. Overwhelmed by a vision of him, sated with drink, calling upon her to sing, she began to suck her finger. *Come along, Chickadee, a little love song for your father.*

She could see him now, standing by the gangplank. A sharp wind blew into the harbour but Jeronimo appeared not to notice it. Esmee could see the golden hairs on his forearms bristling with the chill, still bright against his fading tan. From habit he fingered the tarred pigtail that held his flaxen hair in place, intermittently scratching his scalp. The back of his shirt billowed out and the canvas of his drawers clung damply to his thighs. He stood with legs apart, leaning forward into the wind. As the ship moved beneath him Esmee could see bare toes tense against the wooden deck.

He turned his head towards the horizon and, following his gaze, Esmee knew that soon the wind would change direction. Then they would be ready to sail. At such a moment there was always the same air of expectancy.

She had long since lost count of the number of crossings they had made, yet still each voyage kindled a flicker of excitement, even in her father. The day that feeling stopped, she knew Jeronimo would leave the sea forever.

Meanwhile the passengers were beginning to come aboard, clambering how and where they could to set down their loads.

Esmee's eye was caught by one man, younger than most, the gold of his hair and beard making him out like a beacon amidst the dark

15

uniformity of his companions. He was taller than average, well-built, and he carried himself in a fine, upright manner that made her forget for the moment where she was. As she watched he took it upon himself to help the heavily laden and the older men to find a comfortable space aboard the ship. For a moment Esmee had the feeling that there was another kind of life away from this cabin, one which she could only imagine, where people were good to each other. She opened the door wider and stepped up on to the deck.

The stranger was back on the quayside picking up goods. He paused to speak to one of the seamen who was on the point of disembarking. The sailor turned and pointed in Jeronimo's direction and the young passenger bounded back up the gangplank. His actions were nimble, the movement of a healthy man. He hardly seemed to notice the weight of the load he carried. As he reached the Captain, his youth and vigour were clear to see. Esmee moved closer so that she could hear.

'Captain Jackson?'

'Who asks?'

'Samuel Rushworth, sir. I have the honour to be in charge of the passengers on this voyage.'

'Do you now?' Jeronimo's voice could not conceal his resentment. Looking into the visitor's face Esmee registered the clear, unwavering gaze of an honest man, the eager demeanour of one who is intent on doing a good job. This was not the sort of man with whom her father could strike a bargain – one that would benefit them both and no questions asked. For a moment she felt as if the barren normality of her life was in danger of being swept away. The feeling was exhilarating yet dangerous.

Casually her father asked the stranger: 'What would you be wanting?'

'To check that all is well, see the quarters for the planters. I should like to be assured that there are sufficient supplies for us all.'

'Would you now?' Jeronimo's smile concealed an all too familiar contempt. Esmee knew her father's thoughts. Before him, for all his height and beef, his clear blue eyes and golden beard, stood a man barely past youth – and a landlubber to boot. Five minutes out to sea and he'd be heaving his guts up over the side. She felt the need to put him on his guard.

Rushworth said: 'May I look around?'

Esmee saw her father's eyes narrow. He was not used to being

16

questioned. Here, on the deck of his ship, he was God. No man challenged him.

As she watched, he bowed, an exaggerated show of courtesy. Holding the gaze of Samuel Rushworth, he said: 'Feel at liberty to go where you like, sir.' He swept out his arm, offering the ship for inspection.

As they both disappeared from view, a picture of the young man's face – his honesty, his innocence – was imprinted on Esmee's mind. He could have no idea what her father was like. She felt an overwhelming urge to warn him. Resting her cheek against the windworn edifice of the mast, she thought: Do be careful. Once we weigh anchor that will be all the liberty you'll get.

'What are you doing?'

Esmee jumped so much that her heart seemed to ricochet against her ribs. She had been so preoccupied with the thought of Samuel Rushworth that she had not heard her father's approach.

Before she could move, he grabbed her arm.

'You little fool! D'you want all and sundry to see you?'

Leaning close so that she could feel the heat of his breath on her cheek, he said: 'D'you want these holy fathers lusting after you? Stealing your maidenhead?' He continued in a low, confidential tone: 'Believe me, Chickadee, your girlhood's the greatest prize you've got. Lose that and I'll make you regret it.'

Hastily she stumbled back down to the cabin, her father close behind. Relaxing his hold, he seemed to change his mood. Flinging himself on the couch, he said: 'Go on, speak to me in French. That's a novelty, that is. And Spanish. Good job we've had all these foreign types aboard. They've taught ye something useful at least.'

Eyeing her shrewdly, he added: 'I hope that's all they taught you. You've not let any of them . . .?'

'No!'

Like quicksilver his expression changed. He looked her over, suspicious, calculating. For a terrible moment she saw in his eyes the same hunger that enveloped him when a new consignment of slaves came aboard.

Pulling away she began to recite: '*La mer est belle, comme une dame.*'

He grunted in satisfaction. 'Don't you let none o' them puritans see you, you understand?'

Nodding her head, she slipped back into her corner, crouching

17

down, trying to be swallowed up in the shadows.

This voyage was fraught with uncertainty. Esmee was always afraid, always on her guard, but for the first time there was something else. As the thought of Sam Rushworth came into her mind again and again a far more dangerous feeling swept over her. It was called hope.

THREE

As Samuel Rushworth boarded the *Destiny* for the final time, he was plagued by misgivings. He tried to tell himself that anxiety was only natural. In the past he had made several crossings to France and the Low Countries, but never had he undertaken a voyage of this magnitude. What was more, even if they survived the crossing, at the end of it they still faced the unknown. A catalogue of dangers ticked themselves off in his brain: fever, Spaniards, tornadoes, Caribs. His mind reeled with stories of just such disastrous adventures as the one they were about to undertake.

But there was something more. Although his uncle, Lord Craven, was an experienced trader, having many times both bought and commissioned naval craft, Sam feared that this time he had made a grave mistake.

In spite of the *Destiny*'s less than pristine appearance, as far as Sam could tell the ship was still seaworthy – and certainly Captain Jackson had experience – but it was the character of the man rather than his abilities that disturbed him. Could he be trusted? Would he abandon them along some swamp-infested coast, then return to England to claim his fee? It was entirely possible he already had plans to sell them all into slavery.

As Sam arranged his boxes and bags he could not stop the onslaught of such thoughts. One thing was certain: before they sailed he would send word to his uncle warning him not to pay up unless Jackson brought back written confirmation that all was well.

He became aware that someone was approaching and looking up, almost groaned aloud, for hurrying towards him, his face stiff with intensity, was the Reverend Praisetogod Shergold. As Sam stood up, he thought: In choosing this Minister my uncle has made another

19

mistake. There could hardly be another man of God alive who burned with such religious zeal.

Before Sam had time to speak, the Minister said: 'Master Rushworth, I must insist that you have words with the Captain. He has refused my request that we hold a prayer meeting before we set sail.'

Sighing inwardly, Sam said, 'You and our passengers are free to worship whenever you see fit.'

'He will not permit the crew to take part!'

Reasonably, Sam asked: 'Do they wish to do so?'

Praisetogod jerked back his head, his eyes huge with disbelief. His skeletal face worked feverishly. 'As shepherd to the souls of all those aboard, I must insist. Otherwise we cannot in conscience sail with such a heathen at our helm.'

With sinking heart, Sam said: 'I will speak with Captain Jackson.'

Cursing under his breath, he went to do so. Even as he approached there were signs of impending departure. Nippers scrambled barefoot among the rigging: agile, diminutive, dizzily high at the top of the three masts. On the deck teams of crewmen strained to raise the grey canvas, and the cargo was being checked over to make sure that it was secure.

Raising his voice, Sam called out: 'Captain, I have a request from the Minister that before we start our voyage we all join in asking God's blessing upon us.'

'No time.' Jeronimo shook his head, backing away to add emphasis to his words.

'A few minutes now might save a much longer delay. I fear the Minister feels unable to sail with you otherwise. He has a very tender conscience.'

Sam met the Captain eye to eye. Jackson's face was shrewd. He might be many things but he was not stupid. With a sigh he called out: 'All right, lads, just this once. As soon as we're at sea, I'll sort things out.'

Reluctantly the men assembled in the mist, still hungover, aching from the strain of moving the cargo aboard, suffering the effects of their last night in port. The passengers stood in a group, almost cowed by the enormity of the journey facing them. In silence they all waited.

Now that his entire congregation was present, the man of God stood on a coiled length of rope to provide himself with a pulpit.

20

As Sam joined them he thought that everything about the Minister suggested doom. Only his eyes, slate-coloured and fearsome, sparked with fervour.

In a voice wavering with emotion and with a gaze that surely saw into hell itself, Praisetogod Shergold raised his voice and began to lash the congregation with his invective.

'Holy Father, look with contempt on all these frail beings! Burn out the evil that lurks in this ship! Strike every man present with torments until the very devil is driven into the sea . . .'

The passengers stood with bowed heads, a few assenting to the justice of his words. Along with the crew Sam gazed blankly at the preacher, sharing their disbelief, knowing that every day would bring torment enough without inviting it through divine intervention.

Mercifully the tirade came to an end and everyone streamed back to their various activities. Sam returned to his pile of stores. He distracted himself by ticking off the list of things he had brought with him, having taken advice from experienced travellers.

Apart from his bedding and linen, he had twelve pairs of russet shoes, for he had been warned that black shoes turned mouldy and rotted in the twinkling of an eye. In the dank, poisonous climate that might face them, where worms burrowed into the soles of the feet and thorns thick as dagger blades lay in wait, it was essential to be well shod.

A pistol, powder, parchment, writing materials, wax lights, and of course a prayer book, were secured in a wooden box which bore his name in black lettering. In addition he carried eating utensils, a stewing pan, and his own chamber pot to ease the calls of nature during this hazardous crossing.

Sam tried to think positively about the life ahead of them but his motives for going were ambivalent. He was still smarting from the loss of his position as commissioning agent with the King's navy. On the face of it he had been dismissed because he had spoken out against an injustice. He had never been the sort of man to remain silent while bigotry reined, but the very fact that he was linked by blood to the Craven dynasty had gone against him too.

This had prompted his uncle, Lord Craven, to think of emigration. His plan was to take his entire family to the Indies and there found a new colony, but they had to tread with care. The chances were that King Charles would not permit them to leave the country.

Others had talked of similar ventures and been denied permission – after all, the mass emigration of noblemen reflected badly upon the court.

As a result, a vanguard was to go ahead to pave their way, and Sam was responsible for their physical well-being.

As he thought about it he felt ashamed because there had been another reason for his dismissal that his uncle knew nothing about. Sam had never intended it to happen, but during the winter months he had found himself conducting an affair with Leonora, Lady Righton.

To say that he conducted the affair was to imply that he had some control over events, which in fact he had not. Leonora had pursued him with single-minded determination, and he in turn had been swept along by the pleasure – and the danger – of it. He hadn't loved her but the heady prize of sexual gratification had blinded him to everything else.

Unfortunately the aged Lord Righton was an advisor to the King on nautical matters, so when the affair came to light, as it was bound to do, it was almost inevitable that the noble lord would use the excuse of Sam's puritan connections to rid himself of such an insolent puppy.

Anyway, it was no good fretting about it. If God willed it, then he and his travelling companions would found a new colony, a truly free and just society where men could follow the dictates of their consciences without fear. Perhaps the affair with Leonora had served some useful purpose after all.

Sam did not know any of his fellow passengers but their strength must lie in their unity of purpose. By this time next year, with God's good grace, they would be well on the way to making their settlement self-sufficient – and their sponsors rich. Not that they had any sponsors yet. That was for Lord Craven to arrange.

The echoing thud of wind against canvas alerted him to the heightened activity around him. Many passengers were now at the rails, gazing with mixed emotions at the land of their birth. Slowly Sam rose to his feet.

The last act that he had performed before boarding the *Destiny* was to visit his cousin, Serenity Craven. Both her father and Sam's step-father, the crusty Lord Silchester, had agreed that a union between Serenity and Samuel would be a good thing. Now they were formally betrothed.

22

Sam's feelings on the subject were disturbed, complicated. Of all his family, he loved his uncle the most. Aeneas Craven had been more like a father to him, a friend, the one person on whom he could rely. Sam would never let him down. To be a good son-in-law was now his mission in life.

Serenity was pleasing enough to look at but . . . Other anxieties plagued his already troubled mind. On the surface his cousin was so good, so devout, and in theory these should be excellent qualities in a wife, but Sam feared that beneath her show of piety there was something else, a hard, spiteful streak.

It was ignoble of him to think in this way, perhaps he was wrong, but even supposing he was, he still had doubts about the wedding. Unlike his uncle, Sam was not a devoutly religious man. He was leaving England for reasons other than some narrow doctrine. Justice and tolerance were more important to him than the strict interpretation of Christian dogma.

If it turned out that Serenity was a truly good woman, bound by strict codes of religious observance, then her piety would cast a pall over their future. It was foolish to think he himself could live up to such ideals. If on the other hand she was what he suspected, a spoilt, selfish girl who cared little for anything but herself, then she would not live up to his ideals. At the thought of his own standards, a treacherous sense of failure enveloped him – what he believed and what he did were two different things.

People pushed past him intent on witnessing the historic moment of casting off. He wandered back to the rail for one last, suddenly nostalgic look at England, but the memory of his cousin intervened.

He thought: Perhaps I do not deserve her. A tormenting voice added: Perhaps you do not want her.

FOUR

Lifting on the turning tide, the *Destiny* sailed smoothly out of Tilbury. At first she was nudged along by a following wind and she made one brief call at Plymouth to take on more passengers. She then struck out towards the south, hugging the coast of Spain before picking up a good trade wind to carry them on towards the Verdes.

At Bella Vista they stopped for water. A long boat was sent ashore to fill the quarter casks, repeating the journey many times until every pipe and butt aboard was filled. From then on, they would not stop until they reached Barbados. At the very best they would hope to be there in forty-two days.

Obeying her father's command, Esmee spent most of her time in his cabin. Only after dark did she venture out, avoiding the passengers, hiding herself by dressing in her bulky canvas togs.

For the first time since she could remember the barber surgeon had not shorn her hair. At certain times of the day she would glimpse her reflection in the single pane of glass that glazed the cabin's narrow window. The image was wavy, distorted, but the sight of her hair, the feel of it, carried her back to an earlier voyage when among a group of pilgrims leaving for Virginia, was a baby boy. The child was only two weeks old. His parents were young, demure in their dark clothing, but an almost tangible aura of peace emanated from them.

Once, when they thought they were alone, Esmee saw the young man kiss his wife. The woman closed her eyes while their mouths made long and gentle contact, and when her husband drew away, she smiled at him. Her expression was so serene, so happy, that Esmee had thought about it for weeks.

Then one day the woman let her hold the baby. 'Take care now. Support his head. He's that precious.'

Like holding eggshells, Esmee cradled him close. He was light as a guillemot. She clasped his tiny fingers, wondering at his perfect ears, smoothing the wispy fluff of his hair that was so like her own. It was a miracle. Gideon was the child's name. Esmee vowed that if ever she had a child she would call him Gideon and kiss his father as the baby's mother had kissed her husband.

Combing her fingers through her own sprouting locks, she wondered how she would ever find such a life for herself.

Her only other knowledge of love came from the unlikely source of Ezra. Somewhere in a village near Portsmouth Ezra had a family. When he was feeling mellow he sometimes talked of his wife as if she were a goddess, an angel. Even on long voyages, he alone of the crew did not force himself upon the black girls.

Distant conversations came back to Esmee, Ezra's voice husky and nostalgic: 'There was a time when I was horny as the rest, but now I've got everything I want in my Ada.'

'Is she beautiful?'

'Perfect as Eve.'

'Then how can you bear to be away from her?'

Ezra sucked the stem of his clay pipe, making rhythmic tutting noises, considering her question. When he answered his voice was dreamy. 'Ada's my wife, but the sea's my mistress. When she calls, I have to go.'

About two years ago Ezra had returned home to find that his wife was dead. The sweats had taken her. His children were married, working. They had moved on. It was then that he had started to grow old but even in his lonely times he had a secret, hidden place in his head where he went to remember. Esmee had no such place to go.

During the daytime she took to wearing the emerald gown so that she might grow accustomed to the strangeness of it. Perhaps in this rich, womanly guise she too would find an elusive love.

As she was fastening the ribbons one morning she became aware that somebody was outside the door. It was not her father for the person was still, waiting. A cold sense of fear gripped her and she drew back into her corner, making herself small. She tried in vain to hear above the pounding of her blood. At last the person went away and a reassuring silence returned. Esmee let out her breath with a great gasp of relief. Thank goodness, no one had seen her. But she would have to be careful.

25

*   *   *

'Is our good Captain wed?'

The question took Sam Rushworth by surprise. He was enjoying a few moments of solitude at the stem of the ship, marvelling at the spume, running in parallel crests until it clashed with the choppy after-flow of the *Destiny's* wash. The water was so turbulent that he could clearly see the keel of the ship as it sliced the water. Beneath them shoals of fish played tag. Of all the people on board, Praisetogod Shergold was the companion he least welcomed.

Biting back his irritation, he answered, 'I don't know.'

'Would his wife travel with him?'

Sam thought it unlikely. To Shergold he said: 'Why do you ask?'

'I – I've seen a girl. Not a decent woman.' The Minister's pale cheeks flushed, implying that the female on board was a slattern. He added: 'She don't look English.'

Sam shrugged, thinking it was none of his business, but Praisetogod would not let it rest.

'You must find out. We cannot in all conscience travel on this ship if fornication is rife.'

Sam chose his words carefully. 'Minister, seamen have their own codes of conduct. If the Captain has a "companion", I don't think he'll take kindly to our interference.'

Praisetogod's eyebrows rose in horror. 'You surely do not condone such iniquity? If the girl is sinful she should be punished, have it whipped out of her. If, on the other hand, she is held against her will, then we must rescue her.'

Sam sighed. 'I'll speak with the Captain, relay to him your fears.' He felt burdened by the scruples of the man of God. At the back of his mind he thought that their purpose in founding a new colony was so that people might follow the dictates of their own beliefs and not have other standards imposed upon them. By challenging custom aboard the ship they were in danger of doing just that, forcing their own morals upon these seamen.

But then, there were some things about which you had to speak up. Perhaps the Minister was right in his views. It would do no harm to find out if the girl was a willing participant or held against her inclination.

Reluctantly he knocked at the door of the cabin, wondering what he should say. Nobody answered. He was about to walk away when he thought he heard a sound inside. He knocked again. Now there was absolute silence but it was not the same thing as emptiness. He felt sure that someone was there. Uneasily he lifted the latch and put his shoulder to the swollen door.

The cabin was tiny and stank of sweat and alehouses. Disorder reined. As his gaze encompassed the room he was aware of the faintest movement to his right. Half hidden behind the door, he looked round to see a young girl crouched into the corner on a pile of sacks. She looked cowed as a whipped bitch, her eyes huge with alarm.

He stretched out his hand to calm her. 'There's nothing to fear. I just wondered if . . .' Thin and dirty she might be, but the girl was beautiful. Quite beautiful. Immediately he thought of a hind: slender, graceful, poised for flight. Her skin beneath the grime was a smooth, warm brown. Her black hair was jaggedly cropped but where it grew longer it curled in tight spirals. Her nose tilted, small and delightful, and her half parted lips were full, richly pigmented, utterly intoxicating. But her eyes, her huge eyes, green against the dark hue of her face . . .

For an eternity Samuel gazed at her. Something happened to him. He knew that from this moment his life would change.

Trying to take control of the situation but falling back on Shergold's prejudice, he said: 'Are you the Captain's wife?'

The girl continued to stare at him. She blinked quickly, still silent. In an attempt to reassure her, he said: 'I – we did not realise a lady was on board.'

'What the . . .'

Sam's pathetic attempts to recover himself were overtaken by the unseen arrival of the ship's captain. Jackson barged his way past, his chin jutting aggressively. 'What the devil are you doing, sniffing round my quarters?'

'Captain, I apologise. I had no intention of . . .'

Jackson swaggered up to him, throwing back his head. Looking at the girl crouched in the corner, he said: 'Got designs on my daughter, have you?'

Without taking his eyes from his unwelcome visitor, he reached out and grabbed Esmee by the arm, hauling her to her feet.

'This is my Esmeralda – well named, don't you think?' He twisted her this way and that, jerking her arm to make her move. Eyes lowered, she displayed herself, reluctance showing in every movement.

'Pretty as a picture, ain't she?' said Jackson, sneering at his companion's confusion. 'Growing into a real fine gal – one that a discerning gentleman 'ud pay well for.'

Sam's face burned with shame. Want the girl he did, totally and utterly. Never in his life had such a powerful emotion engulfed him. It was not simply lust, it was total and utter bewitchment. He knew it was useless to deny what was written all over his face.

Pressing home his advantage, Jackson said: 'I'm taking this pretty prize to the islands to find her a "husband".' His emphasis on the word indicated that the opposite was true. 'Speaks French, she does, and the Spanish lingo. Sings pretty as a lark and knows her manners. Ripe for training she is, if you get my drift.'

Sam felt himself growing angry. 'You are going to sell your own daughter?'

'Sell? Come, Mr Rushworth, what do you take me for? I'm merely looking for a gentleman of culture who knows how to appreciate an exotic bird like this, someone to take care of her if ever I should be prevented . . .' He raised his eyebrows and Sam knew that he was taunting him, making an offer – if the price was right.

Backing away, Sam said: 'I wish you well, Captain. I am sure you want what is best for your daughter.' He glanced in embarrassment at Esmeralda who was looking at him with what seemed like entreaty. He did not know what she wanted. In an effort to make things right, he said: 'I assure you that your daughter is safe from every member of our expedition. On this I give you my word.'

As he stumbled back outside, disturbed, shaken, his mind was filled with a vision of this wild, beautiful girl. Among all his other emotions, he had an overwhelming desire to rescue her – but from what, and to what end?

Again he thought that if it had not been for his affair with Leonora Righton he would not be here, on this ship, with this beauty. The other side of himself reminded him: You were happy enough until you saw her. But now he *had* seen her and there was no wiping away the vision, no unfeeling the emotion that even now threatened to sweep him away.

He forced himself to think of his uncle, and in Lord Craven's wake, Serenity, his betrothed. Serenity. So cool, smooth as thin ice and just as dangerous, threatening to pull him under.

Like cold water on hot iron, his soul steamed with the turbulent clashing of ice and fire.

FIVE

The following day several of the passengers fell sick of the flux. The illness was severe – fever, foul-smelling excrement, runny mucus, blood. Without treatment it was clear they would die.

For the first time since his encounter with Esmeralda, Sam managed to put her out of his mind. The passengers needed more of everything – water, food, medicines, blankets. He went to seek out Captain Jackson.

Jeronimo was about to retire for the night. At Samuel's approach he stood blocking the doorway to his cabin, frustrating any chance that Sam might have of seeing his daughter. The act had a deliberately provocative air about it.

Fighting down his dislike, Sam said, 'Captain, I must speak to you. There are sick men aboard. I hear you have given orders restricting the rations.'

Jeronimo raised a cynical brow. Sam knew that he was spoiling for a fight.

The Captain said: 'We have a long way to go. We don't know when we will reach land.'

Sam rose to the challenge. 'You think it is better to weaken the passengers now, when we may make good time and arrive with provisions to spare?'

'That's my order.'

'But some of the passengers may die.'

'I never guaranteed they would all live.'

His words shocked Sam into raising his voice. Too late he realised that this was what Jackson wanted. 'That's unforgivable! I protest . . .'

'Protest all you like. Any further insurrection and I'll have you clapped in irons. Now, kindly go below decks.'

Sam thought fast. He had no authority to challenge the Captain. One word from Jackson and the crew would probably throw him into the bilges. This was no time for a mutiny. He tried another tack.

In a more reasonable tone he said: 'It is my uncle, Lord Craven, who commissioned this ship. If you want to be paid, Captain, you had better treat those aboard like human beings.'

He saw the man hesitate. Suddenly Jackson grinned, but his eyes were black with malice. When he spoke he sounded conciliatory but the mocking nature of his words was clear.

'You must understand, sir, that I am responsible for everyone aboard. Such a duty weighs heavy. If I waste stocks now, others may suffer later. However . . .' He raised his voice as Sam started to object. 'However, I do not wish the sick to suffer.'

Calling out to the mate, he said: 'Get Mr Rushworth whatever he needs from the stores – but only for the sick passengers.' With a smile he added: 'The rest of us must tighten our belts.' Then, with an exaggerated bow, he stepped backwards into his cabin and closed the door.

Sam stood where he was, feeling humiliated and angry, but there was no time to dwell on his own hurt pride. The suffering passengers needed him.

Apart from the afflicted, the lower deck was deserted. The healthy voyagers, fearing contagion, had withdrawn from the stench and were taking their chances in the fresh air. Sam could not blame them. The atmosphere below decks was foul, but he had undertaken to care for the pilgrims and care for them he would.

He did what he could to make them more comfortable: cleaning them, keeping them warm, slaking their thirsts with the cordial he had brought for his own use.

As the night progressed the wind grew stronger. Each time the *Destiny* dipped and tossed she added to the misery of the sick. Finally, after being flung off his feet by a sudden violent bucketing, Sam scrambled up on deck to see what was happening.

Captain Jackson, his mate and an older seaman called Ezra were standing together, heads tilted back, gazing up at the rigging. High up a sail was flapping violently in the storm. With each gust it became further entangled in the ropes, threatening to tear and blow away.

'Who tied that?' Jackson's tone was terse.

No one answered.

The *Destiny* gave another sickening plunge, sweeping the feet from under those on deck. From all quarters men protested pain and fear. Only Jackson remained upright.

Cursing, he moved forward and began to climb the rigging, agile, sure-footed, going up and up until he looked no bigger than a gull. Sam watched tight-lipped as the Captain struggled with the sail. He felt a grudging admiration for the man.

Almost as if the wind was determined to frustrate his efforts it suddenly changed direction. An angry gust lifted the canvas and pulled it half away. As Jackson made a grab for it, the rigging sagged then tightened across the spar where he had a precarious hold. The rope formed a ruthless and ever-tightening tourniquet about his fingers.

Jackson cried out but his words were carried away on the gale. Even so it was clear that he was in trouble. After a few moments he seemed to lose his footing and for a terrible eternity he hung there, high above the deck, suspended only by his trapped fingers.

'For Lucifer's sake, get me down!'

Nobody moved. Time seemed to freeze and there was a horrible fascination about the situation.

Without allowing himself to think, Sam began to shin up the mast, clumsily, sick to his stomach with fear. The increasing distance between himself and the deck seemed elongated, taunting him, drawing him down so that he was afraid some devastating force inside himself would make him jump. He was terrified of heights.

Looking up, Jackson's legs were only a few feet above him. He was flailing about, scrabbling for a foothold. Getting one arm tight around the mast, Sam reached out and guided the man's foot on to a spar, then he eased himself higher so that he could reach the trapped hand.

The sight sickened him. Two of Jackson's fingers were being systematically sawn away. At any moment the vicious rope would cut right through and send the man plummeting down, for he was barely conscious.

'Hold on to me. Quickly, man, put your good arm around my neck.' He yelled at the Captain and saw the flickering eyes as he fought to remain in control.

Taking the weight of the man, Sam used all his strength to ease the rigging just long enough to get the fingers free, all the time afraid that he might trap himself in the process. With a moan of agony, Jackson's arm dropped to his side. One finger had gone and a second hung by a thread.

Sam heaved with nausea, having his own life and death struggle. Turning his head aside, he made his way down, first one foot and then another, guiding Jackson with him. At last hands were reaching out for them, taking the strain, lowering them on to the welcoming solidity of the deck.

Dimly Sam became aware that a young boy knelt at his side, facing away from him and towards the Captain. His mind was detached, ranging about to find some distraction that would enable him to get a grip once more on reality. He was struck by the way in which the boy was tending to his master. With wry amusement he thought that there must be some saving grace in this harsh man to inspire such loyalty.

At that moment the boy turned his head and with a jolt Sam gazed at the sweet, smooth profile of Esmeralda. In the salt-lashed gloom, her skin and soft hair were beaded with spray. A surge of excitement burst through him.

Her small, bare foot was resting against his thigh and the pressure of it was a joy. He lay very still, reluctant to end this delicious contact.

Meanwhile a sawbones had arrived. Without ceremony, he unrolled the sacking package he carried and took out a slender blade.

Realising what was about to happen, Sam's stomach muscles clenched. He must not disgrace himself. Breathing deeply, he shakily sat up, gulping back the spittle that filled his mouth.

The surgeon said: 'Right. Hold him down. Somebody grab his wrists.'

'You should purify the knife first – baptise it with flame.'

Esmee's voice was strong amid the cacophony of noise from the storm-battered ship. Men stopped and stared at her.

Before the sawbones could object, Ezra fetched a flint and a candle. Finding shelter between piles of stacked canvas, he made a light. The blade was passed through it.

With a glare at Esmee and a grunt of dismissal, the surgeon went to work.

Jackson growled his pain, swore and cursed, but even as the

damaged finger was severed he did not give full vent to his agony. Again Sam was sobered by the man's courage.

After the wound was cauterised and bound, Esmee sat back. Sam saw that she had blood on her cheek, and her canvas drawers stretched magically across her thighs. He longed to reach out and touch her. Her eyes were wide with emotion.

Along with old Ezra, she helped Jackson up and propped him against the foot of the main mast.

Impatiently he shook them off and yelled: 'Rum!'

A jug was pushed into his good hand.

His face was alternately grey and yellow but when he spoke, his voice was strong.

'Who tied that rope?'

Above them the storm had abated but the torn canvas still flapped. Those about him glanced at each other then away. No one was going to admit to such an error, or implicate anyone else.

'Don't! It was an accident!' Esmee glared at her father.

Beneath the outrage Sam could sense her fear and his heart melted in the face of her courage.

Jackson looked at her. 'Accident, Chickadee? A ship can't sail with accidents like that.' Addressing them all, he said: 'Don't be such fools. I shall work it out. First thing tomorrow morning, I'll have every man flogged until I get to the right one . . .'

Sam wondered what it was that gave Jackson such a hold over his men. Was it just brutality? He doubted it. Men like Jackson had some inner drive, a ruthlessness that made others obey them even when it was against their own interests.

For the first time he caught Esmee's eye and his thoughts scattered. Her eyelids flickered and she looked away from him. He wanted overwhelmingly to comfort her.

Keeping her head averted, she slipped past him and made off in the direction of her father's cabin. He watched her go, aware that Jackson was watching him closely.

Exhaustion and shock made him incredibly tired. He would have to do something about the floggings, he would have to do something about Esmeralda, but for the rest of the night there were the sick to tend. Heaving himself up, Sam walked unsteadily back to the torments of the hold.

SIX

Alone in her father's cabin, Esmee's mind was awash with emotion. Thoughts of the storm, of her father's accident and Samuel's bravery tossed her about like a chick dashed against savage rocks. Try as she might, she could not find her way into calmer waters. But one thing above everything else weighed her down. In rushing on to the deck in her sailor's garb, Samuel had seen her for exactly what she was, a common shameless piece of flotsam, no different from the other guttersnipes who escaped the sewers to serve as cabin boys.

In Samuel's world surely no woman would ever parade herself in canvas shirt and breeches. Without being told, she knew that it would be viewed as indecent. Her foolish dreams of being his princess crumbled into dust.

For the first time she cursed the garments that had until that day sheltered her from notice. Defiantly she changed into the emerald gown, then to keep her trembling hands occupied she scrubbed at the bloodstains on her breeches until her knuckles were skinned. As she pounded the rough cloth it dawned on her that Jeronimo's crude protection was all that she had.

Her turmoil was heightened by the arrival of her father, half carried into the cabin by two of his crew. With difficulty he scrambled into his hammock, nearly tipping himself out the other side. All the time he was mumbling to himself. He was very drunk.

The crew withdrew, sheepishly avoiding her eyes. She guessed that they were glad to be away from him and she glared at him with distrust.

To ease the tension, she said: 'If you'd fallen and broken your neck, who would have looked after the ship then?'

34

Jeronimo took a swig from the jug he still clutched in his good hand. He belched. When he spoke, his words were slurred.

'Me, die, Chickadee? Don't fret yourself. I've got a pact with the Devil, I have. I'll live forever.'

'Don't say that!' Esmee's insides tightened and she looked round hastily in case some beast from hell should suddenly enter the cabin.

Jeronimo grunted, thinking to himself. When he spoke, he wore a foolishly benign expression. 'Don't you worry. If your old father were to die, the *Destiny* would be yours.'

'Mine?' She stared at him in disbelief.

'Who else? Now come and say thank you.' He began to blow on his injured limb as if to cool some burning pain.

Esmee backed away, shaking her head, but already the rum had claimed him. Within seconds he was snoring.

Quickly she left the cabin and made her way to the deck. Nobody was aboard. A rash of stars splashed light on to an otherwise black world and in the ensuing greyness she could make out a school of porpoises. They travelled in formation, keeping pace with the ship, leaping like hurdlers. A few feet ahead a shoal of flying fish made an acrobatic dash for safety, some landing on the very deck of the *Destiny*. Esmee pushed them towards the rail with her foot, watching them flop back into the silver mayhem, giving them at least a chance of survival.

Her gown was thin but she ignored the cold. While she had been below decks someone had secured the sail and the wind, calmer now, carried them on at a steady pace. She fancied that some giant was blowing them along, his lips pursed in a continuous gentle outpouring of breath, like a man cooling his porridge.

For a while she closed her eyes and let her mind explore what her father had said. She was certain that he had only just made it up, but supposing he did die? Supposing she owned the *Destiny*? A whole range of possibilities clamoured for her attention but she did not follow any of them through.

Below in the hold the animals moved restlessly. Separated from them by a wall of stores, the sick men retched and groaned. In the stern of the vessel, healthy men tossed in their sleep. Esmee looked around her. Apart from the watch there was still no one in sight. Here, amidships, she was alone. She felt safe, invisible, strangely powerful.

She tried to imagine what would happen if Samuel came on deck.

She could almost feel him standing next to her gazing out at the silver-flecked waves, the star-studded heavens. Perhaps he had not recognised her in her canvas clothes. But she had seen his eyes: the surprise, and then what? Shock? Disdain?

Tendrils of grey began to separate the navy blue of the ocean from the black velvet of the sky. The reality of her situation pulled her back to earth. With a sigh she made her way back to the cabin.

To her relief Jeronimo still slept and she suddenly felt overwhelmingly tired. Curling up in her corner, she tucked the folds of her gown over her feet to keep them warm and sought refuge in sleep.

Almost at once she began to dream.

Three men sat in a tavern. The cloying smell of rum and the aromatic waft of dried tobacco mixed with the stink of stale sweat. Esmee knew they were in Barbados.

Hands resting on their haunches, the men leaned forward, hungry, expectant, gazing at a girl crouched in the centre of the floor. It was herself.

With her bare feet she could feel the dusty earth beneath the rancid straw. Her skin tingled with dry heat and the smoky fumes from the fire stung her eyes. The faces that studied her were so clear that she knew she would recognise them anywhere.

The first was large and jowly, tufts of tangled black beard mingling with the mane of hair that hung to his shoulders. About his brow he wore a spotted kerchief. His mouth, half open, revealed blackened, broken teeth. She turned her head away from the waft of decaying breath.

The second was small and thin, his nose sharp as a cutlass, eyes pale and hungry in his emanciated face. Wispy hair hung lank about his neck and a large sore was weeping pus from the corner of his mouth. Esmee gagged.

The third man, yellow-haired, face lined by the elements, regarded her with a half-smile, mocking, greedy, a glint in his shrewd green eyes, choosing, selecting . . . It was her father.

Esmee screamed.

She awoke to an empty cabin, trembling, expecting the men still to be there. Of them all, she'd feared her father the most.

A knock on the cabin door brought her safely back to the day. Cautiously she opened it to see old Ezra.

'Your pa says you're to come on deck, missy. Everyone's to be assembled.'

36

'What for?' She smoothed the crumpled gown over her hips and raked her hair with her fingers.

'Captain's hell-bent on finding whoever tied that rigging.'

Esmee's heart missed a beat. She should have known it! Fearfully she followed the old man outside.

Up on the main deck the assembly split into two separate groups. It was a natural division: the crew on one side, looking sullen, rebellious; the passengers facing them, their faces anxious, mystified.

Jeronimo stood in the centre. In his good hand he held a bull whip. His injured arm rested across his chest. His face was grey and every now and then he bent forward, rocking slightly as if from pain, but he paid the limb no attention.

Looking around him, he said: 'There's some missing.'

Ezra answered: 'There's sick men still below.'

'Get them.'

A few moments later Samuel Rushworth appeared on deck. Esmee drew in her breath at the very sight of him and slipped back out of sight.

Confronting Jackson, Sam said: 'What do you think you're doing? There are two men below at death's door.'

'Fetch them.'

The sick men were carried up and laid, groaning, on the deck. One of them immediately vomited and lay in the mess, whimpering to himself.

Ignoring them, Jackson addressed the gathering. 'Yesterday one of the crew failed to carry out his duties. He was slipshod. I won't have that. It near cost me my life.' He looked around slowly, his green eyes moving from man to man. His voice dangerously low, he said: 'I'm waiting for the scum to own up – or shall we start the floggings?'

To a man the crew lowered their eyes, refusing to meet his gaze. The passengers looked at each other in dismay.

Esmee's mouth was dry. She fought the urge to run away. Clinging to any form of comfort, she thought: When this ship's mine, I'll never flog anyone.

As nobody came forward, Jackson surveyed the crew again.

'You.' He pointed with his whip at one of the younger seamen. The lad's face blanched.

'It weren't me, Captain.'

'But we'll start with you anyway.'

37

The mate and the appointed whipper closed in on him and the lad tried to back away. Already he was yelping.

A distraction to his right stopped the men momentarily. Esmee looked round and to her amazement Samuel Rushworth was peeling off his fine linen shirt. Flinging it aside, he stepped forward.

Esmee had lived close to men all her life but this man's torso was more beautiful than any she had ever seen. For the most part the crew were scrawny men, tight-muscled but lean. Only her father, who ate better than his men, was broad in the shoulder, but he was older and his build was smaller. She covered her mouth with her hand to hold back her mingling love and fear.

Facing her father, Rushworth said: 'You can start with me.'

'Passengers don't count.'

'Why not? You said you were responsible for everyone. We in turn feel responsible for each other. If someone made a mistake, then we're all equally to blame.'

Behind him one or two passengers shook their heads uneasily but no one spoke. The atmosphere was so tense that Esmee found it difficult to breathe. She wanted to rush forward and shield Samuel with her own body. Whatever happened next would be terrible. There would be no turning back.

Glancing at the whipper and his mate, Jackson said: 'Hold him.'

They released the trembling lad and grasped Samuel by the arms. He made no attempt to resist.

Staring at Jackson, he said: 'You want the culprit punished. That's not unreasonable. I'll strike a bargain with you.' Looking round, he said in a louder voice: 'If the man owns up, I'll pay Captain Jackson compensation. When we get to our destination, the guilty party can be set ashore with us to work off his debt.'

With the exception of those too sick to know what was going on, no one was moving. The assembly waited for Jackson's response. In his disconcerting way he suddenly laughed.

'I must say, I admire you, Mr Rushworth. You'd make a fine magistrate.'

In the ensuing silence a single muffled sob broke the air. A young boy, little more than a child, moved forward. Almost incoherent with fear, he said: 'I couldn'e help it. I tried but the wind was too strong. I didn't know this would happen.'

Sam reached out and patted the boy's arm. To Jackson, he said: 'You have your culprit. I have five guineas in coin. Will you take that?'

Jackson shrugged. There was a subtle new unity between the passengers and the crew as they waited for him to reply. Esmee knew that her father was aware of the danger of losing face. Flinging aside his whip, he said: 'Five guineas for two fingers, Mr Rushworth? You drive a hard bargain.'

The tension eased and men shuffled with relief. Just as it appeared to be settled, the Captain added: 'I'll take the money and let the boy off the whipping, but he's got to learn his lesson.'

Turning to the mate, he said: 'Load him up.'

There was a murmur of disquiet from the crew, mystified silence from the passengers. Esmee felt her heart sink. This was one of her father's favourite torments. Looking across at Samuel Rushworth, she caught his eye and gave a warning shake of her head, begging him not to interfere. She knew that her father had been pushed far enough. He had to claw back some of his power. Cross him now and he would react with violence.

The boy, Ignatius, was dragged across the deck, his wrists bound and his arms stretched out until they were near pulled from their sockets. In this position he was bound to the capstan. Nearby three members of the crew began to load cannon balls into two nets. There were fifteen in all.

It took two men to hoist them up and the burden was flung across the boy's shoulders. Under their weight, he sagged, held upright only by the cruel rope about his wrists. He was crying.

To old Ezra, Sam said: 'How long will the boy be expected to stay like that?'

'"Til tomorrow, I reckon.'

'Tomorrow? The weight will break his back! He'll be crippled for life.'

Ezra shrugged. 'The Captain's a hard man,' he conceded.

Doing a quick calculation, Sam raised his voice. 'Captain, seeing as you're hell-bent on punishing the boy, I think we should reduce the compensation. After all, you can't expect both.'

Giving his words time to sink in, he added: 'For every hour he stays there, I shall deduct a crown.'

'I never agreed to that!'

'And I never agreed to . . .' Sam looked across at the tormented child. Producing the coins, he held them out so that everyone could see. He asked: 'When will you release him? In one hour? If so, I shall hand over five pounds.' He removed one crown. 'In two

39

hours?' He went to take back a second crown, but Jackson snatched the money away, his face dark with anger. 'Give me the five pounds.'

For a moment he simply stared at Samuel then once again he seemed to draw back from a direct confrontation.

To the mate, he called out: 'Cut the nipper down at the next watch.'

With a wry nod of his head, he added: 'Well now, Mr Rushworth, you're determined to have your own way, aren't you? Is there anything else aboard you object to?'

Instinctively Sam turned his head in Esmee's direction and she met his eyes. Their clear, honest compassion made her heart soar, but the look was not wasted on her father. With a sudden savage ferocity he grabbed her, pulling her forward, shaking her until her teeth rattled.

Keeping his eyes on Samuel, he hissed at her: 'What are you doing, flaunting yourself here on deck?'

She could think of nothing except that it was Samuel, not she, who was in real danger. With a superhuman effort she tried to suppress her fear, to hide her pain.

Shoving her roughly, her father said: 'Get down below deck and stay there. If I see you up here one more time, it will be you not that nipper across the capstan.'

Again, for the briefest second, she met Sam's eyes. He looked outraged. As he opened his mouth to speak, Esmee implored him with a last look not to interfere. Summoning as much dignity as she could, she walked across to the companionway and stumbled down it out of sight.

A terrible sense of hopelessness bore her down. She was the child of a cruel, treacherous man. If Samuel felt anything for her it was as he did for the boy lashed to the capstan.

As she pressed her bruised arms, finding the tender places, one question burned in her brain: What could a kind a noble man like Samuel Rushworth ever want with such as her? The answer was glaringly obvious. Nothing.

SEVEN

Over the following weeks, more passengers fell sick of the bloody flux. Regularly Praisetogod Shergold came to pray with the afflicted, urging them to cast off their sins so that God might see fit to restore them to health. His exhortations were to little effect and within two days, five of the ship's passengers and four of the crew had died.

It fell to Praisetogod to perform each funeral service and he did so with zeal, commending each passenger to God, condemning each crew member to the Devil, and consigning the corpses to the sea.

Samuel, as both nurse and undertaker, found little time to rest. When exhaustion drove him to close his eyes, he was assailed by unresolved problems. What was he to do about Esmeralda? To escape from his worries he indulged in wild dreams of rescuing her, smuggling her from the ship and on to some island paradise where they would live in harmony, or challenging her father to a duel for the right to her heart. The reality was very different.

When he tried to clear his mind he was faced with stark and unpalatable facts. First of all, whatever his feelings, he could never be more than a benefactor to her. He had given his consent to his betrothal to Serenity. He would not betray her. He could never betray his uncle.

There was another more immediate problem. Before the settlers had set out from England it had been agreed that this advance party should consist only of unmarried men. Theirs was to be the harsh and dangerous task of carving out a new settlement from hostile surroundings. Unity of purpose, trust in each other and faith in God were to be their tools.

Although Sam did not entirely agree, it was generally held that women were by their very nature weaker, more inclined to self-indulgence. They could not help but arouse both passion and division among men. Hence it had been expressly agreed that no woman should be part of this community until it was firmly established, by which time decent puritan girls would be shipped out from England to take on the roles of wives and mothers. How, then, could Samuel even think of taking Esmeralda with him?

The thought of her wild, exotic beauty, surely designed by God – or was it the Devil? – to inflame men's passions, filled him with immediate and all-consuming desire. Would not other men, deprived of women, be equally stirred, and then what sort of chaos would follow? Meanwhile, they sailed ever nearer to Barbados.

In a moment of torment he confided his dilemma to Praisetogod Shergold, citing a hypothetical but similar case.

Praisetogod had no doubt as to the best course. His advice was sharp and clear. 'If this man is betrothed then he must fight all devilish attempts to lure him into sin through weakness of the flesh. 'Beware this girl, I can feel that she is evil. She will ensnare a devout Christian, cause his damnation. Such a temptress is surely Satan's own creature!'

Sam struggled to paint a more rational picture. 'But if the girl be ill used by her father, should he not . . .?'

'Honour thy father – that is the Commandment! No ifs or buts. If this harlot defies her patriarch, then God will heap coals of retribution upon her. Go and pray, my son. Resist temptation!'

In despair, Sam walked the deck, immune to the spume stinging his eyes, the constant dipping of the deck beneath his troubled feet. There seemed to be no answer.

He encountered Ezra keeping watch. 'When will we reach Barbados?' he asked.

'Tomorrow, mebbe. Assuming we're on a true course.'

'What happens if we aren't?'

Old Ezra nodded his head as if confirming some theory to himself. 'The island's devilish hard to find. If we overshoot 'tis wellnigh impossible to go back against the winds. Captain just might decide to continue.'

There was some small comfort here, some gleam of hope, but as the hours passed, Sam knew that sooner or later he would have to act.

In order to keep Samuel from danger, Esmee spent the next few days in the cabin, giving her father no excuse to find fault. The hours hung heavy. Since the night they had set sail he had made no further reference to his plans for her but she knew that it could only be a matter of days before they reached the first of the islands. What would happen then? Would he really take her ashore and sell her to one of his cronies? She began to scrabble about in her mind for some glimmer of hope, but try as she might there was little to offer comfort. The only way was to escape – but to where and to what? Thinking of the destination that awaited Sam and the planters, she wondered if she could hide until they reached the island, then get ashore, unnoticed and conceal herself until the *Destiny* set sail. Once she was safe she would offer herself to Samuel, as his maid, his hand servant, or his own true love.

Her daydream was interrupted by the arrival of Jeronimo, carrying a bucket of water.

'Here. You'd best get yourself washed up. We should reach Barbados by nightfall. We'll be going ashore and I want you to look your best.'

'What's going to happen?' Cold water splashed over her feet as he banged down the bucket. She ignored it. Something far more serious was to come.

'Happen? I'm going to introduce you to some friends of mine.'

Before she could reply, there was a knock on the cabin door. Without taking his eyes from her, Jackson called: 'Come.'

The door creaked open and Sam Rushworth bowed his head, taking a tentative step into the cabin. Esmee's heart leaped. At the very moment she needed him, he had come to her rescue.

'Captain, I must speak to you.'

Jeronimo raised his eyebrows. Esmee knew that he was feeling pleased with himself and that Sam's arrival offered a further chance of amusement.

Samuel said: 'I have come to ask you not to call at Barbados.'

Jackson looked at him in surprise. 'You must be the only man aboard who does not wish to set his feet on dry land.' He eyed Sam curiously before saying: 'We must land. We need to take on water and fresh fruit. Besides, I have letters to deliver to the Governor and –' he gave a glance in Esmee's direction '– I have some business of my own.'

Esmee blushed with mortification. It was almost as if it was she, not her father, who was conducting this shameful trade.

Samuel said: 'I – I have been thinking. I would like to make a bargain with you. It concerns your daughter.'

He looked at her and she lowered her eyes. She knew that her entire future was about to be decided by his next words.

Sam said: 'I have little money but my uncle . . . I will make you a promise. If you will agree to take Esmeralda back with you and hand her over to Lord Craven, I guarantee that he will pay you twenty guineas on my behalf.'

'Fifty.'

'I – it may be years before I have that much!'

'You forget that I shall have to keep her. It will be months before we get back to England.'

Esmee could not look at them. They were bargaining over her like dogs sparring over a bone. Her worth was being measured out in guineas. Her father's greed and Sam's patent disapproval humiliated her in a way she would not have believed possible.

Samuel sighed. 'So be it. When you hand Esmeralda over, in good health, my uncle, Aeneas Craven, will pay you fifty guineas – on condition that you do not see her again.'

Esmee looked at her father, searching for some sign that he cared, but he merely grinned. 'You drive a hard bargain,' he jeered, and held out his hand.

Ignoring it, Samuel said: 'I would ask that you permit your daughter to leave this cabin. I should like to walk with her on deck. She needs fresh air and exercise.'

'Think you own her, do you?'

Sam scowled. 'I am thinking of her well-being.'

'So am I. She ain't yours till I get payment.'

Sam raised his voice. 'Do you think I would do her harm? Do you think I'm some oaf who will ill use her then cast her aside? In that case, I will go straightaway and write you a letter to give to Lord Craven. Then you will have your guarantee.'

Jeronimo made a gesture of compliance. He said: 'So be it. Walk the decks then. Sweet talk the girl. Makes no odds to me.'

Weighed down by shame, Esmee obeyed her father's nod of the head and fled from the cabin with Samuel following behind. She began to suck her knuckle, seeking comfort. She felt worse than she had ever done in her life. This man, her hero, had bought her like a common slave in a market. She was his property now, not a princess, not even a free woman. Her earlier dreams seemed too foolish to bear.

She slowed to a halt and Sam rubbed his strong brown capable hands together, eyeing her with an expression which she could only interpret as pity. She knew that her body smelt dirty. But there, slaves were always dirty. A tear fought its way from under her lid and wavered on the curve of her cheek. She dared not draw attention to it by wiping it away. In despair she thought: He does not even care enough to keep me with him. I am being shipped back to England like a sack of cane, for strangers to enjoy.

Sam said: 'Right then, shall we walk?'

She followed behind, unable to look at him. He glanced round at her several times before saying: 'I don't know how much your father has told you, but he – he had plans to marry you off while we were here and I felt that perhaps you wouldn't . . .' He seemed to be struggling for the right words and Esmee fought to keep her expression blank, not to show her feelings.

Sam tried again. 'I – as a result, I thought that it would be better to send you back to England. My uncle, Lord Craven, is a man of great honour and kindness. He will take you into his household.'

'I am to be his comfort slave?' Her voice wavered dangerously.

'No!' Sam shook his head. His expression was shocked. 'You don't understand. You aren't a slave at all.' He hesitated. 'My betrothed lives with her father. I am sure that she will be kind to you, help you to be a – lady.' He paused, eyeing her as if he doubted such a transformation were possible. Esmee's eyes pricked again with tears of humiliation. His betrothed! What a fool she'd been to think he might care for her.

He started to talk again. 'I myself will be several years here in these islands. It is my duty to take control of whatever place your father finds for us until such time as other settlers come from England. In the meantime you will be safe. Believe me, it is for the best.'

For the best? She could not dispel the sense of shame, of hurt and rejection.

In silence they both stood with heads bowed. Awkwardly Sam looked out across the endless ocean.

'What birds are those?' He spoke to break the tension, adding: 'I have seen them hundreds of miles from land and yet they never appear to rest.'

Esmee looked up at the dark wheeling silhouettes which seemed to balance on invisible air currents. Hardly trusting her voice, she

45

said: 'We call them sea hawks. Sometimes they rest on the backs of turtles. They dare not land on the water for fear of being pulled down by the fish below the surface.'

As she spoke she thought she was just like the birds. If she remained long in Sam's company she would be sucked under by her feelings for him.

Before she could stop herself she asked: 'Could I not come instead to the island with you?' Even as she spoke she could hear the hope in her voice and cursed herself for betraying her feelings. Frantically she tried to claw back some vestige of dignity, adding: 'The settlers know so little of life in the tropics. You are going to need people with experience.'

After too long, he replied: 'That would not be possible.'

Esmee turned away. The pain of his rejection crucified her. With an ill-concealed attempt at indifference, she said: 'Of course, I would prefer the climate of England.'

She began to walk back towards the cabin and when he did not speak, she added: 'Thank you for your interest in me. I bid you good night.'

'Esmeralda!'

Her heart lurched as he called her by name. Slowly she turned to face him. He looked pained, at a loss. He said: 'Forgive me. It isn't what you think. I too would wish for a different future but as it is, my duty to my family and to this mission mean that I must act in a responsible way. Please say that you understand?'

She didn't. All she understood was his beauty, the vivid blue of his eyes that bathed her with their longing. All her self-imposed strictures to keep away from men were forgotten.

For a blissful moment she thought he was going to take her in his arms and she was oblivious to everything but his presence, but suddenly other voices began to intrude. They were no longer alone. With an audible intake of breath, Sam stepped back.

Away to the west, the distant haze that had seemed no more than a darkening shadow between land and sea was transformed into a first intimation of land. Barbados. The name was repeated by the settlers gathering on deck.

Sam bowed his head, accepting defeat. To Esmee he said: 'You must not go ashore at Barbados.'

She looked at him enquiringly and he added: 'Your father might change his mind. About . . .' He shrugged, clearly embarrassed at referring to the nature of their bargain.

As she lowered her eyes, reduced to a piece of merchandise again, he added: 'But before we reach our final destination, I hope you will agree to promenade with me one more time?' As if some explanation were needed, he said: 'Exercise is good for the soul.'

She nodded, drawing comfort from the prospect, and even as she watched he was swallowed up in the clamour of pilgrims looking ahead to their new beginnings.

EIGHT

Long before they reached the Indies, Jeronimo Jackson knew exactly where he would find the perfect island. He had been there before on one of his roving voyages, looking for spices and new crops to take home.

Its disadvantage was that it was some eighty leagues further west, adding considerably to his regular journeys. Its advantages, however, were manifold. The island was only small, not much bigger than six miles long and perhaps four wide, but it had all the essentials to sustain life – fresh water, a good fertile soil, a heavily wooded interior and an abundance of edible plants. It was uninhabited. To himself, Jeronimo called it Fortune. He could not wait to get there but first he had this other call to make.

As he had predicted, that same evening the distinctive outline of Barbados, with its high central tangle of trees, finally emerged from the haze. Jeronimo had stopped there many times before and was not keen to linger although he knew his passengers were counting the seconds until they set foot on dry land. In his view the settlement at the Bridge was an unwholesome place, too low-lying and susceptible to bad vapours.

Now that he had no business of his own to conduct ashore, he suggested that they should stay only for a few hours, setting sail again the following morning, but to his annoyance Samuel Rushworth announced that he had a letter of introduction to a planter called Sir Hastings Hawthorne and insisted on looking the man up.

When Jeronimo could not hide his irritation, Rushworth added: 'If I am to establish a successful settlement wherever we find land, then I need to gain all the knowledge that I can.'

Jeronimo took the helm himself and guided the *Destiny* into

Carlisle Bay, fretting at the delays ahead. Some twenty ships rode at anchor there and he scanned them to see if any of his cronies might be ashore.

It was true that they would have to take on water and he did have a letter to deliver to the Governor, but that would not take long. Still, he brightened at the prospect of a few hours drinking away from his holy passengers.

During the voyage he had conceived an unreasoning hatred of Rushworth. Such a saint! He despised the man's decency but the uncomfortable thought remained: that most of all he envied him his youth, his unconscious ability to attract Esmeralda like a moth to a flame. Jeronimo spat into the wind.

As they dropped anchor in the bay and the first boats were lowered, he consoled himself with the thought that he could spend some time looking around for a profitable cargo, or indulge in a few pleasant hours' distraction in one of the stews, but even as this occurred to him, the prospect of such a pleasure was snatched away.

As Jeronimo made to leave the ship, Sam Rushworth approached him. 'When I visit Sir Hastings on the morrow, I should be obliged if you would come with me,' he said.

'Why?'

Sam did not immediately reply and Jeronimo felt a malicious pleasure in his confusion. 'You think that I might sail without you, Mr Rushworth – or do you perhaps fear that I might find some better deal than the one I struck with you for my daughter?'

Seeing the settler's anger, he added: 'Don't worry yourself. I wouldn't find a better bargain anywhere.'

At first light the next morning Jackson accompanied his unwelcome passenger to see over the plantation. He felt uneasy. It was low tide and the exposed mud stank, its stench permeating the whole of the bay. The Bridge Town was only just recovering from its latest outbreak of the plague. So many men had died that there had been barely enough left alive to give them a burial. Many had been flung straight into the bogs and now the water was contaminated by rotting bodies. This was no place to linger.

'Let's not miss the tide,' Jeronimo said to Sam, but the younger man ignored him. Instead they traipsed around the estate while Samuel inspected acres of sugar cane, toured woodlands and pastures, ginger and cotton fields, boiling houses and cisterns, and studied the construction of Sir Hastings's house.

49

Jeronimo cursed and fretted. He wanted only to be away. It was still the dry season. He needed to get his unwelcome human cargo unloaded before the rains came and be on his way home. Aboard he still had barrels of biscuit and butts of ale which he could sell in Hispaniola, or exchange for sugar or woods and spices.

As he trailed behind Hawthorne and Rushworth, he calmed himself by considering the voyage so far. All in all he was pleased with the outcome of this mission, not least with the bargain he had struck with Rushworth for Esmeralda. The thought of it cheered him up. None of the planters or privateers in the Main could have been persuaded to part with half that amount for a girl, not even a pretty thing like his daughter.

The sight of Sam Rushworth, avidly swallowing every piece of information offered to him by Hawthorne, increased Jeronimo's feeling of victory. This Englishman, with his high moral views and sense of duty, made life devilish hard for others. Thinking of his daughter, Jeronimo knew that in Sam's situation, he would have taken the girl somewhere quiet, had his fill then cancelled the agreement, thereby saving himself fifty guineas. But Rushworth would never do that. He was a man of honour. Slapping his thigh with sudden good humour, Jeronimo thought to himself: What a burden!

Five days out of Barbados, word spread among the passengers that their destination should be reached the following morning.

Esmee, confined to her father's quarters and sustaining herself with thoughts of Sam's half declared feelings of love, began to panic. If he did not come to her this evening then there would be no further chance for them to be together. As the hours darkened, her fears increased.

With every passing second her confidence seeped away. Perhaps she had been mistaken about what he felt? She began to realise that his words could be open to different interpretations. When he had hinted at wanting another future for himself she had assumed that he had meant one with her. Now she admitted to herself that he could have meant any one of a dozen things. When he had called her name, perhaps it had been pity, not love, in the tremor of his voice.

A sudden desperation gripped her as she came face to face with the devastating reality of her future. In essence she had been purchased by a dutiful nephew as a gift for his wealthy uncle. Samuel, so kind that he gambled with his health to care for the sick, so brave that he risked his neck to rescue her father, so compassionate that he faced a beating to protect a young boy, was prepared to buy her for another man's pleasure. True, he might have done so out of kindness, because her father could not be trusted to find her a decent home, but the knowledge that he was capable of such an act reduced her to despair.

She jumped to her feet, feeling an almost panic-stricken urge to get out of the cabin. She wanted to run and run, to get away from herself, only there was nowhere to go. Brimming over with pain, she wrenched the door open to find the exit blocked by the figure of a man. Samuel.

'Esmeralda?' He looked at her in concern, adding: 'I was just coming to see if we might take a turn around the deck?'

Her feelings were so out of control that, try as she might, she could not hide them.

'Whatever is wrong?' He reached out and touched her shoulder. She shook her head, not trusting herself to speak.

Sam gave a sigh. 'You are distressed. What is it? Are you ill? Are you afraid of going back to England?' He hesitated. 'Are you afraid of your father?'

She continued to shake her head. In the recesses of her mind Samuel's mention of her father made her realise how little he knew about her. Fear of Jeronimo had been with her all her life. It was nothing new. Nothing to get upset about. It was a fact of life.

'Come.' He led her out into the narrow corridor, finding a quiet niche between bales of canvas intended to make tents for the settlers' early nights ashore.

He turned her to face him. 'Now then, what is it? You must tell me.'

He took her by the shoulders, forcing her to meet his eyes. Eventually she blurted out: 'I was afraid . . . afraid I should not see you again.'

He pulled her closer, resting his cheek against the crown of her head so that she could not see his expression. Her own cheek nestled against the linen of his shirt, absorbing the warmth of his body.

Finally he pulled back and looked down at her again. He smiled tenderly, reassuring her with his eyes.

'You have nothing to fear. My uncle is truly a good man. He is not the sort to betray a trust.' After a moment's hesitation he added:

51

'And I am trusting him with something infinitely precious.'

'But you are sending me away.'

By way of reply he held her close again.

All her life Esmee had learned to distance herself from men's looks, and from their touch. Now her body seemed to have a will of its own. Here, close to Samuel, her arms longed to close about his waist, her breasts to flatten themselves against his chest, her mouth to seek his out. She wanted to press ever closer to him, to feel his answering arousal, for him to fill the emptiness inside her.

'Esmee.' Sam was pressing back against her. His mouth found her neck, her shoulders, his hands crushed her breasts. For the first time in her life she gloried in a man's hunger for her. Then, with a supreme effort of will, it was he who drew back.

'No. This must not be.'

Esmee hung her head in shame. She had exposed her own need to him and he was rejecting her.

He said: 'One day . . . Perhaps one day things will be different.'

'How?'

He did not answer.

Tears began to flow down her cheeks. She could not prevent them. Until this voyage she had expected nothing from life. Sam had taught her the cruellest lesson of all – that there was beauty in the world – and now he was stealing it away from her.

'I shall never see you again,' she said.

'You will. One day I shall go back to England.'

'To marry?'

'That is a long time away. It is for God to decide.'

She bowed her head. This puritan God held a power over men she had never known before. At sea there were always powers to be appeased – the winds, the tides, fevers – but they were external forces which could be influenced by sacrifice or ceremonial. They did not control a man inside so that he was helpless to shape his own destiny. Samuel's God held his very heart, his will. Against Him there was no intecession.

Sam said: 'We must have faith. I shall pray for you every day.'

Esmee said nothing. Crushed by despair, she knew it would never be enough. She turned away and started back towards the cabin.

'Goodbye, Samuel.'

'Esmee!'

In order to survive she did the only thing possible, she closed her ears and hardened her heart to the man who had become dearer to her than life.

Standing on the deck of the *Destiny*, Samuel received his first glimpse of the land that was to be his future home. His mind was in such a turmoil that his only wish was to find Esmeralda and put things right, but already the planters were coming up on to the deck. He could not deny them their wish to share this historic moment. Instead he stared hard at the distant rolling bank of breakers tumbling over an outcrop of rocks.

His visit to Sir Hastings Hawthorne's plantation had not been reassuring. In spite of the wealth of information he had received about land clearance, sugar cultivation, corn crops, timber, the fact remained that the colony of Barbados could not survive without regular supplies from England. Sam feared that the same would apply wherever they settled.

Then there was the vexed question of slaves. Leaving aside the moral issue, Sir Hastings had assured him that a negro could pay for himself in eighteen months, but from what Sam had seen, the need for security to prevent them escaping, the incidence of sickness and the brutal imposition of punishments, all added to the weight of a planter's difficulties. He turned away from this latest worry and looked back out to sea.

In spite of his own confusion, he could not help but share the settlers' awe at the sight of the smooth, inky blackness of the waters, at times kissed by indigo as the sun skirted a few pale clouds. Away in to the distance the sea suddenly changed to aquamarine, warning of shallows beneath. The whole was a moving tapesty of infinite patterns.

As the passengers gathered, the dark outline of an island transformed itself from an indistinct hump into a clearly layered land mass – dense trees at the crown, vibrant grassy slopes skirting the middle, and sable-coloured sand mottled with sun-splashed cream edging the irregular coastline.

Sam's heart began to beat faster. Somehow he managed to push thoughts of slavery, thoughts of Esmeralda, aside. Later he would find a chance to talk to her again. He must make her understand. They could not part with her thinking badly of him.

Searching among his belongings, he drew out the log he was keeping each day in readiness for the time when he would report on their voyage to his uncle. He recorded his first, emotional impressions.

Praisetogod gathered the faithful and, echoing his name, thanked the Almighty for their safe arrival. It was a premature step. Around the coastline, rocky outcrops and sudden shallows made it impossible to land. For several hours the ship battled its way against the wind to the leeward side of the island, finally reaching what seemed to be the only navigable habour.

Sam tried to concentrate on the landscape ahead of him. On each side of the channel, high cliffs offered a natural fortification. This was where they would settle.

At his side, Praisetogod said: 'I think we should call this place Emmanuel, in thanks to God.'

Sam did not reply. He already knew that this island, with its lush green gown of vegetation, must be called Esmeralda.

As the *Destiny* was guided into the shallows and the anchor tossed over the side, Samuel was among the first to leap into the water and wade ashore. The sea was warm as blood and he felt a strange, almost giddy feeling as he stepped above the water line, planting his feet firmly apart in the scorching sand in order to keep his balance on this unnaturally still land.

Several of the passengers fell to their knees and touched the ground with their lips. Others had tears in their eyes. It was an emotional occasion.

Behind Sam, Jackson was already organising the unloading. When he perceived one of his crewmen to be too slow about his business, he lashed out with the hide whip which was his most constant companion.

Sam had little time to absorb anything of the landscape. Already the settlers were gathering around him, waiting for guidance. In truth he was not sure what they should do first. He did not want to look a fool in front of the seamen and neither did he feel able to ask their advice. He therefore made it his first priority to pitch tents, high enough up the beach to avoid the tide but not too near the woods in case of surprise attack from man or beast.

It was Ezra who took pity on him, offering a few words of encouragement.

'Best to collect some timber first. You'll need fires to cook on and to discourage wild beasts. You'll have to pen the livestock too. And you'll need barbacus – bed frames to keep you dry at night and away from climbing pests.'

'Such as?'

Ezra shrugged. 'Snakes, spiders . . . any number of things.'

Sam tried to hide his alarm. 'Have you been here before?' he asked.

Ezra shook his head but said: 'I've been to a dozen other islands. They're all different and yet they're all the same.'

Sam nodded at him, his face feeling tight with anxiety. He had the dreadful feeling that his own ignorance would land them all in disaster. Assuming an air of confidence which he did not feel, he sent a party off to collect wood and water. In the meantime the pile of stores was growing ever bigger.

'How many men will you leave me?' he asked as Jackson finally waded ashore.

'Don't know that I can spare any.'

Sam felt the frustration he always did when face to face with this man. Trying not to lose his temper, he said: 'It was part of the agreement. You promised to make up the numbers.'

'Have you forgotten I too lost men with the flux? I can't sail this crate single-handed.'

In the end, Jeronimo offered five crewmen: a small, wiry monkey of a man named Hezekiah Martin, a sharp-faced sailor called William Axe, a sickly youth known as Rory, young Ignatius who had endured punishment for neglecting the sail, and old Ezra. Looking at them, Sam wondered if they would be more help or hindrance.

'When will you sail?' he asked Jackson, trying to put some normality back into the situation.

'With the tide. If we don't go then we'll never get past the rocks.'

Sam nodded, too dispirited to speak. It would be foolish to pretend that he wanted Jackson to stay, but the thought of facing his responsibilities caused his belly to knot. And then, of course, there was Esmeralda.

Looking across at the *Destiny* he thought he saw somebody on deck. The figure was there for only a moment then he, or she, disappeared.

Jeronimo followed his line of sight. 'Is there anything you've forgotten?' he asked, his voice malicious, taunting.

'Nothing.' Sam turned away, unable to say what he wanted. Show Jackson the intensity of his need and the Captain would home in on it like a hawk on a fledgling. In any case, what was there to say? Esmeralda could not stay and he could not go back. There was an end to it. It was the bleak and immutable truth.

Jackson rubbed his hands together and Sam glanced at the mangled fingers. The Captain seemed impervious to the so recent injury. Again he wondered what this man was made of.

Aloud, Jackson said: 'I'll chivvy the men along, collect what we need to get us to Hispaniola.' Flippantly he added: 'We'll be gone at first light so don't bother to see us off.'

From the deck of the *Destiny* Esmee watched as the crew unloaded stores on to the beach of Samuel's island. Samuel himself was on the sand, surrounded by planters. Even from a distance she could see that he looked distracted and a faint hope lingered that he might suddenly come wading back to the ship to take her ashore. After a few moments he looked across at the ship and she quickly drew back out of sight.

Turning her head, she could see her father knee-deep in the water, encouraging his men with a curse here, a blow there. She knew that he would be anxious to move on quickly for there was no cargo readily available on the island to take back to England.

She tried to fight down the nightmarish feeling that once they left this place Jeronimo would break his word to Samuel and sell her off at the next port. Even if he did not, the idea of being taken to England and handed over for some noblemen's pleasure was a worse prospect than she could bear.

For a while she felt incapable of thought then her head cleared. She made up her mind. Whether or not Samuel came, tonight she would escape, wade ashore and hide in the woods until the *Destiny* sailed. By the time her father missed her it would be too difficult for him to turn back against the tide. Since she would make the decision, Samuel need not feel guilty. Once they were together his natural feelings would overcome his qualms.

Almost immediately it occurred to her that her father might check out the cabin just before sailing. She would have to wait until the very last minute then slip over the side.

Now that she knew what she was going to do, the black burden lifted. Best to get some sleep and be fresh for the morning. Esmee curled up in her corner, thinking that this would be the very last time she slept in her father's cabin.

Yet sleep would not come. She felt a strange sense of anxiety. Much as she wanted to be away from here, in leaving the ship she was abandoning the only security she had ever known. Out there was – what? Out there was Samuel. He was betrothed but what did that matter? Nearly all the men she had ever known had wives or sweethearts somewhere across the globe. With the exception of Ezra it seemed to make precious little difference to them. Anyway, Samuel's other life was a world away. She swallowed down her fears.

Sometime after dark her father stumbled into the cabin, grumbling to himself. As usual he stank of drink. Lying very still Esmee pretended to be asleep, listening as he lumbered about bumping into things. Finally he hauled himself into his hammock and within seconds he was snoring. Meanwhile she lay awake hour after hour.

As the smoky wisps of dawn curled their way above the horizon she heard Jeronimo drag himself from his bunk. Esmee feigned sleep, waiting for the moment when he left the cabin so that she could make her escape. But as her father went to pass through the door, he hesitated. Without seeing, Esmee knew that he was looking at her. She heard him grunt to himself then after a moment he stepped outside. Seconds later her fate was sealed by the heavy sound of a bolt being drawn across the cabin door.

NINE

There are certain times in a man's life when all thought, all normal activity, seems suspended, as if the enormity of the moment sweeps away the ability to think or feel. For Samuel, standing on the shore of Esmeralda Island, it was just such a time.

Gazing at the outline of the *Destiny*, he felt paralysed by his inability to influence events. Everything that he wanted was there, twenty yards out to sea, embodied in the person of Jackson's daughter. He had only to swim out and bring her ashore. Nobody would try to stop him. As the elected leader of the expedition, nobody would argue with him – and yet he had agreed that no woman should form part of this community. He could not be the one to break this vow.

While his companions began to fashion themselves shelters of a sort on the white sand above the shoreline, he elected to remain on guard, knowing that sleep would be impossible.

Throughout the night he watched the black silhouette of the ship. The air, so hot the evening before, was now cool and a heavy blanket of dew soaked his hair and clothing but he made no attempt to find warmth. Gradually his body was becoming as cold as his heart.

As the first hint of dawn intruded into the night sky, he heard rather than saw the activity aboard ship. Before long the outline of the *Destiny* was transformed as her sails unfurled. He listened to the groaning of ropes as the great anchor was hauled aboard, strained his ears to catch the odd phrases that drifted on the wind. Standing immobile, icy as marble, he watched his happiness drift away.

Perhaps a mile out from shore, the *Destiny* began to curve towards open sea and finally her diminutive outline was eclipsed by

58

the rocky peninsula to the north of the island. Captain Jackson, the *Destiny*, and Esmeralda were gone.

One by one the planters began to emerge from their tents, looking across at the empty space where the ship had anchored last night. Each was cut off in his own private world. Pushing aside his own turmoil, Samuel prepared to take charge.

'Right,' he said, 'first of all we'll divide into four groups.'

'Surely first of all we must pray, build ourselves a place of worship?'

Sam felt his flesh tingle with irritation but he swallowed back his feelings, turning instead to Praisetogod Shergold. The Minister stood slightly apart from the rest of the men as if afraid of moral contamination. He too had suffered his share of sickness and his narrow face was ravaged, yellowed by fever, emaciated by the vomiting that had tormented him throughout the voyage. He looked older than his years, being only in his late-twenties, but his pale, sunken eyes still gleamed brightly with zeal.

'Reverend, I think the Lord will understand if first we give some thought to the needs of our bodies. If we should all die then the noble purpose of our voyage will never come to fruition.'

'If we have faith in God, He will protect us.'

Sam felt a grudging admiration for this man's fortitude. To ward off further objections, he added: 'Perhaps first of all we should all be silent in prayer?'

He glanced at the men around him: the pious settlers intent on a higher mission, the lean, indifferent crewmen, hardened by a lifetime at sea, stripped of finer feelings by those sights they had witnessed, the punishments they had experienced. Soberly he thought: Between these men of God and the men of the ocean is a void wider than heaven and hell.

When prayers were over, he said: 'This morning, one team will begin to clear that site over yonder.' He nodded to a plateau of land to the north of the inlet where a tangle of vegetation made an impenetrable wall. 'I want it cleared, flattened and areas marked out for six dwellings. You can slash the undergrowth away and burn it.'

Turning to the group of men to his right, he said: 'And I want you to take axes and go into the wood up there and select some good timbers. Group three,' he looked to his left, 'will start digging out fields for cultivation. We'll take it in turns, day by day, to split the labour.'

To the final team he announced: 'For today you will separate. Three of you will take the shallop and go fishing. Stick near to the coast and make your way around as far as you can without losing sight of the harbour. Look out for anything of interest and report to me – and bring back food we can cook at sundown.'

This left two members of team four, plus Praisetogod and himself. With sinking heart Sam realised that the Minister would always be his companion.

'Right,' he said, thrusting the thought away, 'the rest of us will begin our exploration of the island. We shall catalogue streams, rivers, plants, birds and animals, and anything else which might be of use to us.'

They each ate a portion of biscuit washed down with ale from the one cask grudgingly put ashore by Jackson, then they again attended prayers beneath a large palm tree where one day soon the village square would be.

'Keep it short,' Samuel said to Praisetogod. 'We need to use the day well, get as much done as we can.'

'Duty to God comes before everything.'

The sermon finally at an end, Samuel, Praisetogod, Seaman Axe and old Ezra plotted their course north. William Axe, armed with an eponymous weapon, hacked a path ahead of them. With sticks and musket butts, Samuel, Shergold and Ezra beat the undergrowth to afford some clearance. Progress was painfully slow.

The heat and moisture was such that it produced trees taller than Sam had ever encountered, their trunks seeming to reach up to the very heavens. The spreading branches formed a dark canopy through which light penetrated in sharp, jagged shafts, leaving pockets of black on the ground below. He tilted back his head to study the jungle roof. Nothing was familiar. Never had he seen such birds, such an array of colour. Never had his ears been assaulted by such a cacophony of sound.

'Mind your step.' Thomas Axe's warning brought him back to earth, where the undergrowth at his feet teemed with insect life. He was just in time to see the smooth green movement of a snake swallowed up by parting leaves.

'Is that poisonous?'

The men about him shrugged. There was nothing for it but to pick their way ahead.

After a while they reached something of a clearing. Trees with shaggy fibrous trunks formed a near circle where sunshine penetrated to the ground. The long smooth leaves seemed to act as a cradle for pendulous green sickle-shaped fruit that bunched beneath them.

'I wonder what these might be?' said Sam, running his fingers over the outer casing.

'Plantains.' Old Ezra took a knife and cut a bunch from the tree. 'They'm good to eat, boiled or fried.'

Sam nodded his head, heartened that someone among them should have some local knowledge. He asked: 'How do we know what is safe to eat and what not?'

Ezra screwed up his eyes as he looked into the branches above. 'Watch the birds,' he said. 'Don't eat anything they avoid.'

It seemed like good sense. Sam asked: 'And what of the birds? How do we know which are fit to each and which not?'

Ezra shrugged. 'Some taste good as chicken, others are more like fish than fowl. See there?' He pointed into the trees.

Sam followed the direction of his finger. 'That white bird with the yellow bill?'

'Aye. The one with the long tail feather. That's a tropick bird, plump as a partridge. Makes good meat.' Ezra raised his musket and brought one down. The bird flopped to the ground then lay in a crumpled heap on the damp soil, twitching until its head gently sank to the earth.

Ezra wiped his hand across his mouth, nodding to himself. As he picked up the dead bird he said: 'Trial and error, that's the only way.'

Sam shouldered the burden of the plantains and they trudged ahead, Praisetogod raising his voice and obeying the dictates of his own name.

After some two miles' walking they came to the northern coast where the island rose fortress-like from the sea, the cliffs offering little chance of any surprise landing. Seabirds clung to the crevices below them. Samuel refused William Axe permission to be lowered over the edge in search of eggs. One thing they did not have in their party was a surgeon. If any man fell sick or was injured he would have to take his chance.

For a while they stood looking out across the restless blue of the waters. A short distance away to the north, another island, cone-shaped, poked its head from the enveloping ocean. One day soon

Samuel would sail across and explore it.

By now they gauged that it was late afternoon. For the sake of speed he decided to return along the path they had already hewn over the hills. It would do no harm to take a second look. Perhaps it would become one of their highways: Rushworth Street. Sam's lips twitched with amusement.

Tomorrow they would travel south, again through the centre of the island, and after that they would make their way around its coastline.

'What's that?' It was William Axe who alerted him, pointing into the shadows of the woods where a dark, solid shape rooted among the trees. Samuel screwed up his eyes, trying to make out the creature's outline. In the shade it appeared to be black. Moments later a familiar grunting sound reached them.

'It's a pig!' Before Samuel could stop him Shergold raised his musket, already primed, and took aim at the shape. The flash, the blast and the squeal were almost simultaneous. 'Thanks to God!'

'Damn you!' Samuel turned in anger then strode towards the writhing creature. 'You fool! This is a sow – look, she was near time to farrow. We should have captured her.'

Ezra said: 'This pig is not a native of these parts. She must have been left here by rovers. Like as not she's the only sow on the island.'

Sam glared at the servant of the Lord and added: 'And you've killed her!'

Praisetogod went white, but not with remorse. When he spoke his voice vibrated with emotion.

'Captain Rushworth, your tongue offends the Lord! I demand in His name that you fall on your knees here in this clearing and ask forgiveness for your blasphemy!'

'Blasphemy be . . .' Samuel bit his tongue. Fighting his annoyance, he struggled to be calm, saying: 'Minister, your actions have deprived us all of a valuable source of sustenance. I must remind you that while you have the spiritual care of our party, it is I who am in command and responsible for our bodily welfare. Never, ever forget that.'

The Minister glared at him and Sam knew that this was a battle of wills. Then, with a dramatic gesture, Praisetogod fell to his knees, abasing himself, throwing handfuls of soil and leaf mould into the air. 'Lord, Lord, forgive this sinner. He knows not what he does!'

Tight-lipped, Samuel looked at the wide-eyed expressions of the two seamen. William Axe raised his eyebrows a fraction, unable to disguise his amusement, and Samuel relaxed. Suddenly he felt confident, in control. If it came to making a choice then he knew that the men would obey him, even if he was in conflict with the shepherd of their souls.

Reaching out, he helped Shergold to his feet, saying, 'That's enough, man. I entrust my spiritual welfare into your capable hands, but meanwhile it grows dark. You can finish praying when we get back.'

So saying he turned on his heel and his three companions followed. By this simple action Sam knew he now had the authority he wanted.

TEN

Aeneas, Lord Craven, was a man devoted to hard work. In many ways he found it a burden but it seemed that fate had marked him out to be an ascetic and a recluse. He consoled himself with the thought that there was some divine purpose in this. Only by following his own nature could he truly serve God.

Despite his best intentions there were times when Aeneas envied his younger brother that elusive gift of popularity. Endymion Craven was handsome, almost Spanish in appearance, an unashamed dandy. He also had the ear – and some said the heart – of Queen Henrietta Maria. Aeneas sighed philosophically, thinking that Endymion's popularity at court was a great advantage when it came to affairs of business. God was good indeed.

He glimpsed himself in the wavy reflection of the leaded glass window, drawing back his head slightly the better to see: slender, dark-haired, his thin face was marked by hollow cheeks and deep-set, brown eyes. He drew comfort from the knowledge that it was a likeable enough face, sensitive, cultured, wearing well for his forty-two years. He brushed back the hair that clung to his cheek, knowing that it was the same, nondescript brown that crowned so many heads in England, whereas Endymion with his black locks ... In every way Aeneas felt himself to be a pale reflection of his brother.

But one thing he did have was his father's title and the estate that went with it. In this he knew that God had been wise indeed, for Endymion was incapable of paying attention to detail. Within a year the estate would have been frittered away, sacrificed to gambling debts or gifted to pretty women.

His deliberations were cut short by a knock on the chamber door.

The latch lifted and, turning, Aeneas watched with pleasure as his daughter Serenity walked into the room. His face relaxed in an expression of tenderness. Before him stood a maid on the threshold of womanhood. Her thick hair was corn-coloured, but she was distinguished by eyes as black as those of her Uncle Endymion – eyes that came from Aeneas's mother. Disloyally he was grateful that his child, the only fruit of his body, did not resemble her own pallid, uninteresting dam who had died, God rest her soul, when the girl was three. Since then he had remarried but that wife too had died, and now, with the benefit of both dowries, he preferred to be alone.

Sometimes Aeneas was fearful that his overwhelming love for his daughter would in some way anger God and cause him to take Serenity away – a stark reminder as to whom Aeneas's first loyalty belonged. Already the thought of her marriage to his dead brother's son tormented him. He quickly shut out the dread.

'Daughter?' He waited for her to reach him.

'Papa. A letter for you – from Samuel.' She blushed becomingly.

Aeneas held out his hand. A feeling of violent jealousy enveloped him but he fought it down as shameful. What was more natural than that a young girl should feel excitement at the prospect of hearing from her betrothed? Thinking of his handsome nephew, with his healthy, youthful physique, Aeneas felt ashamed of his gloomy reaction.

He nodded to Serenity to be seated and perched himself on the table which was littered with documents. His expression thoughtful, he untied the ribbons around the letter and held it at arm's length, the better to see. The missive was thick, water-stained in parts, faded in others. It bore the date 15 April 1634. It was now 21 July.

Quickly he skimmed through the first half, taking in its contents with mounting excitement. Finally putting it aside, he said: 'My dear, your cousin writes with splendid news. He appears to have fulfilled his mission. With Captain Jackson he has discovered an island as yet uncharted. It lies to the south of the Spanish Main. He urges that I apply for a patent to husband it.'

Serenity returned her father's smile, nodding encouragement. 'That is splendid news, Papa.'

Getting up, he said: 'Jackson left behind members of his crew to help Samuel take possession then sailed to Barbados. This letter was transmitted from there.' He sighed with satisfaction, his mind racing with possibilities.

65

He continued to read on but this time the news was not so much to his liking.

'. . . I regret imposing upon you in this way but the girl, Esmeralda, has known no other life except aboard ship. I feel certain that you would wish to give her the opportunity to experience a truly Christian home. With this in mind, I have agreed to pay Captain Jackson fifty guineas to part from her, which I shall repay you, as God is my witness . . .'

Aeneas gave a gasp of disbelief. Surely his nephew was deranged! Looking up, he found Serenity watching him, her arched brows raised in concern. Fighting down his misgivings, he said: 'Sam has performed an act of kindness, rescued some child from moral danger.' He did not mention the money or her imminent arrival.

Reading on, his worst fears were confirmed: '. . . The island is truly God-given, a veritable paradise, green and fruitful. Jackson calls it Fortune but in view of its verdant nature, I suggest that we call it Esmeralda.'

To Serenity, he said: 'It seems that the island as yet has no name. Jackson refers to it as Fortune, but fortune can be good or bad. I feel it should be called something more fitting.' He hesitated before saying: 'Samuel describes it as a place of great peace and calm. I therefore think it appropriate that the island should bear your name: Serenity.' He smiled rather grimly to himself.

'Oh! Thank you, Papa.' The girl deposited a kiss upon his brow.

Folding the letter and crushing it between tense fingers, Aeneas said: 'With God's good grace, by this time next year we shall have colonised this island and established there a truly Christian community, dedicated to the service of the Lord.'

'I hope so.' Serenity seemed to hesitate, uncertain as to whether to voice her thoughts. When she did Aeneas knew that God was already testing him, demanding a price for his disloyalty.

Eyes large with entreaty, she said: 'I feel that God has a purpose in bringing this island into our hands. Please, I beg of you, as soon as I am of age, will you allow me to be one of those who gives her service to the Lord in taking the gospel to this new world?'

'I – this cannot be. You are my heiress.' His heart thumped painfully. Trying to calm himself, he said: 'In the fullness of time you will marry Samuel and bear heirs to this estate.' At the thought of his daughter in childbirth, the black fear of losing her clawed once more.

Serenity said: 'Perhaps it is the Lord's wish that you should remarry, have an heir of your own?'

Aeneas shook his head, not allowing himself to consider the suggestion, but as if sensing his inner doubts, the girl added: 'This time you are wealthy enough to marry for love.'

'Ah.' Again he shook his head, threatened by some long-suppressed regret. Blotting it out, he took her hand, his heart inexplicably heavy. 'No, child. My posterity lies with you.'

Now it was Serenity's turn to look regretful.

Aeneas squeezed her fingers. With a strange mixture of hope and fear, he asked: 'What troubles you, daughter? Is your cousin not to your liking?'

She shook her head. 'Oh, I like him well enough, Papa. He is a fine man, but . . .' She looked away. 'I shall always obey you, honour your wishes, no matter what. But perhaps God has other plans for me.'

With an uneasy heart, he feared that indeed it might be so.

The inaugural meeting of the Serenity Company took place at Craven House, which stood large, square and imposing, on the south bank of the River Thames. Those present included two dukes, an earl, seven gentlemen and Aeneas Craven's brother, Endymion.

A week had passed since the arrival of Samuel's letter and during that time Aeneas had had the relevant part of the document written out by his secretaries so that ten copies could now be circulated among those present. He knew that finding an island was only the beginning. Now he had the uphill task of raising funds, persuading men of wealth and influence to invest in this, his most cherished project.

When the good lords and gentlemen had had a chance to pass the time of day together and refresh themselves with wine, Aeneas rose to his feet. He was aware of a tightening in his chest and the mixture of curiosity and scepticism on the faces of those about him. He cleared his throat and the room fell silent.

'Gentlemen, I hope that later on you will take time to peruse the document before you. In the meantime, I will outline its salient points.' He smoothed the linen bands about his neck, moving his head slightly from side to side as if to release himself from the constraints of his collar.

'Some eight months ago I personally financed an expedition to the Caribbees. My intention was twofold. As you will all be aware, the Spaniards have virtually overrun the islands of that part and named them as their own, but although they have laid claim to them, many are still unoccupied. Others have proved difficult to colonise.' He paused for breath, waiting an extra second to add emphasis to his next words.

'There is a third factor. Much of that area has yet to be explored. For all we know, other islands, nay, even continents, might still exist. With this in mind I commissioned a ship, the *Destiny*, with a brief to find a suitable location for the growing and harvesting of new crops. I am pleased to report that such a place has been found.'

The men gathered in the room were still. Aeneas knew that he had their interest but not necessarily their support for what he had in mind. Underlining each word, he added: 'On the fourteenth of April this year, my nephew Samuel Rushworth, along with a vanguard of decent, God-fearing men, landed on Serenity Island.' He felt his cheeks colour at the name but pressed on quickly. 'My nephew has stayed behind with the party to guard it for our benefit – I say "our", gentlemen, because when you hear more about it, I am convinced that your enthusiasm will match my own.'

For the moment at least that enthusiasm was in abeyance Aeneas sat back on the edge of his table, resting his hands on his thighs. He leaned forward.

'Serenity Island is a godsend. My nephew reports that it is hilly, well-wooded and easily defended. He has found only one natural harbour which will be simple to fortify. Any ships approaching will have to pass under the scrutiny of this place if they wish to land.' He sat back, inviting his guests to share in this good fortune.

'I have to tell you that the island is abundantly blessed with fresh water. It is fertile. Dyewoods grow in some quantity. Captain Jackson has sent back evidence of spices. There may be much more.'

Gauging the moment to be right, he said: 'It is my intention to set up a company for the express purpose of colonising this place. I am confident that there are rewards to be had and I am led to believe that His Majesty will not be averse to granting me a patent.' He glanced at Endymion who had the ear of the Queen. His brother gave the merest inclination of his head.

'How does this affect us?'

Aeneas turned towards the Duke of Silchester, married to his dead brother's widow, grateful for a focus. Addressing his remarks to the honourable lord, he pressed his case.

'I sincerely believe that there is sufficient wealth there to allow every man here present to benefit. You will appreciate that initially there will be some outlay. A ship will have to be bought and provisioned. Men will have to be found to go there and begin planting. The rewards will take a while to reach us, but when they do ...' He opened his hands in a gesture that hinted at limitless possibilities.

'You said that your intentions were twofold?'

Aeneas turned back to Lord Silchester. 'I was just coming to that.' He addressed the rest of the gathering. 'I know that there is not a man among you who has not suffered in some way for his sincerely held beliefs. Not a day passes without one of us, or those like us, being punished for our faith in God. For myself, I fear our country moves ever nearer to Popishness. While the Queen openly practises her faith it is difficult to imagine that things will change.'

He glanced at Endymion, puritan in name but a courtier at heart, and felt a moment's unease because he used his brother's worldly contacts to gain advantage. It did not lie easy with his conscience.

Pushing his worries aside, Aeneas said: 'My second, or perhaps my first, intention in finding this island is to enable us to establish a new settlement there for those of our faith. If Englishmen cannot worship God as they see fit, then I deem it my solemn duty to find a place where a truly Christian community can thrive – one based on the principles we all embrace.' He looked round at his friends whose faces betrayed nothing.

'My intention is that this should be primarily a mission. To this end I have chosen each of you 'specially to hear what I say. Any man who embarks on this venture must first and foremost put the purity of men's souls above any advantage to his pocket.' He leaned back, saying: 'I have already spoken with John Hampden, John Pym and the Earl of Warwick. I have their interest and support. There are many more out there who would fight for the chance to invest in this venture but I do not want their money. I want yours, the commitment of truly Christian men. What do you say?

Shuffling among his audience preceded low-toned discussion and men turned to neighbours or friends to air their views. Aeneas sat back, withdrawing himself from the debate. He felt breathless, on the verge of an undertaking that might change not only his own life but ensure the creation of a venture in which he passionately believed.

Endymion was in close conversation with the Duke of Silchester:

rich, fiercely puritan, shrewd in matters of financial gain. Endymion's long black hair hid his expression but in the Duke's movements Aeneas could read his acquiescence. Aeneas found his brother's manner smoothly persuasive and once again his ambivalent feelings towards the young man disturbed him. Much would depend upon how the Duke responded. Silchester's hard-headed business acumen would sway several others.

Aeneas calculated that to make the project viable he would need twenty investors, each willing to put forward two hundred pounds. These would include himself and his brother. If those present agreed then they in turn would attract other reliable puritan supporters. Only then could the venture begin.

After a while the room became silent. With unspoken accord the men drew apart and resumed their seats, looking towards Aeneas, ready to pronounce their verdict.

Barely able to disguise his nervousness, he stood up.

'Gentlemen, is there agreement among you?'

It was the Duke of Silchester who appointed himself spokesman.

'Craven, we will need further time to consider all the implications. There are questions to be answered.'

'Of course.' Aeneas nodded his understanding, still waiting.

His voice gruff, his pugnacious face registering caution, Lord Silchester said: 'In principal, we agree.'

Thanking God, Aeneas thought: Now our mission can truly begin.

ELEVEN

No sooner had the *Destiny* left Samuel's island than Esmeralda fell ill. She feared that the malady was inside her head, for as the shores of the island faded so her will to live seemed to diminish with them.

As the days passed the sickness spread to her body. At first her gums felt sore then her throat started to plague her with a razor-like pain whenever she tried to swallow. Her body burned hot as Africa and even had she wished to, she could not eat.

Her father was moved to anger. 'Pull yourself together, girl. This Lord Craven ain't going to pay good money for a bag o' bones.' He poked her with his foot but she could not be bothered to move out of the way.

'Come on,' he said, his tone more kindly. 'Eat a little of this mush.'

She pushed away the tasteless mash of biscuit soaked in bone stock. If God was good then he would permit her to waste away before this journey was at an end.

After four days they called at St Christopher to take on more passengers, travelling home on the profits of their labours, intent on finding wives.

'Stick to your cabin,' Jeronimo warned. 'These men have been a long time without women. I ain't having you spoiled at this late stage.'

Esmee curled up in the dark and closed her eyes. She felt nothing.

While the outward journey had, by and large, been uneventful, the return journey was plagued by disasters. Many men fell sick. The rigours of the past months had already weakened them and they quickly succumbed to fever. Esmee alone, praying for release, was denied the deliverance of a watery grave.

Two days out of St Christopher, Jeronimo discovered that three of his seamen had jumped ship. Already the crew was reduced to a minimum. If bad weather were to strike they would be hard put to keep the *Destiny* on course.

As if stalking its sickly prey, a vicious storm blew up. While still two weeks away from land, the main mast, weakened by constant battering, splintered and fell, crushing one seaman and casting another, who had the misfortune to be in the rigging, into a raging sea. He was not seen again.

For several days they drifted out of control, then the wind abated and Jeronimo managed to hoist such sail as he could, battling against an unseasonal nor'-easter. With consummate skill he got the *Destiny* back on course and coaxed her along, mile by mile, until at last the hazy tip of the Lizard marked the homeward strait. The ship finally hobbled into Plymouth three weeks after Samuel's letter reached England.

Once ashore, Esmee felt increasingly sick. The land, strangely rigid after the rhythmic undulations of the sea, left her body feeling as if it moved of its own volition, making her dizzy, threatening to send her crashing to the ground. All the while the chasm of her future loomed before her.

Jeronimo took her to an inn and insisted that she lie flat on a narrow cot. She had no time to wonder at the luxury of the bed for the whole room seemed to swirl like a tornado. Ignoring her protests, he forced a scalding measure of geneva down her unwilling throat. It burned the infection which grazed her flesh and went some way to numbing the pain.

It was three days before the land sickness ceased and the fever with it. During that time Jeronimo went out on business of his own. On the third afternoon he returned with an array of garments.

'Right, I've ordered a tub and hot water. Get those things off and clean yourself, then dress in these fine feathers. Tomorrow we're going to see this lord.'

Still feeling weak, Esmee did not move, until Jeronimo dragged back the covers. Then, shakily, she eased herself from the cot. She would have liked to stay at the inn forever, as long as she could sleep and blot out all thought.

When the water arrived, Jeronimo hung around the room, waiting.

'I'll not disrobe till you leave,' she said, feeling suddenly rebellious.

She sensed his reluctance but he pulled on his boots and made for the door, saying: 'Wash that stink out of your hair. Gentlefolk are fussy about that kind of thing.'

There seemed nothing else to do. It took Esmee the best part of an hour to comb the tangles from her hair. Washed and soaped and rinsed with rosewater, the knots were transformed into soft, springy curls. For so long had her scalp been shorn, or clipped short and coated with layers of grime, that for the first time she realised her hair was not black but the deepest burnished brown. She fingered it with interest, finding an unaccustomed glimmer of hope in the silky feel of each lock.

Freshly scrubbed, her skin too was toned to a warm bronze that glowed and promised the return of health. In the polished pewter of a plate, she looked at her face, its shape refined by her recent illness. It served to emphasise the smooth curve of her nose, the mulberry pouting fullness of her mouth. To her surprise she thought: I could almost be beautiful! The dense blackness lifted.

Standing with the candlelight behind her, she gazed at her naked self reflected in the window glass. She looked with newly awakened interest at her body, its slim waist, the flat belly almost hollow in the aftermath of illness. Shyly she looked at her own breasts, cupping them, feeling the warm pliant weight of herself. The brown, puckered nipples grew hard as she fingered them. She had seen such breasts on the slave girls delivered to her father's cabin.

Suddenly afraid that he would return, she hastily began to dress, struggling into an unfamiliar shift, fumbling with strings and ties until she was clothed in a brown dimity gown. Awkwardly she secured the lace bands about her throat. Now a stranger looked back at her from the window – demure, finely apparelled, a match for any of the ladies of the dockside.

When he came back, Jeronimo pronounced himself pleased with what he saw.

'I've sent word to say we'll be calling tomorrow morning. Just you keep quiet and I'll do the talking.' He gave a satisfied grunt. 'This time tomorrow I'll be the richer by fifty guineas. Not a bad dowry eh, Chickadee?'

'I – I'm to marry this lord?' Esmee's heart jolted at the prospect.

Jeronimo laughed. 'You dolt! His sort only marry rich meat.' He shook his head at her naïveté. 'No. Normally chickens like you can be picked up for ten a penny, but that foolish Rushworth doesn't seem to know the cost of such merchandise.'

He looked pleased with himself, then coming out of his reverie, said: 'I don't know what His Lordship will have in mind for you. Perhaps his nephew has sent him instructions.' He came closer, looking her over, eyes bright with avarice and something more.

Esmee pulled back but he grabbed her arm. 'Just you listen, girl. You know how to please a man, don't you? Just you be good now, do what the old man wants – no matter what. If you satisfy him then perhaps I can bring in more chickens on the next voyage – nice ebony ones. These lords'll pay well for virgins, I'm certain of that.' He squeezed her arm, hurting her, but she bit back the pain.

Jeronimo said: 'Just you take note of what I tell you. This could be the beginning of a good business for me.'

A sense of outrage welled up in her. Unable to stop herself, she shouted: 'And what about me? What do I get from this?'

'You?' Jeronimo looked at her in surprise. 'What do you expect? You'll have a roof over your head and good victuals.' Suddenly sly again he added: 'And when Rushworth comes back, hungry from his exile, he'll be ripe to fall into your bed. That's what you want, ain't it? You'll have learned a few tricks by then. If he's foolish enough to pay fifty guineas for you now, by then he might offer you the moon.'

Aeneas was less than pleased to receive Captain Jackson's message. The more he thought about it, the more convinced he was that his nephew was the victim of some fraud. Besides, he did not want the inconvenience of having a savage girl in the house. And what about Serenity? Surely such a companion would not be good for her? Then he began to wonder if perhaps this was not some sort of trial: God testing him out to see if he was a truly compassionate man, a good Samaritan.

Trying to quell his doubts, he concentrated instead on the issues that had to be resolved for the new colony of Serenity Island. There was so much to think about.

His most important task was to arrange the next voyage. Some of the shareholders had already put forward their two hundred pounds, and a victualler had been sounded out to amass stocks of all vital supplies. Rather than go to the expense of commissioning a new ship, it had been agreed to make use of the *Destiny* again. After all, Captain Jackson, rough as he was, knew the route and would have first-hand knowledge of what the planters would need.

His thoughts were interrupted by the announcement that Jackson had arrived. Remembering the purpose of this visit, Aeneas hastily raced through his alternatives: refuse to take the girl at all; offer a token amount to cover her passage; or accept his nephew's instructions and pay over the money. Ruefully he realised that the cost of this child was equal to one-quarter of a share in their great venture. No girl was worth that.

The footman returned with his visitors and Aeneas pushed all thoughts of the company and its needs aside. He made up his mind. He'd refuse to take the girl off the Captain's hands. If Jackson became difficult, then he'd look elsewhere to commission a ship.

'Lord Craven?' Stepping into the room, Jackson snatched his hat from his dusty hair and nodded awkwardly. Wiping the back of his hand across his mouth, he said: 'It was a good voyage, sir – one you'll no doubt be planning to repeat?'

'No doubt.' Aeneas leaned to one side, trying to get a glimpse of Jackson's daughter but she was right behind her father.

Preparing to state his case, he started: 'We congratulate you, Captain, on a job well done. In due course you will receive the amount owing to you. We will of course be thinking of other trips. But before we talk about that, what is this nonsense about your daughter?'

'Nonsense, sir?' Jackson shook his head. 'There's no nonsense. Mr Rushworth said he'd written to you. And he gave me this agreement.' He held out a crumpled document.

'So he might have done –' Aeneas started to say, but at the same moment Jackson let the paper slip from his fingers. As he bent to retrieve it, the girl hiding behind him was at last revealed.

Aeneas stood very still. He felt the skin of his jaw tighten.

The girl stood with her head bent forward. The shawl that had been used to cover her hair had slipped down and she was bareheaded. Rich near-black ringlets tumbled forward, obscuring her face. Her demeanour was one of demure – or perhaps defeated – acceptance.

'My dear?' As Aeneas spoke she raised her head a fraction. For a brief moment she looked up and he felt his throat grow dry. Before him, regarding him with large eyes, green as newly sprouted lime leaves, was a creature of great beauty.

'This is your daughter?' he said to Jackson with ill-concealed surprise.

'Aye. I've never denied it. When her mother died I did my best to raise her, though a life aboard ship ain't the best place for a – lady.'

'And your wife?'

'An Ebo woman.' Jackson moved forward conspiratorially. 'Some of those black gals are a treat, real quality they are.' He grasped Esmee's wrist and pulled her forward. 'I reckon there's royal blood in these veins – foreign blood, of course, but the girl's got breeding.'

Aeneas hardly heard what was said. He could not tear his eyes away from the mirage.

'Speaks French and Spanish, she does, and sings like a linnet – go along, Chickadee.'

Aeneas shook his head impatiently. Suddenly he wanted Jackson out of the house. But he would not, could not, send this beauty away with him, not back into the clutches of such a ruffian. For a second he thought of his nephew and a spasm of raw envy shot through him.

Aloud, he said: 'Not now. Come back tomorrow and we will talk about the next voyage. In the meantime I shall honour my nephew's bargain. You can leave the girl here.' Already he had delved into his pouch and drawn out a fistful of gold coins. 'How much did you say?'

'Fifty.'

Aeneas paid up without demur.

TWELVE

As her father left the room Esmee found herself face to face with her new master. She stole a glance at him, keeping her face averted so that she would not have to meet his eyes. Now that the captain had gone, he seemed to relax. Like most people, Jeronimo intimidated him in some way. Only Samuel had stood up to him and he was thousands of miles away.

After a prolonged silence, Lord Craven said: 'There is nothing to fear, my dear. You will be well taken care of here. I am sure my daughter will look after you.' He hesitated. 'Have you been raised to worship God?'

Esmee risked another glance at him. He was old, possibly nearing fifty. He wore buff-coloured breeches and a brown stomacher over a very fine, full-sleeved shirt. His frame was thin and his hands reminded her of delicate claws: soft, with clean, trimmed nails. Remembering Minister Shergold, she said: 'I have attended prayers.'

The man nodded his approval. She thought that his face was quite plain but gentle. His hair and eyes were brown and his skin had a tawny haze to it. When he opened his mouth he showed a set of regular, yellowish teeth.

Without looking away from her, he rang a bell and moments later the man who had ushered them in came to answer his call. To the servant Aeneas said: 'Fetch my daughter.'

Esmee fixed her eyes on the floor. She knew that he was still looking at her and could not prevent her eyelids flickering with embarrassment. To stop her fingers from trembling, she clasped the ends of her lace bands and twisted them around.

'Sit down, child.' Aeneas stepped back and indicated a settle near to the fire. Esmee sank on to it, focusing on the hearth to avoid his gaze. The sweet scent of apple logs mingled with smoke was drawn upwards into a wide chimney.

As Lord Craven busied himself with some papers that lay on his table, Esmee took the opportunity to study the room. It was even more splendid than the chamber at the inn. Low-ceilinged and rectangular in shape, it was panelled in squares of light, warm wood, divided alternately between plain squares and blocks of carving. The room contained three chairs and on the floor, silky beneath her bare toes, were real rugs. As if this were not splendid enough, the whole was lit with up to six flickering candles, not the tallow sort that they used on the ship but rich, honey-scented beeswax. This man must be very rich indeed.

At that moment the door opened and, glancing up, she saw a girl of about her own age come into the room. Although short of stature she moved in a graceful, floating way, high-headed and haughty. His Lordship put his arm about her shoulders and drew her close.

'Serenity, my dear, this is Esmeralda. God has given us this opportunity to take her in and teach her the path of righteousness.'

Esmee looked momentarily into the girl's sharp black eyes. She was reminded of a bird of prey, an owl perhaps, creamy of colouring but with a dark, disapproving gaze. She felt her cheeks grow hot.

The girl did not smile. Her displeasure was obvious. The man spoke to her softly and his tone was almost wheedling. He said: 'It is Samuel's wish that we help Esmeralda. I am sure you will wish to oblige him.'

At his words Esmee's heart plummeted. This superior girl was Samuel's betrothed!

Serenity was a long time in answering. When she did, she addressed her father but continued to fix Esmeralda with her cool, critical stare. 'And you, Papa? Is it your wish that we should undertake this burden?'

Her father did not reply but looked uncomfortable. The girl continued: 'It is God's commandment that a daughter should obey her father. Therefore, since you appear keen to accept this – this duty, then I shall of course help you to do so.' Turning from Aeneas, she drew herself up as if about to face some ordeal. Her next words confirmed her mood. Composing her features resolutely, she said: 'I shall look upon it as a trial, like one of the torments that plagued Job, sent by God to test his faith.'

78

Esmee listened in dismay. Whatever else she had expected, it was not to be viewed as a form of punishment. Forgetting herself, she said: 'Six months aboard my father's ship and you'd know what punishment is!'

'Be silent, girl!' Serenity's cheeks suffused with indignation as she looked to her father for support. He turned away. Undeterred, the girl said: 'It seems you do not know the difference between a lady of quality and a woman of the serving classes. I am a lady of quality whereas you – you are – well, even lower than a servant. You speak only when spoken to.' Seeing her father's pained response, she added in a more reasonable tone: 'It is God's will that we all fulfil the roles He has given to us. If God has seen fit to send you here as some sort of test to us, then we shall do what we must to teach you how to behave, and of course how to serve our Lord, but never forget your place.'

To Esmeralda's relief His Lordship intervened. He seemed to speak on her behalf.

'Serenity, my dear, I fear that Esmeralda has not had the opportunity to learn about such things. She has been raised at sea. I trust that you, with Christian charity, will guide her to the path of righteousness, remembering always that she cannot help her ignorance.'

Ignorance! Esmee shrank with shame, then thought: Just put you two on the deck of my father's ship, then we'd see who was ignorant!

Serenity's eyes narrowed. It was clear that she was not used to any criticism, however mild, from her adoring father. Quite forgetting where she was, Esmee watched in fascination, having only the experience of her own father to make a comparison.

As if anxious to make amends, Aeneas slipped his arm through his daughter's, saying: 'I strongly sense that today is a great day in our lives. God has given us a sign. In order to please Samuel, and to prove ourselves as true Christians, we will do as he requests.'

Looking at Esmee with large, moist eyes, which contained many messages she could not interpret, he pronounced: 'From henceforth, we will strive to make this girl into a lady.'

As the months passed, Esmee found herself undergoing a transformation. She learned many things, taught to her by her new mistress, always pronounced in a cold, critical tone that implied she found Esmee wanting.

'No decent woman would be seen with her hair uncovered' – this in response to seeing Esmee's lengthening locks, bouncing into tight, silky spirals. 'Only pale skin is beautiful. No God-fearing man would look upon a dark, coarse-skinned woman.'

Over the months, sheltered from the constant glare of sunlight and the harsh beating of the wind, Esmee's skin had grown paler, taking on a golden, pampered look. She was aware of the spitefulness in her companion's tone. From the approving glances of Lord Craven's brother, Endymion, and the indulgence shown her by Lord Craven himself, Esmee wondered if Serenity's pronouncement could be true.

At first Esmee found it difficult to walk in the slippers that were presented to her but gradually she grew used to the elevation of their heels and she learned to glide, her shoulders back, her head lowered in a modest, maidenly way, eyes downcast, instead of striding out like a common bawd.

But these changes were on the outside. Inside too she absorbed a new way of living. New rules applied. She must not steal. She must never blaspheme. For everything that came to her, she must give thanks to God.

Although from their demeanour she could tell that the Cravens disapproved of her father, she was nevertheless urged to honour him and never to voice disloyal feelings.

'Pray for him. Ask God to bring him back from the brink of hell and show him the path of righteousness!'

Esmee thought of Minister Shergold's impassioned cries. She had no time for such prayers, but she did have prayers of her own. They were never voiced aloud. If ever Serenity were to have the merest hint of their content she would surely explode with anger. Daily, nightly, Esmee prayed that Samuel, dear handsome Samuel, would come to claim her.

Serenity's voice intruded into her reverie: 'Remember, if a man should address you, always keep your eyes averted. Never give him the opportunity to read anything other than the love of God into your expression.'

In spite of her claim to humility, Serenity never tired of reminding Esmee that as a body servant, she was ordained by God to wait upon her mistress. Whenever Aeneas was present, he included them both in whatever interested him at the time. Esmee was aware of his smile, his encouraging approval of everything she did. On such occasions she would sense her companion's annoyance, see the compressed lips, the malevolent eyes. Serenity would flash Esmee a hostile look and she would feel helpless in the face of Aeneas's approval and Serenity's spite.

When her father left them, Serenity would be sharp and shrewish, demanding onerous services. Combing the girl's golden hair, laundering the linen she wore next to her skin, Esmee grew very familiar with the person of her mistress. Ignoring the dictates of her new religion, she could not help but compare herself favourably to the woman she served.

Serenity was fair enough of face and well enough formed, but would any man choose such a crab for a bride?

There was little time to dwell on such considerations for under Aeneas Craven's guidance, a whole range of new accomplishments were wished upon her. Esmee learned her letters. She painstakingly copied out receipts. She mastered the complexities of keeping accounts.

Already she spoke French and Spanish but it was with the vocabulary of the gutter. Tutors were engaged to instruct both her and her mistress in these foreign languages. To her secret pleasure, Esmee took easily to the task, learning quickly.

'Such base tongues are Popish, the work of the Devil!' Serenity flung her slate aside pettishly. She said: 'I shall ask Papa to desist from teaching us such heresies.' But for once Aeneas did not concur. While Esmee became more fluent, Serenity sought refuge in criticism.

They also received instruction in painting and embroidery. Their voices were coaxed into sweet instruments of praise for their Maker. Esmee knew that she sang well. Serenity took pleasure in condemning the catches that her servant knew as blasphemous, but when Esmee learned a new repertoire of hymns, it was to her that people turned, listening with rapt attention. It was very gratifying.

One evening, when Serenity remained in her chamber suffering from an ague, Esmee found herself dining alone with Lord Craven. Faced with his undivided attention, she felt ill at ease.

'Is anything amiss, my dear?'

Esmee glanced up into his kind eyes, reassured by his concern, liking the thin, aristocratic face. With Serenity away she did not have to be on her guard.

'I thank you, sir, but I am well.'

He sighed as if the news was a relief to him. Sitting back, he said: 'Esmee, my dear, I find myself wondering if you are happy here?'

'Oh, yes, I am truly happy.' She did not need to stop and think. If it were not for Serenity, she would be almost in heaven.

Lord Craven hesitated. 'I find myself wondering about your life before you came here.'

It was then, for the first time, that she spoke her history out loud. 'I was conceived upon the body of a girl younger than I am now.'

Lord Craven drew in his breath and Esmee stopped uncertainly. 'I – I was conceived in pain, on a black girl's terror and on the flow of a sailor's lust.'

Lord Craven drew back. 'You have witnessed such things?' he started. Then, his voice hardly a whisper: 'You have experienced them?'

Esmee shook her head, trying to explain about her father's dinahs, adding that her own virginity was the prize for which fifty guineas had changed hands. Demurely, she reassured him: 'I am quite untouched – I am truly pure.'

She thought about the male bodies that had been part of her life. Unwashed, smelly, performing all manner of masculine acts before her eyes as if, in her canvas shirt and drawers, she were blind or invisible.

Sometimes in the dark of Jeronimo's cabin she had touched herself, feeling for that missing organ, knowing she could never experience whatever it was that the sailors felt. It seemed to torment and pleasure them equally. She wanted to know what it felt like to be hungry for women, avid for satisfaction, restless as caged beasts.

Sometimes two crewmen would lie together barely concealed, working themselves into a frenzy that seemed part violence, part agony. She was fascinated yet afraid, but familiar as she was with these men and their bodies, not a single one ever attempted to treat her as they did the slaves.

Of this she had, of course, been glad. But neither did any of them speak of her as they did of their wives and sweethearts, with words of tenderness and longing. Something kept her apart from them. She was like no other woman. She wondered if it was fear of her father, or something about herself, something that made her offensive to men.

Aeneas shook his head, intruding into her worries. 'I had no idea.'

He seemed to struggle with his thoughts. In the end he simply repeated: 'I had no idea.'

Esmee feared that she had offended him. Keeping her eyes lowered in the manner which Serenity had taught her, she said: 'My only wish is to serve God.'

'My dear.' Aeneas came to sit beside her. Although she did not look up, she knew that he was studying her closely. His eyes rested upon her face, her bosom. Hesitantly, he reached out and took one of her hands.

'My dear. If you were able to have anything you wanted in this life, what would you choose?'

Esmee thought quickly. The answer was simple – to be with Sam – but she hesitated to say so. Instead she replied: 'One day I would dearly love to return to Samuel's island.' Then, thinking of what he would like to hear, she added: 'I – I should like to serve the Lord.'

'You mean Serenity Island?' Aeneas corrected her. He seemed to take pleasure from her confession, adding: 'I too have such a wish. I have thought long and hard since the news reached me of the island's discovery. I truly believe that God is calling me to go there, but not yet. First I must oversee the plans from this end. As Secretary of the company, there is much for me to arrange.'

He raised her hand and rested his lips against the back of her fingers, adding: 'It is Serenity's wish also to go there and serve the Lord.'

Esmee kept very still, not wishing to prolong the physical contact between herself and her guardian. She turned her thoughts to the island, sensing danger at the thought of Serenity and Samuel together, but Aeneas's next words drove every other thought from her mind.

'I have received reports that the *Destiny* sailed yesterday for the Indies. She has taken more settlers to strengthen our colony.' He paused thoughtfully and added: 'It is a great venture. I myself have paid for four dozen catechisms for the comfort of the labourers.' Again he kissed Esmee's fingers, as if his thoughts were in the Caribbees – but his body was close to hers. His maleness unnerved her.

Aeneas turned towards her. He smiled tenderly and said: 'The Lord knows how lonely, how empty, my life has been since the death of my wife. Apart from Serenity, I have no heir to follow me.

Now I am convinced that it is God's wish that I should act. In coming here, my dear, you have given me a sign.'

Esmee felt confused. She waited for him to make himself clear. There could be no mistaking his next words.

'I have decided to bring new blood into the Craven line. No matter that you bring neither wealth nor land. No matter that you are of foreign blood. We are all God's creatures. You bring something far better – youth, freshness, a willingness to serve God, and the prospect of new life for our family.' He squeezed her fingers until they hurt and moved restlessly in his seat. Leaning forward, he said: 'God has sent you to me and I shall not disappoint Him. Esmeralda, my dear, you shall be my bride.'

The news was so devastating that she remained silent. She looked at his old man's hands, holding hers, and thought of her father's words: 'Do what the old man wants, no matter what.' She began to shake her head.

Sensing her distress, Aeneas rose from his seat and pulled her close.

'Don't, my love. There is absolutely nothing to fear. I shall guard you against all evil.' He cradled her to him and she could feel his thin body beneath the fine linen of his shirt. His fingers massaged her shoulders, intent of soothing her. She had to fight with herself not to draw back.

Holding her away from him, he looked into her eyes, searching for the truth. 'Does the thought of marriage frighten you?'

She shook her head, unable to admit to her repugnance.

'Then what? Surely your father would not disapprove?'

At the thought of Jeronimo's plans, she gave a snort of contempt. Seeing Aeneas's confusion, she said: 'My father would be most pleasantly surprised.'

'Then you have no other objection?'

Inside she screamed: Of course I have. You are old! You are thin and scrawny. You have no fire in your heart. You are NOT Samuel! Aloud she said: 'I have never considered. What of your daughter?'

Aeneas shook his head. 'In marrying, I shall relieve Serenity of the obligation to provide an heir to my estate.'

'Then she will not marry . . .?' She stopped herself in time from mentioning Samuel's name.

Aeneas shrugged. 'That will be for her to decide. Like myself, she must follow the dictates of her conscience. She might choose

84

fulfilment in marriage, or in doing God's work in some other way.' He repeated: 'That is for her to decide.'

And me? Esmee thought. Do I have no right to decide my future? She wondered what would happen is she should refuse. Then, over and above the prospect of marriage, was the knowledge that as Aeneas Craven's wife, she would one day be making the journey back to Samuel's island, back to Samuel. A hundred things might happen between now and then, but as long as she was going back to him, that was all that mattered. Drawing comfort from this tender hope, she said: 'I would always wish to do God's will.'

THIRTEEN

During the winter months the shareholders of the Serenity Company were much occupied in drawing up rules and regulations for the governing of their island. It was a long process. Each clause was hammered out in such detail that it was the third week in February before the document was completed to their satisfaction and Jeronimo Jackson had permission to sail. It was now up to him to deliver the papers to Samuel Rushworth.

This delay in agreeing the conditions and laws gave Jeronimo time to patch up his ailing ship. It was no easy task for her hull was rotting and her sails paper thin. Had he been a religious man he would have prayed for good weather to coax her across the Atlantic.

He had another reason to be grateful for the delay. One morning he awoke to a vague itchy feeling around the top of his penis. When he went outside to piss his water began to sting. Cursing, he went about his duties, hoping this was just some minor irritation.

Over the next few days, however, things grew markedly worse. His cock grew red and swollen. Pissing became an agony and he was subject to frequent and painful erections which it was impossible to relieve.

He thought angrily of the slatterns who frequented the taverns where he spent his time on land. One of those whores had infected him. Going ashore he purchased some mercury pills, some papers of cooling powders and balsam drops. He also bought a nanny goat and brought her aboard the ship.

'Cap'n's got the pox,' remarked Thomas Warner, the carpenter. 'Best to keep out of his way, he'll be moody as Hades.'

Jeronimo knew from experience that the treatment would take forty-four days. Night and morning he purged himself with the mercury and bathed his penis in the goat's milk. Fashioning a probe from a piece of green hazel, he cleaned out the yellowish-green matter which ran from him.

At night he lay with his legs apart, the covers raised to let air circulate around his infected parts. An angry rash had spread across his thighs. It was impossible to sleep. He vowed that when they reached the Indies he would find himself a nice clean virgin for the return journey. He wasn't going through this again. By day he went about his duties as if nothing was amiss. When they sailed, the infection was at its height.

In total he was carrying ninety men to join the new colony. Such was the press of stores and supplies they carried that there was barely room for each soul to lay his head. Once they reached their destination they would be dependent upon what they brought with them, plus whatever the first group of pioneers had managed to grow.

Idly Jeronimo wondered if the settlers were still alive. In his experience many a new settlement was wiped out by disease or savages before it ever became established. Anyway, it made no difference to him. He would unload this human cargo, cruise around until he found the most profitable goods to bring home, and return as soon as possible. He was only pleased that this time there seemed to be no Samuel Rushworths aboard to question his authority.

The new men fell roughly into three classes. First there were the planters who were paying their own fares and who would receive free land in return for a share of the profits from their labours. These were respectable men, driven from the old country by dissatisfaction with the religious bigotry they found at home. Although not wealthy, they shared the company's ideals. Jeronimo was pleased to find them so preoccupied with their religious grievances and the prospect of a new beginning that they seemed immune to the privations of the journey.

The second group were poorer men who had elected to go to the colonies in the hope of improving their prospects. For the most part their fares were paid by the company. At six pounds a head, Jeronimo guessed that he should make a healthy profit.

When they reached the Antilles they would be expected to work the land in return for their food and clothing and a wage of five pounds a year. Jeronimo soon recognised that while they paid lip service to the new religion, their main interest was in improving

87

their lot. These men had known empty bellies and slept beneath the stars. Smugly he thought that they too would not complain much about conditions aboard the *Destiny*.

Socially the third group were superior to the other two, being the sons of more affluent guild and craftsmen. They consisted of boys of about fourteen years of age. Like many a boy in England, they were beginning an apprenticeship. The same conditions would apply to them. At the end of their indenture, however – assuming that anyone lived that long – they could expect to be rewarded with land and a share in the colony's profits. But first of all they would labour for free, accepting only their keep in return for their efforts.

Laying in the dark, Jeronimo grimaced to himself. The first voyage had, against his expectations, proved profitable. He had ended up with over a hundred guineas, including the sale price for Esmeralda. For a moment he wondered how she feared. It was merely idle curiosity. He had no real desire to see her or have news of her and yet the memory of his daughter was disturbing. She aroused in him an uncomfortable mixture of emotions but he refused to define them. He felt angry with himself that she could affect him in this way and tried to dismiss her from his mind as not worth thinking about. He was not entirely successful.

When Lord Craven had visited the ship just before its departure, Jeronimo's first thought was that Esmeralda was proving a disappointment and that the old man wanted his money back. Jackson was ready to take her off the noble lord's hands – for a price. However, nothing was said so he assumed that she was giving satisfaction. He wondered whether to chance his arm and bring back a consignment of black girls. Best to wait and see what was on offer in the market places of Barbados or Jamaica.

Even without the benefit of Jeronimo's prayers, the elements were kind to the *Destiny*. Once the voyage was under way she made good time and they stopped only once to take on essentials: water, sugar, plus cotton and tobacco plants to be cultivated on the island. A commercial crop was a priority.

Jackson also collected six pieces of ordnance for the colony's protection, for once news got out that their venture was successful, who knew what opportunists might try to take advantage of it for themselves?

As they sailed the last miles, the pox had all but gone away and the state of the *Destiny* was Jeronimo's main preoccupation. Patch her he might, but she would not endure many more crossings. He shrugged into the wind. There were always ways and means of getting another ship. Meanwhile, this time tomorrow, they would be at Fortune Island . . .

FOURTEEN

'Today is a special day, for as far as I can tell it is exactly one year since we set foot on Esmeralda Island.'

Sam stopped writing and gazed along the white expanse of shoreline. Here and there its smooth curve was broken by a rock, unnaturally black against the paleness of the sand. Down by the water's edge, an occasional piece of wood or a coconut lay stranded by the high tide. Far into the distance he could see one of the settlers, too small to identify, gathering pieces of driftwood.

Sam sighed heavily and leaned back into the shade of the palm that supported his back. The beauty of the evening only added to his heaviness of heart. He was a man chastened, punished because he had dared to think he had control over his destiny. The seasons, the true masters of the island, had taken pleasure in teaching him otherwise.

During those first weeks Sam had grown increasingly confident about the success of their mission. His early fears had proved groundless and in spite of the yawning gap between the devout settlers and the godless sailors, they seemed to adopt an unspoken commonality of purpose. The sailors prayed and, Minister Shergold excepted, the colonists turned a blind eye to the occasional game of dice or bawdy song. There was no strong drink, and no women present to disrupt their brotherly calm.

In spite of the heat, the men laboured energetically and within a few weeks the first communal houses were completed. The newly divided plots were planted with seeds brought from England and in the balmy climate the delicate plants quickly took root, hungrily feeding from the fertile soil. They soon grew strong. Potatoes and turnips pushed up vibrant leaves while experiments with flax and corn promised success.

There were some setbacks. The sheep quickly sickened and died, but the hens flourished. Chicks hatched. The flesh and eggs of the parent birds were supplemented by myriad fowl from the surrounding countryside. Sam soon discovered quam, plump as turkeys, and the booby birds were so tame they could be captured without any need for musket or sling.

There was a shortage of tools and powder but my mutual agreement the men shared and economised. Their spirit of brotherhood was heartening.

The rains came in June. At first they were welcome. Sam felt a positive surge of excitement as he stood bareheaded, his face lifted to receive the baptism of the first shower. But after a few days, the intensity of the downpour, the slippery paths and flooded huts, brought the first uneasy qualms.

Around the tenth day of September Sam wandered down to the beach as usual. It was a blustery day of low grey cloud. He had the feeling that something was different. The wind had swung round to the south, lifting his hair, blowing fine grains of sand that stung his face. As he listened he began to realise that although the wind was rushing, the boughs shaking, beneath the superficial noise of the elements there was silence. He felt suddenly uneasy.

As he wandered down to the waterside he became aware of another unusual event. The tide, which normally skipped up across the damp sand, had retreated farther than he had ever seen it. It was almost as if some force of nature were holding it back.

Thomas Axe came to join him.

'I don't like the look of this.' He pointed towards the distant rollers. In silence they both watched concentrated spirals of what looked like smoke, far on the horizon. As they stood there the outlines grew larger, black cones now, skimming the water's surface, heading unerringly towards them.

Almost before there was time to remark on it, the gusts of wind grew stronger, gaining momentum until, too late, Sam recognised that a storm of unbelievable proportions was upon them. As he called out for the men to take cover, the hurricane speared the island like a lance.

Sam raced for the harbour, desperate to secure their single shallop before it was tossed to destruction by the angry waves.

'Help me!' he shouted to Hezekiah Martin and planters Swift and Roach, who came struggling after him.

91

Straining against the current, ineffective as kittens pitting their strength against a mastiff, they struggled to shift the boat, forcing her inch by painful inch away from the devouring waves. Inside, Sam felt a painful terror. They faced a rage so mighty that man and his ingenuity were as nothing. Against it only prayer could intercede.

A snapping sound, sharp as musket fire, rent the air above them. Even as they turned in the direction of the sound, a mighty palm, reaching sixty feet towards the heavens, tore itself up by the roots, tumbling in their direction. The upper branches caught the edge of the shallop, but worse, far worse, as it struck the ground it crushed Hezekiah Martin beneath it, the force driving his body into the sand.

He screamed, a long, single note. The three men let got of the vessel, but pinioned as it was by the palm, the waves could not claim it. His heart contracted to a solid knot of fear, Sam struggled to the injured man's side. Hezekiah was half buried by sand, hands outstretched in a cruciform. His mouth moved soundlessly and from the corner of his lips a dribble of blood oozed its way down his chin.

'Hezzi, be still! We'll have you out of this.' Even as Sam spoke, e heard the hiss of breath, the bubble of fresh blood coursing from his companion's mouth. Frantically he looked down at the trunk of the palm, realising in one terrible moment that a single sharp protrusion, barely a branch, had punched its way into Martin's chest cavity. His life's blood spread in a leisurely pattern across his body and down into the hollow of the ground.

'Hezzie.' He repeated the man's name, impervious to the shifting sand, the stinging spray from the ocean.

Behind Sam, planters Swift and Roach dragged at his clothes to pull him away, desperate to find shelter from the eye of the storm. He shook them off.

'Hezzie.' Flinging himself face down beside his companion, Samuel gripped his wrist. He started to pray, an urgent jumble of words, beseeching God to effect a miracle cure. Hezekiah Martin mumbled incoherently and, tensing his tortured frame, began to struggle, whimpering like a child after a nightmare.

'Hush, Hezzie, hush.' As Sam watched, the man worked his mouth furiously, his lower lip beginning to tremble, then slowly, slowly, something somewhere put out the spark that had given Hezekiah life. His sightless eyes, gazing into the storm, were slowly covered by the sand.

When Sam finally came to his senses, the worst of the storm was over. In its place, a cold, spiteful wind prodded him. Like his dead companion, he was partly buried. Slowly and painfully he pulled himself up, his trembling legs barely holding his weight. Fearfully he staggered his way back up the beach, towards the settlement of New Bristol, named after his home town, with its six wooden houses. The sight that greeted him froze his heart.

All but two of the houses were demolished, like piles of matchwood flung carelessly across the clearing. The others were damaged, the thatch of their roofs bedraggled and hanging in wisps. Of the livestock there was no sign.

Sam called for his companions. 'Where are you?' He was appalled by the thought that perhaps he alone had survived. Within moments, however, settlers emerged from the two remaining houses: one ... two ... seven men. Abel Roach came out of the woods.

There was nothing to say. Each man was beyond speech. Heads bowed they drew closer, distant yet united in their common grief.

'This is God's punishment on us. We should have driven out the evildoers among us!' The sound of Shergold, castigating the wickedness of the sailors, dragged Sam back to the present.

'Enough, Minister! If this is God's punishment then let us show compassion to those who remain.' Sam closed his mind to the horror and began the task of seeking out the dead or dying, rescuing what little that remained of their belongings, organising a burial party to dispose decently of their departed. Praisetogod sanctified the ground next to the site planned for their church. The cemetery was born.

The memory of that day and the weeks following weighed on Sam like cannon balls. He had a fleeting memory of young Ignatius, loaded down aboard the *Destiny*. At that time he had longed to be away from the ship but now he would have given anything to see her sails, have news from home and the company of other men.

In the months since the hurricane, the survivors had worked resolutely, rebuilding the huts, replacing the devastated crops with anything that looked as if it might be good to eat or sell. The cow and chickens had gone, escaping into the hinterland or killed by the storm. The little remaining gun powder had been blown to the wind so that hunting was possible only with knives and home-made spears.

The wet season ended as sharply as it had begun. Soon the skies were once again clear and the atmosphere dry as an oven. Sam began to wonder if they had built their town in the right place. They had settled for the cliffs around the harbour, but the nearest source of water was from an inland spring some two miles away. It took precious energy to fetch it.

He made it his job to begin laying wooden pipes to channel the water to the settlement. It was a slow, laborious struggle, hollowing out trunks to act as an aquaduct. The gully grew by only a few yards a day. At the same time he ordered guttering to be made for the houses to channel the rains into cisterns – if ever it rained again.

Slowly the repair of the shallop progressed so they would soon have access to the sea again. Meanwhile, work on the land was a torture in the unrelenting heat.

Whenever the weight of his burdens beame too great, Samuel turned for solace to that secret place in his heart where he could be with Esmeralda.

He did so with a mixture of shame and confusion. Here he was, a man experienced in the ways of the world back in London, a man entrusted with the creation of this colony and all its souls. Here he was, someone who had allowed himself dalliances in the past and enjoyed communion with women, but always too sensible hitherto to be touched by foolish sentimentality. Then, almost in an instant, this slip of a girl with no breeding and no prospects had turned him into some love-sick swain.

Was it true what they said, that mariners could be bewitched by sea maidens? Or was this the love he had scoffed at in Sir Phillip Sidney's verses or Will Shakespeare's sonnets? Was it something to fight against or something to embrace – a love that knew no boundaries, a love that would overcome everything to fulfil itself?

He tried to shake off these thoughts but once again they drew him back to that place he visited every day, every night. Over and again he played out the same private pageant, with himself composed and confident, freshly bathed and well apparelled, the master of his own destiny. Esmee, eyes luminiscent with love, waited in some secret cove, arms outstretched in welcome. The ritual of holding her, kissing her, making love to her in a hundred different ways, pronouncing her his wife for all to see – even if only in his imagination – helped him to believe that such a future was possible.

Sometimes he visualised her seated at his uncle's table: cultured, demure, miraculously transformed into Aeneas's daughter, free and

94

equal and eager to wed with him. He wondered: in the past year could Aeneas have educated her, accepted her so totally that she might truly become Samuel's bride with his uncle's blessing? He held an imaginary conversation with Aeneas, explaining why Esmee and not Serenity would make the perfect match for him, his uncle agreeing that Serenity's own choice would be for a different future. A picture froze in his mind of Aeneas taking Esmee's hand and placing it on top of Samuel's own, enclosing them both in his avuncular grasp and saying: 'I give you my blessing.'

Reluctantly he put the daydream aside. As the months passed, the vision grew harder to sustain and before any of this could happen, he had to complete his duties here, shape a paradise out of this hell.

'If we are to survive here we need some native labour.' William Axe cut into his reverie, adding: 'The company should buy in a load of bucks.'

Sam shrugged, his mind still absent in that distant dreamland. Every instinct told him that the bringing of forced labour, slaves, into the island was against everything they stood for but he was too exhausted to put forward his arguments.

Since the storm, four more men had died, overwhelmed by weakness and disease. Of the original forty pilgrims who had elected to stay behind when the *Destiny* sailed for home, only seven remained: William Axe, Abel Roach, young Ignatius, Ned Swift, old Ezra, Minister Shergold and himself.

Thinking about all that had happened, Sam wondered how much longer they could hold out. He tried to be positive, to believe that with sufficient men and stores, the right tools and arms, they could still succeed. But would they, could they, struggle on until the day, if ever it came, when Lord Craven's promised ship returned?

There was no one on watch to spot the dim shadow that heralded the arrival of the *Destiny*. The first inkling the settlers had of her presence came with the alarm calls of the terns, fluttering up in agitated flocks as their habitat was disturbed by the trampling of alien feet.

So unexpected was the arrival that Sam, hearing the hubbub, came running barefoot from one of the shacks, expecting to find Caribs or wild boar about to attack them. Instead he saw a crocodile of men lugging boxes, crates, furniture and containers up the incline from New Bristol harbour.

He did not move. It was almost as if the dream that had sustained him over the past months was playing tricks on him, taunting him in the daylight. He nearly dismissed it as a mirage. The sight of Captain Jackson broke the spell.

'Mr Rushworth, I thank God that you are in good health.'

The Captain's habitual sarcasm galvanised Sam into action. Without replying he scanned the new colonists, looking, fearing, hoping that by some miracle Esmeralda might be among their number.

Sensing his distraction Jackson produced a cumbersome package wrapped in oilcloth. 'I bring you instructions a-plenty from the good Venturers.'

Sam took the package but did not open it. 'Is all well in England?' he asked, needing to hear his own voice. 'With my uncle? His family?'

Jackson's narrow lips twitched. 'Your uncle appeared to be in good health when last I saw him. Anything you need to know will be in there.' He nodded towards the package.

Setting his turmoil aside, Sam started to recount the events of the past year. The presence of so many men seemed suddenly threatening. He felt himself assailed by the sound of voices, overwhelmed by the plethora of goods piling up around the settlement.

Dredging up his energy, he addressed the new arrivals, explaining how the past months had unfolded, trying to paint a balanced picture of the potential of their paradise and the evils that threatened it.

His audience was silent. Relief at having reached dry land showed in their tired eyes. They nodded sagely at his warnings but Sam knew that they had no idea of the reality he was trying to portray.

That evening, when the new arrivals had found a place to pitch their tents and were fed and sheltered, he took the company's instructions into a forest clearing so that he could study them in peace. The title page caused him to grunt: ' "Regulations for the Administration and Government of the Serenity Company ..." ' The name reminded him of his duty to his betrothed. That her name, not Esmeralda's, should grace their endeavour, seemed like a bad omen.

As he read on his heart grew heavy for it was clear that the Venturers had no inkling of what he and his men were facing.

In disbelief he read through the rules and regulations that were to govern the new colony. The sheaf of papers was at least an inch thick and each section was filled with minute detail. They numbered thirty-five articles in all.

With a bitter-sweet mixture of pride and unease Sam saw that he was now appointed Governor of the colony. Among the *Destiny*'s cargo, Jackson carried a mace as a symbol of the new Governor's authority. With six others whom he personally should appoint, Sam would have the power of martial law and the right to appoint magistrates. He alone would have full jurisdiction over life and death. His tired soul rebelled against the responsibility.

Again he skimmed the resolutions. In this earthly paradise, sin was to be unknown. Purity would reign supreme. The playing of cards or the throwing of dice was banned. If men needed distraction then a game of chess would be permitted.

Whoring, drunkenness and profanity would be severely punished. Church services must be attended by all. The Minister was to have his own house and be supported in his spiritual labours with food and sustenance provided by his flock.

All those imported to the colony, men, women and children, would be required to swear an Oath of Allegiance to the crown.

Sam laid the papers aside. At the thought of women coming here, his feelings for Esmeralda swamped him. Hastily he flicked through the sheaf of papers looking for any personal word from his uncle, any communication from home that gave some clue as to her well-being. There was nothing. He felt uneasy. In normal times Aeneas was a scrupulous correspondent.

His search was interrupted by the arrival of Jackson. Guiltily Sam pushed the papers aside as if he had been caught out in some sin.

'How long will you stay, Captain?' he asked, trying to assume an air of calm.

'A few days. Seeing as you have no cargo for me take back, I shall have to look elsewhere.'

Sam bit back any retort at the implied criticism. He said: 'Next time you call, pray God we will have had more success.' He ignored Jackson's cynical smile.

The older man said: 'You need some niggers. Those well-meaning Christians out there ain't up to this sort of work. I'll see what can be done.'

'That's something the company will have to decide. I don't hold with slave labour myself.'

Jackson raised his brows quizzically. His expression was mocking but he said nothing, instead adding: 'I've brought you some figs and oranges. Perhaps you'll have better success growing them.'

'Perhaps.' Sam would not ask if the Captain had any news of his daughter, but that night he scribbled a formal letter to his uncle, as Secretary of the company.

'I send my earnest wishes to your noble self and to your daughter, my cousin. Being now Governor of this place it seems that I will be here for several years at the very least. I wish you both God's protection and excellent health and hope that before I die, I shall once again cast eyes upon you.' He could not bring himself to refer to Serenity as his betrothed. The quill faltered as he added: 'I trust that the responsibility for the girl, Esmeralda, has not proved too great a burden and that she grows in goodness and in health.'

Sitting long into the darkness, wild words of love circling in his head, the quill grew dry. In the end he could do no more than sign his name.

FIFTEEN

As soon as the *Destiny* had taken on fresh fruit and water, Jeronimo made a quick dash back across the Caribbean. His destination was the Spanish island of Jamaica.

Anchoring offshore he ordered his crew to remain aboard, then set off accompanied by only two reliable officers. As they rowed the shallow vessel into the harbour it drifted with deceptive ease, weaving its way among a mêlée of ships. Jackson studied those craft tied up with an expert eye. He soon spotted what he was looking for.

A pinnace of some ninety tons was hove to at the edge of the harbour. Her paintwork was bright and her sails still had the stiff, creamy look of new canvas. A gilded figurehead gazed proudly across the harbour and along her side she bore the name: *Evangelina*. Jeronimo nodded to himself with satisfaction.

Ignoring the *Evangelina*, he ordered his men to moor by the quay and, leaving them aboard, went ashore. Although he and his ship were English, nobody challenged him. As a known slave master and regular trader, the Spanish authorities turned a blind eye to his activities.

The moment he stepped ashore the heat from the dockside assaulted him. Sweat trickled from his armpits. The sun beat down on to him, soaking his back. He resisted the temptation to seek relief in any of his old haunts. For once he had no desire to hunt down his usual drinking companions.

The harbour was bustling with activity. Everywhere men were loading and unloading cargo while planters and merchants haggled over tempting goods. Stopping only for a word here, an enquiry there, Jeronimo picked up sufficient information about cargoes in need of transport. Business was done quickly and efficiently – a

99

handshake here, a quick exchange of gold there and the transaction was complete. Soon, a consignment of goods for shipment to England would be transported down to the harbour.

Before returning to the *Destiny*, Jeronimo made a detour to the slave market. He was in a good mood. Perhaps he could pick up something worth shipping home and, besides, he was feeling well again. A little company for the journey would not go amiss.

It was not a day for regular trading but a few dealers had brought in produce for sale. Jeronimo eyed them with disappointment. They were mostly refuse slaves, those who had arrived too sickly or maimed to be purchased straight from the slave ships. There was certainly nothing pleasing to the eye that might tempt some country gentlemen to buy a pet for his family. He shrugged.

As he was leaving the market, he noticed a child crouched behind a pathetic-looking woman. He peered at the youngest through the swollen, ulcerated legs of the mother. Reaching out he grabbed it by the arm, realising that it was older than he had at first imagined. Although it hung back, there was no more weight there than a sparrow. Pulling it up, he looked down at its genitals to identify the sex – a bitch.

The woman gave a moan of protest, reaching for her daughter, turning a stark, imploring face towards him. Jeronimo pushed her back and dragged the girl with him.

'How much?' he asked the trader.

'A thousand.'

Jeronimo spat and gave a snort of disbelief. 'I'll give you ten.'

The trader looked offended. 'Such a pretty pet. A good wash and she'll shape up nicely.' He eyed her budding breasts.

Jeronimo noted the tribal scars on her cheeks. There were also some smaller marks that were the legacy of smallpox. He felt heartened. In buying a slave there was always the risk of catching that dreaded scourge. He ran his hand over his own unblemished skin. The fact that this girl had already had the disease raised her value. There was always a market in England for slaves who had already suffered the smallpox. Aloud, he said: 'Eighty.'

'Eight hundred.'

They went through the pantomime, settling on five hundred pesos.

The mother continued to moan and implore in her own native gibberish but Jeronimo ignored her. As he paid over the money and pulled the girl with him, the woman made a lunge for them but was brought up short by her shackles.

Dragging his new purchase behind him, Jeronomo did not look back. The mother's eerie wailing was soon lost amidst the shouts and bustling of a busy port.

He flung the girl into the bottom of the boat where she crouched stiffly as if made of wood. Ignoring her, he ordered the two seamen ashore, leaving them to guard the newly purchased merchandise that was now being loaded on to the quayside. Then he jumped into the boat and rowed himself back to the *Destiny*.

As he passed the *Evangelina*, his lips creased in the semblance of a satisfied grin.

That night, half the crew of the *Destiny* left their ship with the scurrying silence of rats. Armed with cutlasses, their bare feet noiseless on the decks, they scrambled down the sides, took to the boats and paddled their way across to the *Evangelina*.

The ship slept at her berth. Only two days into harbour, her crew were either ashore or sleeping off the effects of recent trips on land.

The *Destiny*'s crew worked with silent efficiency. Within minutes every living soul aboard the *Evangelina* was either knocked senseless, stabbed through the heart, or heaved, still heavy with sleep, into the harbour waters.

Working with years of experience, the sailors hurried ashore, transported the waiting cargo into the holds, untied the *Evangelina*, raised just sufficient sail to coax her out of her berth, and eased her into deeper waters.

At the same time, those still aboard the *Destiny* steered their tired craft up the narrow channel and into the mooring so recently left by the *Evangelina*. Within half an hour, the newly purchased cargo and the entire crew of the *Destiny* were back aboard their new ship and making full sail out of harbour.

SIXTEEN

After his proposal of marriage to Esmeralda, Aeneas found himself in a kind of limbo. Having plucked up the courage to ask her, he had thought it would all then be so easy. In his head, he'd already sent for the priest, announced his intentions to the world and lived out a life of extraordinary joy with this beautiful woman.

The reality was different. He felt a peculiar sense of paralysis whenever he even thought of discussing it with Endymion or Serenity. Once the word got out, scorn, amusement, derision would greet his plans. He told himself he did not care, or at least cared only for the opinions of his immediate family. In reality, though, he couldn't face being a laughing stock.

For days he agonised over how to tell them, avoiding Esmeralda in case she should question him. In the end, it was to Endymion that he confessed his plans, his face burning, the words tripping him up as he tried to make it sound reasonable, which it did not, even to himself.

On hearing the news, Endymion Craven leaned back in one of Aeneas's fireside chairs, placed his hands on its arms and took a deep breath. When finally he spoke, it was in a ponderous, almost disbelieving way.

'My dear brother, I fear you have lost your reason.' He gave an incredulous laugh. 'If you want the girl, have her. She's a pretty enough thing to turn any head. Take her to your bed and do what nature calls for, but marriage ...' He shrugged his shoulders in a gesture of disbelief. When Aeneas did not reply, he added: 'I don't know in what circumstances you came by her, but if money changed hands then she is yours to do with as you wish.'

'No!' Aeneas protested. He did not want to even consider that

Esmeralda might agree to his proposal because she felt herself to be under duress. To his despair, he blushed with shame at the thought of the fifty guineas he had handed over so readily, albeit on Sam Rushworth's behalf. A treacherous thought reminded him that as Sam had not repaid him then Endymion was right: Esmeralda was legally his.

The thought of Sam, with his powerful physique and youthful zest, only added to his misery. He could not let himself dwell on his nephew and the lad's own plans for Esmeralda.

Miserably he imagined his nephew's concern when Jackson arrived at Serenity Island without some personal letter from himself. Surely Sam would suspect that something was wrong? But even as Aeneas blamed himself, he knew that he could not possibly have written and explained, for how could Sam ever understand his uncle's feelings?

Endymion said: 'If you want a wife, look around you. There are young, tempting brides of good family galore at the court. Just think what it is that you are seeking – another fortune? Another title? Or is it just a good *poke*? If it is the latter, then take your dues. You are feeding the girl, clothing her. Let her earn her living.'

Aeneas would not follow Endymion's cynical train of thought. It pained him to think in such a way. At all costs he would hang on to his ideals.

Endymion studied him thoughtfully before adding: 'The King will certainly not approve of such madness.'

'That is why I intend to do what I always thought was required of me – go to Serenity Island and begin a new life there.'

Endymion thought for a moment. 'Then who will run the estate – or are you planning to part with it?'

Aeneas knew that his brother was thinking of his own advantage. Dashing Endymion's hopes, he said: 'At first I shall appoint a bailiff. Someone I can trust. Then, with God's good grace, Serenity will come with me and wed her cousin as planned. When Samuel has served his term as Governor, they can return here and he will oversee things for me.'

'Sam Rushworth?' Endymion gave a dismissive shrug. 'He's no more than a boy.'

'He is but two years younger than you.' To himself Aeneas added: And a sight more responsible.

Endymion tried again. 'Do you seriously think that the shareholders of the company will be happy about their founder behaving in such an irresponsible way?'

Aeneas felt offended. He tried again. 'I consider marriage to be the most responsible of acts. I have given great thought to the needs of our line and new blood is called for. I have prayed about this. I know that it is God's will.'

Aeneas met his brother's eyes, asking for some understanding, but Endymion shook his head at such folly.

Knowing that he was not going to win, Aeneas sought to change the subject, saying: 'How go things with the company? Have you any news?'

Endymion said: 'While you have been so preoccupied with your affair of the heart, you missed the last shareholders' meeting. I have here the minutes.'

He held them out and Aeneas took them, chastened by his failure to attend to his duties.

Endymion said: 'I think you will approve of most things but there's one . . .' He made a gesture that implied the outcome had nothing to do with him, adding: 'The shareholders don't like the company name. "Serenity" does not slip easily from the tongue. It implies a certain lassitude, a lack of drive. They approved and passed a resolution to call the company and the island by an alternative name. In future they shall both be known as "Eden".'

Aeneas felt as if he had been slapped. The change seemed like a personal insult to his daughter and a lack of respect for himself.

Endymion stood up and smiled sardonically. As he made ready to leave, he said: 'It is to Eden Island that you will be going, brother. I congratulate you on your intended marriage. I only hope that you and your little Eve will find the paradise you hope for.'

Downcast by his brother's response, Aeneas found it even harder to raise the subject of marriage with Serenity. At the same time, he knew that he had to do so before she heard it from some other source. A sense of gloom settled over him, brought on by the knowledge of his own weakness.

In bed that night he could not sleep. Gritty-eyed, he examined his conscience, trying to be honest with himself about his failings. In essence he did not wish to hurt anybody, which was surely a good thing, and yet he could not be certain whether it was kindness or cowardice that sometimes held him back from pursuing his own ends.

With a sigh he turned over. Left to himself he wanted a simple life with simple pleasures. Unease gnawed at the edges of his mind. Surely that was the essence of his religious belief? And yet there was another side to him which was enchanted, if not to say bewitched, by beauty in all its forms. Was not the fine carved oak staircase that he had recently commissioned an example of this frailty – or the silver in the side cupboard, the silk Cathay carpet, the portrait of Serenity that hung in his bed chamber, dressed in white satin, pearls at her neck and wearing her mother's ruby brooch?

At the thought of that portrait a tide of guilt threatened to submerge him. Perhaps he could make a case for displaying a painting of his daughter, but what about those other treasures he had truly hidden away: objects of great beauty but which sprang unequivocally from the devil-touched Popish religion?

He tried not to visualise them but already they were in his mind, rich, priceless, to be treasured – he had almost said *worshipped*. Here was the source of his true failure, in the covetous love of these symbols of Catholicism.

In order to test his faith he knew he should dispose of them, but how? He could not give them away. Even to admit to having them was to hand a weapon to his enemies. What sort of credibility would he have then, branded as a secret Popish sympathiser?

Serenity, of course, did not know of the artefacts' existence. Had she done so she would have been outraged. There would be no such dilemmas for her. Aeneas's moral obligation to destroy these works of the Devil wrestled with his outrage at the thought of desecrating such things of beauty. Sleep would not come.

He lay back on the bolster, listening for the night sounds of his home: the creak of old timber, the gentle spitting of a dying fire, the restless sigh of a hound in the kennels outside. These were the rhythms of a sleeping household.

Carefully he eased himself from the bed, crept across to the door and lifted the latch. It flew up with a resounding clang that set his heart thumping in response but as its pace slowed, he heard only the distant lapping of the river.

In his parlour Aeneas lit two candles in the sconce to the left of the fireplace. Like a blind man he fingered the panelling along the wall, counting to himself until he found what he was looking for. Pushing hard with his thumb, he depressed a peg concealed in the corner of one of the panels and with a click it swung back.

Aeneas's heart continued to thud, both with the fear of discovery and the guilty anticipation of pleasure. Reaching inside the cavity he drew out a simple silver box. With tingling fingers he placed it on the table, then unhooked the clasp and raised the lid. His mouth dry, he lifted out a package and carefully unwrapped it. Almost reverently he picked up the first of the objects.

In the palm of his hand, no bigger than a hen's egg, lay a painting of the Virgin Mary. With his head Aeneas knew that this was a heresy, a graven image of a human woman raised to god-like status. With his heart he looked on a face of exquisite beauty, both in form and expression. But what really moved him almost to tears was the richness of the *lapus lazuli*, her gown so blue that he could almost imagine being swallowed up by it. Tiny as the painting was it seemed to fill his whole universe. Reluctantly he laid it aside to examine the second object in the box.

Again it was small, perhaps two inches long and one and a half inches wide, a crucifix of gold, its entire surface encrusted with jewels.

Aeneas struggled to be calm. In his hand he held something not only of great beauty but also of great value. They were living in dangerous times. In the past houses such as his had been razed and every object of value destroyed, leaving the owner destitute, even if he escaped with his life. Anything secreted behind the panel and tucked into the niche in the solid stone of the wall would be safe. Endymion, with the Queen's favour, would have a line of communication to the Spanish court. Best to put these treasures away and forget about them, in preparation for a rainy day.

He looked at the cross one last time, with its pearls and rubies and emeralds. The green jewels brought his thoughts back to Esmeralda. She was his first priority. As he tenderly wrapped the madonna in linen and secreted it, he thought: Is Esmeralda just another example of my weakness for beauty? But no, he would not admit that. It was the beauty of her soul as much as her body that drew him to her. He had no reason to feel guilty in this respect. Tomorrow he would inform Serenity of his intention to marry then all would be well.

Aeneas at last confessed to his daughter after supper the following evening, having dismissed Esmee from the room. He would have liked to have his betrothed beside him but he did not want to risk having her insulted by Serenity's response.

Stumbling, embarrassed, he struggled to find the words that would best convey his feelings. As he spoke, his daughter's eyes grew large and black with spite. She rose from her chair and stepped back as if pushed by some unseen force.

'Papa! You cannot mean it! Surely you would not even conceive of such a union!' Her mouth hardened as the implications hit home. She continued: 'The girl is from the gutter, little more than filth! I know – I *know* that she is a witch. She has bewitched both you and *Samuel* and now she threatens to steal my very inheritance!'

Aeneas struggled manfully to make her understand. His very future depended on winning her co-operation for he could not conceive of a life without his daughter's good will.

Calmly, he said: 'Nonsense, my dear. It was you who wanted a different future for yourself instead of simply marriage. Now both our wishes can be fulfilled.'

Coming closer, fighting down his anxieties, he said: 'There is nothing to fear. You know that whatever you decide about your own future, I will make full provision for you in my will.'

Browbeaten by his daughter's thunderous frown, he said: 'If Esmeralda were to bear me a son, then the estate would of course pass to my male heir, but if that does not happen, then you would still be my heiress. This I promise: when I die, I shall leave Esmeralda provided for, but if there is no male child, the estate shall be yours. There now, there is absolutely nothing to worry about.'

'You love her more than me!' Serenity pouted and stamped her foot.

'Nonsense, sweetheart. You are my girl. You always will be. Try to understand that a lonely man needs ...' He did not have the words to convey his newly awakened lust to his daughter. Shamefaced, he said: 'I am not the sort of man to wear my feelings lightly, I do not believe that that is God's way.'

He was shocked when Serenity replied: 'Well, I think that you should do so. Anything would be better than to bring such a creature into our family. Why, she's some heathen's spawn!'

'Enough!' Aeneas found his patience wearing thin. If his life with

Esmeralda was to be bearable then he had to instil some discipline into his daughter. Uncomfortably he knew that he had left it too late. Then, because he could not bear to cross her, he said: 'Is there anything that you would like as a wedding gift from your papa? Name it and it shall be yours.'

He watched his daughter thinking, calculating. Moving closer to him she rested her cheek against his chest, his small child again, wheedling, loving. She said: 'If I marry Samuel and if I bear a child before – before your new wife, would you settle the estate upon my son, your true grandson?'

Aeneas could not think through the implications quickly enough. To buy time he said: 'That means you still intend to marry Sam?'

Serenity raised her eyes and he looked into their black, unfathomable depths. Demurely she said: 'Of course, Papa. It is your wish that I should do so, thereby strengthening our family ties. Our family name means so much to me. Naturally I shall do as you wish – and any child that I conceive with my cousin will be a true Craven.'

Aeneas sighed, having no answer. Hugging Serenity to him, he said: 'But Samuel is now Governor of the colony. He will not be returning here for several years. Even if we were to go there, it would not be until next year at the very earliest.'

Demurely, reminding him of a kitten as she rubbed her cheek against his, Serenity said: 'Then I shall have to wait. Patience is God's way. There is no rush. Perhaps you too should take time to consider your actions?'

Before he could demur, she added: 'Esmeralda is young. There is plenty of time for her to conceive.' She looked into Aeneas's eyes and he saw her maidenly cheeks turn pink. He sighed. His haste to marry Esmeralda, to experience the delights of her body, now seemed indecent. Sadly he thought that he would have to show some self-restraint and like his child wait a sensible length of time. The uncomplicated joy in his feeling for Esmeralda was marred.

He released Serenity and walked to the window. Outside, there were lighter flecks of green among the winter-worn trees. They hinted at a new spring time. Such rebirth was in stark contrast to his sudden disappointment. He tried to draw comfort from common sense. Perhaps it would be better to wait until Jackson returned and then formally ask for Esmeralda's hand?

The thought of the uncouth captain with his ruthless green eyes added to Aeneas's despair, but gallantly he fought to find some comfort. As soon as they married, they could leave straightaway on the next voyage to the colony. There they could start a new life away from the cynicism of the English court.

He was aware of his daughter standing behind him. At the back of his mind he suspected that she was urging him to wait because she did not want to give her rival any advantage of time in the race to conceive a child, but he pushed the thought away as unworthy.

With a sigh, he said: 'So be it, child. I shall delay any thoughts of marriage until next spring. When Captain Jackson returns I shall formally ask for Esmeralda's hand, after which we shall all three leave for the colony. There, you shall marry Sam.'

Swallowing down his disappointment, he added: 'To whichever of you a son is born first, either to yourself or Esmeralda, then to him shall pass the Craven estates.' Grasping at crumbs of comfort, he added: 'It will be for God to decide.'

SEVENTEEN

The shock of Aeneas's proposal reduced Esmeralda to the same state of panic she remembered when first her father said he was going to sell her. She had grown used to her way of life with Lord Craven and had assumed that it would last forever. Within moments a few words threatened everything that had grown safe and familiar.

In some ways she was worse off because since she had come to live with the Cravens she had never ventured out alone. The neighbourhood outside their front door was as alien to her as the jungles of Africa.

Esmee tried to imagine sneaking out at night and finding her way to the docks, there to board a ship for the Caribbean, but beyond that was a black tunnel. At the end of her tunnel was the lure of arriving at Samuel's island and being welcomed amid tears of joy. The reality of taking even the first step overwhelmed her.

She wondered what would happen if she told Aeneas that she had changed her mind. Of course he would be angry. She thought too that he would be hurt, and he had been so kind to her that she did not want to lose his good opinion. Unwillingly she had to admit that he was the one person who stood between her and jeopardy.

She thought too about Serenity. From her behaviour it seemed unlikely that Aeneas's daughter knew of her father's intentions. If the girl suspected that he planned to make Esmee his wife then she would surely be viciously angry. At the prospect of outwitting her mistress, Esmee felt a faint glow of exhilaration. It would almost be worth marrying Aeneas just to spite his daughter.

Throughout the next day she dreaded coming face to face with him for fear of what he might say, but when she did glimpse him in the corridor he seemed to avoid her. He was not present at meal-

110

times and for once Serenity seemed to imitate her name and maintain a serene silence.

As more days passed and nothing was said, Esmee began to think that she had imagined the whole business but then, as she passed Aeneas on the stairway, he reached out a hand and patted her arm. In a low voice, he said: 'My dear, I think we should wait until your father returns.' At the same moment Serenity came gliding down the stairs and he pulled back as if caught out in some shameful act. The matter was not mentioned again.

As the weeks passed there were some changes. Esmee moved from the small attic cubby-hole she had occupied since her arrival into a roomy chamber on the first floor. At the same time a woman was employed to look after both herself and Serenity. Her name was Hannah Hardy, she was large and matronly and her manner brooked no argument. Her role was never made clear, but Hannah ran their lives with slavish attention to detail, making each waking moment a labour in the service of the Lord.

Esmee did not sleep alone for Hannah now occupied a truckle bed that in the daytime fitted neatly beneath the huge four poster in her new chamber. She was never out of the woman's sight.

There was a subtle change in Serenity too. On the surface she began to treat Esmee as if she were more of an equal, but it was in a slightly amused, smug way, as if she knew something that Esmee did not.

When they dined with Aeneas he seemed ill at ease and at such times Serenity smiled with ill-disguised triumph. It was very unnerving. Meanwhile they seemed to act out their roles as if they were part of a tableau.

The news of her father's return from the Indies in October startled Esmee awake. At the thought of seeing him all the old anxieties came tumbling back. She felt as if she had woken suddenly from a dream so vivid she no longer knew what was real and what was fable.

It was soon widely broadcast that Captain Jackson had arrived back in a different ship, a fast new pinnace with the name *Destinnee* badly painted across the hull. Simultaneously, complaints reached the Eden Company from the Spanish Ambassador. An act of virtual piracy had taken place in the very harbour of Spanish Town, Jamaica. Questions would have to be answered, people punished, compensation paid.

Esmee feared that this time her father had gone too far. She wondered if they would hang him from his own yard arm. Worse was the thought that because of his crime, Lord Craven might see fit to throw her out, not wanting the child of a pirate beneath his roof.

News of Jeronimo Jackson's arrival seemed to act like touch paper in the Craven household. Aeneas looked tight-faced and Esmee guessed he disliked the prospect of confronting her father with his crime. Aeneas was essentially a man of peace who would not wish to cause his captain trouble. Dismally she thought: If only my father could be the same.

Above everything else, Esmeralda knew that there would be news from Samuel although she did not know how she would get to hear it. It would certainly not be from Serenity. She comforted herself with the thought that perhaps Lord Craven would announce it at a mealtime, or when his brother Endymion came to call.

This sudden link with Samuel, however tenuous, stirred up such a storm of feeling that she wondered how to endure each calm, passing moment. Without news of him she would surely suffocate in this narrow choking existence.

She looked at Serenity seated opposite her. Her mistress seemed calm and unruffled, but there was a certain grim determination about her. Esmee knew that the other girl shared none of her feelings for Samuel. Inwardly she cried out against the injustice. How could he marry a woman who did not love him? She would not even consider that he might love his betrothed.

'Papa?' Serenity rose from the table with a polite bow to her father. She bent forward to kiss him on the brow and as she did so her eyes met Esmee's. Her black stare was provocative, contemptuous, and Esmee's courage threatened to fail her. Serenity gave the impression of someone who knew that there was a prize to be won, and that she was determined to win it . . .

Jeronimo Jackson presented himself at Craven House the day after the *Destiny* docked. He was surprised to find that word of his new ship had spread so quickly, and even more disconcerted by the furore his action had caused.

'What else was I to do?' he asked Aeneas, seated opposite his employer. 'If you wanted me to come back with a good cargo, if you wanted something seaworthy to carry the next contingent across the ocean, then I had to take action.'

'But you stole a ship!'

'I exchanged it. The old *Destiny* was bigger than this one – that's a fair exchange.'

Aeneas sighed. 'The Spaniards demand that you be punished. They want compensation.'

Jackson shrugged it off. 'There's a goodly supply of timber aboard. Offer them half.' He did not mind the loss. He would still make a profit and he had what he wanted most: a new ship.

'They will insist that you be prosecuted.'

Jeronimo homed in on Aeneas's unease. Whatever the reason, His Lordship seemed unhappy at the prospect of a trial and Jackson did not think it had anything to do with the company.

Some shrewd instinct made him ask: 'How fares Esmeralda?' To his satisfaction he saw his employer's face colour.

'She is well. I – I wish to speak to you about her.'

Jackson waited. His blood pumped faster. In His Lordship's confusion he sensed the chance of a profit.

'I trust she is still a virtuous girl?' he said, suspecting Aeneas had been tampering with his prize. No matter that the old man had paid handsomely for her, now was the time to act the injured father.

Aeneas looked affronted. 'Of course she is. She's a good Christian maid, only lacking the benefit of a wise husband.'

Jeronimo smirked. 'You have someone in mind?' he asked, unable to hide his amusement.

'Your daughter needs kindness. She shows every promise of making an impeccable wife. That is why I – I have decided to do you the honour of making her a part of my family.'

'How?' Jeronimo sat back and studied his flushed companion. Let the old man sweat. If he was hot for Esmeralda then he could pay for her a second time.

'I intend to marry her, if you have no objection?'

Jeronimo pulled a face as if the prospect of entrusting his daughter to this man caused him some misgivings. 'We-ell . . .'

'I know she has no dowry,' Aeneas intervened, clearly trying to claw back some advantage.'But I'd be willing to overlook that.'

Jackson raised his shoulders in a gesture that said: So be it. Aloud, he said: 'Perhaps she'd be happier in another profession? Black girls are notoriously difficult to please.' His expression implied that Aeneas's sexual potency might not be up to keeping such a bride happy.

Aeneas flushed, this time with anger. 'Your daughter is not a whore. She understands well enough the holy state of matrimony. I am confident that she will be a good and faithful wife to any man who risks taking her on.' Standing up, he continued: 'After all, her upbringing is bound to raise some doubts as to the present state of her virtue.'

Jackson grinned, enjoying the game. 'I'll examine her myself if that's what you're worried about. I know enough about virgins to give you a fair opinion.'

He saw the shocked look on Aeneas's face and bowed his head, giving in with a good grace. 'You want my blessing, is it? Then you have it. My daughter is yours. I give her to you.' He hesitated. 'As your father-in-law, you might find it more convenient if I were to be a part of this new venture of yours. Perhaps a share in the company as a wedding gift from my new son . . .?'

Aeneas looked away. A nerve twitched in his cheek. Carefully he said: 'I don't hold that sort of power. Ours is a democratic venture. All the shareholders have to agree before a new member is appointed.'

By Craven's tone Jeronimo knew that the good men of the company would never under any circumstances welcome him to their number. He grinned good-naturedly. He could wait. There would be other times when Lord Craven's wealth and influence would come in useful.

'Well then, God bless you,' he said, standing up. 'I feel confident you can come to some arrangement on my behalf with the Spaniards. It might be an embarrassment if I were to be charged with piracy.'

Aeneas's face grew tighter. Blinking back his discomfort, he said: 'My brother has some influence at court. He may be able to smooth things over.'

'Good. Now, I have brought back some correspondence from the island.' He handed over Sam's reports and recommendations. Before Aeneas could look at them he added: 'I have another suggestion to make. That colony ain't going to last five minutes without proper labour. Between now and the next sailing to the island, I intend to go to Africa and pick up a load of natives. I'm sure we can come to some agreement about a price.'

Aeneas shook his head. 'I can't hold with such a traffic. It is against God's good laws.'

114

Jeronimo sighed and sank back into his chair. He did not speak for several seconds and when he did so, it was slowly, spelling out the facts as to a none-too-bright child.

'You have no idea what it is like in the Caribbees, have you? You have no concept of the heat. It takes white men and drains them dry. They fall like flies at a window.'

When Aeneas did not speak, he added: 'You'd be doing the blacks a favour, taking them from a heathen shore and instilling Christian virtues into them.' He paused to give weight to his next words. 'Believe me, your colony is doomed if you don't have black labour. Look, I'll even forego making a profit. You can have the slaves for what it costs me to get them – that's how important it is.'

'Then what is in it for you?'

'I see the colony as an ongoing concern, one where I can trade regularly. If it fails I shall have lost a market – and you and your friends will have lost your investment.'

Aeneas looked crestfallen. With a sigh, he said: 'I shall raise it at the next company meeting.'

Jeronimo rose to his feet again, feeling well pleased with the way that things were turning out. He said: 'I shall go to the Guinea Court come what may. If you don't want the merchandise, I can always sell it elsewhere.'

Aeneas shrugged, accepting defeat. Before his visitor could leave, he said: 'I forgot to tell you. On your next voyage to the island I shall be coming with you. I shall be bringing my daughter – also my bride.'

Jeronimo's heart gave a jolt. He felt suddenly unnerved by the news and angry with himself for letting it show. For the first time the reality of Esmeralda as Lord Craven's bride hit home. His mood changed as quickly as the weather. Curtly he bowed his head so that Aeneas should not guess his feelings, then without speaking he left the room.

From her chamber window Esmeralda watched the top of her father's flaxen head as he entered Craven House. She sat very still, straining her ears for any sound that might give a clue as to what was passing between the two men downstairs.

Her father's presence filled her with potent fear. Like onion skins, layer upon layer of memory peeled away, revealing aspects of him that she would rather not remember: Jeronimo in a black temper,

115

Jeronimo overfilled with drink, belligerent, violent, then frighten-
ingly sentimental.

Once she thought she heard a creak on the stair. Rigid with appre-
hension she drew back into the window recess, fearing that he was
coming to take her back, but the creak was followed by silence.

After about half an hour the front door opened and she listened
to the sound of farewells. Straining to see the path below, she witnessed his departure. His step was confident. Clearly he did not
expect to be hanged. She wondered what sort of trick he had played
on her unsuspecting guardian.

She did not have long to wait. Moments later there was definitely
the sound of steps on the stair followed by a tentative knock on her
chamber door. In answer to her call, Aeneas himself stepped inside,
being at pains to leave the door ajar so that their meeting could be
chaperoned, albeit at a distance.

'Esmee, my dear, your father was just here. He – he was in something of a hurry so he did not stay to pay his respects.'

She shrugged. Acts of courtesy by Jeronimo were so unlikely that
she knew the excuse was Lord Craven's, not her father's.

Aeneas looked ill at ease. Not meeting her eyes, he said: 'I took
the liberty of discussing with your father my hopes that we should
wed. He raised no objection.' He glanced up quickly and she saw his
embarrassment, a silent entreaty that she would raise no difficulty.
Compared with the prospect of returning to the *Destiny*, marriage
with Aeneas was a happy alternative. She kept her eyes lowered as
Hannah Hardy had instructed her and Aeneas seemed to take heart.

He said: 'Captain Jackson is sailing shortly for Africa. Now we
have his blessing there is no need for us to delay the ceremony.'
He hesitated. 'It might be – difficult for my daughter to come to
terms with our marriage. She is very devoted to me and naturally
does not wish to lose my affection.' Swallowing down his discomfiture, he added: 'As my own flesh, she will of course still come
first in my feelings.'

Esmee nodded to show that she understood. In fact she had no
way of gauging what Aeneas's feelings might be, either for herself
or for the spiteful girl he had fathered.

With a sigh of relief, he continued: 'When your father returns,
we shall be joining him on his next journey to – Eden.' He struggled
over the name and Esmee knew that he was smarting from the imagined slight now that their island no longer bore his daughter's

name. Thinking of Serenity's chagrin, she smiled to herself.

He continued: 'I am confident that my girl will find comfort in joining her betrothed. Once on the island she and Samuel can marry – and you and I can begin our new life together as I believe God intends.'

Her amusement at Serenity's discomfiture was short-lived. It was hard to decide which was worse: the thought of submitting to Aeneas's tentative advances, or witnessing the union between Serenity and the man that Esmee loved.

Thinking of the past months, when thoughts of marriage had seemed to be forgotten and she had been free to dream her dreams in peace, she heartily wished that she could go back to sleep.

EIGHTEEN

As Lord of the Manor of Westlingham in the county of Berkshire, Aeneas had himself appointed the Minister of the church in that parish. Believing the man to hold views sympathetic to his own, he decided that his wedding should take place in the village. When he sent for the priest to announce his plans, however, he received an unpleasant surprise.

'I am not at all sure that such a marriage is possible,' the Minister announced, clasping his hands over his rotund belly.

'How, not possible?'

The man looked abashed. 'Let us just say that not all of God's creatures have souls.'

For a moment Aeneas did not understand, then a wave of anger washed over him as he realised what the Minister was implying.

'Are you saying that my bride is not human?'

'No. That is . . . Let us just say that some of the lower sort are heathen, not designed to be part of God's congregation.'

Aeneas threw down his gloves in a fury. 'Such a view is abominable! I cannot believe what I am hearing. My betrothed goes regularly to church. She leads a blameless life. She can read and write and she fully understands the nature of the Christian way.'

Still the parson looked unconvinced. He said: 'You must understand, My Lord, that I would not wish to insult God by conducting a ceremony that was not acceptable to Him. After all, if a man should come and ask to be wedded to a dog . . .'

Aeneas swore. 'Damn you, man! How dare you compare my betrothed to a dumb beast! A white man's blood courses through her veins, as it does through yours and mine. If you mean to imply that she is some lesser creature . . .'

The Minister shook his head. 'Please do not misunderstand me. I am merely trying to point out that sometimes there are difficulties. There is no clear instruction about this. I need time to consider. Has the – er – young woman been baptised?'

Aeneas hesitated. The thought had not occurred to him. Recovering his poise, he said: 'If not, she shall be so without delay.'

He let out his breath, calming himself, seeking for a way to reason with his priest. He said: 'I fear it is you who face a crisis of conscience. For myself I believe that all men are part of God's congregation. Those who say otherwise do so because it is in their interest to pretend that some men – slaves – are lesser mortals. Only in this way can they justify buying and selling their own kind. I cannot accept that view. Nowhere in the testament will you find it voiced. Now, you had better take time to consider exactly what it is that you believe.'

The Minister was instantly placatory. Nodding his head, he said: 'I am merely trying to point out that there are sometimes difficulties. However, since you assure me that the – er – lady, is fit to undertake these vows, then we shall of course call the banns.'

'No. I no longer wish to be wed in this place. I shall go elsewhere, where my wife is revered for what she is: a good, chaste woman of intelligence. She shall not be wed on sufferance.'

The Minister bowed his head. 'As Your Lordship sees fit.' He hesitated. 'I hope this little misunderstanding does not prejudice my appointment here?'

Aeneas snorted: 'Go and search your conscience.'

Afterwards he could not settle. The Minister's views distressed him greatly. He wished there was someone to whom he could turn for understanding but when he thought about it, no one had declared themselves sympathetic to his feelings for Esmeralda – except perhaps her father, and his motives were hardly creditable.

For a moment he nearly weakened. Perhaps they were right: Serenity, Endymion, the priest. Perhaps he was making a fool of himself. Perhaps he was bewitched. But when he walked into the parlour that evening and saw Esmeralda bent over some tapestry work by the light of the fire, his heart overflowed with love. He would marry her if it was the last act of his life.

The marriage between Aeneas, Lord Craven and Esmeralda Jackson was solemnised on the eleventh day of November 1635 at the Church of St Michael in London.

To Aeneas's relief, when he announced his plans to the incumbent of the church, the man raised no difficulties. The service was modest, a simple exchange of vows and prayer books. But to his sensitive ears, Aeneas suspected that the sermon which preceded the ceremony contained guarded warnings. The message was: As you sow, so shall ye reap, implying that an unwise choice of partner would remain so for life. It was not a sentiment to his liking.

There were few persons present. Although Aeneas extended an invitation to all colleagues and family, neither Endymion nor Aeneas's brother-in-law, Lord Silchester, saw fit to attend. No member of the Eden company was present. Only Serenity, her mouth compressed with disapproval, stood martyr-like behind the bride, a living symbol of a daughter's submission to the will of her parent.

Turning to look at his bride, Aeneas drew heart. With her eyes downcast, her face obscured by a veil, so still and graceful, he thought her the most beautiful, pure, priceless gift from God that any man could deserve. He was blessed indeed.

Esmee felt as if a frozen lump of ice had been placed inside her stomach, resting just beneath her ribs. It would not melt. She suspected that her heart had stopped beating for she was cold as marble, there in the body of the church. A tiny part of her mind that seemed to be working all by itself, wondered if a witch had hexed her.

That morning she had woken early with the thought: Today I am to be wed. She did not really believe it. It seemed more like a leftover feeling from her disturbed dreams.

When Hannah Hardy appeared, she allowed herself to be dressed in a kind of half-sleeping state. She had seen men so entranced in the Americas, after they had smoked mysterious weeds known to the Indians.

Even when they reached the church and she was led from the carriage and up the aisle by one of Lord Craven's distant cousins, she still thought: At any moment I shall wake up. Standing in the gloom of the building, the physical discomfort of her chilled body finally stirred her from her apathy.

Aeneas was at her side, looking at her. Through the lace of the veil she could see his brown eyes, moist with emotion. They crinkled at the corners as he smiled at her and she quickly looked away.

She became aware of a silence in the church and realised that the Minister was looking at her, waiting for some response. He repeated his words.

To her amazement she realised that her consent was required to the union. Until that moment she had not questioned that she must simply do as she was told.

When asked to make a declaration, she could barely find the voice to do so. It was only as she whispered: 'I do consent,' that she realised she might have said no.

Back at the house of which she was now mistress, there was an air of false jollity. With a terrible sense of loneliness, she knew that those present were trying to make the best of a bad job.

Aeneas plied his guests, mostly members of his household, with sweet wine from the Palatinate States, presented as a wedding gift by Endymion, with the cryptic message: 'God's blessing, brother, you are going to need this!'

Esmee sipped the wine cautiously. It was smooth and she quickly emptied her beaker, warming to the comforting sensation as it flowed into her belly, at last melting the ice. A second measure swiftly followed the first. It relaxed her enough to swallow a few mouthfuls of the wedding breakfast that awaited them.

A meal of fresh bream topped with oysters, and quail stuffed with chestnuts, was followed by syllabub and iced berry fool. Sitting at Aeneas's right hand, Esmee nodded and bowed in response to the stilted remarks of his guests. Opposite her, Serenity fixed her with a gimlet stare, cold as the icy waters across the South Atlantic. After an eternity, the signal was given that Esmee should retire.

Serenity, her face carved in granite, sought permission to leave the table at the same moment. She moved wordlessly from the room and preceded Esmeralda up the stairway to the gallery above. As she reached her chamber door, she snapped: 'I trust that your rutting won't keep me awake!'

At the thought of the violent activity about to be thrust upon her, Esmee physically recoiled. She could feel Serenity's venom wafting in the air like acrid smoke.

Mistress Hardy, puffing up the stairs in their wake, seemed unaware of the remark. Pushing open the bedroom door and ushering Esmee inside, she said: 'Come along, child. Into bed with you.'

Fighting down her fears, Esmee entered the bed chamber. A

121

nightgown of cambric lay across the quilt, the neck and sleeves trimmed with lace that she herself had pinned during the summer months. The gown was simple, virginal. Thinking of those warm evenings when she had stitched and sewn, she felt cheated. She had never realised that the garment was intended for this sacrifice.

Hannah Hardy unlaced Esmee's gown, peeled off her stockings, unpinned her cap and loosed her hair. It sprang back in bouncy ringlets and Hannah tutted to herself.

'Such a pity your locks aren't long and straight.'

On top of everything else, Esmee felt the burden of not living up to her maid's idea of beauty.

The chemise that lay next to her skin was stripped away and she was aware of the other woman glancing at her. She felt her cheeks burn and hastened to cover herself. As the nightgown tumbled down over her body, Hannah said: 'Such a pity about the hue of your skin, but otherwise he won't be disappointed.'

At the thought of what was to come, Esmee reached out to stay Hannah, wanting to hold her back, hoping to be saved from her husband's demands, but there was a cold light in the servant's eyes, the spiteful look of a spinster witnessing the transition of a younger girl from child to woman.

Esmee let her hand fall back. She lay down on the linen sheet, her body feeling brittle as eggshells. She pulled the coverlet up to her chin and watched Hannah's retreating back. The door clicked shut and she was alone.

Aeneas came in quietly. Esmee had a fleeting glimpse of his voluminous nightshirt and the embroidered cap on his head before she closed her eyes. At sea she had witnessed what was about to happen many times. It was soulless, brutal and now she had consented to it. Dear God, let it be over quickly!

'Esmee, my dear. Do you sleep?' Hesitantly Aeneas pulled back the coverlet and climbed in beside her. He did not blow out the candles that flickered in the sconces above the bed. For a moment he was very still and she knew that he was looking down at her, then he reached out his hand and smoothed a lock of damp hair away from her cheek. Slowly his fingers stoked their way down across her neck and came to rest over her breast.

She drew in her breath with an audible gasp, fighting down the desire to scramble out of the bed and run.

The sound seemed to release him. With a little moan, he fumbled with the opening of her gown, sliding his hand clumsily inside, grasping her nipple between his fingers as if he was a nursing mother. Esmee turned her head away to avoid his breath. She tried to think of the afternoon's service and the promise she had made before Samuel's God to love and obey this man. She endured the intrusion.

'My dear girl.' Her lack of response seemed to give him courage. Reaching down he raised her nightgown and toured the surface of her skin with his fingertips. Her flesh crawled with fear. All the time he drew nearer to the centre of her being. When she could stand it no longer she tried to close her legs but he held them apart with his knee.

'My dear girl,' he repeated, finally touching her in the most sacred place. At the feel of his fingers she panicked and struggled to get up, to get out from under him, but grasping her hands, he forced her once again on to her back, wriggling himself into position. All her fears were back, that life-long knowledge that men were to be avoided at all costs.

He whispered: 'Just help me, my dear. I'll be as gentle as I can.'

As the tip of his cock came to rest in the most sacred part of her, she screamed.

Aeneas stopped. For an eternity he lay over her, his breath indrawn, his hands still clasping her wrists. She felt as if he was suffocating her, crushing her chest until she would die like a drowning soul. Mercifully he drew away.

Sitting up and turning his back to her, he said: 'I'm so sorry. I thought . . . I suspected . . .'

Esmee drew away, pulling her knees up to her chin, gripping the covers to hide her body. This was a nightmare, a living nightmare. How had she come to be here? With certainty she knew that this was an act she could perform only with Samuel. She was immediately immersed in that feeling of magic that had coccooned her when Samuel held her close and his urgency had answered her own. Silently she cried out to him to rescue her. Why had he held back? Why had he not made her his bride there and then so that she would not be lying here, an unwilling virgin in her husband's house?

Her husband. She looked at Aeneas's skinny back. A terrible sense of failure enveloped her. With all her heart she wanted him out of her bed, out of her chamber. She did not know why he was apologising to her.

123

With a heavy sigh he turned towards her. He gave a little sob of his own and she wondered at the awfulness of her failings.

Swallowing deeply he said: 'I am so very sorry. In spite of your father's assurances, I truly expected that after the life you had led you would already be a woman.'

He pulled his nightshirt down over his knees and sighed again. Rising from the bed he said: 'I will not force myself upon you. Perhaps in the fullness of time, when you have come to know me better, you will feel able to accommodate my needs. In the meantime . . .'

Without finishing the sentence he padded solemnly to the door. Lying frozen in her loneliness, Esmee heard the latch to his own door lift, then moments later the creak of the bed as he returned to his lonely couch.

In spite of his failure to consummate his marriage, Aeneas found some consolation in the possession of his new bride. In public she conducted herself with such dignity that she soon won the hearts of those few friends and colleagues who deigned to acknowledge her.

Dear, pure Esmee. He was comforted by the knowledge that if her innocence held her back from the physical side of marriage, he need have no fears that she would cast an eye on those other, younger bucks who so openly admired his good fortune in possessing such a gem.

For his own self-respect he made a point of visiting her in her chamber most nights, where he would spend an hour reading to her or teaching her the rudiments of chess.

Sometimes, when she was absorbed by the game, he would glimpse the globe of her breast beneath her gown and in his mind he would feel again its vibrant weight in his bridegroom's fingers. Once he risked cupping her bosom as she leaned forward to move her pawn but as she froze to a standstill, he let his hand rise, pretending he had meant to brush a spiral of hair away from her shoulder. She looked unbelievably beautiful.

'Forgive me, my dear.'

In the face of her silence, he felt he had to sort something out. Even as he sat there, he longed to possess her. He told himself that he did not mind how long he had to wait as long as the day would come when she would truly be his. After a silence, he said: 'Perhaps when we leave England, when you are away from here, you will feel able to be a wife to me?'

Without meeting his eyes, Esmee nodded.

Aeneas breathed out his relief. He took this to be a solemn promise. He had not told her but her father was already down the coast of Plymouth with a supply of native labour.

In spite of Aeneas's own opposition, the company had agreed to buy the slaves and they would all be travelling to Eden together. Aeneas felt demoralised. He should have asserted himself, stuck to his principles and resigned in protest, but he had not. He wanted too much to sail to Eden and begin his new life. He knew that he was a poor servant to the Lord. Then he comforted himself with the thought that perhaps he could ease the slaves' suffering if he travelled with them.

Esmee had made her chess move and was waiting for him. He opened his mouth to tell her about her father, then changed his mind. He would leave it until tomorrow.

As he moved his bishop he felt an overwhelming rush of elation at the prospect of visiting Eden Island. Everything was settled. Endymion had interceded on his behalf and Queen Henrietta Maria had encouraged the King to grant permission for them to make the journey. Aeneas suspected that the promise of additional English territory in the Caribbean impressed the King more than the prospect of a new Christian community, but no matter, the end would justify the means.

Aeneas's steward would take charge of his London house, a bailiff had been appointed to oversee his estate at Westlingham and his financial affairs were safely in the hands of Oliver St James, solicitor to the Eden Company. He took comfort from the fact that Endymion, while having the use of his brother's house, would not have control of the purse strings.

Aeneas leaned back and watched his wife with a feeling bordering on reverence. Her face was in repose, still as a portrait, while she considered the chess game before her. Aeneas was reminded again of his painting of the Madonna. He wondered whether he should take it with him but immediately decided against it. It would be too dangerous. Not only would it be risky to be found with it in his possession, it was also his insurance in case of trouble.

In writing his will, he had not mentioned it. Endymion knew nothing of its existence. If Aeneas perished on the journey, the secret would die with him.

He wondered if, years from hence, somebody would discover it.

'Check!' Esmee's cry of triumph interrupted his daydreams. Asserting some rights as a bridegroom, he reached out and squeezed her shoulder.

'Time to sleep then, my dear. I bid you goodnight.' His lips rested briefly against her hair and the unique blend of herbs and scents that were her own stirred again his desire for her. Without saying more, he hurriedly left the room to seek some private relief for his growing frustration at his own hands.

For the first few weeks following her marriage, Esmee lived in a state of unease. She tried not to think what might happen when her husband came nightly to her chamber, but as the days passed and Aeneas seemed content with reading to her or playing games, her anxiety began to recede.

Once or twice he attempted some greater intimacy between them – a goodnight kiss that strayed from her temple to her mouth, a hand that wandered from her shoulder to her breast – but when she drew away he immediately expressed his apologies. With amazement she began to realise that she was the one in control. Little by little it dawned on her that she might even be able to bend his will to suit her own.

'Perhaps when we leave England you will feel able to be a wife to me?' he said hopefully one evening as she brushed aside his probing fingers.

Carefully Esmee moved her knight, thus threatening Aeneas's king. 'Check.' She did not answer his question but he seemed to draw his own conclusions. Instead, she said: 'I may be wrong, but sometimes I think Serenity is unhappy at the prospect of marrying your nephew.'

'You think so, my dear?'

Esmee shrugged, uncomfortable in the role of meddler, but a lot was at stake. After a while, she added: 'Serenity is so fair of skin, I fear she may suffer greatly in the tropical climate.'

Aeneas glanced down at his own pale arms and Esmee realised too late that she might be planting doubts about going to the island at all, so she quickly continued: 'It is often harder for women – childbirth and the like.' The thought that Serenity could bear Samuel a child hardened her resolve.

126

'Then do you think we should consider staying in England?' He sounded alarmed.

'No. That is, I am used to such conditions. But I simply thought that if your daughter has the slightest misgivings, then perhaps she should stay here with Hannah.'

Aeneas nodded. 'I will suggest it to her.'

That he had done so became clear the following evening when Serenity came down to supper. Esmee busied herself laying the table with the simple pewter that served for everyday use. Aeneas liked wine with his meal so she crossed to the cupboard and took out three glasses, ignoring Serenity's gimlet stare.

Aeneas had not yet made an appearance and Serenity went to stand near the fireplace, awaiting his arrival before they joined in pre-prandial prayers.

'I hear that you are worried about me,' she started, her chin jutting provocatively. 'Papa passed on to me your concerns about the climate – *and* your fears about my marriage.'

Esmee piled fresh diet bread on to her favourite Delft charger with its warm swirl of vivid flowers. At the mention of Serenity's marriage her hands began to tremble.

'I have been there, you haven't.' She concentrated on the first observation.

Serenity smirked. 'Such consideration – especially over my finer feelings where my cousin is concerned.' She paused for effect then continued: 'But I beg you not to worry on my behalf. As far as the climate goes, I am tougher than you think, and as for my cousin . . .'

She gave a snort of contempt, dropping her mask of pretence. 'Do you think I am absolutely blind? You have your scheming claws into my father and now you want his nephew. Well, I am sorry to disappoint you, *Mother*, but I have every intention of travelling to our island, and no qualms at all about fulfilling my father's wishes in wedding Samuel. In fact, I look forward to being a wife – so just put your doubts out of your mind.'

At that moment Aeneas walked in, hesitating momentarily as he caught the frosty atmosphere, but before he could comment, Esmee excused herself and hurried to the kitchen. Her stomach churned and the thought of food repelled her but she tried to behave normally.

As she went in the cook lifted the brass cauldron from its supporting brigg and stood it down out of range of the fire. Today's was a simple meal – Dutch pudding wrapped in cabbage leaves, plus carrots and turnips simmered in the same pot in a net. While Esmee busied herself untying the pudding cloth, the cook extricated a round earthenware crock that held a pheasant, basted in butter and cooked in its own juices with a liberal sprinkling of herbs. Until half an hour ago Esmee had been looking forward to the dishes but now her appetite had gone. With quaking heart she led the way back to the dining room, carrying the pudding on a trencher.

Both Serenity and Aeneas stood behind their stools at the table. Once the dishes were in place, Aeneas led them in prayers. 'Lord, a blessing we pray Thee on this house. Make our hearts grateful for Thy bounty and look with compassion on all our hopes. Amen.' Esmee remembered the convoluted prayers of the Reverend Shergold aboard her father's ship and gave thanks for Aeneas's brevity.

While her husband carved the bird and sliced the pudding she sat in silence, refusing to meet her adversary's eyes. As Aeneas took his seat, Serenity said: 'Papa, have you told my step-mother that her dear father will be here on the morrow, and that before the month is out we shall be leaving England to start our new lives?'

Esmee darted a look at Aeneas who lowered his eyes in embarrassment.

'No, my dear, not yet.' He spiked a morsel of pheasant and Esmee saw that his hands were shaking.

Whatever his reasons for not telling her, Esmee faced a far more painful truth. Soon they would be going to Eden Island, going to Samuel – and it would be Serenity, not herself, who would be the object of his love.

NINETEEN

Jeronimo had had a good trip. The new *Destiny* was a joy to sail: sleek, fast, responsive, like a good woman. He felt pleased with himself as he retired to his cabin for a few hours' rest.

Tomorrow they would be moving up the coast to Portsmouth then revictualling, ready for the third trip to Eden. The knowledge caused a quickening of his heart. The prospect of transporting Lord Craven and his new bride suggested endless possibilities. He tried to imagine what might happen, dwelling on the fantasy of having Lord Craven in his power, stealing his money, perhaps gaining ownership of the old man's estates, the hand of his haughty daughter . . . all in return for sparing his life.

The daydream was a pleasant one. It kept him from thinking about Esmeralda and that other fantasy that still came to torment him.

Going down into his cabin he closed the door to shut out the grunts and moans from below decks. The noise of the slaves seemed to hover over the *Destiny* like a plague of hornets.

That afternoon his cargo had been taken on deck for inspection. While the entire crew stood guard, armed with knives, whips and muskets, the slaves were hosed off, examined, then given some exercise. Stiff and weak, they had to be prodded to make them jig around until the crew grew bored, then they were herded back down below.

The long chains that ran the length of the hold and passed through the rings on each set of manacles which secured the slaves had rubbed some of them so sore that gangrene threatened. Jeronimo cursed his crew for not looking after the blacks properly. He couldn't afford to lose bucks willy nilly.

129

From their pale skins and fine features, he guessed that most of the slaves, all male, were Fulani. In spite of a long march from the interior to the coast and a prolonged stay in the holding pens, they were still generally in good health. He thought they should stand up to the Atlantic crossing without undue loss of life.

The dinah whom he had picked up on his last voyage to Jamaica jumped up from the pile of sacks where once Esmeralda had slept and backed away from him as he came in, her head bowed in submission. She stood there sullenly, her face half turned away, eyeing him with her black, suspicious look.

'Ale.'

She ran to do his bidding.

When he had sailed from Jamaica he had intended to sell the girl as a pet to some pampered English family, but once he got her aboard and cleaned her up he realised she was not a child but a young woman.

He did not understand her foreign jabber but it seemed likely that she had not long been landed at Jamaica and the rigours of the journey had undoubtedly stunted her growth. Under his calloused hands, the little creature was being coached into a whole range of interesting tricks. One good beating and she had soon come round to his way of doing things.

She wasn't a pretty thing – not like Esmeralda. Her features were coarse and her skin was disfigured by those criss-cross scars across her cheeks. This one wasn't Fulani but from some smaller, pagan tribe. He knew that women were often scarred to make them ugly – keep them faithful. Jeronimo smirked. He had no trouble in that way. No woman would dare to double-cross him, either free or enslaved.

The comparison with Esmeralda had disturbed him in the old, familiar way. Putting the tankard down, he pulled the dinah to him and forced her to sit facing him on his lap. His cock reared and he poked it inside her, then rolled her on to the bunk.

The dinah gave a little whimper as he thrust as hard as he could to get into her. She wasn't very big and he had the feeling of driving up under her ribs to get satisfaction. He suspected she was in pup for she hadn't bled to his knowledge since he had brought her aboard. He wondered if he would dislodge the child. It was idle speculation. A brat would be more trouble than it was worth. Look how long it had taken to get any profit from Esmeralda.

The thought of his daughter excited him so that he came to a juddering and premature climax. Frustrated that his pleasure was cut short, he shoved the girl roughly up against the wall to give himself more space. For a moment he felt sulky, like a child denied a treat, then he became aware of the dinah's small frame squashed between him and the hard board of the cabin partition. Her discomfort brought him consolation and his bad mood disappeared as quickly as it had come. Stretching out, he grinned into the darkness.

Just as he was dropping off to sleep he thought again of Lord Craven and his wife, Esmeralda. His grin widened.

As Esmee stepped aboard the new *Destiny* she was assailed by haunting sensations, all struggling at once to crush her fragile resolve to remain calm. Everything fought to overwhelm her: the sounds of seamen swearing or singing, the dull thud of rope against the deck, the heavy scraping of chests as they were winched down to be stored below.

Then there were the smells – salt, fish, canvas, dirty bodies – all blended into a pungent whole that was part of her earliest memory.

The sight of her father made her falter. She did not deign to look at him as he welcomed her husband aboard, but his mannerisms, so familiar, were as clear in her mind as if she were watching his every move. More spectres of the past came to haunt her.

Without meaning to she moved closer to Aeneas who, sensing her presence, slipped his arm through hers and guided her aboard.

She was glad to be on a different ship. Had she entered the old *Destiny*, the memory of that last journey, and Sam's imprint, would have been too much. She was aware of Serenity standing with a pinched expression behind Aeneas, her skirts lifted to avoid the slime of the deck on a wet morning, and in her wake Hannah Hardy, her eyes large with dismay.

The sight of their fear restored Esmee's confidence enough for her to move away from Aeneas's protective grasp. Holding her head high, she followed him down to the cabin that had been set aside for them.

She thought with a sense of self-mockery of the years she had slept in the corner of her father's cabin on a pile of sacks. Now Jeronimo was ousted from his quarters so that she and her husband could sleep in the narrow bunk that ran the length of the cabin wall.

A second, smaller cubicle had been cleared for Serenity and

Hannah, while Jeronimo himself would sleep in what was little more than a cupboard.

Looking round, Esmee caught a glimpse of a black child, squat and skinny, peering from the entrance to her father's new quarters. Her heart missed a beat at the thought of the girl's role in her father's life. She wondered whether to say anything to Aeneas, but she did not have the energy, or courage, or whatever it took to set a course of action in motion that would anger her father and bring some unknown retribution to rest somewhere – upon her husband, upon the skinny girl, or upon herself? She remained silent.

Esmee looked round the cabin. In spite of their cramped conditions, she acknowledged to herself that it was the height of luxury compared to the conditions endured by the slaves below. Even as they had boarded the ship, the familiar, haunting stench of the hold had dealt another blow to her confidence.

'What is that smell?' Aeneas, storing his trunk half under the couch, and knowing that sooner or later he was bound to knock his shins on the sharp corner, wrinkled his nose in distaste.

'The slaves.'

'Do they always smell like that?' He looked dismayed.

Esmee shrugged. 'They don't stink when they've been cleaned.'

'But your father assured me that they were able to wash regularly. If they aren't being properly cared for . . .'

Esmee smiled at his ignorance. 'It's the ship that stinks. Their smell gets into its very timbers.'

Aeneas's brow furrowed with concern. 'I think I should go and see for myself.'

Esmee slipped off the satin slippers that encased her feet. She suddenly longed for the canvas togs that had for so long been her only clothing. At that moment she remembered the rare good things about being a cabin hand, like riding in the prow of the ship as if on some great white stallion, her body rocking gently with the rise and fall of the waves. She remembered the crew's gentle teasing. Ezra's stories, the warmth of the sun against her skin. Best to concentrate on those things and forget the others.

Aloud, she said to Aeneas: 'It's best you don't.'

In her mind she could see the darkness, the misery, feel the slippery boards of the deck, smell the ghastly stench of piss and vomit. Seeing Aeneas's concerned face, she added: 'You can't change anything so you'd best not interfere.'

Aeneas shrugged it off. Esmee thought: He feels guilty because he thinks he should do something but doesn't know how.

Aeneas took her hand. His eyes were misty with affection. He said: 'Today is a great day for us. The beginning of our new life together. Let us pray for God's blessing on our endeavours.'

Esmee lowered her eyes so that he should not see her own thoughts. Compliantly she sank to her knees in an attitude of prayer. Quietly her husband intoned his supplication.

As she went to stand up he caught her arm, turning her towards him. She sensed that he felt freed from the constraints of his old life. Although she instinctively grew tense, she did not pull away from him.

Ever since their wedding night, when Aeneas had attempted to possess her, Esmee had been troubled by a constant sense of dissatisfaction. It sometimes seemed that her body was at odds with her mind. In her heart she wanted only to be faithful to Sam, to live for the day when it would be he who made love to her. Quickly she pushed away the thought that it would be Serenity, not herself, who would share his bed, but the vision trickled like poison into her mind.

After what she had seen at sea, she freely admitted to herself that she was afraid of the marital act, scared of losing control or being hurt. Yet Samuel would never hurt her. A treacherous voice added: Neither would your husband.

Often she relived all that she had felt during Aeneas's brief time in her bed. Her mind was appalled by the thought of him, old, skinny, timid, yet perversely her body sent out loud messages that it would like to be touched again, to feel fingers trailing over her skin, to give itself up to a tender hand, caressing and soothing. She felt tormented by frustration.

'Esmee.' Aeneas kissed her temple, his lips lingering against her damp hair. He held her close so that her breasts were flattened against his chest. In spite of herself, her pelvis moved forward a little as if seeking out the stirrings of his groin. She closed her eyes, her mind elsewhere, courted by some other, hazy figure who knew how to give pleasure.

'Oh, Esmee!'

The feeling was there again. It frightened and excited her. Aeneas pushed his hand against her, pressing the stuff of her gown between her suddenly hungry loins, and she responded by moving towards

133

him, wanting to protect herself against the knowledge that at the end of this voyage, Samuel would touch Serenity so. But Aeneas hesitated too long, was too tentative in his wooing. The thought of Sam intervened, with his young man's virile body, his handsome face and half-confessed feelings of love. If she could never have Samuel, then she would remain a virgin until her grave. She did not want this old, courtly knight. She drew back.

'Esmeralda!' There was despair in Aeneas's voice. He reached for her again but she slid away.

'Please, Aeneas, this is not the place. Please be patient.' To fend him off, she added: 'Perhaps when we have a place of our own . . .'

If he had insisted, used his masculine power to bow her to his will, she might still have given way but instead he sighed and stepped back.

'As you say, my dear. Only please, I cannot – I cannot wait forever.'

She nodded her head as if she understood and with that he had to be satisfied.

As the days passed, the crossing was marked by few events that seemed likely to stay in Esmee's memory. Aeneas was always kind and considerate, making light of his sea sickness and hiding the debilitating stomach cramps that stayed with him throughout the journey. In consideration for her comfort he even struggled to sleep in a hammock so that she should not feel crowded on the narrow couch.

In stark contrast Serenity wailed her disgust at everything: the ship and its crew, her cabin and the food, the vagaries of wind and ocean swell. Hannah Hardy was sick for most of the voyage and kept to her cabin. The feelings of the slaves could only be guessed at from the cries of despair that echoed from the holds.

Esmee, born to the movement of the tides and the half-forgotten kiss of the wind, revelled in the elements. And all the time the thought came back to claim her: at the end of the journey there would be Samuel. She tried to imagine the moment when she saw him. In her mind, Serenity and Aeneas did not exist. There would be just the two of them, Samuel and Esmeralda, lovers, destined to spend their lives together until the end of time.

Her thoughts were interrupted by the sound of her father, imparting some information to Aeneas. She strained to hear what he was saying but it was of no particular interest.

Jeronimo had not spoken to her directly since she had come aboard. Now, as at every other meeting, he concluded his visit with a curt nod that encompassed her along with her husband. But sometimes she would catch him watching her, his vivid green eyes narrowed from years of enduring the blazing sun, his tawny skin marked with criss-cross lines where the wind had beaten into his face. His body was spare, hardened by years of struggling against the elements. For a moment she was disturbed by this comparison with Aeneas's softness.

She caught a glimpse of his mouth, unnerving her with its downturned grim contempt. On the rare occasions that he smiled, his expression was secret, sinister.

As he turned to go, she noticed the dinah scuttling about the decks and read in her shuttered eyes the message of despair she had seen in every such woman, every female slave at the mercy of her captors. The same expression must have been in the eyes of her own mother. Again Esmeralda faced the black wall of not knowing.

At Barbados they were to go ashore to revictual. In addition, Aeneas carried important papers to be handed to the Governor.

'What a joy it will be to set foot on land,' he said, as they watched the hazy shape of the island transform itself into a solid, sun-touched outline.

Esmee did not reply. For the past few hours she had been feeling increasingly unwell. Her face was damp with sweat yet at the same time she was shivering. She knew the symptoms well enough. The best cure was to lie down and give herself up to the alternate hot and cold and to drink as much as she could lay hands on to assuage the rasping of her throat.

'My dear, are you sick?' Aeneas was immediately the loving husband, concerned only for her welfare.

'It is nothing. I have known it before.' Seeing his fear she gave him a brief smile. 'Really, Aeneas, I just need to rest.'

'My dear, you are hot. Let me find a cloth and sponge you.'

'No. please. You go about your business.' She did not want him fussing over her. As brightly as she could manage, she added: 'We don't want to be delayed, do we? This is just a minor ailment.'

'Then Serenity will sit with you.'

'No!' Esmee answered too quickly. She had already heard her step-daughter shouting impatiently for the time when they would step ashore and away from this pox-infested ship.'

'Then Hannah will certainly stay.'

'No, Aeneas, truly. Hannah is desperately looking forward to going ashore. She has suffered so much on the crossing.'

She took his thin hand. 'I promise you, I am in no danger. You forget that I have spent most of my life on a ship such as this.'

As he went to protest, she stilled his mouth with her fingers. He sighed doubtfully but pushed her gently back on to the bunk, pulling the coverlet over her.

'You are cold now, my dear.'

'I know. It is usual. Please go, or I shall be worrying that you have failed in your mission.'

In the face of her insistence the party made its way ashore. Dragging herself up on to one elbow, Esmee watched from the port hole. Jeronimo had sent the ship's mate to guide them. Esmee guessed that her father would have his own business ashore. Her chest tightened as she remembered those evenings when he'd returned to the ship, drunk and belligerent. Idly she thought: The poor dinah.

She must have been on the point of sleep when the door opened. The creak and the current of cool evening air jerked her awake. It was dark. She tried to hear above the sudden noisy thumping of her heart, to see into the gloom.

'Aeneas?'

The shadowy figure in the doorway moved inside, shutting the door behind him.

'No, Chickadee, it's me.'

Every sense was immediately startled awake. Esmee sat up in the bed and leaned back against the rough wood of the wall.

'What do you want?'

'I've come to see how my little daughter is faring now that she's a rich lady.'

Esmee could not speak. Undiluted fear coursed through her veins.

Jeronimo sighed expansively and moved into the tiny cabin, in the process hitting his shins against Aeneas's trunk. He cursed loudly and his previously jovial tone changed.

'Well, you've got it all now, haven't you? Thanks to me you're one of the gentry.'

Still she could say nothing, wondering how long her husband had been away and hoping that by some miracle he would appear. The fever that had gripped her was banished by this sudden danger.

Jeronimo gave an audible grunt as if his thoughts intrigued him. 'What's it like then, being married to a peer of the realm?'

Esmee hesitated, wondering how best to play for time. Carefully, she said: 'My husband is good – but powerful.'

Jeronimo gave a mirthless laugh. 'Good is he? Under the covers? He don't strike me as a stallion.'

She tried to sound assured but her voice wavered. 'It's none of your concern. Get out of here or he'll hear about it.'

Jeronimo pretended hurt. 'Now then, that's no way to speak to your father.' He came closer and Esmee could not stifle the whimper of terror that filled her throat.

Jeronimo sank on to the bunk. 'Come along now, Chickadee. Tell me all about it.'

'I won't!'

His hand shot out, fast as an arrow, clasping her in a grip of iron. When he spoke she could feel his breath on her neck, hear the spite in his voice.

'Nigh on fifteen years I kept you, watched you grow. Night after night I endured your taunting, watching you flaunt that pretty arse of yours, and I didn't do a thing so that you could keep your prize.'

He leaned closer, dominating her with his menacing presence. His voice hardly above a whisper, he said: 'Well now, it paid off, didn't it? Old man Craven paid up and you're rich and comfortable. Now he's had the prize, I can sample the leavings.'

Esmee screamed. She tried in vain to scramble out of the bunk and past her father but he blocked her way, his fingers still biting into her wrists.

With his free hand he unfastened his breeches and dragged her gown up above her waist. 'C'mon,' he said thickly. He fell heavily upon her, pushing and manoeuvring her on to her back.

'No!' She tore at his hair, his face. Pain, terror, revulsion kaleidescoped as every thrust of his body tore at hers. Razors sliced her tender skin. Grappling irons scored the dark tunnel of her flesh. She fought desperately, suffocated by his weight but her struggles only seemed to drive him harder and he grunted out his lust as he broke and bruised her.

In one great thrust, he tore at her shoulders with his nails, punctured the skin of her throat with his teeth. Juddering, pushing, he drove himself to a halt.

Beneath him, Esmee floundered in a black pit of hurt and disgust.

137

As he pulled out she felt again the pain of his entry.

Her father gave a grunt of dismay. 'Am I deceiving myself or were you still a maid?'

'I'll kill you!' She raked at his cheeks with her nails, kicked with her bare feet, having nothing left to fear. The worst had happened. She could only die and surely that would not be so bad?

He seemed immune to the assault. 'Don't that husband of yours never . . .?' There was disbelief in his voice and a gathering dismay.

'Get out!' Esmee finally freed herself and huddled back into the corner of her bunk, pulling the crumpled gown over her bruised body.

Her father remained sitting, stunned. 'You were still a virgin?' he repeated, looking to her for denial.

'I'll kill you for this!' Her voice ended on a choking sob and she shrank back into her misery, clutching the damp gown. The terrible consequences of what he had done rolled over her, wave upon wave. Then came the thought: Will he kill me to hide the evidence of his crime? Even in this black moment she knew that she wanted to live.

He patted her arm distractedly. 'Hush, Chickadee. Don't take on so. I had no idea.'

Getting up from the bunk, he moved towards the door. As he opened it, he said: 'I can't believe this. I've got to think.' Then quietly he left the cabin and she was alone with her undoing.

TWENTY

Jeronimo was a man cast adrift. Throughout the voyage he had entertained himself with the daydream that sooner or later he would possess Esmeralda. Her sickness and Lord Craven's absence had presented him with the opportunity. Never, ever had he considered that her wedding might be in name only.

He was painfully aware of the repercussions once the truth was discovered – as discovered it would surely be. He sighed. To ravish one's daughter was considered a sin. To rape the wife of a rich man was an act of madness.

He floundered about in his mind to find a way out. He could kill Esmee. A knife in the heart and a few cannon balls tied about her corpse and all evidence could be neatly drowned in the sea. But even as he considered it, he shied away from the act. His heart beat unnaturally fast.

He could equally well wait until Lord Craven returned and then slit his throat, along with that snotty daughter of his and the old hag of a maid. Then he would have Esmeralda back for himself. For a moment the thought of tormenting the haughty Serenity before wringing her aristocratic neck distracted him, but he forced himself to think seriously of his present predicament.

Perhaps he should plead with Esmee to keep silent, reminding her of her ultimate loyalty to him as the man who had both fathered and raised her, but he knew that there was no reason why she should. Anyway, it was against his very nature to beg. The alternative was to threaten but at that moment he felt particularly impotent. In any case, bruised and scratched as she was, it would be impossible to hide her injuries even from her pathetic husband.

He glanced in panic along the harbour's edge in case the party was already returning, but the dock was deserted.

That seemed to leave only one alternative. Gloomily he realised that some of his most trusted men had been allowed ashore, and his mate was with Lord Craven. The thought of another voyage with barely enough men to keep the *Destiny* afloat weighed heavy.

Then there were the slaves. For a moment he thought about cutting his losses and dumping them over the side, but the prospect of losing all that income made him balk. In any case, where should he go? A flotilla would soon be in hot pursuit. He did not relish the idea of being hunted down and cast around in his mind for the most unlikely place to hide.

Perhaps he could confound them all by sailing back against the wind and heading further north. But then, he had time on his side and a fast ship to boot, best to make a run for it. They would have to take their chance, him and Esmeralda.

He felt an unfamiliar fluttering in his chest at the thought of his daughter. While she had been in Lord Craven's care he had banished all thought of her existence – after all, he had convinced himself that he had reared her to make a profit and that was what he had done. But now she was back, and after the events of the evening it tormented him to think of her. This feeling – regret, concern, call it what you will – was new to him. He did not like it.

Shaking his head, he returned to the practicalities. They would set sail without delay, go direct to St Christopher and there sell the slaves, quickly, for whatever he could get. Jamaica would have been better but he dared not risk returning there with the new *Destiny*. After that they would head west and hide out, perhaps along the Moskito coast. From now on, he would keep Esmeralda at his side and with luck he would find a place where no one would ever find them.

When Esmee was certain that her father had gone, she climbed painfully from the bunk and began to clean herself. She worked mechanically, touching herself tenderly where the bruises and cuts sent out shafts of hurt. Her mind was so bleak, so devoid of hope, that she hardly seemed to breathe.

There was nothing left. She was now no different from every slave who had come aboard her father's ship. As the pain welled up in her she realised anew just how much she had wanted to be different. A small voice inside her head said: This is how your mother felt. But Esmee was luckier than her mother, she had Aeneas.

She thought of the feel of his arms about her, his gentle caressing hand smoothing her hair, his soft, reassuring voice whispering against her cheek. Tears poured down her cheeks. It was gone. All gone. Her value to him lay in her purity. His certain shock, his disgust, was the greatest loss of all.

Suddenly she wanted his love back more than she had wanted anything in her life. She knew that in some way she must be to blame. Perhaps if she had behaved differently, been a wife to Aeneas, God would not have allowed this to happen to her. God. Bitterly she thought that this was Samuel's God. What reward did she have for embracing his faith and doing as he wished?

There was another thought, there at the back of her mind, trying to force its way to the forefront. She could not resist it. A shadowy picture of Serenity and Samuel threatened to submerge her. In the face of her own downfall, she would not let them into her thoughts, but they were already there – handsome, honest Samuel, and his betrothed, virginal, pure, the picture of feminine goodness. Serenity. Mentally Esmee let Samuel go. She had lost him. God bless you, my love. She bowed her head in defeat.

Limping across to the door she hooked the single catch, knowing that it would not keep her father out if he chose otherwise, but she did not think he would be back. In all her life she had never seen him so dismayed. She had no idea what he would do next, but over and above everything else she realised that for the first time she had power over him.

With amazement it dawned on her that if she so chose she could have him hanged, have him punished in such a way that he would never again be able to harm a woman. She thought of her mother and all the other dinahs – she could do this for them.

But she knew that she wouldn't. Like a million women before her she would keep quiet about the abomination and in her silence would lie her power. Jeronimo would suffer all right. Suffer every day for as long as he lived. It was some small comfort.

Even as the thoughts spiralled through the turmoil of her ordeal, Esmee noticed the sudden lifting of the ship, heard the familiar noise of canvas being raised. For a moment she dismissed it then, scrambling back on to the bunk, she peered out into the blackness. As she did so, the new *Destiny* swung out into the inky waters and headed for the open sea.

141

*   *   *

In normal circumstances, Aeneas would have enjoyed his visit to Governor Hawsey. This was the first time he had set foot in this tropical wilderness and he wanted to savour every moment. As it was, his niggling concern for Esmee overshadowed every second away from the *Destiny*. Despite his wife's reassurances, he could not stop worrying about her.

The Governor's house was within walking distance of the ship. The building was large, square and roomy. The stucco that coated the exterior glared white beneath pink hibiscus that scrambled up to the palm-fronded roof. Aeneas, a keen gardener, had studied the flora of the Caribbees with interest, poring over accounts and drawings brought back to England. It excited him to see the flowers in their natural state.

The garden sported several orange trees of different varieties, dotted between a profusion of flowers. The air hung heavy with perfume and Aeneas stopped for a moment to breathe in the scent of jasmine and tamarisk. Beneath the sweet aroma he caught a whiff of the cow dung used to bind the plaster walls of the house. It served to remind him that where there is beauty there is also ugliness. He hurried on.

Inside, the house was cool and airy. A few pieces of heavy English furniture squatted about the place, giving the cane stools and couches a light, ephemeral air.

As he was looking around, the Governor came to meet him. Henry Hawsey was a short man with light, sandy hair, his rounded cheeks marbled with minute red veins. In spite of the heat he was buttoned into a heavy woollen coat, liberally decorated with braid.

'Lord Craven, your visit brings me great pleasure. A visitor from home is always a welcome sight.'

Aeneas returned the greeting and answered the Governor's questions as best he could. In between making polite conversation and sipping a strange but refreshing brew concocted from pine juice, he kept seeing alarming pictures of Esmee, delirious, lapsing into a coma and finally slipping away, alone and uncared for, his name half formed upon her lips.

As soon as he decently could he looked for a chance to make his escape. With mixed feelings he noticed that Serenity seemed to be animated for the first time since they had left England. She was surrounded by three or four English officers, young men, clearly avid for female company. It was obvious that his daughter was in no hurry to leave.

In her wake, Hannah Hardy kept a vigilant if indulgent eye on her charge.

Fighting down his restlessness Aeneas sought comfort from the fact that Serenity had made such friends with her chaperone. She had never been an easy girl to get to know. His only regret was that the same amity did not exist between his daughter and his wife. Again fear for Esmeralda was foremost in his mind.

Aeneas loved them both, but if he forced himself to face the truth, then he had to admit that his first concern now was for his wife. Every look, every movement, the carriage of her young body, the beautiful features of her girlish face, all filled him with a reverence that left him in awe of God the Creator. He wondered how he had come to deserve such a priceless gem, yet he could not help but regret his inability to claim her totally for his own. Perhaps, when they reached Eden . . .

At last he managed to chivvy his party away. Toby Scutt, the mate, lit their way back to the harbour, the flame from his rush torch playing hide and seek as a frisky wind blew up. Their route wound between palm-thatched huts, ramshackle, threatening in their silence. The universal stench of decay offended his nose.

Behind him, Serenity and Hannah were deep in conversation. For once they seemed oblivious to the hostile nature of their surroundings. Their voices were low, confessional. He heard Serenity laugh. He guessed they were discussing the Governor and his entourage, those young men so appealing in their uniforms, elegant in spite of the heat.

That Serenity was not immune to a handsome man was something of a relief. Sometimes Aeneas had feared that her godliness precluded her from any other interest in life than service to the Lord. He guessed that Sam Rushworth would hope for a modicum of response from a wife.

Now that he had Esmeralda it did not hurt so much to think of Serenity and Samuel together. On the contrary, sometimes he nursed a guilty wish to be released from his responsibility for her. Only then could he really enjoy his wife, give himself totally, body and soul, to her care and welfare, the joy of his old age.

Even as these thoughts circled in his mind he scanned the harbour for the *Destiny*. At first he could not see her and he looked again, wondering if they were too far along the harbour wall.

A curse from Mate Scutt set alarm bells ringing. 'What the . . .'

'Where is she? Where's the ship?'

Toby Scutt shook his head, frowning. The torch light played across his broad features, illuminating his disbelief.

'She's gone.'

'That's not possible.' Aeneas shook his head, still searching. It was not possible. Not thinkable. 'Why should . . .?' he started. He could not think any further.

Mate Scutt went to make enquiries, seeking out anyone who might have witnessed what had happened. An eternity later he returned to report that the *Destiny* had set out to sea some half an hour since.

'But why?' Aeneas repeated. His mind could not cope with any explanation that occurred to him.

Mate Scutt shrugged. 'P'raps Captain's got his own plans for the slaves,' he suggested. 'Some of 'em was pretty sick.'

'But my wife!' Aeneas clenched his fists in anguish.

Mate Scutt shrugged again. His expression implied that the girl was only a mulatto. Why make such a fuss when there were plenty more in Jamaica, or a dozen other islands?

'Ain't he her father?' he asked, as if that answered everything.

Aeneas insisted on returning to the Governor's house. There, he poured out his tale, confused, lost, still not believing what had happened.

To comfort him, Governor Hawsey set every wheel he could think of in motion. For all his disarming manner, Aeneas Craven was a powerful man. It was wise to pander to his needs.

A pinnace was despatched immediately to pick up the trail of the *Destiny*. During the course of the night, letters were written to the Governors of every English island ordering the seizure of the ship if she tried to land, then at first light the next morning, a barque was diverted to carry the sorrowing husband, his daughter and her maid on to Eden Island.

TWENTY-ONE

'If a ship should arrive this very morning, then I should not hesitate to leave here.'

Sam read the words he had written the day before in his log book and wondered if they still applied. In the months since the *Destiny* had disgorged her last consignment of venturers, there had been little to make him want to stay.

He made a note of the weather, the wind direction, the number of sick planters, the duties he had ordered for the day, all in the hope that this time next year, or the year after, a pattern would emerge that would make the government of this place that much easier.

With regret he remembered that the first part of his log, so painstakingly recorded from the day of their arrival, had been destroyed by a combination of insects and mould. He had rewritten as much as he could from memory but it lacked the spontaneous feel of those first, breathtaking days when they had explored their new kingdom with such high hopes.

With a sigh he sat back in his customary place beneath the big palm in the centre of their settlement's square. Silchester Square they had named it. There was also Warwick Heights, Craven village and Rushworth Street. He grinned sardonically. It was one way to be remembered.

For the most part he was too tired to dwell on anything but his immediate needs: sleep, drink, escape from aching muscles and stinging bites. When his body was at rest, his mind agonised over the infinite problems that beset the smooth running of the island. Everywhere he turned there was some dispute – over land, cultivation, religious observance, division of labour – an entire skeleton of

145

contentious issues. Gloomily he thought that no surgeon could heal this sickly patient.

He tried to shrug off his worries, but wherever he was or whatever he did, they persisted. At first he attempted to involve all the colonists in every aspect of decision making but they simply quarrelled. When that failed he took the reins of government solely into his own hands and bore the brunt of the discontent that rained from every quarter. The arrows of the settlers' anger pierced deep into his peace of mind.

Looking across the square which had been cleared and left bare except for the palm tree, he could see his own, newly constructed house. It was two-storied and made from bricks forged from the yellowish clay that ran in a seam across Eden. Next to his house stood the church, also a brick building, a simple square with a deeply pitched roof to keep out the torrents of rain that had seemed to last for months.

There was some small comfort in the knowledge that apart from the church, his home was the only building not to be built of wood. It gave it an air of permanence, a symbol of his status that often felt very precarious.

Stiffly he got up, folding his documents and wrapping them in oilskin before slipping the cylinder into a hollowed cane, which he carefully plugged with wax.

Inside the house he fumbled around in the dark, not wanting to attract more insects. He was tired. Feeling his way up the ladder to his sleeping platform, he pulled off his boots, shirt and breeches, and slipped under the netting that kept the worst of the pests away.

Not for the first time he thought that perhaps coming to the island had been a cowardly way of escaping from his grievances at home. And his misdemeanours. He should have stayed there and faced them. He wondered if the island's present difficulties were not God's punishment on him personally – sending torments to remind him that he could never run away.

He remembered the sense of powerlessness that had faced him back home, and the naive hope that by finding a new world perhaps he could construct a paradise here on earth. That idea now seemed laughable. He was embarrassed by the thought of that other Sam, so shallow and self-assured.

As always, the one thing that stopped him when he thought of returning to England was the prospect of marriage to Serenity. He turned impatiently on his sleeping frame. The thought of a wife tormented him. He wanted one: a beautiful, wise girl whose wit and passion matched his own. Esmeralda. The thought of his cold, puritanical betrothed dredged up yet more pain. What should he do: return to England and embrace this marriage as some sort of test or remain where he was and try, against all the odds, to pull this disparate group and this treacherous climate into some sort of paradise – or Eden?

The thought of Esmee was clawing at the edge of his mind but his reverie was disturbed by the sound of a single shot. Immediately he was out of bed and into his boots and breeches. Grabbing his musket, he raced for the look-out above the cove. The shot had come from the watch.

'What is it?' He climbed up beside the man and scanned the distant ashen strip that marked a dawning horizon.

'Sails. Just one craft, I reckon.'

Sam found it, little bigger than a butterfly's wing, way out to the east but moving in their direction. From the formation of the canvas he was already certain that it was not the *Destiny*. He swallowed back the disappointment and immediately wondered if it might not be a Spanish armadilly, patrolling the waters in pursuit of intruders. It could not be long before the dons came sniffing the air, sizing up their strength, making ready to oust them from their prize.

Nodding his thanks, Sam descended and rallied the rest of the watch. Soon the cannon was primed and ready. If the ship were foolish enough to come too close, then a well-aimed shot would warn her off. In the meantime the whole of the colony scrambled down to the beach, armed and ready to fend off trouble.

''Tis an Englisher.' Thomas Axe's shrewd eyes were the first to pick out the pennant that flew on the approaching ship. There was a collective outrush of breath, a lowering of weapons and a new impatience to see what would happen next.

A distant shout from on board was carried away by the hiss of the surf, but the tone was friendly. Men waved from the beach and Sam's spirits lifted. This new arrival could only bring relief from the monotony of the past months. He wondered if it was in direct answer to the words he had written the day before in his log. Was this a sign that he should return to England? How was he to know?

Two islanders rowed out to meet the ship and guided her directly into the harbour. As her sails were furled and she settled easily

147

beside the makeshift wooden jetty, Sam stepped forward, his body tense with expectation.

'Welcome to Eden.'

The Captain was unknown to him, but his nationality alone was cause for celebration. As Sam watched, others were beginning to crowd on deck. He saw someone who reminded him of his uncle and as he looked again at the man, realised with disbelief that this surely was Lord Craven. Sam waved but his uncle did not return the salute and again for a moment he thought that he must be mistaken. Seconds later he became aware of the girl standing beside the man, her face set into an expression of triumph. Serenity.

Sam's hands began to tingle. Hastily he scanned the other passengers but he could not see the one person he wanted to set eyes on more than any living being. There was a third person, a woman, but she was not the girl of Sam's dreams. Having negotiated the steep ladder from below decks, the stout, matronly figure stood awkwardly as if the sea was still intent on upending her. Her face was damp and grey. Whoever she was, she was not Esmeralda.

At last they prepared to come ashore. Sam hurried to help them down the plank, his mind buzzing with questions. He felt an incongruous mixture of delight and unease. The ship pulsed with the restless uneasy movement of the waves.

First ashore was the senior officer. Sam held out his hand in greeting. 'Captain, welcome. I am Governor here.' The Captain responded by returning his grip. In unison the two men turned to the hunched figure of Lord Craven.

'Uncle.'

The older man stumbled on landing and Sam took him by the elbow to steady him. For the first time he detected signs of age in his relative. Until this moment Aeneas had always seemed the same: wise, calm and untouched by time. Sam said: 'This is such a surprise. I had no idea you intended to visit so soon. Have you come to stay?'

Aeneas did not reply and there was no chance to say more before Serenity too was teetering on the edge of the board. The Captain took both of her hands as if they were made of eggshell, helping her gently ashore. Sam noticed that she raised her eyes almost coquettishly towards the man, her confidence taking Sam by surprise. Then she turned to face him.

'Cousin.' He nodded, cheeks growing hot with confusion. He

tried not to think what her arrival meant in terms of their intended marriage. The girl's cool black eyes sparkled with triumph, doing little to reassure him.

'Cousin Samuel.'

Sam turned back to his uncle, once again taking his arm, encouraging him with a nod of his head to speak. He desperately wanted some explanation.

At last Aeneas spoke. 'Samuel. Thank God that you are here. There is such trouble.'

'Trouble?' Sam's first thought was that the company had been disbanded, or else a dispute had arisen over ownership of the island. His uncle's next words took him totally by surprise.

'It is Jackson. He has run off with my wife.'

'Wife?' Sam frowned in confusion.

'I –' Aeneas stopped as if he had blurted out some indiscretion. Fighting to find the right words, he added: 'It is a long story but the fact is, I am wed and Captain Jackson has kidnapped my wife and stolen her away, together with all our stores.'

'Do you know where he has gone? Has anyone given chase?' Sam still could not come to terms with these startling events. For a fleeting moment he wondered how this affected his inheritance prospects but pushed the thought aside as unworthy. As much as anything, it brought home to him that life continued whether he was there or not, leaving him with a gloomy sense of his own unimportance.

Remembering what his role was, he threw off his own concerns and said: 'Come, Uncle. Step ashore now and take some rest. I am certain that something can be done. Indeed, I will go myself and find Captain Jackson, if only you will explain what has happened?'

Aeneas looked so exhausted that the Captain of the barque intervened. 'Captain Richard Jordan at your service, sir. I will explain all.' He indicated with a subtle nod of his head that they should wait until later. Aeneas threw him a grateful glance.

He went ahead on the Captain's arm and Samuel and Serenity walked together.

'I had no idea that your father was thinking of marrying,' he said, to break the silence. 'Is his wife ...' He waited for Serenity to enlighten him.

When she spoke her voice was condescending as if it was she and not Aeneas who was the parent. 'My father seems to have lost

149

his reason.' A strange smile twitched about her lips as if she was amused by the turn of events.

'Is the lady someone I know?'

Serenity flashed him a look. Her mouth turned down in derision and not for the first time Sam felt that there was another side to his cousin which sat badly with her saintly deportment.

'I should not disturb yourself,' she said by way of a reply. 'She is of little account.' She gave a bright smile as if the subject of her father's marriage was already dismissed. Tossing her head, she said: 'No doubt, though, you will be anxious to get our cargo back. Amongst the rest, there is a valuable consignment of slaves aboard.'

Sam frowned. 'I do not wish for slaves.' When Serenity looked surprised, he added: 'It is my wish that every man who sets foot on these shores shall be free.'

'Even savages? Heathens?'

'Every man can come to God.'

She shrugged at his intransigence, saying: 'The company thinks otherwise.'

'It is I who am Governor here.'

For several seconds they were silent then Serenity said: 'If you are disturbed at the thought of Papa's new wife, I can assure you that whatever he might say to the contrary, she is no more than a foolish diversion.'

She moved closer and lowered her voice. 'To be honest, I fear he may have regrets about marrying her at all so . . .' Her expression hinted that it might be best if the bride were not pursued but left to Captain Jackson's mercy.

Serenity tucked her small hand under Sam's elbow and her head was close against his arm. Towering over her, he felt none of the protective warmth that had once inspired him when Esmeralda had so shyly paraded with him on the deck of her father's ship. Esmeralda . . . He opened his mouth to ask where she was, then thought better of it.

As they reached Rushworth Street, Serenity said: 'Perhaps you are right about the slaves.'

Sam was just thinking that the girl had one saving grace after all, when she added: 'Many of them were sickly anyway, hardly worth bothering about.'

Tightly he asked: 'And my uncle's wife?'

She shrugged. 'If God so wishes it, she'll turn up. If not . . .' She

150

raised her shoulders in a fatalistic gesture.

They had reached Sam's house and for a moment the conversation ceased as they went inside. Serenity stood looking around the room and Sam could see her barely disguised contempt. He said: 'We must get her back. If we do nothing, we are as guilty as Jackson.'

Looking into her eyes he saw no compassion. For a moment he thought: She and the Captain are of the same stock, essentially ruthless and brutal. It was a terrible discovery.

He fussed about, getting his visitors settled. Serenity and Hannah were packed off to get some rest in his own bed and Sam accepted the tub of brandy that Captain Jordan had brought ashore, with gratitude.

'Take some of this.' He insisted that Aeneas should drink some, relieved to see a hint of colour begin to return to his uncle's cheeks.

'Can you tell me exactly what happened?' he asked, as Aeneas gazed into nothing, his knuckles showing white against the jug.

There was a catch in the older man's voice as he said: 'You don't owe me anything. The debt is cancelled.'

Sam wondered what he was talking about. Perhaps the journey and the shock of his loss had upset his reason.

For a moment Aeneas raised his eyes and Sam gazed into their pain. His uncle's expression was one of almost sheepish regret.

'Uncle?' Sam waited for an explanation and when Aeneas failed to speak, looked to Captain Jordan. Concisely, the officer outlined Lord Craven's visit to Governor Hawsey, then his hasty return with the news that his wife had been abducted and the action they had taken to date.

This was now a family matter. Sam knew that he must act. To Jordan, he said: 'What are your orders?'

'To make myself available to you.'

'Right.' Turning to Aeneas, Sam spoke slowly, wanting to reassure him. Gently he said: 'You need have no fears. As soon as the Captain has had a rest and refreshments we will go in pursuit of your wife.' He paused. 'Would you like to tell me about her?' When Aeneas did not speak, he hesitated before adding: 'Serenity seems to think that you might have some – anxieties about your marriage?'

For the first time a spark of life showed in Aeneas's tired eyes. He looked both disappointed and angry. 'Serenity would be happy if my dear girl were never seen again.'

Sam was surprised at the intensity of his uncle's feelings. 'You must love her dearly,' he said.

'I do, Sam. I do.' Aeneas turned again to him and his eyes were wet with remorse. 'Forgive me, nephew.'

'There is nothing to forgive.' For a moment Sam thought that Aeneas was embarrassed by his weakness in displaying his tears but as the older man continued to shake his head, it dawned on him that there was something else.

'Forgive you for what?'

'For marrying Esmeralda.'

'For marrying Esmeralda?' Sam repeated the words because somehow his ears had not taken in what he had heard. Perhaps there was another Esmeralda. Perhaps he was having a vivid dream.

'My Esmeralda?' he asked, his brow furrowing with disbelief.

'She isn't yours. Don't you see? It was I who paid her father. What could you have done for her?'

What indeed. Sam felt nothing. It was the same numbness that had cocooned him when he had learned of his mother's death. The same feeling that had protected him when, as an eight-year-old, he had gazed aghast at his roan pony, her hind leg hanging by a thread.

Now it blocked off his emotions, laying a blanket over the pain that was a hair's breadth away from engulfing him.

'I see. Well.' He had nothing more to say.

Esmeralda. Lady Craven. In Aeneas's bed. His hands on her.

He rose to his feet. To Jordan he said: 'Make yourself comfortable. Perhaps I could ask you to stay here with my uncle? If we are going to sail this day then I have much to do.'

Esmeralda. His aunt by marriage. Step-mother to his intended bride.

He stumbled down to the shoreline where a sun gentle as a calf's breath was warming the dripping clump of mangrove that fingered its way out into the encroaching tide.

Esmeralda. Wife of Aeneas for all the world to see. For all the world to know.

Booby birds, plump and clumsy, bobbed and nodded to each other, performing their ritual dance. A declaration of what? Love? Commitment? Til death do them part?

Esmeralda!

Opening his mouth Sam roared her name into the emptiness and the echo came back across the whispering sea, ghost-like, invisible.

Esmeralda. Lost to him, unreachable, elusive as the air.

He thought of Serenity's words: if God intended her to be found then that was how it would be. If Samuel found her it would be to bring her back to his uncle, back to Aeneas's arms, his kisses, back into his possession.

Esmeralda. The thought was shameful. He must find her. He must rescue her from Jackson and return her to where she rightfully belonged.

He must.

TWENTY-TWO

Esmee had no idea how long she had been in the cabin. She stood with her back pressed against the door, straining to pick up any hint that her father was returning, then slowly it dawned on her that now the *Destiny* was at sea he would have other things to occupy him.

Her thoughts tumbled into some bottomless chasm. There was no way back and the way forward was fraught with danger. As her legs grew too shaky to support her she stumbled back to the bunk. She had a terrible feeling of moving again into the very arena where she had been raped, as if in so doing she would suffer the same agony again, but there was nowhere else to go.

Gingerly she perched on the edge of the bunk and tried to think what to do. She let out her breath in a long gasp, trying to ease the muscles that bunched tightly in her belly. If she was to survive then she had to escape, from this cabin, from the ship and from her father's hold. There was only one thing to do.

She had no idea how many of the crew remained on board. In any case she guessed that fear of her father would surely outweigh any sympathy they might feel towards her. Some of them she had known since childhood, but she could not rely on their support or protection.

There was the dinah, but she was young and cowed and probably incapable of understanding. Even if Esmee could win the girl to her side, they would hardly be a match for the hardened men who manned the ship.

That left the slaves. In Esmee's experience, the shock of abduction, the hardship and sickness suffered on the voyage, added to the fear of their alien destination, made them incapable of fighting back.

True, she had seen some men resist, the brave ones making a

desperate life or death bid to regain their freedom. She had seen them punished too, beaten, starved, strung up until their arms were separated from their sockets, driven crazy with thirst, branded, punched, their toes or fingers crushed – but only when they were too far gone to be of any possible use.

Dragging out Aeneas's trunk, she took out his pistol. Powder and shot were carefully stored to keep them dry. Loading and priming the gun, she laid it carefully on the bunk.

The act strengthened her resolve. Picking up the gun again, she went to the door and opened it. There was no one in sight so she scrambled up the ladder to the deck. The silhouette of the bosun moved gently with the motion of the boat. He seemed to be the only person on deck.

Quickly Esmee tried to calculate their direction. From the hint of light on the far horizon she guessed they were travelling east – or was that the dusk and they were headed west? What would her father do? Where would he go?

She ducked back down and into the companionway, keeping her head low to avoid the roof. To reassure herself she clutched the gun tightly in her hand. Its weight seemed symbolic of its power.

When she reached Jeronimo's cabin she opened the door and stepped inside, the gun held in front of her like a crucifix to ward off evil. Her father was not there but the dinah, hunched in the corner, leaped to her feet and gave a wail of fear.

Esmee shook her head and held out a hand to calm her. She beckoned the girl to her and after a desperate look round, there being no escape, the dinah crept forward, a step at a time, like a cowed dog expecting a beating but too scared to disobey.

Esmee tried the few words she knew in several African languages: Mandingo, Ibo, Yoruba, Ashanti. The dinah did not respond, so she reverted to English.

'You come with me. We're taking charge of this ship.'

The dinah looked hard at her from under her brows. There was a shiny purple patch on her left cheek. It looked inflamed and puffy. This sign of the other girl's suffering confirmed her in her intention.

Taking the dinah by the wrist, Esmee slipped back outside and led the way stealthily towards the hold. As she stopped to check, the dinah shook her head, imploring.

'I'm not going to shut you down there. I want *you* to help *me*.' Esmee nodded encouragement.

The dinah shook her head more insistently and Esmee added: 'My father, the Captain, is a *bad* man. You help me.'

'Bad.' The dinah nodded her agreement. Esmee thought in amazement: In spite of all you have suffered, you have still learned something of my father's language.

She nodded her approval.

Signalling to the girl to keep out of sight, she stepped forward and lowered herself down into the hold, her feet feeling for the rungs of the ladder.

The stench was immediately overpowering. She had an almost panicky feeling of suffocation and had to fight the desire to scramble back up.

'Who's zat?'

She came face to face with a sailor, propped against the bottom of the ladder, a whip in his hand.

'It's Esmeralda.' She recognised Tolly Cross who had made regular sailings with her father ever since she could remember.

Cross looked away and Esmee thought: He knows. He knows what my father did. Her heart fluttered painfully. She said: 'The Captain wants you. He's up on deck.'

Cross hesitated, eyeing her and the dinah uncertainly.

Esmee outstared him. In Aeneas's house she had learned how to command. 'You'd best hurry,' she said. 'Leave me the whip. I'll keep an eye on things.'

Tolly Cross looked down at the gun and Esmee tilted it just enough to underline the fact that she nursed a lethal weapon. With a quick wipe of his hand across his mouth, he nodded and skipped up the ladder.

'Quick.' Esmee looked along the length of the deck. Each side was shelved with planks, three rows deep, about eighteen inches apart. Stacked on the shelves was the merchandise: row upon row of men, lying on bare, slatted boards, linked one to the other by heavy, rusting chains through padlocked shackles.

Silence fell in the cavernous belly of the ship. Only men's breathing echoed like the whispering sea. In the half dark, Esmee could see the luminous questions in a hundred eyes, the mixture of fear and anticipation.

She glanced at the wall behind her where the end of the chain was hooked, high out of reach of the nearest slave. All the time she thought: What am I unleashing? What will happen if I set them free?

Nearby, a man vomited, retching out his misery. A few feet away she could see a foot, half raised and stretched out as if to ease the agony of a deep abrasion, constantly chafing against the iron of the shackles. She reached up and, lifting the chain, let it drop to the ground.

Immediately there was a mad flurry of activity. The nearest man leaned forward, pulling the chain out of the manacles, clumsy in his urgency. He passed the end of the chain on to his companion. The noise of rattling metal was deafening.

Esmee raised the pistol. Liberated, some standing, some crouching, others too weak to raise themselves, the men all looked in her direction.

'*Ka ji Hausa?* You understand Hausa?' she asked.

'I.'

One of the slaves stepped forward. He scrutinised her with black, intelligent eyes. His face was emaciated, his skin dull as if it had lost its bloom. He was naked except for a filthy scrap of rag about his loins. His ribs showed in rungs down towards his hollow belly but his shoulders were broad. His wrists and ankles were pale pink, rubbed sore. Esmee's heart sank. She must act quickly, establish some control before the slaves became a mob that swept her away along with the crew.

'*Sarike che.*' I am in charge. She spoke uncertainly, her grasp of the language incomplete.

The man continued to stare at her. From his expression she feared that the authority of a woman would be ignored. She tried again. '*Ban ka bawa ba.*' You are no longer a slave. She pointed the pistol in his direction just to remind him that neither was he in charge.

The silence seemed to last forever, the man simply staring at her. The pistol began to shake in her hand. At last he spoke.

'*Suna Musa ne.*' My name is Musa.

'Esmeralda.' Lady Craven, she thought. The wife of a powerful man.

Musa acknowledged that he understood. For a moment they stared at each other then he said: '*Ruwa.*' He nodded his head towards his companions. Water.

Esmee indicated the barrel that stood in the central aisle of the deck, always just out of reach of the slaves, a cruel symbol of the power of the traders and their ability to offer or withdraw life. The barrel was nearly empty. She remembered that they had not been in port long enough to take on supplies.

157

She nodded and the man moved forward, taking the slimy wooden cup and dipping it into the tepid scum in the barrel, then offering it to those too sick or damaged to fend for themselves.

She watched him work and was reminded of Sam Rushworth, a man with a gentle, humane concern for those less fortunate. Quickly she pushed the thought from her mind.

As the man returned for more water, she said: '*Ban kashe bature ba.*' You will not kill the white men.

He stared at her and her confidence threatened to crumble. A boy, perhaps a little younger than herself, came to join Musa and he put his arm about the lad's shoulders.

'*Ubanshi,*' he said. I am his father.

Esmee immediately remembered her own father. She said: 'Can you sail a ship? Can you overpower the crew – but without killing? Any man who kills, I will shoot him.' She brandished the pistol to make her point.

The man shrugged. Turning to the slaves, he spoke quickly. Esmee did not understand. It was not Hausa, nor any of the languages that she knew.

In response to his words there was a murmur of accord. Those who could walk followed their leader up the gangplank stealthily, tensed for the show-down ahead. They filed past Esmee and she realised too late that she should have stopped them.

She felt the terrible weight of her betrayal. She was sacrificing every man up there to the mercy of these prisoners, who would surely be turned into animals by their brutal misuse.

Even before the first slaves reached the top of the ladder, Esmee heard her father's voice in the gangway, followed by the almost simumtaneous crack of a whip and an answering scream. With an angry howl the slaves still in the hold clambered ahead, climbing over each other in their haste to get out and wreak revenge on their hated captors.

The dinah moved closer and in the dark Esmee reached out to give her a reassuring pat. She felt no such comfort herself. The girl will be safe, she thought. She is one of them.

Above them, pistol shots crackled above the howling of the Africans. Battling bodies hit the boards over their heads, falling with the dead weight of discarded cargo. Without realising it Esmee found she was holding the dinah's hand.

Together they crept forward, feeling their way along the

companionway, fingering the second ladder that led to the quarter deck. The howling had subsided and the air now buzzed with the angry hum of men for whom revenge is assured.

Esmee took in the crowd of naked Africans, standing stiffly, easing limbs long weakened by lack of use, still blinking in the unaccustomed light. Their eyes were focused on the foremast where the remaining crew members formed an ever-decreasing group as they pressed back against each other to avoid their captors.

Esmee's father and his bosun stood apart, their hands secured behind their backs. Blood dripped from a cut across Jeronimo's cheek but he seemed unaware of it. His feet were planted firmly apart and he thrust out his chin, challenging and aggressive as ever. His eyes were fixed firmly on the man named Musa, who held Jeronimo's cutlass.

At that moment her father saw her. 'Get away, Chickadee!' Fixing Musa with his hard stare, he said: 'Touch her and I'll rip your balls off.'

Letting go of the dinah, Esmee pushed her was through the throng.

The Africans parted to let her by and Musa turned to face her.

'Who is this man?'

'The Captain.'

Musa scrutinised her face and she looked away from him.

Quietly he said: 'Then he must be punished, as the one who has inflicted such a wrong upon us.'

'No!'

She did not ask herself why she did not want her father to die. The reason was too dangerous. If she thought about it she would fall into a bottomless pit and suffocate. She only knew that she did not want to be responsible for his death – not like this.

'Who is he?' Musa repeated.

'My father.'

Esmee was aware of nothing but the man's eyes upon her as if he was trying to see into her soul. Finally, he turned to the slaves and said: 'Take these men down below. All of them. Chain them up. Deny them water.'

'No!' The violence had to stop. All of it. Countermanding Musa's order, she said: 'Lock the men in the hold.'

The slaves looked from Musa to Esmee and back again. She knew that this was a decisive moment. If she wanted to keep control then she had to impose her will.

She met Musa's eyes and he tossed his head, challenging her, but she could see that his mind was working, assessing the wisdom of what she said. He was also assessing her and, with a sudden fluttering of her heart, she knew that she did not wish to be found wanting.

The pistol weighed heavy in her hand. Could she use it against this African? Was this the only way to keep control? She was certain he could read her thoughts. He spread his arms, almost as if offering himself as a target.

Her eyes not leaving his face, she repeated: 'Lock them in the hold.'

After a moment's hesitation Musa acceded to her command. She drew in a deep breath, relief flooding over her. Of all those present, she did not want to shoot this man.

As the slaves bundled the sailors below, Musa bowed his head as if acknowledging her authority. She was certain he was not the sort of man to give in to someone he did not respect. She had a heady feeling of passing some undefined test.

He said: 'Do you know how to navigate this ship?'

'Where do you want to go?'

'Back to Africa. To Calabar.'

She gasped. 'You can't! It's thousands of miles. Weeks away. You would need stores, and anyway the winds are against you. Can you read the charts?'

He shook his head and she could see the weight of his predicament pulling him down.

A wave of exhaustion began to claim her and, lowering the pistol, she sank back against the rail. Musa said: 'You are weary. Go to your quarters, you and the girl. I'll make sure that you are safe.' He indicated the dinah with his head.

Esmee was unwilling to relinquish her newly won control but at the same time she knew that the dinah was exhausted and could not be left alone. Looking again at the African, she did not believe he would let her down.

Musa said: 'If it is possible we will all return to our homes.'

Home. A painful sense of loss engulfed her. Tears stung her eyes. Where was home? Craven House in London? Here on this ship? Some distant island where Samuel would marry Serenity?

Looking up at him she said: 'I have no home,' and taking the dinah by the hand, sought shelter in her husband's cabin.

That night the slaves, drunk on hope, set about raiding every corner of the *Destiny*. From the port hole Esmee glimpsed men dressed in a curious assortment of garments – canvas breeks, stockings, her father's best scarlet jacket that he wore only when visiting town, shifts and skirts stored as trading gifts for the wives of influential natives. About their necks they had beads and one or two wore women's caps. The bizarre sight of them posturing on deck did little to reassure her.

Starved, until that day deprived of hope, the slaves quickly made short work of the meagre rations remaining on board. They also discovered the barrels of brandy secreted under Jeronomo's bunk. As the noise level grew, Esmee barred the door and sat with the pistol trained on the entrance, prepared to defend herself and the dinah to the death. But nobody came. The euphoria was short-lived. Too weak to stand the sudden inrush of strong spirits, the men quickly succumbed to vomiting then sleep.

Meanwhile, the *Destiny* continued on her unmapped journey to an unknown destination.

'You sleep. I watch.' Esmee pointed to the bunk, not wanting to lie there herself and relive her ordeal.

The dinah shook her head. 'You sleep.' She indicated that Esmee should be the first to rest.

'What are you called?' She felt again a sobering respect for this girl who had obviously endured so much in the last few months.

The girl raised her eyebrows then pointed to herself. Esmee nodded.

'Yinka.'

'Yinka.' The girl had a name and a history but they did not share enough language to spell it out. No matter, they shared feelings, the mutual unspoken sameness that binds women together.

Esmee looked at Yinka, noting the fullness of her belly. She suddenly felt sick. This girl, the dinah, was no different from Esmee's mother. Had she too been so young?

Like Esmee's mother Yinka had remained longer than normal on board. Like Esmee's mother she would give birth to a child – a girl with green eyes? Would the dinah die and Esmee's father keep the baby, watch her grow until . . .

She swung round quickly, trying to get away from her own thoughts. To Yinka, she said: 'You sleep.'

At that moment somebody pushed against the door, rattling the

161

handle. Esmee jumped, turning to face the doorway, the pistol in her hand.

'Who are you?'

'*Musa ne.*'

Esmee unbarred the door and pulled it open. The African greeted her with a nod of his head. He carried dried meat and biscuit and a jug of ale.

'For you.'

She took it, suddenly realising how hungry and thirsty she was. She began to soak the hard grey meat in the liquid, dip the weevil-bitten biscuit to soften it enough to bite. Beside her, Yinka waited.

'You eat.' Esmee felt humbled by the girl's assumption that she was an inferior, a servant to wait until she was bidden. Hungrily, Yinka helped herself to the tack.

Musa stepped into the room, looking around him.

'We have trouble,' he said. 'Our men are used to sailing dhows, paddling canoes. They know their own coastline, they know the heavens above them, but this place is foreign to us.'

'Then release my father. He will take you to safety.' Jeronimo alone knew these waters.

The African looked doubtful. 'He will surely take us somewhere to be sold.'

'Not if you promise him his life.' Even in this extreme situation she knew that her father would still argue, still challenge his captors. Feeling an unreasonable sense of disloyalty, she added: 'I will warn you if I think he intends to break his promise, if he is taking you somewhere unsafe.'

Musa nodded. 'Then I will do as you say.' He glanced behind him. 'I think a storm may be coming.'

Esmee screwed up her eyes, peering through the wavy glass that gave the sea and sky the same brownish hue. The *Destiny* was moving with a gentle rhythm, but fast. She could only see where they came from, not where they might be going, but something about the sound of the wind, its increasing speed, made her uneasy.

She repeated: 'Get my father.'

Leaving Yinka to sleep, Esmee accompanied Musa on deck. He spoke a few words to one of his countrymen, and two of the slaves set off in the direction of the hold.

Esmee thought of the other men below decks, the sailors she had known for so long and so well. To them at least she owed a loyalty.

To Musa she said: 'I insist that you give them food and water.'

'We already have. Do you think we are beasts?'

She looked away from him, embarrassed by her assumption.

A scuffle drew her attention from the man beside her. Two slaves were struggling up from the lower deck, her father held between them. Pulling and tugging, he swore at his captors, tossing them this way and that as they tried to restrain him.

'Let him go.' Musa faced his prisoner. 'You. You will navigate this ship and take us somewhere safe.'

Jeronimo looked to Esmee for translation. 'What does he say, Chickadee? I don't understand his jibberish.'

'He doesn't understand yours.' She defied her father to look away. His face was grey, his flaxen hair a tangled mess. The manacles chinked as he moved his wrists and she saw that they were bleeding.

Her voice struggling to be firm, she said: 'Now you know what it feels like.'

'You are on their side?'

'No.' She faltered. 'I simply want to go to Eden.'

Jeronimo glanced at the Africans. He nodded conspiratorially. 'And them? Do they want to go and work there for nothing?' He moved closer to her, she stiffened, pulling back from him.

He said: 'He hasn't touched you has he? If he has, I'll castrate him myself.'

Esmee spat back at him, 'He hasn't touched me.' Then echoing Musa's words: 'He isn't a beast.'

Undaunted, Jeronomo tried again. 'We can work this out, you and me. You tell them I'll take them somewhere safe, then we'll sail to Eden like you want. Once we're there, it will be easy enough to overpower them.'

'It was I who set them free.'

'What for?' He looked at her in disbelief.

'What else should I do – let you carry me away and make a slave of me like my mother? Like Yinka?'

'Who?'

'The girl who bears your child.'

He shrugged philosophically. 'That's how it is. A man must take what he can get wherever he finds it.'

'So must a woman.' She glanced at Musa then back at Jeronimo. 'If you want to live, you will navigate the *Destiny* to a safe haven

163

where these men can hole up until the winds change, then you will sail them back to their homes.'

'Back to Africa? You really think I would do that?'

'If you want to live.'

He pulled a face which said: So be it. Then his green eyes narrowed. 'You'd better watch out for yourself, Chickadee. Don't go thinking this native'll treat you any better than a white man would, because he won't. He's a savage. You ain't one of them. If you want to get back to your noble husband, if you want to be a lady again, then you'd better remember who is the only person who can take you there.'

Aeneas. Esmee thought of his thin, gentle face, remembered his love and care. She wanted to go home to him. She looked at Musa, watching the exchange with dark, intelligent eyes. He had treated her with respect. He had been merciful to the crew. As escaped slaves, their future would be grim should they ever be captured.

Loud enough for both men to hear, she said: '*Jirgin ruwa, ya tashi na rashin hadari.* Sail them somewhere safe.'

TWENTY-THREE

In all conscience, Sam felt that he must allow Captain Jordan a minimum of rest before returning to sea, although with every passing minute Esmeralda was being carried further and further away. The thought went round in his brain like a frenzied hornet but even as he fretted and chafed, the wind changed direction and any hope of leaving harbour that day was dashed.

Reluctantly he returned home only to find that his uncle had a visitor. As Sam walked in the Reverend Shergold rose from his knees and turned to greet him. Serenity too was at prayer, her hands against her breast, head bowed demurely, a perfect vision of modest purity.

Praisetogod welcomed Samuel almost as if it was he who was the host. 'Governor Rushworth, pray be seated. We have all asked God for the safe return of Lord Craven's wife.'

Sam looked across at his uncle who made a brave attempt at a smile. Regretfully Sam informed him that any chance of putting to sea was lost until the morrow at the earliest.

Praisetogod added his own observation. 'Do not kick against the pricks, my son. God will have sent this wind for a purpose – and I think I know what it is.'

Inwardly Sam groaned.

As they talked, Serenity rose to her feet and went to stand beside the Minister. For a moment Sam felt as if he was facing a deputation, then his cousin spoke.

'Reverend Shergold has pointed out to us that the presence of unmarried women on the island might cause complications within the community.'

Sam said nothing. He had no desire to think of anything other

165

than the need to get Esmeralda back. Petty jealousies among the planters were the least of his worries.

Aeneas added: 'I fear he may be right, Sam. I am solely to blame in bringing the ladies here unannounced.' He turned his head towards the fifth person present. 'I have already raised the subject with Mistress Hardy and she recognises that in the circumstances an early marriage might be wise. Can you suggest anyone whom she might wed, without causing conflict among the other planters?'

Hannah Hardy, standing outside their uneasy circle, flushed bright pink and her expression was expectant, like a hungry man offered an unexpected meal. Sam shook his head. A line of disembodied faces flashed through his mind. What were they supposed to do, draw lots for her?

Aloud, he said: 'Perhaps it would be best to wait until Mistress Hardy has had time to meet the island residents.' He was about to add that he personally thought it was best if people made their own choice, when Serenity said: 'As it is, there is no point in our delaying. You and I must take our vows, Samuel.'

'I –' Her words struck him almost like a thunderbolt.

Seeing his shock, Aeneas cut in: 'I hope I have not done wrong, nephew, in bringing your bride to you?'

'Yes – no. Er – would it not be better to wait?' He scratched around for any straw to save him from this particular drowning.

'Wait for what?' His cousin's black eyes were bright, probing. There seemed to be an almost indecent haste in her intensity.

He tried again. 'Would you not at least want a wedding breakfast? I – I haven't even got clean linen.'

'That is no matter. I realise I shall be facing hardship here. That is surely part of God's test.'

There had to be a way out and yet it was too late now to begin expressing his doubts. Besides, what was the point of freedom if he could not have Esmeralda? For the first time Samuel truly understood the meaning of heart ache. He turned towards the window to hide his pain.

'There is no reason why you should not take your vows now.' Praisetogod was taking control. As Sam was about to refuse, he caught Aeneas's eye and saw in his uncle's expression a mute pleading. In spite of the fact that Lord Craven had stolen away his very reason for living, Samuel still could not let him down.

The ceremony was so brief he hardly noticed its passing. Within minutes he was transformed from bachelor to bridegroom. As he formally kissed his bride's pink cheek he saw the sharp satisfaction in her eyes.

Too soon the night descended. Sleeping accommodation was arranged for all the new arrivals. In deference to the need for privacy of the newly weds, Lord Craven and Hannah returned with Captain Jordan for one final night aboard ship.

In spite of Serenity's disapproving stare, Sam helped himself liberally to the brandy that Captain Jordan had delivered. He said: 'I shall understand if you would prefer to have your own chamber.' The house already possessed two sleeping areas, acknowledging the fact that one day the Governor would be a family man.

'Surely it is usual for husband and wife to sleep together, especially on the first night of their marriage?'

It was not the answer he had expected. All his life he had seen his cousin as somebody cold, an unlikely lover. Now it felt as if she was taunting him, even questioning his virility.

As he bowed his head in assent, she said: 'It is my father's wish that our first-born son becomes his heir.'

Before he could comment she added: 'I realise he had hinted that you would inherit the estate in your own right, but you would surely have no regrets if it passed instead to your son?'

He could not digest the implications of this. To buy time, he asked: 'What if his wife . . .?'

'My father has prayed about this.' Serenity hesitated. 'It is his decision that the first-born boy, either to ourselves or to *that* woman, shall inherit the estate.' He heard the venom in her voice.

Now he knew the reason for her impatience to wed. Keeping his tone level, he said: 'Then you are anxious to be the mother of that first-born?'

She made a dismissive gesture.

He too raised his shoulders, thinking they were in the hands of fate. Aloud, he confirmed: 'It will be for God to decide.'

It was well over a year since Samuel had made love to a woman. On the occasions when he had thought about it, two scenarios had come to him – the relaxed and fleeting release with a lady of pleasure, or the exalted and lifelong union with the woman he loved. Now he lay beside a woman about whom he understood nothing. He hesitated to reach out and touch her yet he could sense her impatience.

With every passing second the tension increased. His voice unsteady, he said: 'Serenity, I will try not to hurt you.'

'Just do it.'

He was aware that she had drawn up her nightgown and spread her legs. Miserably he slid across and lowered himself on to her.

'Ouch!'

'I apologise.'

He pushed and stabbed at her, the brandy blunting his senses. He knew that she was feeling pain, but she merely sighed fretfully and felt for him, guiding him to the right place. 'Now, go on.'

She cried out as he deflowered her and he completed the process with a sense of humiliation, not wanting to display his feelings in any way. It was with nothing but relief that he finally pulled away and lay desolate in the dark.

Esmeralda. The dream of the wedding night that had sustained him for the past year was in ashes.

Into the darkness, he said: 'I hope I didn't hurt you too much?'

'No more than I expected.'

'Good night then.' He lay tense and unfulfilled, the weight of his betrayal upon him. His thoughts reached out to some distant place where the woman of his dreams was back in the clutches of her father. Esmee. Please understand that I never intended this.

To Serenity he said: 'If the winds permit I shall be sailing tomorrow morning.' He turned his back on her and hoped for the comfort of sleep.

By way of reply she rolled towards him, pulling at his arm. 'In that case you had best take me again for I might not have conceived the first time – and it is imperative that we have a baby soon.'

'No.' But even as he spoke, his treacherous body, hungry to wipe away the so-recent sense of failure, betrayed him once again.

In spite of the still contrary winds, Sam insisted on putting to sea at first light. Both he and Captain Jordan agreed that Jackson was unlikely to make for any of the English islands so they decided to aim for those outposts held by the French, the Dutch or the Spanish. While there were plenty of uninhabited islands, Jackson's priority would surely be to find a market for the slaves.

The voyage was difficult and dangerous. Everywhere they called they met with disappointment. Nowhere, it seemed, had the *Destiny* attempted to put into port.

Their failure left Samuel increasingly desperate and Captain Jordan impatient to return to his normal duties. When Sam suggested moving on, Jordan said: 'I fear you will not find her. There are hundreds of islands out there. Some are not even charted.'

Sam did not reply. He found it hard to hide his torment. Reasonably, Jordan added: 'I know nothing of this Captain Jackson, but in his shoes I should dispose of the lady quickly, either by selling her or . . .' He ran his hand across his throat.

Sam's heart plummeted. He could not let himself think past the first alternative.

'If she has been sold then I must follow up every avenue. No matter what it costs, I shall endeavour to buy her back.' He felt his guilt begin to show. The Captain must surely wonder why his uncle's wife was so important to him. Realising too late that he was making matters worse, he said: 'I owe it to my uncle. It is a matter of honour. He has been like a father to me.'

'Then would you have me put you ashore somewhere?' Captain Jordan forestalled any arguments by adding: 'I must return to Barbados.' He paused, picking his words carefully. 'To travel alone on a foreign island is to court disaster. As sure as there is light, you will find yourself taken up and either imprisoned as a spy or sold into servitude. My advice is that you should go back to Eden and carry out the duties assigned to you there. You have done all you reasonably can.'

'You don't know her. You don't know Esmeralda.' Sam was prepared to be thought a fool, willing to risk an indiscretion, to face anything in order to get her back.

All the time a demon kept niggling at him, asking: Did she enter into this marriage willingly? His uncle was not the sort of man to coerce people into doing something they did not want. *Esmeralda, in Aeneas's bed, wanting to be there.*

He tried to concentrate on something practical. It was true, to find a solitary girl in this vast sprawl of islands would be like searching for the proverbial bodkin in a haystack. Perhaps, just perhaps, during his absence she had turned up. When he got back she might be there, safe and well – along with her husband. He almost groaned aloud.

There seemed nothing else to do. Aware that Jordan was watching him, he nodded his head in defeat. 'All right, Captain. It is as you say. We will go home.'

Jordan looked out across the horizon where a jumble of clouds piled high. He frowned. 'I don't like the look of that sky. We'd best make sail.'

The barque began the return journey, making fast speed now that she was going with the wind, but as the hours passed, Richard Jordan, studying his charts, making regular readings, looked increasingly dismayed.

'We're being carried off course.'

'Where are we headed?' Sam looked at the empty sea.

'I don't know. We're further east than I imagined. We seem to have lost our bearings.'

Sundown came with such suddenness that they were all taken by surprise. Raindrops the size of dinner plates began to hammer the ship. All the time she pulled away to the north-east, like a bitch on a lead, determined to go her own way.

'You think we are in danger?' Sam asked, making it his business to stay with the Captain even though neither of them had slept for twenty-four hours.

'I don't know. I don't know where we are. I thought I knew these waters well, and yet . . .'

Jordan reduced the sail to a minimum, hoping to slow their progress until daylight. The lowering clouds buried the stars so that sky and sea were the same inky black.

'Land to starboard.'

The solitary call as the first wisps of light appeared had every man on the quarter deck rushing to the rails. There, hunched low in the waters, was a large land mass, rising to a wooded ridge.

'Where are we?'

Captain Jordan shook his head. He looked puzzled. 'According to my charts there shouldn't be any land here, especially not of that size.'

The ship continued her gentle drift.

'Do we land?' asked Sam. He felt something of the same excitement that had gripped him when they'd first set eyes on Eden, not knowing what they might find. Anything was possible.

'We have to. We should identify this place, chart it.' Jordan removed his hat and scratched his scalp, fluffing up the thinning hair.

'If I'm not mistaken, this could be Fonseca.'

'Fonseca?'

'Aye. The Spaniards call it San Bernaldo. There are accounts of it but I don't personally know anyone who has been there.'

The sense of anticipation increased. They might be the first Englishmen to set foot there. If it was not Fonseca, they might be the first white men. Perhaps they would claim it for the Crown. Esmeralda Island. Sam shook his head at his own persistent foolishness.

As dawn lightened, the barque seemed to drift naturally towards a gap in the rocky shoals. 'I think this could be it.' Jordan was wide awake, eyes straining towards the hazy landscape.

They came easily to land in a rocky cove and waded ashore. The sand beyond the waves was honey-gold in the early light. A dark skirt of lush vegetation spread along the coast in both directions, as far as they could see. Bird song, varied as a sonata, trilled invisibly from the trees.

'This place is quite a size.' Sam screwed up his toes in the warm sand, revelling in the sensation as the smooth grains trickled beneath his feet. Excitedly he wondered if there was some divine purpose in their coming here. Could it be that Jackson had chosen this very spot to hide?

'What do we do now?' he asked.

'Make camp. I'll send a shooting party out. There's an abundance of wood.' Jordan moved a few yards up the beach towards a sandy hillock. Bending down, he began to scrape the sand away. After a few moments he stood up with a grunt of satisfaction. 'Just as I thought. Turtle eggs.' He held out the white, leathery globes.

As Sam attended to the fire, he wondered for the first time if the island might be occupied.

'Could there be anyone else here?' he asked Jordan, the next time the captain came by.

'We're on the north coast. After we've rested, we'll make our way round to the south. If there is anyone, they'll have spotted us.'

'Might they be hostile? What nationality would you expect? Indians? Europeans?'

Jordan shrugged. 'Whichever, the longer we are left in peace, the greater the likelihood that anyone living here is friendly.'

The shooting party returned with an assortment of wild fowl, some yams, two coconuts and a huge hand of bananas: the making of a splendid meal. Herod Samson, the ship's cook, hobbled his way around the fire. Swathes of ebony smoke drifted above them, carried over the trees and away to the south.

They waited impatiently for the meats to cook, teased by the smell of roasting flesh. At last they ate hungrily, not thinking beyond the immediate pleasure of filling their bellies. The water gathered from a nearby river, flowing briskly towards the bay, was fresh and sweet.

For a while they lay on the sand, digesting their meal, but soon Captain Jordan organised them into groups, one to stay with the ship, one to comb the immediate vicinity and the others to spread out and circle the island.

Sam went with three of the crew, heading for a steep outcrop to the east. From this distance it looked unlikely that they would be able to get round the point, but as they drew near, making good progress along the damp, firm sand, he saw that the rocks were easily climbable. The tide was going out, leaving a legacy of seaweed and shells.

As they rounded the point, the beach to the south mirrored the one they had just left. As far as they could see, smoky blue waters stretched to infinity. Mangroves extended twisted fingers into the sand. A scurry of crabs hastened for the shelter of the tortured roots.

Sam was the first to spot a spiral of smoke. At first he wondered if they had walked further than he thought and that it came from their own fire, but the bay ahead was empty. No ship marked their landing site. In any case, they would have met up with the party of men travelling west.

His companions hesitated.

'I think we should go back.' The eldest of the three, called Lugger by his mates, perhaps because of his oversized ears, drew to a halt. The younger men looked to him for guidance.

'We ought to go and check,' said Sam. He couldn't go back now, not without knowing who was there. Common sense told him that it wasn't Jackson – after all, there was no ship – and if it was some native tribe, he was anxious to see them. So far he had not encountered one indigenous Indian.

'I'm going back.' Lugger did not wait for further discussion. Turning on his heel he strode purposefully along the way he had come. With the merest hesitation, the other two hurried after him, glancing now and then over their shoulders as if they expected Sam to stop them.

He continued to face in the direction of the smoke, turning once

172

or twice to see if his companions had changed their minds but they were already at the point and scrambling up the rocks.

With a sigh he started walking ahead. He was unarmed, clearly not a threat. He hoped that someone might speak English.

As he drew near he caught the smell of rancid meat. Just above the tide line he could make out signs of human habitation, piles of as yet unidentifiable objects, but placed in such a way that he knew they were there by design and not chance.

His heart rate increasing, he took a deep breath, wondering what he should do or say. Slowly he walked on towards the fire which smouldered damply. A large pot hung crookedly over it from which a putrid smell wafted in his direction. Wrinkling his nose in distaste, he halted and looked around him. There was no one in sight.

A few huts woven from palm leaves formed a half circle near the trees. The piles he had noticed before were skins, perhaps from goats. All around, the sand was stained with circles of burnt ash where other fires had burned, and by dark reddish discolorations which he thought were probably blood.

The stink from the pot was so offensive that he turned away, but some curiosity made him take one quick look inside. The sight froze his blood. There, in the simmering liquid, among badly plucked bird joints, was unmistakably a human arm, the hand outstretched as if in some last agony.

He backed away, stifling a shout, hell-bent on finding Jordan and the crew of the barque.

Suddenly he was aware that there was someone behind him. It was hardly a movement, more a shadow, stalking, waiting. He froze where he was, fighting the urge to swing round, fearing yet needing to know what fiend lurked in his shadow. Was it a wild beast or a human hunter?

He turned as calmly as he could to be confronted by three, dark-skinned men. Each carried a spear, the base resting against the ground. They regarded him with sloping, impassive eyes.

Sam had never seen men like them before. They were not like the slaves: brown-skinned, frizzy-haired, wide-featured. They were certainly not like any European.

By his own standards they were quite small, but that offered little comfort. All the wild tales he had heard circled in his brain.

Their bodies were thin, narrow-shouldered, their legs long and spindly. The skin had a coppery, almost yellowish sheen. For covering they wore some sort of leather apron. They regarded him impassively, their cheeks broad, their eyes almost sickle-shaped, their noses long and slightly hooked. Surely these must be Caribs!

Still the men did not move. Their hair, black as any that Sam had ever seen, was straight and lank, cut to just below the ears, from which heavy wooden plugs protruded, presumably as some bizarre form of decoration.

His only hope was to bluff it out. Surely, sooner or later, Jordan and his men would arrive.

'I bid you good day.' He spoke out clearly, hoping that the tone of his voice would show his friendly intent.

The Indians did not speak. They continued to stare at him, unmoving.

'I am with others,' said Sam. He looked around him, hoping that someone might be visible, but there was no one.

With a slight bow of his head, he added: 'We do not intend to stay.' He pointed out to sea, trying to signify that that was where he was headed. Some instinct made him place his palms together and bow, taking a step backwards as he made ready to depart.

The movement seemed to prod the Indians to action. They all three began to speak at once: strange, incomprehensible sounds. Sam looked from one to the other. By the rising pitch of their language he knew they were excited. All the time the thought of the arm in the pot, a few feet away, made him tremble.

He must not show fear. He knew that. Old Ezra's tales came back to him. ' "There'm lots o' Indians round about – Moskitos, Darians, Arawaks – but the ones to look out for is the Caribs. Fearsome as hell they be." ' It all came back to him: the grizzly details, polygamy, cannibalism, even breeding their own children for the pot.

Looking at these alien men, he feared it could be true.

He wondered whether to make a run for it but those spears, razor sharp, would be as fast as any pistol. He stood and waited, giving himself up to his destiny.

Moments later another group of Indians emerged from the forest. There were about a dozen of them, men, women and children. They carried the limp body of a pig. Speared in several places, its blood dripped in beads across the sand. As they saw Samuel, they all turned silent and still, and the original three began to recount their discovery in excited tones.

174

One of the hunters stepped forward. He was an older man, a hint of grey in the straggly hair around his face. For some reason the grey hair reassured Sam. Like other humans, these people aged, were subject to the same natural laws that governed his own life.

The man carried no spear and about his neck he wore several thick necklaces made up of dozens of human teeth. Instinct told Sam that this was their chief. He would not let himself think that perhaps his own teeth could end up embellishing his host!

The man studied him intently. Cautiously the other Indians crept closer. Any conversation was interspersed with gasps of amazement.

Suddenly he realised they had probably never seen a white man before. The boldest reached out and touched his hair, leaping back quickly in case it harmed him. Another, then another, touched his skin, his clothing. He forced a smile, nodding at them.

Somebody began to laugh and the infectious sound soon had them all hooting with amusement. Sam continued to grimace, knowing that this show of high spirits did not necessarily mean they meant him well.

The most daring began to open his shirt, tearing the strings to reveal his pale flesh beneath. He thought of tender meats, the pot. Only with the most heroic effort could he stand his ground.

Now they were swarming around him like dogs at a bone, pulling his arms, squabbling with each other for the right to explore him, prodding his belly, peeling off his clothes.

'No!' He began to struggle as they lifted him off his feet, dashed him to the ground and stripped him naked. Without clothes he was more vulnerable than ever. In one corner of his mind he still found time to wonder at the strange fact that, even in this extreme danger, embarrassment at his own nakedness featured high in his feelings.

They pulled him back on to his feet again, laughing, pointing at his genitals, wondering at the fuzz of reddish hair that flowered in his groin.

The chief raised a hand and immediately the others fell silent. Sam tried to maintain some dignity. He stood straight and faced his captors. God forgive him for his sins. If he was about to die, he would do so bravely. But the pot . . . Not the pot!

To his amazement, the chief bent his head forward and removed one of the ropes of human teeth. Holding it out he shook it, indicating Sam should put it on. Swallowing hard, he placed the macabre ornament about his neck and nodded his thanks.

175

The chief continued to survey Sam while two of his men helped him into Sam's shirt. One of the sleeves was turned inside out and they seemed to have great difficulty in mastering the complexities of the garment. Finally the chief nodded to himself, swathed in the linen which dwarfed him as it clung to his damp body.

He had a hasty discussion with two of his men – his sons perhaps? There was clearly agreement among them. Turning in unison they signalled to someone behind them. Head bowed, a young girl stepped forward. The chief nudged her with his foot and she took a few steps closer to Sam.

The chief, with a gesture that was universally recognisable, offered the girl to Sam.

He did not know what to do. Somewhere in the back of his mind were the rudiments of a story that Ezra had told him, about a man captured by Indians. He had been honoured, given the chief's daughter, and then, unwilling or unable to join in an act of marriage with a savage girl, had refused the offer. Angered, the chief had had the man staked out on the ground, his privates severed, his eyelids slit off, his tongue removed, then left him to die.

He had been found a week later by his comrades, still alive but a lunatic.

The girl did not look at Sam. Her head was turned away and her eyes were fixed firmly on the ground, but every now and then she gave a small, bubbling giggle.

The other females twittered like birds, whispering together, laughing aloud, their faces animated for the first time.

'I thank you.' Sam looked with despair at his gift. She was small, even for an Indian. He guessed she was no more than thirteen years old. Her skinny torso was marked by two small, cone-shaped breasts. A woven skirt the size of his kerchief concealed her front, but her smooth buttocks were bare.

Sam felt his own private parts shrivel to the size of walnuts. What was he expected to do?

To his immediate relief, one of the chief's sons fetched a cloak made of goatskin and draped it round Sam's shoulders. It was not enough to cover his nakedness but he held it round him as far as he could to shield himself from prying eyes.

The men led him forward, inviting him to sit down outside one of the huts. Some sort of gourd was brought and to his horror, Sam watched his new bride dish up a helping of the hellish stew. He gagged. He could not eat it even if it cost him his life.

Utterly out of control, he vomited up the contents of his stomach on the stunted grass in front of him.

The Caribs did not seem to be offended. One of the chief's sons kicked sand over his regurgitated last meal and, to his eternal relief, the maid tipped the stew back into the pot. The stench drifted towards him and he had to swallow hard so as not to be sick a second time.

The chief, already seated, held something out to him. Hesitantly he took it, hardly daring to look into his hand, afraid that some instinct might make him drop whatever it was. It felt light and damp.

Cautiously he opened his hand to reveal a wad of what looked like tobacco, only greener. It had a potent, herbal smell. The chief placed a similar wad in his own mouth, pushing it with his tongue into the hollow of his cheek. He nodded to Sam to do the same. Reluctantly he did so. The acrid taste of the tobacco, or whatever it was, trickled over his tongue. He tried not to swallow and was relieved when moments later the chief spat a gob of green spittle towards the fire. Sam did likewise.

He had no idea how long he had been here. He was certain that Richard Jordan would arrive at any moment, but a quick glance along the beach in both directions revealed no one. Meanwhile, the village women were busy dismembering the pig.

The arm. The human hand! Sam tried to blot out the image of some man like himself being butchered in this same, indifferent way.

The pig was skewered and its flesh held directly over the fire. Its fat dribbled on to the flames, hissing and spitting. After too short a time, both Sam and the chief were served with undercooked pieces of pork, the chief by a girl, presumably one of his wives, and Sam by the child whom he had received as a gift.

The tobacco had taken away the worst of his fear. He gnawed at the meat, nodding an approval he did not feel, forcing the lumps down. His child bride brought him some sort of drink in a coconut shell. It tasted fruity, slightly sharp. Without allowing himself to think, he drained it back.

After a second draft, he realised his head was growing fuzzy. This was some sort of intoxicant. He must keep his wits about him.

The Caribs were relaxing around the fire, drinking and talking in low tones. A toddler waddled over to Sam and stared at him. He

177

nodded at the child and its mother came to gather it up, giggling in the high-pitched way that he had heard the women laugh that afternoon.

Already it had grown dark. He wondered if under cover of night, he could make his getaway. He felt strangely drowsy. Someone was stoking up the fire, others were gathering up their spears and covers.

The girl, who had been sitting with the other women, now came over to him, reaching out and pulling at his arm. Unsteadily he got to his feet. She led him towards one of the huts and although he knew that he should protest, explain the he was a married man, he did not feel able to find the words.

Ducking inside the hut, he let himself be pushed down on to the goatskins that lay in one corner. The girl pulled his cloak away from him. For the first time in an hour, he remembered he was naked.

'No. You must go to sleep now.' He pushed at her shoulder but she ignored him, kneeling up beside him and taking his cock in her hands where she rolled it with practised fingers.

'No. You mustn't do that. It's not right.'

He tried to sit up but in response she knelt down on all fours in front of him, wriggling her pert little behind in his face.

Everything seemed slightly out of focus. He put out his hand as if to judge the distance between herself and him. His hand landed on her rump and he smoothed it as he might have done the rounded arse of a pony, patting her warm, smooth skin.

Gradually his fingers found their own way to the crevice between her legs. He could not stop himself. She stuck her behind further up in the air and braced herself for his entry. There was nothing else to do. Clumsily he climbed on top of her, balancing himself on his knuckles, and penetrated her.

She was quite still, taking his weight, patient as a donkey burdened by some heavy load. When he had finished he wondered if he should cuddle her, but she simply stood up and left the hut without looking back.

Sam lay down again, trying to get his breath back. He needed to clear his mind. Now was the time to escape.

Quietly as he could, he got up and crawled across to the entrance to the hut. As he pushed his way past the skins covering the doorway, he was aware of two shadowy figures. He had a guard!

Flopping back down inside he wondered if he could cut his way out of the back, but even while he was thinking about it, the effects of the wine and the sex, the lack of sleep and the fears of the day, crept over him, closing his lids, wafting him away to a dream world.

He awoke to the sound of shouts. Already it was light and his eyes protested at the harsh brightness. His head pounded heavily as he crawled his way outside.

What he saw made him forget everything. There, coming along the beach, were half a dozen of his comrades, heavily loaded with an assortment of goods.

'Thank God!' Sam spoke out loud and made to go forward to meet them but was immediately surrounded by the Caribs. He had no choice but to wait while they sent their own delegation to greet the sailors.

For a while they stood in conversation, then the whole party returned. Sam looked with joy at Richard Jordan. He nodded enthusiastically at him and Jordan smiled reassurance.

The chief had taken up his seat outside the central hut and Jordan was invited to sit before him. With a wave of his hand the Captain indicated his crewmen who began to unload their goods, placing them before the chief as gifts.

The Carib nodded his satisfaction. He looked across at Sam then said something to the girl. She scuttled across to join him. Clearly he was reaffirming that she was a gift, in repayment for the generous assortment of ship's biscuits, beads, combs and scissors, petticoats and barrels of rum that were piled up around the old man.

The chief signalled to his men and they began to examine the goods, exclaiming in wonder at each new item. Sam noted with relief that every one of the sailors carried a pistol as well as a dagger.

Captain Jordan indicated the barrels of rum and, getting up, opened one, taking a beaker and filling it. He held it out to the chief who sniffed it cautiously then sipped it. He pulled a face, his head jerking back in surprise, but after a moment sipped the fiery liquid again.

Jordan nodded encouragement. He opened the two other barrels. Soon, every member of the village was helping themselves, pouring out liberal measures, draining it back, exclaiming, laughing. The noise grew more raucous. The girls began to dance, their splayed feet thumping on the sandy turf, breasts bobbing in time to the rhythm of a hollowed gourd over which a tighly stretched goatskin gave out a resonant echo.

Jordan, still smiling at the chief, his eyes never leaving the man, edged his way nearer to Sam. Without looking around, he whispered: 'Let them get through this lot. Soon they'll be paralytic. Then we move. Fast.'

Sam nodded, hope coursing in his veins. The Caribs grew more outrageous. They laughed and danced, then some of the younger ones began to copulate, mounting their women like dogs, as Sam had done the night before. He felt a wave of shame pour over him. He looked at his gift, happily nodding her head in time to the music. He remembered the feel of her and his treacherous cock stirred.

Gradually the saturnalia died down. Men, women and children began to sit down, then lie flat where they were. The drummer's beat became increasingly erratic. Finally he simply stopped playing and slid sideways, already snoring.

'Quick!'

Jordan stood up and crew followed suit. No one bothered with them. Sam glanced at his bride. She was curled up like a puppy, her face resting on both her hands.

A momentary feeling of tenderness and regret touched him. Such a little thing, a young, wild animal, behaving as nature intended. Carefully he stepped over her and with the others began to run back along the beach, round the point, down to the water's edge, and finally, thankfully, waded out to the waiting ship.

TWENTY-FOUR

As Esmee watched from the quarter deck the members of her father's crew clambered up from the hold. They came out into the fresh air, taking deep breaths and blinking in the early morning sun. With groans of relief, they stretched their legs and aching shoulders. As the *Destiny* pitched and rolled each man seemed to have lost his natural balance. There was no fight in them.

Musa, standing at Esmee's side, remarked: 'You would not keep animals in such filth.' She did not answer but his words struck her with force. Until this moment she had not allowed herself to face the implications of her father's transatlantic cargoes. Now she wondered at her own blindness in not recognising the inherent evil. With dawning realisation she thought: It should not be like this.

The slaves stood around the prisoners, vigilant, nervous in the face of their new-found power. They had little to fear for they outnumbered the crew by three to one. In any case, now that the sailors were unarmed they posed little threat. Besides, the Africans needed their skills.

Esmee eyed the crew uncomfortably. Would they see her as a traitor? With a sudden sickening jolt, she wondered what would happen if by any further twist of fate her father should regain control of his ship. Her fingers grew damp as she gripped the pistol.

There was something incongruous about the bright clear morning and the fierce, persistent wind. The deck of the *Destiny* dipped and rose in a stomach-churning rhythm. The high wind was coming from the north-west. Battling against it was a thankless task.

Already at the wheel, her father was cursing quietly to himself, the sound of his words rather than their meaning reaching her above the roar of the mounting gale. Remembering who she was, a free

181

woman and the wife of a lord, Esmee went over to him. He was flanked by three of the slaves, armed with an ugly assortment of knives.

She asked: 'Where are we going?'

Jeronimo did not reply. Esmee felt angry with herself because she was still afraid of him. She felt even angrier because, in spite of everything, he continued to represent some bizarre form of security. The slaves, having shown a mercy and humanity which would credit a saint, even now made her uneasy.

Finally he answered. 'If I can get this bucket on course, we'll head for the Darian Coast.'

He showed no real concern at finding himself a captive on his own ship. There was no hint either that he blamed her for her betrayal.

Esmee tried to reason with herself. It was his own fault. If he had not – she could not use any word to identify what he had done to her – if he had behaved differently, they would not be in this situation. It was all of his own making.

The crew were dispersed to carry out various duries and, with the exception of the guards, Esmee found herself alone on deck with her father. For the first time ever she felt herself to be on an equal footing with him. Now was her chance.

To Jeronimo she said: 'What was my mother called?'

He did not answer, pretending a concentration on steering the ship which she knew came naturally to him.

She repeated the question.

Jeronimo shrugged. He looked uncomfortable. 'How do you expect me to remember after all this time?'

'What *do* you remember?'

He threw her a glance, raising his shoulders dismissively. 'I was a young man then. It was my first command. I had lots to think about.' As an afterthought, he added: 'I treated her well.'

'Then why did she die?'

'People just do.'

Her stomach knotting with emotion, she blurted out: 'Why did you keep me?'

'Why?' He looked surprised. After a moment he added: 'What else should I do? Now, Chickadee, that's enough.'

His shoulders were hunched and Esmee knew she was probing some dark corner where he would rather not go. She tried again.

'What was *your* mother called?'

Jeronimo gave a snort of contempt. 'You don't want to know about her.'

'I do.'

He swayed with the rhythm of the ship – and something more. When he spoke he looked away from her, throwing the words over his shoulder. 'There's nothing to know. Tamar Tilly, that's what they called her. The biggest whore in Christendom.'

She shook her head. 'Where did you live? When you were a child.'

'Anywhere. Everywhere. We never stayed anywhere long enough to belong.' He spat over the side. 'My mother spawned brats galore.' He fell silent, lost in thoughts of his own, finally saying: 'Don't ask who my father was. It's of no consequence anyway. I left when I was about eight and went to sea.'

Esmee saw him blink and with dismay recognised a long-buried hurt resurrected in his eyes. She had not credited him with such feelings. She was silent.

The wind was getting higher. She could hardly hear him above its wail, but she caught his last words.

'I'm sorry for what I did to you, but I didn't know, did I? Anyway, I was drunk.' She delved in her mind for something to say but no words would come.

The sun disappeared with shocking suddenness, almost as if it had gone into hiding. Black clouds raced overhead, discharging angry rain, crackling with a sudden, vicious jet of lightning.

'This is gonna be a bad 'un,' Jeronimo shouted above the noise. He turned his head towards her and she saw misgivings in his expression.

'You'd better get below, Chickadee. Secure yourself to something strong.'

Esmee did not move. The slaves guarding her father were thrown this way and that. They began to wail. Slipping and sliding across to the rail, they scrambled up and headed for the comparative shelter of below decks.

There was a sudden feel of every man for himself. Only Jeronimo, drenched, his face set with determination, remained at the wheel. His shouted commands to his crew were lost in the wind. In any case, there was no one near enough to hear except Esmee, who clung to the main mast, hugging it as if it was the most precious thing in the world.

'Get below!' he screamed at her. She met his eyes again and saw in them genuine alarm. She stared back at him, suddenly paralysed by the danger.

He yelled at her: 'Go, you little fool! Remember, if anything happens to me, the *Destiny*'s yours.'

Picking her moment between the pitching and tossing, she ran towards the companionway, fell against the door, wrenched it open and tumbled down the ladder. She could do no more than sit down in the corridor, her back and feet braced against the partitions, waiting for the barrage to subside.

She wondered where Yinka might be. She tried to calculate how long the girl had been aboard, anything to take her mind off the deafening assault that raged around her.

Dimly, shouts and screams combined with the roar of wind and the harsh hissing of the waves. Here, in the darkness of the corridor, she felt totally alone.

Suddenly there was a cracking sound, so loud that everything else was drowned out. The *Destiny*, already buffeted like a leaf on a stream, juddered violently as it was blasted by some heavy object. The mast!

Esmee fled from her hidey hole, driven by the certain knowledge of this new danger. Flinging open the door of Aeneas's cabin, she fell inside as the *Destiny* tilted back to starboard. She landed across the bunk, nearly on top of Yinka who was clinging on to the narrow rail that ran along the edge of the bed.

'Are you safe?'

Yinka did not answer but her face told of both her terror and relief at finding another human soul.

Esmee wedged herself in beside her, and in the blackness of the cabin Yinka clung to her. Above the roar of the tempest, Esmee uttered words of comfort.

The storm lasted for perhaps an hour, perhaps a morning, Esmee did not know. She had become so inured to the battering that at first she did not register that it had eased. At last, letting go of Yinka, she stumbled across to the door, tripping over the dross that had tumbled down during the worst of the assault.

She felt her way up on to the deck. The sight that greeted her nearly stopped her heart. Rent canvas, broken spars, barrels burst open, rails split assunder. The *Destiny* was badly damaged.

All the time she looked around her. No man stood on the deck.

Jeronimo ... She knew with terrible certainty that he had been swept overboard. Walking to the leeward channel, denying to herself that there was any real urgency, she surveyed the grey waters, swirling in infinite patterns. No living creature showed above their surface.

'What has happened?' She turned to find Musa behind her.

'My father. He has gone.'

'*In Allah ya so.*' If God wills it. He bowed his head.

'The *Destiny* is mine.' She spoke the words without believing them. The enormity of the damage, the loss of the man who had seemed invincible, numbed her.

One by one, seamen began to appear on deck, brushing down their soaked clothing, wringing water from hair and sleeves, dabbing at cuts and bruises. Esmee ordered a head count. There appeared to be eight crewmen and seventeen slaves remaining. Many of the men were missing, swept overboard – drawn to their deaths by the ferocity of the storm. Others were wounded, limbs broken or bodies trapped beneath falling freight.

Leaving Musa to organise the care of the injured, Esmee made her way back to her father's cabin. Inside, the same chaos greeted her. All his belongings were scattered about. Her heart beat fast. She expected to see him there, to hear his voice. She still felt the same mixture of fear and reluctant admiration for him. Too late they had held the first conversation of their lives.

Dragging out her father's chest, Esmee soon found what she was looking for. Clumsy in her haste, she struggled out of the brown woollen dress that Aeneas had admired so much. With a gesture of abandonment she kicked off her satin slippers and, as if putting on a new personality, dressed herself in the shirt and drawers favoured by her father. Now, clothed in a seaman's garb, she felt herself to be once more a part of the *Destiny* – and the designated leader of her crew.

Picking up things as she went, she righted the table that normally stood wedged between Jeronimo's bunk and the wall, replaced the lamp, his log, quills and the empty inkwell. Her hands trembling she spread out the crumpled maps.

Musa, a man from far inland, had surrendered his authority to her. Tolly Cross, the bosun, was looking to her for instructions. She swallowed hard, trying to get a grip on the present. Her duty now was clear. It was up to her to get the *Destiny* safely into port – but which port?

The vision of Jeronimo was back again, hands on the wheel, implacable, indestructible.

' *"We'll head for the Darian Coast."* ' That was what he had intended. She had no other thoughts of her own.

Jeronimo Jackson. Her father. Cruel. Unloving. Fearless. An enigma. In some curious acknowledgement of his memory, Esmee said to herself: 'We'll head for the Darian Coast.'

Following the chaos of the slaves' liberation, the imprisonment of the crew and the confusion of the storm, no one aboard the *Destiny* had had the presence of mind to take any navigational readings. As a result, with the death of Jeronimo, Esmee had no clear idea of where they might be.

Along with Nathanial Rouse, the navigator, she studied Jeronimo's charts. Too late she tried to recall the wind speed and direction since the last entry in her father's log. The storm had been so violent that neither Esmee nor Nat could tell for certain either how far they had drifted, or even in which direction. How long ago had that been – ten hours? Twenty? More?

'I reckon we must be hereabouts.' Nat Rouse stabbed at the vellum of the chart, his finger veering several leagues to the west at the last moment.

Leaving him to his deliberations, Esmee went up on deck and studied the skyline, hoping for some clue, but the ocean was empty. At the back of her mind she wondered what they should do if they met another ship. In their weakened state and with half the crew missing they were in no position to fight. For certain the *Destiny*, crippled by her broken mast, would have little chance to outrun a predator. Meanwhile she limped onwards.

Ordering a watch to be kept, Esmee went again below decks where she encountered Musa.

'*Sannu da rana.*' He greeted her in Hausa, adding: 'I hope you have rested.'

Esmee nodded, thinking that he had probably not slept since his release. In the confined space of the companionway she realised how tall he was. Overnight he had found a canvas shirt and some breeks. The trousers were too small and strained across his upper legs which, in spite of the weeks of confinement, were still muscular. The sun-bleached canvas emphasised the smooth, clean brown of his forearms.

186

'You've washed.' The discovery took her so much by surprise that she blurted it out.

Musa raised a questioning eyebrow. 'There is no shortage of sea water,' he replied. 'And we are a clean people.'

Esmee felt ashamed of her outburst and of her own unkempt state. As soon as she could she would send for water and bathe.

Looking at Musa she thought of Samuel. Although he was the antithesis of Sam – dark as Samuel was fair, lithe in build as Sam was broad – his calm, compassionate manner and self-respect attracted her in such a way that she wanted his approval. The knowledge annoyed her. Free at last from her father's control, she had no wish to be beholden again to any man.

Musa coughed, drawing her attention back to him.

He said: 'We need to come to some arrangement with the men.'

As he stepped aside to let her pass she was aware of his physical presence. She guessed he was at the height of his maturity, perhaps thirty years of age.

Pushing her thoughts aside she skipped up the ladder and into the fresh air, sending an order for every man to assemble on deck. Unthinkingly, as the men appeared, she took her place on the spot so often occupied by her father. She had the strange feeling that he was there too, relinquishing the mantle of command to her. Drawing in her breath she vowed that her captaincy would be very different from his.

As Musa came to join her she noticed that the crew and the slaves divided naturally into two groups, each staying with their own kind, the one suspicious of the other. Esmee raised her voice and silence fell around her.

'Every man here, black or white, is in danger. We have a crippled ship and we are lost. If we are to survive then all of us, *all* of us, must work together. There is no longer free man and slave, no black or white, no man or woman. We are all the same.'

Her own words sounded portentous. She looked at the expressions on the faces of her father's crewmen. To a man they changed from disagreement to deep thought, acknowledging the sense of what she said. As Musa translated, an identical expression stole over the features of the Africans.

'Where are we going?' It was Thomas Warner, the carpenter, who asked. His question brought Esmee face to face with an unsurmountable problem. The crew would want to return home. The

187

slaves also wanted to go home. Somebody was bound to lose. Whatever they did, they needed to repair the ship and find supplies both to feed them and to finance their return voyage.

Knowing that the very future of the *Destiny* depended on what happened next, she side-stepped Thomas's question, saying instead: 'You must all work together, according to your skills.'

The men looked at each other then across at the opposing group. After an eternity Thomas Warner stepped forward. 'Any other carpenters?' he called out. As Musa translated two of the Africans came to join him. The three men looked uncomfortably at each other then by mutual consent set off to find tools to begin the job of repairing the stricken ship.

In the same way healers, sailmakers, coopers and cooks were identified. Suddenly there was no question of free man or captive. Those of like skills found themselves bound by a previously unthinkable brotherhood born of necessity.

Esmee closed her eyes and sought for inner strength. She looked up to find Musa watching her. 'You are very clever,' he said, and she felt her cheeks grow hot.

Looking around, he asked: 'Where is the young girl?'

Esmee followed his gaze and realised Yinka was missing. She felt uneasy and, excusing herself, hurried down to Aeneas's cabin. As she walked in she found Yinka hugging herself and rocking in distress.

'What ails you?' she asked, fearing that the girl had suffered some injury during the storm.

Yinka shook her head. Her child's face was troubled, her eyes round with worry.

'Tell me.'

Yinka stared at the ground. Finally she said: 'I piss myself like baby. I bleed.'

Esmee had no direct experience of childbirth but she knew the signs. Yinka's face was grey. Spasms of pain tightened her already taut abdomen. Esmee took the girl's hand.

'Your time has come. The baby.'

Seeing the girl's fear, she sought to calm her but Yinka drew away.

'Baby bad. Father bad.'

Esmee shook her head. 'Baby good. You love baby.'

Seeing Yinka's disbelief, she added: 'I love baby.'

Would she? Could she? She suddenly felt frightened. The thought of this baby, a part of her father, a repetition of her own unwelcome arrival into the world, made her want to run away. All the time she thought: If I want to believe that I am special, then this child must be special too. She did not know if she had the courage to make it so.

Yinka began to pace the cabin, a difficult task for two steps brought her across its breadth.

'Sit down.' Esmee pointed to the bunk.

Yinka shook her head and continued to roam like a caged beast.

To keep herself occupied, Esmee sought out some linen to make bands for the child, a sheepskin jerkin to wrap it in.

Yinka began to moan, clutching her belly, bending double to contain the hurt. Helpless, Esmee watched.

The minutes dragged by. No sooner had one bout of pain subsided than another started. Yinka burbled to herself in her own language, at one moment grasping Esmee's arm for comfort, at the next pushing her away as if to escape from the pain itself.

After what seemed like hours, the girl crouched down on the gently moving floor of the cabin. She strained and groaned, screamed and cursed. Esmee watched, repelled yet intrigued. As the girl wailed her torment, her hands went down to cup the black, rounded protrusion that began to tear its way out from her womb.

Instinct made Esmee fall on her knees and hold the child's emerging head. 'Push, Yinka. Push!'

Suddenly it was there, a slimy, blood-stained creature, face contorted with the discomfort of its journey.

Yinka fell back against the bunk. The baby was followed into the world by its afterbirth. Esmee, paralysed by events, still held the child away from her as if she wanted someone else to come and take it away. There was no one.

'It is girl?'

Yinka's question woke her up. Lifting the trailing birth cord, she looked at the child.

'It is girl.' Her heart plummeted. Another girl. Another Esmee.

The baby rolled its head slowly as if tasting for air. It made small, snuffling noises. All the time Esmee knew that she was watching her own arrival into the world. Its eyes opened in a leisurely, uncoordinated way and she saw that they were dark, almost blue-black.

The discovery seemed to release her from her nightmare. This

189

baby was not her. It was the dinah's child. Its skin was paler than Yinka's but darker than her own. The knowledge set her free.

Distantly she recalled something about tying off birth cords. She did it as much by instinct as knowledge. Fetching water, she washed the babe and wrapped her in the linen. When she had finished she washed Yinka, cleared up the mess, and got the girl into the bunk. She persuaded her to hold her baby. Seeing her doubts, she said: 'She has your look. What will you call her?'

As Yinka raised her brows, Esmee nodded at the infant and repeated: 'Name?'

'Sole. Mother.'

Esmee nodded her understanding, wondering where Yinka's mother was. Wherever she might be, she would never have the blessing of knowing this, her granddaughter.

Tamar Tilly ... Esmee too had a grandmother. She could still hear her father's contemptuous tone, but she felt no such emotion towards her unknown relative. Who knew what sort of life she had endured? At least she now had a name, one more tiny piece for Esmee to add to her own history.

Gently she persuaded Yinka to put the child to her breast. It snuffled for a while then fell asleep. Seeing the exhausted girl begin to doze, Esmee placed Sole in the box that had held her father's clothes, padded round with his old shirts. To herself she thought: Welcome, little sister. This is part of your inheritance.

The arrival of the baby was greeted with pleasure by the men on board. From the broken crates and barrels, Thomas Warner set about fashioning a crib. Tolly Cross gave Yinka ten pesos. Nathaniel Rouse presented the babe with a gold chain that he had taken once from an Indian prince. The slaves had nothing to give but their blessing, but the child's presence on board seemed to give the ship a new sense of purpose.

Yet in spite of the co-operation of everyone on board, the *Destiny*, still crippled by storm damage, drifted without any clear direction.

Thomas Warner, having carried out a survey of the ship with his African counterparts, sought Esmee out to report on her condition.

'We've done what we can – Cap'n.' He used the title with the merest hesitation and Esmee felt a surge of exhilaration knowing that her position was now established.

Thomas continued: 'We've replaced some of the planking but

below decks water is seeping in fast. We've set up a twenty-four-hour rota but the pumps are hard pushed to cope.' He paused before adding: 'We need to get ashore.'

Esmee nodded her head. She already knew that the ship needed caulking to seal her joints. She also needed careening to rid the hull of the accumulation of weeds and barnacles. To do this they must take her out of the water, but where?

Thomas cut into her thoughts. 'Then there's the mast.'

By now they had set a course south by south-west. At worst they had missed Tobago and were drifting into the Spanish trade routes. At best they might find a sheltered inlet not shown on her father's charts. Meanwhile they were down to the last barrel of beer and dependent on what they could catch to eat.

'A ship to starboard!'

At a cry from the watch, Esmee ran for the quarter deck, screwing up her eyes to see. There, emerging from the morning haze, was a large, heavily masted galleon. She did not need to ask. It was a Spanish man-o' war, patrolling the area for enemy craft.

'Shall we prepare to fire?' Thomas Warner asked, coming up beside her.

'I – ' Esmee hesitated. The *Destiny* carried four cannon. Soon the galleon would be within range yet she feared that to open hostilities was to risk their own safety.

To Thomas she said: 'Perhaps we can slip by without being noticed.'

He shook his head and she knew that without the benefit of proper sail they were helpless to stop their relentless drift in the ship's direction.

Taking her father's pistol she went to the rails and looked across at the distant craft. Even as she stood there, she heard the faint cry of alarm as the sailors aboard the man-o' war spotted them.

Taking careful aim at the prow, she waited.

The response was swift. Even from a distance they would see that the *Destiny* had been dismasted. They homed in on her like a cat on a fledgling.

'We come in peace. Peace.' Esmee's message, bellowed through cupped hands, went unacknowledged. All the time the craft was bearing down upon them, her canvas full with the benefit of the wind.

With sinking heart Esmee saw that she was heavily armed. Black devil cannon yawned from the length of the ship's sides. At any moment they would open fire. On the deck many men gathered, the glint of knife and cutlass reflected by the sun.

The crew of the *Destiny* was helpless. Their ship could not outrun this gargantuan though ungainly predator. They continued to drift nearer, as useless as a bird with a broken wing.

Now they could see the enemy clearly: black-haired, brown-eyed men with skins burned copper by the sun. Even from the distance of twenty or thirty yards, Esmee could feel their relish, sense their impatience to attack. They must outnumber those on board the *Destiny* by at least three to one.

'Let us pass!' she shouted again but the ship, her name now clear, had lowered sufficient sail to allow her to draw alongside. Within seconds grappling irons from the *Vaya con Dios* were thrown across to the crippled *Destiny* and Spanish sailors were scaling the sides, armed to the teeth with daggers and guns.

'Fire!'

She did not know who had called out, but there was no need to give the signal for already the crew were exchanging volleys with their attackers.

'Stop!' She knew that it was too late. In any case, it was useless. If only they had waited she might have been able to talk her way past the Spanish Captain, or at least bargain for their safety.

The fighting was fierce and bloody. At her side, Matt Harbottle received a wound in the belly. He fell to his knees, wailing, clutching at the cataract of blood that flowed from the jagged hole.

For a moment Esmee froze, watching the scene in horror, but there was no time to worry about him. Round and about her others were killing and being killed.

Esmee fired, hitting the man who had attacked Matthew Harbottle. The force of the recoil threw her back against the rails. She fired again at the invading seamen, but it was already clear that they had the upper hand. Overwhelmed, the surviving sailors dropped their weapons and raised their hands, looking for some mercy.

'Who is your leader?' The Captain of the *Vaya con Dios* was incongruously elegant amid the carnage. He surveyed the remaining members of the *Destiny*'s crew, each held fast by one of his number.

'I am.' Before anyone else could speak, Esmee took command. The Captain's eyebrows shot up in surprise. He was a youngish man, long-faced and dark-eyed. His curving lips had a superior, fastidious set. He wore his hair long and curled, a popinjay among the ravenous hawks of his crew.

The men surrounding them chilled Esmee's heart. Their faces were cruel, avaricious. Systematically they roamed among the crew of the *Destiny*, searching them for weapons or anything of value, ripping away amulets, stealing kerchiefs as they took their fancy. There was little of any real worth. Two of the Spaniards grabbed her arms, forcing her hands behind her back. She did not expect mercy from any of them but at least she would do her best to preserve the crew's lives.

Her voice threatening to betray her, she said: 'I am Captain of this ship. We hit a storm. We are bound for Eden Island.'

The Captain surveyed them, eyes lingering over the slaves. A grin contorted his features. '*Inglese?*'

Esmee nodded. In Spanish, she replied: 'We come in peace.'

'Filipe de Ortega.' The Captain removed his hat and bowed low, smiling, clearly enjoying himself.

Sensing they were in terrible danger, she said: 'My name is Esmeralda. I am the wife of Aeneas, Lord Craven. My husband is even now at Eden Island. If you will escort us there, Capitano, you will be handsomely rewarded.'

At this, Ortega laughed. 'You, Señora? Such a pretty, exotic bird. You the wife of an English lord?' He spoke quietly to his officers who stood around him like seconds at a duel. They began to guffaw.

'It is so. If you harm us, any of us, you will have the English court to answer to.' The words flowed, hardly making sense even to herself but she did not know what else to do. There on the deck, a few feet from her, Matthew Harbottle was breathing his last, an unearthly wail bubbling from his blood-filled lungs.

'Please, Capitano, we ask only to go in peace.'

Her pleading seemed to amuse him even more. Bowing again, he said: 'Lady, I know your ship. She is the *Evangelina*. She belong my brother. You and crew are boucanniers. I hang you up, like fruit in tree.' He made a choking noise as he acted out his plans for them.

'No!' Esmee searched desperately for some excuse. She said: 'There is no man on this ship who is a pirate. If it is, as you say, a stolen craft, then we know nothing of it, I swear to you.'

Captain Ortega laughed. 'You speak pretty word, lady. But now you my prisoner. You come work with me. I have good sugar plantation. Need plenty men. You all come work for me.'

'No!'

His mood changed. His voice suddenly low and vicious, he said in Spanish to his crew: 'Take them below. The sick and wounded, throw them overboard.'

Esmee, still restrained by two of the Spanish sailors, watched helpless, horrified, as Matthew Harbottle was tossed into the water. Others followed: crewmen, slaves, anyone unfit for work.

Even as the thought came to her, Esmee heard a single, high-pitched scream – Yinka and the baby!

Seconds later members of Ortega's crew emerged from below, one dragging Yinka by the arm, a second holding Sole high above his head.

Esmee found the strength to break free. Turning, she called to the Captain: 'My Lord, this is my servant. She – she attends my child.'

'Your child?'

The seamen who held the baby thrust it out for his captain to see. Ortega raised his eyebrows. 'This? This is child of an English lord? I think not.' He pulled a cynical face.

Esmee was beside herself with panic. Her voice rising hysterically, she shouted: 'She is! Look, can you not see the resemblance to myself?' He was unmoved. She sank to her knees in front of him, her only thought to save the baby.

'Capitano. My Lord. I will give you anything you ask if you spare us.'

'What have you to give?'

Esmee hesitated. 'If you spare us, you will have the thanks of the King of England.'

Ortega snorted disbelievingly. 'You know the King?' he asked, the merest hint of uncertainty in his voice.

'I do.'

He shrugged off his disbelief then the sneer was back. He said: 'You are generous, Lady, but do you not realise that your gift is mine already? In fact, everything aboard this ship is now mine.'

Esmee bowed her head. Fighting her trepidation, she said: 'Then if you will permit me to keep my servant and my child, I myself will be a faithful servant to you – in any way that you want.'

Ortega laughed. 'You are kind, madam. But me, I have no great interest in you or your servant. My taste is more ...' He looked over the men on board, his eyes coming to rest on Edrize, Musa's son.

For a moment Esmee did not understand, then as Musa shouted a protest, she remembered the partnerships that existed between some of the crew. She bowed her head, ashamed of her own relief. All the time she thought: I am saving my own skin, but I am condemning Musa's boy to the Captain's mercy. There was nothing that she could do about it.

Behind her Musa gave a grunt of pain as one of the Spanish sailors struck him. She glanced round quickly to meet his eyes, pleading with him to hold back. The baby could still be spared. Edrize would keep his life. One thing at a time.

Ortega nodded to the sailor who held Yinka's child and to Esmee's intense relief he handed Sole over. She held the baby close, cupping her tiny chin. Tears of exhaustion spilled down her cheeks. All the time she was aware of Yinka's stricken face. She prayed that the girl would hold her tongue, not give the lie to the claim that Sole was Esmee's child, knowing that the offspring of a slave would have little value to a man like Ortega, whereas his doubts about Esmee's status might just be enough to save the baby.

Aloud she said: 'I thank you, Captain. If I cannot comfort you in any other way, I guarantee to work hard in your service – as long as my daughter and my servant are with me.'

He raised his shoulders in an expansive gesture. 'Then so it will be, Contessa Craven.' He grinned again at the suggestion that Esmee might be the wife of an aristocrat. His lips twisted at his own, dangerous sense of humour. He added: 'Now you will be servant of Filipe Ortega – a slave with a slave of your own. Is most unusual I think.'

Esmee bowed her head. In her arms, Sole squirmed with the uncomfortable movement of a babe whose belly is either too full or too empty.

Ahead lay the prospect of what? Captivity. Grinding labour. Disease. Punishment. There were only two ways to end this: escape or death. For the moment escape seemed impossible. Esmee looked round at her companions, both black and white, and in their present desperate straits saw little hope of survival. It would all depend upon her.

To Captain Ortega she asked: 'Where do you take us?'

He raised an eyebrow, underlining her audacity in daring to ask. After a moment's pointed hesitation, he answered: 'We go to San Bernaldo.'

San Bernaldo. Esmee frowned. That was the island the English called Fonseca. Her father had known the Caribbean Sea as well as any man. The island was marked on his charts and yet, in all his years of sailing these waters, he had never been able to find it.

TWENTY-FIVE

With the exception of young Edrize who was transferred to the *Vaya con Dios*, all those remaining aboard the *Destiny* were taken captive. Four of the Africans were immediately dragged away to man the pumps while the rest were consigned to the hold. Slave and sailor alike were roughly bundled down the ladders and shackled together, forced to lie in the filth from which they had so recently escaped.

'Please, the baby,' Esmee pleaded with their captors but her appeals went unheeded. Seconds later she and Yinka too were pushed after the men, down into the cloying blackness. The only concession granted to them was to remain unchained, for the shackles and manacles were too big to fasten around their ankles or wrists.

'My baby!' Yinka rocked her daughter and set up an eerie wailing. Esmee stood in the dark, her arm around the slave girl, trying to think what to do. From the sounds above, the Spaniards were preparing to take the *Destiny* in tow. Esmee's stomach rebelled at the stench but there was no escape from the suffocating air. As her eyes grew accustomed to the gloom she led Yinka to one of the shelves away from the men and encouraged her to lie down. Only little Sole's cry and her mother's howls pierced the subdued silence of the other prisoners.

Patting the girl's shoulder, Esmee said: 'Feed her, it will give her comfort.'

Leaving Yinka, she felt her way along to the lines of men, her feel slipping in the liquid filth of the hold. At last she found Musa, his head bowed in despair.

'We must escape,' she said.

'My son.' He seemed to be unaware of anything else and Esmee felt the magnitude of his anguish. She did not know what to say. Reaching out she squeezed his arm as she had done to Yinka, offering impotent comfort. His bare flesh was cold to the touch and she felt a sudden hungry urge to move closer to him, to warm him and seek out comfort for herself.

Musa said: 'There is nothing we can do now. I have to rescue my son. You must look to the girl.'

With sinking heart Esmee knew that he was right. For the moment they were powerless. As she was about to leave him, he reached out and pressed her hand. She took comfort from the knowledge that even in his present anquish, he was essentially a strong man. Nodding in the darkness, she made her way back to Yinka and climbed in beside her. They lay close together, the babe snuggled between them.

Her thoughts stayed with Musa and his devotion to Edrize. She wondered what he felt for the mother of his child and was gripped by an irrational wave of jealousy, imagining the tenderness between them. The feeling swelled, sucking her under as Samuel crept into her thoughts. Samuel, wed to Serenity, the father of her children.

Hours passed but nobody came to offer them food or water, or any relief. Esmee thundered on the hatchway with her fists but her calls were ignored. Her thirst raged and she was overwhelmed by a sense of hopelessness. All she could do was try and conserve her energy in the hope that when the chance came, they would be able to escape.

After an eternity she picked up the sounds of canvas being lowered, then the familiar squealing of an anchor chain. At last the darkness was shattered by light as the hatch was lifted away. Several Spanish sailors dropped into the hold and began to release the men, pushing them impatiently up the ladder. Stiff and cold, the prisoners' limbs refused to obey them and their slowness was rewarded by kicks and blows.

As they came on deck, Esmee looked around her. The *Vaya con Dios* was anchored a little to starboard. The *Destiny*, being smaller, was nearer to the shore but both ships were some way out, away from the shallows that separated them from land.

A long, creamy beach undulated as far as the eye could see, running down to frothing turquoise water. Dark vegetation formed a barrier, and behind that lay a seemingly impenetrable mass of jungle. Silhouetted on the skyline, incongruous in this tropical wilderness, was a scattering of windmills.

At the water's edge a group of men waited, gazing across at them. They shouted a greeting to Ortega's sailors.

From the *Vaya con Dios* a boat was being lowered. Aboard the *Destiny* the Spaniards began to drive their prisoners to the rail, threatening them with sticks and cutlass blades. If they tried to resist, their captors threw them bodily into the water. 'Get yourselves ashore.'

'I can't swim!' Tolly Cross struggled to get away but he was man-handled over the rail, landing with a splash and a yell in the sea.

Yinka turned a stark face to Esmee, shaking her head. It was clear that she too could not swin. 'Baby drown!' she wailed.

Esmee could not swim either but she looked at the waves and saw with relief that the tide was coming in. If they could keep their heads above water they should be washed towards the sands.

'Hold on to me.' She grabbed Yinka by the hand, forcing her to put her arms about her neck, Sole secured between them. As one of the Spanish seamen approached, she drew in a deep breath and plunged over the side, taking Yinka with her.

She seemed to fall forever, the wind whipping past her, then the roaring, sucking water pulling her down. All the time she held Yinka's hands fast about her, pushing her own head back, reaching up again for salvation.

For too long they were buffeted about, struggling to keep their mouths above water, then suddenly Esmee felt the swirling sand beneath her feet. She staggered and forced her way forwards, dragging Yinka in her wake. Together they fell on to the sloping shore, sinking down on the damp, gritty solidity of land.

For a while Esmee simply lay panting on the beach, Yinka gasping at her side. Sole added her protest and Yinka hugged her baby close. Seeing the girl scoop up a handful of sea water, Esmee cried: 'Don't drink it! It will make matters worse.' As Yinka ignored her, raising her hand to her mouth, Esmee dashed the water aside. 'Soon.' she said. 'Soon I will ask them for water for all of us. Be brave!'

With an outrush of breath Esmee turned to look back at the sea. Other men were wading ashore, some helping their companions, others on their hands and knees crawling up to the beach. Esmee scanned the shoreline then the ocean but there was no sign of Tolly Cross. She jumped up and began to run along the sand but she could not see him.

'Tolly?' She turned to Musa who himself had just struggled ashore, dragging one of the slaves with him. Musa too looked round but then shook his head. In that moment Esmee remembered that it had been Tolly who had guarded the slaves the night she had set them free. She fell silent, wondering what Musa's feelings must be.

From the *Vaya con Dios* a boat was being rowed ashore. On board was Captain Ortega with several of his officers – and young Edrize, held fast at the Spanish Captain's side.

'My son!' Musa made to run towards them but Esmee grabbed his arm.

'Please, no! There is nothing you can do now. You must wait – for all our sakes,' she pleaded with him, and he looked away then hung his head. She said: 'Don't despair. We will all get away from here.' But even as she spoke she thought again of Tolly Cross and knew it could not be true.

As the prisoners set foot on the beach they were immediately grabbed by the waiting Spaniards and hustled inland. The hinterland, seemingly impregnable from the sea, was in fact dissected by a roadway leading through the bush. Along this they travelled.

By the side of the road men worked in gangs: widening the pathway, filling in ruts, cutting away timber. A team of mules passed them, loaded high with brush and logs. No one acknowledged the men from the *Destiny*. In the bowed heads and hooded eyes of the workers, Esmee read fear and regisnation. Her own courage struggled to sustain her.

As they came out of the jungle she was stunned by the panorama before her. Ahead of them, sheltered in a natural valley, was a settlement of some size. To their right stood an assortment of stone and wooden buildings. Round about, men were working on them, repairing thatch, replacing warped timbers, tinkering with pieces of metal. Their swishing and banging created its own discordant music.

To the left a jumble of sheds and palm-leaf dwellings tumbled to the valley floor. Outside a few sickly-looking people squatted on the dusty earth, attending to cooking pots, but Esmee's gaze was drawn ahead, to a vast tract of land which had been cleared of its natural vegetation. Across this ravaged landscape, row upon row of men armed with picks and hoes worked to break up the earth. In the searing heat their bodies gleamed as if they had been polished. With a lurch of fear she saw that no back was unscarred.

A single, strong male voice rang out across the valley, rhythmic, plaintive. Soon an answering chorus picked up the refrain as picks and shovels rose and fell in a regular rhythm, binding the work gang into one continuous act of toil.

Sickness rose in Esmee's belly. Her tongue felt huge, glued to the dry palate of her mouth. 'Please, we must have water.' She turned to the man who held her by her arm. 'If we do not, we shall all perish.' The Spaniard shrugged as if such a decision was outside his jurisdiction.

Esmee forced herself to look ahead, half blinded by the brilliance of the sun. High above the plantation, dominating the skyline and fronted by vivid terraced gardens, was an imposing building. Two storeys high, its outer wall was punctuated with stone arches giving way to a huge brick edifice, glorious in its intricacy. Esmee wondered if it was some sort of temple.

There was no time to stare. She suddenly realised that her companions were being separated. Poked and prodded, struck with bull-hide whips, the men were being driven on down towards the tumble of huts. Esmee and Yinka alone remained. Their guard began to drag them on along the road, through the fields and up towards the palatial building.

'Musa!' Esmee called out to the African, and he turned his head and shouted something in return but above the babble of voices, the cries of the sick and the hubbub of the plantation, his words were lost.

'Where do you take them?' she asked the man who held her.

'To the field gangs. Today they build their own shelter. Tomorrow they start work.'

'And us?'

Their captor gestured with his head towards the temple. He said: 'Is Capitano Ortega's house. You work in kitchens.'

In silence they followed him up the hill and through the gate. The gardens were heavy with the scent of myrtle and jessamine. They represented a place of cultured, tranquil elegance, far removed from the frenzied violence outside the walls.

An arched doorway loomed huge as the entrance to a cathedral. Esmee and Yinka were pushed inside. Immediately the stifling heat of the day fell away. The rooms were high-ceilinged, immense, airy. For a moment Esmee stood in blackness until her eyes grew accustomed to the muted light.

On the floors, cool tiles decorated with vividly coloured pictures of gods and monsters soothed their feet. As they passed through, Esmee glimpsed heavy Spanish furniture, exquisitely carved screens, silk carpets. It reminded her of some huge place of worship.

The kitchens were at the back of the house. As they went inside they were once more assailed by heat. An assortment of pots and pans bubbled over fires and the smell of roasting meat, the rich aroma of boiling fruits, tormented Esmee's thirst, tortured her with hunger. To the man she said again: 'Please, we must drink.'

With a nod of his head he indicated a pail on the floor from which a large grey hound was slaking its own thirst. Unable to contain herself, Esmee pushed the dog aside, ignoring its snarls, and dipped her hands into the tepid liquid, holding it out to Yinka so that she could ease her agony. 'Not too much.'

She stayed the girl with her hand as she greedily guzzled from the pail then at last, tears of relief pricking her eyes, immersed her own lips in the stale water.

Her captor then handed her into the charge of a large black man who was busy tasting the contents of one of the pots.

'Cesare, I bring you more labour. See to them.'

The man turned a round, glistening face in their direction. In the gloom the whites of his eyes appeared luminescent. His body was huge, a mass of wobbling black flesh over which a calico shirt spattered with cooking stains stretched alarmingly. When he spoke his voice was incongruously high.

'You work, hard hard,' he said by way of greeting. 'Captain he get plenny mad you no work.'

'Please, can we not first eat? We have had nothing for two days.'

Cesare looked them over, his eyes resting on Sole. After careful thought he pointed to a cauldron standing on a low wooden table. 'In there. Plenny lob lolly.'

Esmee strode across to the pot and looked inside. It contained a glutinous mess of stodge. Her hunger was such that she grabbed a handful and stuffed it into her mouth. It was thick and tasteless, unsalted, and only added to her still persistent thirst. She turned to look at the other pots from which such enticing smells filled their air. Cesare, following her gaze, shook his head.

'Only lob lolly for slaves. Every day. Is cheap. Nice maize. Nutritious. You live on that. On water.'

Taking pity on them he said: 'First you come alonga me. I show you quarters.' He preceded them through the back door and across a courtyard to what Esmee thought at first were stables, a series of cubicles constructed of rough wooden planks. Stepping inside Cesare pointed to one of the many identical stalls, the only furnishing being a floor covering of husks from the canes. He said: 'This for house slaves. You live here. Rest now. Tomorrow you start work, quick quick.'

Esmee ducked through the doorway. The barren hut offered little in the way of comfort. She was still hungry, still thirsty, the mush of the lob lolly coating her throat.

Taking Yinka's hand, she pulled the girl down into the scratchy trash from the cane fields, saying: 'You feed Sole now, then rest.' Seeing the girl's bleak expression she added: 'Don't fret. We will soon get away from here.'

Esmee closed her own eyes but felt exhausted beyond the point of sleep. Somehow she had to get out and explore the island, discover how many men Ortega had, make contact with Musa. She missed his reassuring presence. She missed him.

As Yinka's breathing became regular, she scrambled up and went to the doorway, peering out into the still fearsome heat. At the end of the lane one of the overseers was positioned in a place where he could keep an eye both on the slave huts and the entrance to the kitchen. Any exploration would have to wait until after dark.

She sank down again, her limbs aching with fatigue. The only way of escape would be by sea. The *Vaya con Dios* was too big for them to handle and the *Destiny* – or the *Evangelina* – was no longer seaworthy. Perhaps there were other ships. Perhaps there were other slaves willing to risk an escape. Perhaps . . . Her mind could cope with no more. Sucking on her thumb for comfort, she curled up beside Yinka and sent up a prayer to Samuel's god, and through him to Samuel.

'Please help us get away from here. Please, please don't let Samuel wed Serenity. I know I am married to Aeneas, but it isn't a true marriage. Not one of love. Once Samuel and I are together we will prove the strength of our feelings. Nothing else will matter.' There being nothing else that she could do, she gave herself up to a dreamless slumber.

TWENTY-SIX

Esmee awoke to the sound of the four o'clock bell, summoning the slaves to the fields. For a moment she lay very still, trying to remember where she was. A rustling sound nearby made her open her eyes. A few inches from her foot a scorpion, big as a rat, scuttled away and under the rough planking of the hut. With a scream Esmee leapt up and was immediately gripped by nausea. Her heart thundered and she drew in deep breaths, seeking to regain control. Her limbs felt like lead, her shoulders ached and she had slept awkwardly, ricking her neck.

Outside it was still dark. With no covering to pull over herself, the cold night air had permeated the very heart of her. She longed for some hot, comforting broth to still her churning stomach, warm her being, ease the torment of her thirst.

At her side Yinka still slept, curled into a little ball, Sole cradled against her. Shakily Esmee reached out and touched the babe. With relief she found that she had absorbed sufficient heat from her mother to keep out the worst of the cold. This exclusive pairing, with warmth passing from mother to child and back, added to her own sense of isolation.

Unsure what was expected from them, Esmee roused Yinka and together they made their way to the kitchen.

'You come start work, quick quick!' Cesare greeted them at the door. In his hand he held an evil-looking, blood-stained chopper. On the bench a partially dismembered pig bore witness to his activities. Following Esmee's gaze, he said: 'I make good jelly – pig meat, calves' foot, cockbird.' He nodded to a stool beside the table on which lay a dead cockerel. To Yinka he said: 'You pluck big bird now.'

From his expression, the sudden softening of his face, Esmee knew that he felt sympathy for the young girl and her baby. Slyly he pushed a jug towards her. 'You drink, quick quick.'

Looking across at Esmee for her approval, Yinka lifted the jug and drained the contents. White froth coated her upper lip as she set it down again. After a moment's hesitation Esmee walked across to the bucket of water by the door, set out for the dog. There she slaked her own thirst.

Her pleasure that Yinka had found some way of easing her lot was marred by suspicion, wondering what return the huge man might exact for his favours, but she clung to the hope that kindness alone guided his actions.

During the morning she cleared the kitchen fires, fetched wood from across the yard, swept the downstairs rooms and oiled the massive cedar floor in Captain Ortega's bed chamber. The room was cool and airy and from the window most of the surrounding countryside was visible, saving only the sugar mills, the curing sheds and the negro houses. Esmee scanned the landscape, hoping for some clue as to what might lie beyond the plantation, but as far as she could see there was only forest.

She turned to study the room itself. It was dominated by the Captain's bed. The structure was larger than anything she had before encountered. At least seven feet in width, almost square in shape, it was supported by four huge curved posts, decorated with vines and birds and pairs of explicitly male cherubs. The whole was curtained with a rich brocade in shades of green, imitating the jungle outside. Captain Ortega himself was nowhere to be seen.

Esmee crept into the corridor and peered into the other rooms, hoping to find Edrize, but they were empty.

Around eight o'clock she was called back to the kitchen and set to breaking eggs into a crock to which was added nutmeg and cinnamon and a generous measure of rich, moist sugar. All the time her stomach cried out for sustenance.

Cesare personally supervised the cooking of the porridge. He fussed around as neats' tongues, pickled herrings, cold meats and potato bread were laid out. Esmee caught the tantalising whiff of cheese cake, flavoured with sharp, mouthwatering lime. In desperation she swept a handful of crumbs from the kitchen table, stuffing them into her mouth to soak up the acid that tormented her.

When the breakfast had been delivered to Captain Ortega's dining

205

room, Esmee was given the task of carrying pails of lob lolly and buckets of water to the fields for the delectation of the workers. Jugs of mobby, a fermented potato juice, were served to the white servants, while simple water was given to the black slaves.

At last Esmee encountered Musa along with a gang of other men. The sight of him was like a distant beacon in the fog, promising home and safety. He was stripped to the waist and trickles of sweat left clean channels meandering across his dusty skin. Like a scarlet ribbon across his left shoulder, a lash mark gaped, fresh and raw. Flies buzzed around the wound, settling greedily. About his neck a newly forged iron collar chafed the skin.

'Musa!' His predicament threatened her fragile calm.

'Esmee.' He reassured her with a look. Bending his head, he scooped up a handful of water from the pail, drinking deeply, then taking a second measure he threw it over his face. She watched it run down across his jaw and seep beneath the slave collar, washing away traces of blood.

'You are hurt?' Hesitantly she held out the pail of lob lobby but he shook his head. She looked despairingly at the unappetising stodge. 'You must eat, even if . . .'

Musa said: 'Today is Saturday. I am told that at the end of the shift we will get our week's rations – two mackerel and a hand of plantains. I will eat then.'

'That is not enough.'

He shrugged. 'Tomorrow we are given a day's rest. Men go crabbing. We are each allowed a patch of ground to grow food. I can begin the cultivation.'

She shook her head impatiently and to forestall her he asked: 'And you? How are you being treated? Have you eaten?'

She side-stepped the question, saying: 'The cook has taken Yinka and the baby under his wing. We will not starve.'

'Have you news of Edrize?' She heared the anxiety in his voice, saw the fear in his eyes, and sadly shook her head. 'Not yet.' To distract him she asked: 'Is the work very hard?'

'Hard enough. The soil is like rock. We dig holes to plant fresh cane. They have to be deep and wide. We are the "A" gang. Ours is heavy work.' He indicated another group of men nearby, saying: 'My friends there carry dung to the field all day long.'

Even as he spoke the men were wearily hoisting great wicker baskets filled with dried manure on to their heads.

Esmee said: 'We must escape.'

'We will, but it will take time.'

Already the overseers had begun to chivvy the gangs, lashing out impatiently at anyone who was slow in moving.

Musa said: 'I will try to see you every day.' He hesitated. 'If you see Edrize, tell him to have courage. Tell him his father will come for him.'

Esmee nodded. In contrast to the cold of the night air, the sun threatened to boil them in its smothering humidity. Sweat beaded her body and trickled down her back, between her legs, under her arms. She felt incredibly tired.

As Musa moved away she heaved up the buckets and turned back. Raindrops the size of her fists began to lash the parched earth. Along with everyone else she ran for cover, making her way to the kitchens.

Inside, Yinka was seated on the stool earlier occupied by the dead cockerel. Sole was at her breast. She sang softly to her child in a high voice, the sound untamed as a tropical breeze.

Esmee put down the buckets. She felt increasingly unwell. Inside her head there was a strange, buzzing noise. She seemed to be looking at the world through a dark tunnel. Her chest felt constricted, her mouth bitter.

'Yinka.' She tried to speak to her friend but the words were inside her and would not come out. Again she tried to call out but everything was moving further and further away. Then, with an intake of breath, she felt herself slipping into an endless silence.

After a while Esmee heard voices but they were still a long way away and she could not recognise any of them. She tried to remember where she was. Somebody shook her arm impatiently, but she ignored him.

Her mind was preoccupied with the mystery of parental love. Yinka, Musa . . . both were chained to their children by a bond stronger than any iron links. Had her own mother felt the same? Involuntarily her hand came to rest on her belly. Bile rose in her throat as she thought how much Yinka hated Captain Jackson and yet loved the fruit of his violence.

'Esmee, please wake up!' Yinka's voice penetrated her darkness, anxious, frightened.

'You get up now, quick quick.'

As Esmee struggled to open her eyes she came face to face with a truth – one so terrible that until this moment she had not allowed herself to admit of its possibility. A knot of nausea gripped her, forming an almost physical lump deep inside her. This sickly presence symbolised another reality – one that could no longer be denied.

Since Jeronomo had come to Esmee's cabin she had not bled. Perhaps it was too early to tell, but there are some truths which go deeper than any fact.

She opened her eyes wide. Yinka was bending over her. In her arms she held Esmee's half-sister. In a devastating moment of admission Esmeralda knew that in her own belly too her half-sibling was taking root.

Part II
The Year of our Lord
May 1637

TWENTY-SEVEN

Your name is Gideon. You are both my brother and my son. I don't know what I feel about you. Not yet. Already I see that you have your father's eyes. My eyes. If people knew of the circumstances of your birth they would feel repugnance, but it is my secret and I will never tell. No one knows. Only me.

Esmee ran her thumb across the soft skull of her baby. She could feel an answering pulse that beat in time with her own. She did not know how old he was – five minutes, half an hour? She did not know the day, or even the month for certain. It was May – or perhaps the end of April – or the beginning of June. She must ask, find out soon before she became muddled and lost count of the days.

She felt calm. A sense of well-being wafted over her like the peace that follows a storm – and his birth had been stormy enough. She never knew there was such pain, such loneliness. Now she wanted to sleep, to escape to another world.

Inside the hut it was dark and stuffy. Flies droned sleepily as if they too were enervated by the heat of the day. Outside, the distant noises of the plantation drifted on the air. Already harvesting of the sugar crop had started.

Across the island a westerly wind blew, hot as Hades, whispering with an eerie, echoing hiss through the canes, making the dry leaves confess their secrets. Esmee closed her eyes, listening for some wind-borne message.

Her indisposition at this of all times was an inconvenience, or so Cesare had told her. This was the busiest season of the year. Esmee wondered how that could be possible. In the months since her captivity, every day had been packed with endless labour.

In one respect alone the field slaves had the advantage in being

211

permitted a day of rest. This was denied to the house slaves, but even so Esmee knew they were luckier, sheltered from the fiercest heat, spared the casual beatings that befell her friends, occasionally given presents by their mercurial master. Sometimes they were even allowed to clear the debris of a meal or drain the dregs of the wine that graced Captain Ortega's table.

Esmee stretched and in answer the babe moved against her. His tiny arms seemed to flail in the air as if feeling for the confines that had so recently held him safe, then came to rest on her breast. He seemed reassured, comforted by the feel of her warmth. A rush of tenderness flowed through her. Tears pricked her eyes.

She thought she heard the door of the stable open and somebody step inside but could not be bothered to look up. She wondered if it might be Cesare. Her fears about the big man's motives had proved groundless. When she had no longer been able to hide her condition, his kindness had immediately been extended to her. Esmee knew little about him except that he was a man with no interest in women and a strongly maternal fondness for babies.

'Babby born!'

Esmee heard Yinka's cry of delight, and knew without looking that the girl was bending over them, admiring Gideon, crooning to him in her own baby language. Esmee managed to open her eyes. She felt some small measure of comfort that Yinka too had been spared the privations of field work. Sweating under the relentless sun, it was unlikely she or Sole would have survived for long.

Esmee asked: 'What day is it?'

Yinka shrugged. She was down on her haunches, smoothing the baby's cheek. On her back Sole protested, aware that her mother's attention was distracted.

'What you call him?'

'Gideon.'

'Is father's name?'

'No.' Esmee felt her chest tighten. Even Yinka did not suspect the truth. People would ask, speculate. Here it did not matter but perhaps one day there would be another life away from here.

In the months since her capture she had learned not to have hope. What was there to hope for – that Samuel would rescue her? That Aeneas would send an army to take her home? Either way she would be faced with her guilt. Samuel would believe the child was his uncle's, but Aeneas would know otherwise. Hope of escape brought no comfort.

212

Yinka took charge, cleaning her, swaddling Gideon, chattering like a jay. Esmee gave herself up to it. All she wanted was sleep. Sleep.

When she awoke it was to Gideon's cry. For a moment she did not know where he was then she realised that Yinka had slipped him into the crook of her arm. He was there, squashed against her breast. Groggily she sat up and offered him her nipple. His small, pursed lips clasped her like a life-line, sucking noisily.

Once or twice he seemed to bite on her with his hard, white gums but the feeling was not unpleasant. As he suckled she traced the outline of his face, wanting to see herself in him, looking for some reflection of her own mother.

Again the door opened but this time it was not Yinka or any of her friends.

'Contessa. You have baby.'

Esmee sat up quickly, pulling her blanket over herself. Her heart began to thunder.

As a slave master Filipe Ortega was unpredictable. Esmee guessed that he was very rich, not just from seafaring or planting. The slim profile of his aristocratic face, the cut of his many clothes, told of a man with high connections, a man used always to having his own way.

Often he was indulgent, boorish, treating her to long sagas about his life and loves. Always he talked of young boys, wistfully, intimately, making her feel uncomfortable. Sometimes he was moody, spiteful. She was constantly aware that she was dealing with a viper, sometimes happy to bask in the sun, but always capable of striking a lethal blow.

She realised he was not alone. Standing behind him was another youngish man, well dressed in braided coat and light breeches. He looked like another sea captain.

Filipe spoke to his companion in a low voice and they both laughed. Esmee did not recognise the language. It was neither English nor Spanish. She thought it might be Dutch.

Gideon, tiring from the strain of drawing off his mother's milk, dozed against her breast. Carefully Esmee detached him from her nipple and rocked him to her.

'You have boy? Is splendid.' Filipe bent forward to look at him, clucking at the sleeping infant. Again he spoke to his visitor. Speaking louder he said: 'Baby will be call Filipe, after me.'

213

'His name is Gideon.' Too late Esmee realised she had made a mistake. Ortega's eyes narrowed. His lips set in a firm, vicious smile. Spitefully he said: 'Babies no good. They take mother away from work. He go.'

'No!'

She knew he was playing a game with her, showing off in front of his friend. Trembling, she said: 'But of course he will be Filipe.'

The Spaniard looked pleased with himself. Pulling the cover away from the babe he looked at his small, skinny body, pointed at his genitals and made a remark to his friend. They both laughed.

Esmee covered her baby and held him closer. This man was capable of defiling him. He held the power of life or death over both of them. At any moment he might take Gideon away and harm him. At that moment she knew she must escape soon.

Ortega looked around the room. 'You have food?'

Esmee nodded, knowing that he would inspect the stables in the same way, check to see if the horses had hay.

Affable now, chatty almost, he said: 'I tell my friend Captain Tromp that I have lady work for me – wife of big English count.'

'He isn't a count. He is a lord.'

He translated and both men sniggered. Then he asked: 'This baby is lord's? Like other one?'

Esmee said nothing. She knew he was mocking her. They had given up the pretence that Sole was hers but the evidence of her pregnancy had been before him during the past months.

She asked: 'What day is it?'

'*Sabado.*'

'What date?'

'*Nuevo Mayo.*'

Saturday, May 9, 1637. A very important day indeed.

Gideon burped sleepily and stretched before snuffling back into the folds of her blanket. The Dutch man made some comment and Ortega said: 'My friend say he can see baby is son of lord. He go often to English islands. He pass on happy news.'

Esmee endured their jokes, their stupidity. At last they grew bored and drifted away. Too tired even to fetch the mackerel that Yinka had left for her, she snuggled back down with her child. Her son. For the rest of her life she would strive to protect him.

When Esmee next awoke it was dark and she was not alone. For a second she held her breath, trying to hear above the thumping of her heart, then with relief she knew that her visitor was Musa.

'Esmeralda. You have a fine son.' From somewhere Musa had found a candle and now he lit it and held it high to get the maximum light. Its smoky glimmer illuminated his face, making his cheekbones look taut. His eyes seemed unnaturally bright in the glow. When he moved the chink of metal from his slave collar broke the silence.

Esmee felt a sense of safety now that he was here, as if all her fears were literally drained away. He alone of all the people on San Bernaldo gave her hope. She lay back on the rickety couch that Captain Ortega had given to her in a generous moment, and closed her eyes. She was about to confess to him her fears for Gideon's welfare when she remembered that his own son was already sacrificed to their master's lusts and held her tongue.

Like herself and Yinka, Edriza was classed as a house slave but he did little work. His role seemed to be to wear frilly clothes and always to be at Captain Ortega's side. When Esmee saw him he was silent, not meeting her eyes. It was only to Yinka that he spoke and she said nothing of their whispered conversations.

Many times Musa came to the Captain's house, looking for his son. Always he was driven away by the servants. Many times he had been beaten, but still he came back.

Now Esmee reached out and grasped his hand, greedy for more comfort. In the past months they had learned to know each other's feelings without the use of words. Now escape was foremost in her mind.

Since her arrival she had taken every opportunity she could to explore the plantation but she had not managed to step outside the settlement, bounded as it was by lime hedges, thick and barbed with thorns. As far as she could tell the rest of the island was uninhabited. Captain Ortega's estates represented a solitary piece of Spain in this tropical hell.

Again, as if her thoughts did not need to be spoken, Musa said: 'This week men have been working on the *Evangelina*, repairing her mast. I think it is their intention to sail her away.' He hesitated. 'I think it should be our intention also.'

Esmee sat up, her heart lifting. 'When?'

'I don't know. It will need planning. We will all have to be ready to take our chance.'

215

For the first time the danger of such an enterprise loomed large. She had Gideon's safety to think of now as well as her own. Then there was the question of where they should go.

As if picking up her thoughts Musa said: 'Your father's men will wish to make for home. We will have to bargain with them, find some place where we can live in freedom. Perhaps you have some idea?'

Esmee shook her head. There were dozens of islands, some uninhabited, some already colonised by outcasts. Some had no water. Others were occupied by fearsome native peoples who would brook no landing by others. It was then that she had an amazing moment of insight. Before coming to the island she had disassociated herself from the slaves. As the daughter of a mariner she had unthinkingly included herself among the crewmen. Now, with this talk of escape and finding another island, she automatically felt herself to be with the Africans, one of them by both birth and inclination. To Musa, she said: 'Fear not. We will find a place for us all.'

He was looking at Gideon. There was a distant, pained look in his eyes. In a low voice he said: 'I remember when Edrize was born. I remember my other sons and my daughters.' He shook his head to dislodge the sadness.

Esmee felt an answering jealousy at the thought of his past, his life about which she could only guess. She knew he wanted to go back. She too wanted to go back but the paradise she dreamed of did not exist. Instead there was Aeneas – and Samuel wed to his cousin.

Her thoughts were interrupted by a disturbance somewhere outside. Above the evening noises of the plantation the air was rent with a doleful wailing. Esmee looked at Musa and he lowered his eyes.

His voice very solemn, he said: 'Another funeral. Today, Plutarch, one of the men from the boiling house, was killed. He was crushed when his arm became trapped between the mill stones. He bled to death.'

Esmee covered her mouth, thinking of the horror. Evening funerals were all too familiar. She said: 'That is the second death this week. Yinka told me, one of the men took his own life.'

Musa's silence confirmed the truth of it. Squeezing her fingers, he began to talk.

'Many of us believe that when we die we will return to our homes

216

and our families. For most of us it is the only thing that makes life bearable. The lad had been caught stealing. He found a length of rope intended for a mule's halter and took it home to mend his hammock. He truly believed that nobody wanted it.'

Expelling his breath Musa released her hand, resting his own against the small of his back and stretching to ease an aching body. Esmee knew that he had difficulty in continuing. At last, he said: 'The overseer found the rope. Rather than face another beating, the boy used it to hang himself.'

He turned towards Esmee and put his arms about her, his cheek caressing the crown of her head. His presence felt like her sanctuary. She said: 'At least he is at rest now.'

She felt Musa grow tense. He drew back a little then, his voice filled with bitterness, he said: 'They would not even permit him a decent burial. His body hangs outside his own hut. They say we must learn once and for all that when you die your body is not transported back to Africa. It rots.'

He held her closer, his lips brushing against her hair. He said: 'These white men have no soul. They don't realise that when you die it is the spirit which is set free.'

Esmee said: 'We must get away from here.' She felt numbed by the abomination that was the plantation.

Musa held her away again and forced her to look at him. 'We will. But first you must lie up and regain your strength.'

Reaching out he picked up the bowl containing the mackerel. Bending down, he broke the fish into pieces and offered it to Esmee, saying: 'You had best eat while you can. If all goes as we hope, then before the next moon we shall be away from here.'

217

TWENTY-EIGHT

Samuel awoke with the ebb of a scream circling around him. He jerked violently, then recognising where he was, fell back on his bed, panting. His nightshirt was damp with fear.

He had had the dream many times before. It was always the same. He was on the island of Fonseca, surrounded by Caribs. There, in the middle of a clearing, was a cooking pot. As he watched, paralysed by some external force, the chief of the Caribs knelt down and lifted up a bundle. He raised the object high, offering it to some pagan god, then rising to his feet he walked solemnly towards the cauldron and dropped the offering in – it was Samuel's child.

Ever since they had left Fonseca he had been plagued by the belief that the native girl would bear him a child, one bred especially to be eaten. Old Ezra, ignorant of what had taken place on the island, had inadvertently spelled it out to him.

'Them Caribs believes that if you eat an enemy, you take on board his powers. That way they think they gain strength. 'Tis the same with children. They think if they eat good stock – babbies well bred – they soak up their future, keep themselves virile.'

'You mean, if the baby has a strong father they will get that strength?'

'That's it.'

Sam hesitated. 'Supposing the father was a foreigner?'

'Even better. They'd get power over their enemies.'

The date was carved in his brain. It was nine months since they had drifted on to Fonseca. At this very minute the girl might be bringing forth his son.

He sat upright, wanting to escape from his imagination.

At his side, his wife Serenity protested. 'What is it? Why don't you lie still? You know I need my rest. You know I get sick when I'm disturbed.'

Ignoring her Sam slipped from the bed, dressed and padded his way outside. It was barely light but already the air was simmering and a cacophony of noise greeted the morning. Parrots vivid as fireworks fluttered in the trees, squawking their greetings as they awoke for the day. Monkeys yawned and stretched, squabbling with their neighbours, chattering in their haste to begin the search for breakfast. The last of the bats were flickering their way back to their roosts, like blackened leaves massing in the white mangrove. The jungle around the village was as busy as a London thoroughfare.

In the square itself there was nobody about. Normally this was a time that Samuel enjoyed, surveying the sleeping community he had helped to create, savouring the peace and privacy that was so rarely his, but just now he would have liked some company, anything to take away the awfulness of the nightmare.

Looking across the square he noticed that a rush light burned in Aeneas's house. His uncle rarely slept. Since Esmee had been lost the old man had gone downhill fast. The life had been knocked out of him. Sam hesitated, wondering whether to pay his uncle a visit, then he dismissed the idea. To Aeneas of all people he could not confess his true feelings.

Away to his left he heard the sound of someone opening a door then striding down the path. It was Praisetogod Shergold, headed in the direction of his church, ready to make his first obeisance of the day.

Sam wished that he could talk with the Minister, discuss with him his dilemmas, but how coud he explain what he felt for Esmeralda, how confess to his fears that he had fathered a child on a savage girl too young to contemplate?

He shrugged, seeking solace in the shadowy contour of the tobacco crop that grew thickly in the surrounding fields. If God was good then they should at last get some return on their harvest. It was not a crop that was universally popular. Aeneas for one was dead set against it.

Pushing his doubts aside, Sam hoped that the processing would go according to plan and that a ship would arrive on time to transport the cured leaves back to England.

He sighed. The work had taken a heavy toll of the planters. It was true what they said – Jackson and others like him – white men were not up to this sort of labour.

The thought brought him face to face with another crisis facing him. A ship was due soon, bringing replacement slaves for those lost when Esmee's father had carried them off. Sam had made his opposition clear both to the council he had appointed to administer the island, and in letters home to the company, but with the exception of Aeneas, his was the lone voice of dissent. In this respect the islanders treated him as if he had lost his reason.

Serenity shared their opinions. She saw the slaves as she did horses, mere beasts of burden. Whenever the subject arose Sam was aware of the disdain with which she viewed his scruples. Sometimes he wondered if he was as weak as she implied he was, but on this issue he had no doubts. He would fight even if it meant resigning his governorship – as he suspected it would.

For a while he watched the frigate birds circling over the shore-line. The birds were supposed to herald the arrival of a ship. He gazed across the ocean but it was hazy and he could see nothing. He felt heavy with disappointment, longing for some news from beyond the island shores.

His thoughts turned to his wife, lying up there in his chamber, her belly rounding with his child. Think of this child, not that other Carib one that might not even exist. If God willed it then it would be a boy. Aeneas had already said that their child would be his heir, now that his wife . . .

It was no good thinking about Esmeralda, what it might have been like if he had had the courage of his own desires. Perhaps Serenity was right and he was weak. Whatever had happened to Esmee since he had sent her to England, it could only be his fault. Another, defensive voice answered in his head: You weren't to know. In any case, what's done is done.

Gradually he became aware of more activity around the settle-ment. Thomas Axe had taken on responsibility for the defence of the island. Every morning at this time he carried out a regular drill. No one was exempt. Out there, beyond the rocks, Spanish warships cruised the waters, predatory as sharks. Eden Island was a solitary English outpost in Spanish waters. The dons waited to see if the colony would fail and the settlers go home. If it was successful, then one day they would attack.

Sam looked at the company of men, drilling inexpertly to Thomas Axe's commands. He knew them all well. This island was too small for there to be any strangers, any secrets.

Gloomily he thought: I am the only man on this island to have a wife. He felt uncomfortable, knowing what people whispered, sensing the covetous way in which Serenity was regarded. *They didn't know what she was like.* It wasn't his fault that he had broken their agreement where women were concerned. He had had no idea that Aeneas would arrive with his daughter.

Painfully, he wondered what sort of impact Esmee would have had on the colony. While the planters displayed an understandable envy at the thought of possessing any woman – even Serenity – Esmeralda, with her sensual, almost innocent beauty would surely have driven them wild. He cursed himself for thinking of her again.

As it was, more women would be coming next year. He shrugged philosophically. They might not be what the planters hoped for. In spite of the company's high-flown ideas, few decent, well-bred girls would voluntarily come to this unknown colony, but there would be other women, poor, fallen women, whom the authorities back home would be glad to get rid of. With or without their consent they would find themselves shipped over to bring comfort to the settlers. Finding some small cause for amusement, Sam thought that Praisetogod would have his work cut out moulding these new arrivals to his ideal.

Jumping to his feet he strode out in the direction of the church. He might as well get himself into Shergold's good books and pray early. His prayers would be kept secret, not ones that Praisetogod would approve of, but perhaps they would do some good.

Removing his hat, he slipped into the building. Inside it was severe in its simplicity. The stark whitened walls were bisected by a creamy diagonal shaft of light from a single narrow window. With a sense of desolation, Sam hoped that in this place the light of God might penetrate the darkness of his soul.

Beneath his feet the cedar boards felt cool. His eyes, adjusting to the gloom, took in the roughly hewn wooden pews and the simple table which served as the focal point for the sermon. Here, there was an air of tranquillity which soothed his fears.

In the body of the church Praisetogod was on his knees, mumbling to himself, genuflecting with an almost manic concentration.

Silently Sam sank down and began to spell out his fears – his anxieties about his unborn child, his alarm about the imaginary one, the seemingly insoluble conflict between Minister Shergold and the ordinary planters for whom religion was a more relaxed affair.

Finally he prayed for his uncle, regretting the old man's anguish but knowing that Aeneas's loss was no greater than his own – and one he could not even publicly admit to. When he had finished, Praisetogod was still deep in communion with his maker. Thankfully Sam tiptoed out again, relieved of the need to speak with the man of God.

He was hardly out of the door when he saw Serenity skirting the square, heading in the direction of the church. Quickly he slid back into the shadows, a knee-jerk reaction, not wishing to be seen. As he peered cautiously out he saw her hurrying purposefully up the path. There was something stealthy in her demeanour. She looked like a woman on some secret mission.

His sense of heaviness increased. Once Serenity was inside the church he hurried away, not wanting to face the humiliating temptation to creep back inside and eavesdrop. He did not even question that her purpose in visiting the house of God was to meet with its Minister.

Wandering back towards the square Sam faced the unpalatable truth that if ever there were two like minds, they were those of his wife and Shergold. His main agony lay in wondering how many other people had come to the same conclusion – this place was indeed too small for any secrets.

His thoughts were disrupted by the sound of a cannon shot, one single blast, signalling an approaching craft. Immediately he began to run for the beach in time to see a British vessel making for the harbour. His heart lifted. The birds had been right! Who knew what the ship might carry, what news her Captain might bring? Would there, could there, be news of Esmeralda?

Samuel was surprised and delighted to see that the Captain making ready to come ashore was Richard Jordan.

'Richard!' He waved to the man who answered his greeting. 'This is a pleasant surprise. I did not expect to see you here again.'

Jordan took off his hat to wipe his gleaming forehead. 'Neither did I. The Captain of this pinnace took sick in Barbados and I was charged to bring her cargo on over to you.' He glanced out at the ship. 'There are some sickly slaves aboard. You'll not be able to put them to work at once.'

Sam frowned. 'I did not intend to. After the rigours of such a journey they surely need time to recover.'

Jordan looked at him with a quizzical expression. 'Do I detect

222

that you are unhappy about your new helpers?'

Sam shrugged. 'I find it hard to believe that stealing men away from their land and forcing them to work for nothing is morally justified.'

Jordan observed: 'They won't work for nothing. You'll feed and clothe them. Even the worst masters know that it is false economy to starve their labour force.'

Sam did not answer. When he could not prevent the despatch of the negroes, he had personally supervised the building of quarters for them, insisting that the planters paid attention to details like shade and bedding, covers and sufficient water.

Some of the settlers had complained, saying: 'Let them build their own huts,' but Sam had been adamant, replying with wasted sarcasm: 'If you were buying a horse you would have a stable prepared.'

In theory, for the first week the slaves would be detained in holding pens to ensure they carried no disease. Thereafter they would be divided among the community, to help both with the communal tobacco crops and the individual acres that the planters had for their own needs. Sam's plans were more revolutionary: give the slaves the same rights and conditions as the apprentices. For the present they could expect no say in the running of the colony, but once they had earned their keep, paid back the cost of their transport, then he saw no reason why they too should not have the right to freedom. Catching Richard Jordan's quizzical look, he knew that he was in for a tough time.

As they walked up the steep incline towards the settlement, Sam returned to the other issue that was always with him. He said: 'I've been thinking about Fonseca. I believe we should go back there and claim it for the crown.'

Richard Jordan glanced at him. He looked uncomfortable, or perhaps more disturbed. At last he said: 'It is strange you should say that. Twice I have sailed in that direction. I could swear that my compass readings are accurate, but no matter how often I look, the island does not seem to exist.'

TWENTY-NINE

Aeneas lay in bed watching a lizard which clung to the rough wooden surface of his chamber wall. It was there every morning at about the same time, its body inert, head stretched out to absorb the first warm rays of sunshine that penetrated the room. The creature was so familiar that Aeneas almost regarded it as a pet. In any case he was grateful to it for helping to consume the multitude of insects that inhabited the thatch above his head.

He guessed it was about five o'clock. Already the day shift had taken possession of the forest. He had lived through the noises of the night, finding only the briefest escape in anxious oblivion. Now the too-familiar sense of gloom settled upon him.

His stomach knotted and churned with some unnamed fear. Try as he might he could not accept his destiny. He felt as he had done as a child when he had unknowingly committed some misdemeanour and been soundly whipped for his sins. The same question hung over him. But why?

Why did he feel so guilty, so ashamed? What had he done that was so wrong in marrying Esmeralda? Was it a sin to want what other people took for granted – a wife, an heir, some happiness in conjugal union? He looked to the example of Minister Shergold who denied himself such comforts but could find no justification in following that narrow path.

He had a sudden vision of his brother, Endymion. As children Aeneas, the elder, had always taken the brunt of their father's disapproval. With a sense of injustice he recalled how often Endymion, brash and fearless, had shamed him into some action which brought retribution on both their heads. 'You should know better' – that was what his father always said, punctuating each word with a whiplash.

But Aeneas *didn't* know better. He did not understand the rules. He could not blame Esmeralda for his present troubles. Indeed for once he had acted against his brother's advice. But was it so wrong to have married Esmeralda? Was it a crime to have brought his daughter to this alien land and to have married her to her cousin? Again he remembered Endymion's sneering reference to Eden. It had proved to be anything but a paradise.

He was startled by the sound of thumping on the outer door.

'Uncle! It is I, Samuel.'

'Sam, come in!' Aeneas scrambled from the bed, tangling himself in the insect netting, scrabbling for his clothes.

Moments later Samuel entered his bed chamber. As usual he looked strained and tired. Aeneas felt guilty because he had sent the lad here, burdened him with responsibilities, yoked him to Serenity. In his secret heart he knew his daughter did not make his nephew happy. Sadly he admitted that she seemed incapable of offering happiness.

'Uncle, the time has come. Serenity is in child bed.'

Aeneas's heart jolted. He was immediately confronted with his own disloyal thoughts. *Please*, God, don't punish me again. Whatever I have said, don't take my daughter from me. Don't deny me this grandchild!

Together the two men hurried across to the Governor's house. Long before they reached the fenced garden they could hear Serenity's howls. Aeneas's heart sank.

'She'll be well enough,' Sam said gruffly. Both men silently acknowledged the girl's inherently complaining nature.

When they reached the house the first person they encountered was Minister Shergold. In the cool of the parlour he was on his knees, praying to God to ease the travail of His faithful servant above.

Aeneas saw Samuel's face darken. 'Enough, Minister! My wife is in God's hands. Your prattling will make no difference.'

Shergold scrabbled to his feet. His stork-like limbs flailed with emotion.

'Governor Rushworth, you are a heathen, sir! Have you no concern for that poor, pure lady up there who suffers torment to bring you forth a son?'

'Of course I am concerned, man. She is my wife. *My* wife!'

Aeneas saw the Minister's cheeks colour. Like everyone in the

225

settlement he was aware how much time his daughter spent in church. Only a blind man could fail to notice the dog-like devotion with which Shergold followed her. Sadly, he thought: They are two of a kind.

Serenity continued to scream and moan. Hannah Hardy hurried briefly down for more cloths and poppy juice.

'Is she far advanced?' asked Sam.

Hannah shrugged. 'It should not be long.'

In the eternity that followed the three men kept to their private worlds. Samuel stood at the window gazing out across Rushworth Square. Praisetogod stood in the shadows, rocking himself, his lips moving soundlessly. Aeneas sank on to a stool and wondered how he would bear the guilt if his child should die up there, in agony.

Suddenly the air was rent by the cry of a baby. All three men started, gazing in the direction of the bed chamber. The cry was lusty. After a moment it stopped. No one came down to announce the good news.

Aeneas looked at his two companions. Samuel's face was so taut that his cheeks throbbed. Praisetogod had again fallen to his knees.

'What is it? What is wrong?' Aeneas could bear the suspense no longer.

As Sam moved towards the stairs the mewling started again. They expelled their breath in unison. At least the babe still lived. At the same moment they heard voices above, Hannah exclaiming, Serenity thanking God.

The men turned to face the door, palms tingling, mouths dry with expectation.

At last Hannah Hardy came into the room. Her face was alight with triumph. In her arms she held not one but two swaddled bundles.

'Mr Rushworth, God has blessed you indeed. You have twins – a son and a daughter.'

Sam looked at his uncle in disbelief then, licking his dry lips and wiping his hands on his breeches, he stepped forward, taking one of the bundles. He looked round again at Aeneas, too affected for words.

In that moment, Aeneas felt the curse to be lifted. In the birth of not one child but two, both healthy, God was giving him a sign that he had done no wrong in coming here.

Aloud he said: 'Samuel. God be praised! You are blessed indeed.'

Sam nodded his thanks. He studied the face of the babe he held. Its crumpled redness, crowned with a down of golden hair, offered no clue as to the adult who would some day emerge from this chrysalis. To Hannah he said: 'This is – ?'

'Your daughter.'

He passed the child to her new grandfather and took the other bundle. The boy was fair like himself – and like his mother. His head turned slowly from side to side as if to accustom itself to this new space. Sam held his tiny hand with his own giant's fingers, wondering at this miracle.

'You had best visit your wife,' said Hannah.

Samuel nodded. Aeneas detected an air of reluctance. He was certain there would be no more grandchildren. Never mind, God had proved him right, rewarded him with these prizes.

'What shall you call them?' he said to his nephew.

'The boy must be Aeneas, after you.'

'No. I – I would wish him to bear a name that denotes faith and courage.'

Sam demured. He wanted to offer his uncle some words of encouragement, to assure him that he possessed those very qualities, but the right words would not come. Instead, he said: 'What name would you suggest?'

Aeneas thought for a moment then said: 'Only last night I was reading from the Old Testament. The book of the prophet Zephaniah. I think perhaps it was providential.'

'Zephaniah? You wish your grandson to be known by that name?'

'If it does not offend you, nephew?'

Sam shrugged. He would have preferred something simple, like William or Thomas or even Samuel, but this child was Aeneas's heir. It would do no harm to please him in this matter.

Aloud, he said: 'And the girl . . .?' Their eyes met and they both knew what the other was thinking.

Regretfully Aeneas shook his head, the merest indication, willing Sam not to voice what neither of them should acknowledge. He said: 'Perhaps you should discuss this with your wife.'

Samuel smiled. Unbidden, a name came into his mind. As he moved towards the door, he said: 'Very well. I will discuss it with my wife.'

Leaving his uncle with Hannah and the babies, Sam made his way

up to the bed chamber. Outside the door he stopped, mentally gird-
ing his loins for the encounter ahead. This should be a moment of
exquisite tenderness and yet ... When he had composed himself,
he ducked under the lintel and into the room.

Serenity lay surrounded by pillows and cushions. Her fair hair,
damp from her recent exertions, curled tight about her face. A dew
of sweat still glistened on her forehead, but it was her mouth that
held Sam's attention: pursed, lips drawn down in almost permanent
discontent.

Putting a brave face on things, he said: 'Wife, I congratulate you
on the birth of two such fine children.' Dutifully he kissed her salty
temple and she jerked away.

Her voice sharp with complaint, she said: 'I pray I shall never
have to suffer such an ordeal again.'

Sam did not reply. He had no wish to share a bed with his wife.
There was no joy for him in the act of love. Serenity treated his
courtship with a confusing display of distaste overlaid with discontent, as if essentially she found him lacking as a lover.

'I have been speaking with your father,' he said, to divert his
thoughts.

Serenity barely acknowledged his words. She said: 'On the subject of the children's names – I have discussed this many times with
Minister Shergold. Of course we did not know that there would be
twins but we had considered both sexes. Often we have prayed
about it. I am confident that it would please God if we call our
daughter Purity – or perhaps Humility.'

Before Sam could object, she continued: 'And the boy – what
better than to honour the Minister who has been such a spiritual
comfort to me in these difficult months?'

Sam blinked in disbelief. 'You are not suggesting that our son
should be called Praisetogod?'

Serenity fixed him with her black stare, her pouting mouth ready
to burst into petulance if she was to be denied.

Sam said: 'I have already settled this with your father. As the
child will be his heir, he has the right to choose our son's name. He
is to be Zephaniah.'

Serenity snorted, flashing a lance-like glance at him. 'Why do
you take pleasure in crossing me?' she shouted. Her mouth trembled
as if she was on the verge of tears. 'Why can you not let Minister
Shergold, as a man of God, guide you in these matters?'

228

Sam inclined his head. 'As for our daughter,' he said, 'it is my feeling that she should be called Salome.'

'Salome?' Serenity looked at him as if he had lost his reason. 'How can you even suggest naming her after the woman who took the life of John the Baptist?'

Sam shrugged. 'Rather, I feel we would be calling our child after a dutiful daughter. After all, she was only obeying her mother's commands.' He looked at Serenity, adding: 'I am sure, my dear, that you would wish your daughter to be obedient to you?'

Serenity gazed fixedly at the window. Sam's message was not lost on her. Changing tack, she said: 'I shall not be surprised if our dear Minister refuses to baptise them, seeing that you will not be guided by his advice.'

Sam eyed her ruefully. 'Then if his conscience is too tender to perform the ceremony, we shall have to wait until a new Minister arrives.'

He saw the alarm in Serenity's eyes. The very suggestion that she might be parted from her zealous guide clearly upset her. He knew they were in danger of quarrelling.

He had not seriously intended that their daughter should be called Salome but it seemed that the name had already been accepted, albeit reluctantly. Now he felt that as a matter of principle he should not give way.

To calm the situation, he said: 'Since you have been safely delivered, I shall be making a journey. It is essential that we find new crops to grow on the island. Our cotton and tobacco are inferior and already most of the dye wood has been cut down and shipped abroad.'

He waited for her to respond and when she did not do so, he added: 'We have commissioned a ship with Richard Jordan as its master. It is due any day and then I will sail with him to explore the Moskito Coast.'

Serenity's expression did not change. Sam was relieved at the thought of being away from her, away from Eden with all its problems, but over and above everything else was the hope, however remote, that the course of his journey might, just might, lead him to Esmeralda.

When he left the house he was surprised to learn that a foreign ship had just come into harbour. On going to investigate, he discovered that a pinnace, the *Henrijk*, had hove to, offering to exchange beef in return for permission to lade salt.

Sam promptly agreed. Cows did not thrive on the island. Good beef would be a luxury, and a fitting banquet to celebrate the arrival of his children. He immediately sent an invitation to the Captain of the vessel to come ashore that evening and dine.

As a matter of course he invited his uncle. For a while he hesitated, wondering if he should extend the welcome to Shergold, but decided against it. Tonight of all nights he could not face the Minister's carping.

The Captain of the pinnace was a young man with that combination of blue eyes, light hair and a slightly sallow skin that indicated he probably came from northern Europe. He was flamboyantly dressed with a plethora of lace at his neck and cuffs, and the cut of his jacket emphasised the width of his shoulders and the neatness of his waist.

To Sam's disappointment he had no English, but he was accompanied by a black youth who had an excellent grasp not only of English but also of Spanish, French and the Captain's own Dutch.

The slave was liberally swathed in gold braid: around his cuffs, along the collar of his scarlet velvet jacket, down the seams of his white breeches. This was complemented by gold buckles on his shoes, a huge golden ring in his left ear, and a heavy gold slave collar encircling his neck.

Sam felt dismayed. Not knowing any Dutch himself, he was very aware that this young lad, Scipio, displayed an accomplishment superior to that of all the white men present. Once again he thought that such slavery was wrong.

Sam had ordered the best dinner the island could provide. Turtle, peccary, quam, fried plantain, roast yam, cassava bread, fresh mango and pomegranate, plus of course the beef. It was liberally washed down with French brandy or rum and lime. As the evening drew to an end, and numerous toasts were drunk to Salome and Zephaniah, all those at the table grew increasingly drunk.

Replete and expansive, Sam surveyed his guests. Aeneas sat with his head slumped forward, his eyelids flickering. Sam felt a surge of affection for his uncle, or should he say father-in-law? He would not embarrass him by suggesting he withdraw to bed.

The Captain's conversation became increasingly inconsequential and the translation more difficult to understand. Standing behind Captain Tromp, Scipio continued to interpret every remark.

230

Sam spoke directly to the slave boy. 'Your mouth must be dry. Would you like – that is, are you permitted to drink rum?'

Scipio looked uncomfortable. Bending his head closer to his master, he repeated the question.

Captain Tromp raised a hand dismissively. His voice displaying no emotion, Scipio translated: 'The boy is not thirsty. In any case, slaves are allowed only water. He will wait.'

Sam felt a sudden burst of dislike for the Dutch man. He deliberately remained silent in order to spare the lad the need to speak. As he watched, Captain Tromp caught Scipio's hand and squeezed it, placing the boy's dark fingers against his chest. It was the act of a lover and Sam felt disgust, not for the love of a man for a man, but for the exercise of power the Captain used to gain those favours. He wished that his guests would go.

He realised that Scipio was talking, repeating a monologue for his master.

'This girl, she tells her master that she is a married woman. Married to an English nobleman. And her black as a moor.' Scipio was silent as Tromp laughed, then he relayed: 'Only she had strange eyes. Not brown. Green.'

Captain Tromp hiccoughed. Sam realising too late what his guest was saying, froze in his seat. His mind began to race, pulled in so many directions he was unable fully to grasp anything.

He looked quickly as Aeneas but he was gently snoring.

'Are you saying that you know where there is a young slave woman, one with green eyes who is married to a lord?' he asked.

'That is it. "Contessa". That is what my friend calls her. "My husband is *not* a count, he is a lord." ' Tromp mimicked her words and Scipio translated.

All the time Sam could see her face, hear her voice. 'Where? Where is she?'

Tromp looked surprised. 'You know someone like that? She tells the truth?'

'Where is she?' Sam repeated.

'San Bernaldo. You know it?'

Fonseca! Sam didn't know what to do or say. He did not want Aeneas to hear. He did not want to arouse Captain Tromp's curiosity although it was probably too late.

But Captain Tromp was growing sleepy. He leaned his head back against the boy standing behind him. Turning his face, he said something to the lad and the tone of his voice was husky with innuendo. Scipio looked stony-faced but agreed.

For the merest second Sam wondered if he should try to buy the boy, rescue him, but he realised that was exactly what he had done with Esmeralda: interfered and set in motion a train of events no one could have foreseen.

In reply to Tromp's unanswered question, he finally said: 'I did hear of such a tale once, about a kidnapped lady, but that was long ago.'

By mutual agreement, both men rose from the table. Tromp staggered to his feet, his arm about Scipio's shoulders for support. To Sam he bowed.

'I thank you.'

Sam bowed in return. He could hardly contain his impatience to be rid of his guest.

When Tromp was finally outside, Sam pulled Aeneas to his feet and half carried him to a settle where he laid him down and covered him with a blanket.

He let out his breath with a long gasp to ease his tension. Esmeralda! She was alive. On Fonseca of all places. His blood pounded. Until that moment he had not realised how devoid of hope his life had become. But now he had a mission again. As soon as Captain Jordan arrived, they would set sail straightaway for the island. Then, like a dark whisper he heard Jordan's words: Wherever I look, the island does not seem to exist.

Of course it existed. Tromp had been there. *They had been there.* He pushed his fears aside. Together they would find it again and bring Esmeralda home, back where she belonged.

THIRTY

After Gideon was born Esmee was given a week to lie up and rest. Never had she felt in such poor spirits. Often for no apparent reason she found herself on the verge of tears, not wanting to be alone during the long days, but there was no one upon whom she could call except for a few men who were too sick to work.

At any other time, she would have welcomed the company of the afflicted slaves but now she was afraid to go near them for fear of infecting Gideon with some foul disease. To her distress, every time he cried she was gripped by unreasoning panic. For the first time ever she faced a new nightmare: how would she bear it if her baby died?

The one glimmer of warmth in her darkness was Musa. To her joy he continued to come most evenings, sneaking up from the negro houses, checking on her welfare, reporting on the progress of the *Evangelina*. Always he visited at dusk when the work in the fields or in the boiling houses was cut short by impending darkness. Sometimes he came with one of the crew. Mostly he came alone. Esmee liked it best when he came alone.

During the days she tried to concentrate on a plan for escape. Everything would depend on when the *Evangelina* was repaired. Thereafter they would have to gauge when the moon, the tide and the wind were right, and when the overseers were distracted. She fretted because there were so many things outside her control but at least she could try to think up a system of signals. It was essential that every man was alerted to the right moment − when it came.

At the end of the week she still felt exhausted but her request to Captain Ortega for one more day to rest was dismissed. 'Come, Contessa, already your child has cost me your services for too long.'

Esmee sensed that in Gideon the slave master had found a weapon to torment her. She would never give him the chance to condemn her son for being born. Somehow, the next morning, she dragged herself back to work.

By the end of the day she was exhausted. Gideon was fretful, crying in the night. Esmee felt anguished, fearing that her milk was not flowing.

'You give him to me.' Yinka, with her child's body, had milk to spare.

After Esmee returned to her duties Musa continued to visit. She knew he came in the hope of learning some news of Edrize, but she was aware that he came also to see her. The thought pleased her. Of all the people who had been taken on the *Destiny*, he alone was the one with whom she felt a bond. She did not try to analyse exactly what it was. If she was honest, she was attracted by his self-assurance and dignity, his refined features and inherent maleness. She was attracted by *him*. As she recovered from the birth of her child she could not ignore the restlessness that burned her up, the same restlessness Aeneas had first aroused yet had been unable to satisfy.

She and Musa did not share a common past. They knew little about each other but there was an air of certainty that made her want to surrender herself to him. In every way.

'Hosea King has the flux. I do not think he will last until morning.' Musa, arriving as the sun made its rapid descent, announced the news gravely, bowing his head in respect for Esmee's feelings. Hosea King had sailed many times with her father. He was a cooper by profession, maker of most of the barrels that had carried their water and powder and salt beef. Now he was dying.

The evening was sultry and a lowering sky threatened rain. With every movement a fresh trickle of sweat beaded Esmee's body. Her ankles and shins felt hard and the skin shone tight and angry, pitted by dozens of insect bites. On those rare occasions when Gideon slept, the itching still kept her awake.

She looked at Musa, wrung out by a day under the scorching sun, and was afraid. She felt a strange stillness inside. So many of her father's crew had died that it was impossible to experience any more grief. She remembered that along with the rest of the crewmen, Hosea King had once been Musa's gaoler. She wondered what he must think about the sailors, but his feelings were closed off from her. He looked exhausted. Tonight his skin was stained, dust clinging to the sweat. Esmee realised that normally before visiting her he made some attempt to wash himself. She felt again a wave of respect for this man's pride. Tonight he had come direct from the fields.

He said: 'Several of the men are badly afflicted with yaws. They suffer great pain and fever. Unless they can be cured I fear that they will not be strong enough to attempt an escape. When you feel able to, perhaps you will visit them.' He hesitated and when he spoke again, his voice was bitter.

'Captain Ortega has had them isolated. He treats them by standing them in casks of water with a fire burning beneath, until they cry out with the pain of the heat. He thinks it will cure them but it does only harm. He forces mercury pills down their throats until they vomit and I see only that they grow worse, not better.'

Esmee thought of the huge ulcers, the suppurating smell of pus. Her stomach churned. Dimly she remembered Accubah and her treatments for every ill. They came back to her by rote, those distant accounts Accubah gave her as she lay abed, waiting for sleep to free them from the day.

Aloud she said: 'You must boil up the bark of the log plum tree then add to that the juice of a lime and rust of iron. Apply that direct to the sores. It will cure them.'

Musa regarded her steadily. Anger burned in his black eyes. He said: 'We live in filth. Our food is barely enough to sustain life. Yesterday a cow died. It was badly diseased but the Captain gave it to us as a treat. The servants had first choice. They took the meat. We were left with the skin, the head and the offal. We are expected to be grateful.'

Esmee lowered her eyes. When she looked up at Musa she could see that his own eyes looked unnaturally bright. He started to speak again.

'We suffer the worst heat imaginable. All the while we are beaten because we do not work harder than it is possible for a man to do. We have to get away from this evil place. Work on the *Evangelina* is nearly completed. We must go soon.'

Esmee nodded. She felt guilty because her own captivity was so much easier than his. At night she enjoyed this hut of her own that was luxury in comparison with the sheds in which the field slaves were locked away. Even now Musa was risking a beating by being

235

here. Bitterly she thought that the Captain kept her healthy only to protect himself against infection.

Some nights Musa brought her small gifts of rich molasses smuggled from the boiling house, or a tot of kill-devil made from the skimmings of the sugar vats that transformed the crushed cane into a harsh, courage-giving liquid. Her nostrils twitched at the sweet cloying smell which infected the air of the entire plantation. Harvesting was well under way. The atmosphere was almost frenetic. Always they lived with the threat that the equipment might break down and the cane be left to rot on the ground.

Her heart fluttered at the thought of the punishment Musa might suffer if he was found stealing the fiery liquid. She said: 'You must stop this. You will be whipped, or worse!'

He shook his head. 'You need it, it will give you strength, new heart. Here, eat, drink.'

His kindness brought back her tearful sense of need. Kindness was the hardest gift to accept. She looked at his haggard face. None of the deprivation he suffered could crush the spirit that shone from his dark eyes.

She put out a hand to comfort him. The skin of his shoulders felt damp beneath her fingers.

Musa said nothing. Looking into her eyes, he reached out and laced his fingers about the back of her neck, pulling her gently towards him. For a moment she hesitated, then stood quite still while he untied the strings of the calico gown that covered her. As he peeled the cloth away, he seemed to strip her past with it.

She did not move while he unfastened the cloth that hid his loins. The sight of his erection did not alarm her. As he pushed her gently back on to her cot, she was already opening her legs to receive him.

There was no pain, hardly any fear. Gently, confidently, Musa took control of her body. Esmee gave herself up to him in a deliberate act of severance from her past. It was the first truly free choice she had ever made.

Afterwards, lying with her head against his shoulder, breathing in the smell of him, she felt calmer than she had ever believed possible. They were both silent, together yet caught up in their separate worlds. Her eyes closed and she drifted in the dark half-world of near sleep.

At last the almost physical presence of Jeronimo was washed away. Esmee felt released from her past, from her father's rape, from her husband's fumblings.

236

She did not love Musa, not in the way she loved Sam. She knew with equal certainty that he did not love her. But they were both alone, and there was no going back.

Again, as if he knew her thoughts, he said: 'Some day you will be rescued. You will be returned to your home and husband.'

'No!' She spoke harshly and felt ashamed of the guilty reason why she could not go back.

Musa sat up and looked down at her, tracing the line of her jaw with his forefinger. 'You do not like your husband?'

Esmee shook her head. 'It isn't that. He is a good man. It is just that – after what has happened . . .'

'Ah.' Musa drew apart and Esmee realised that he thought she was referring to their act of love. She did not know what to say.

After a silence, he asked: 'Is Gideon your husband's first child?'

'No.' She could not tell him the truth. She said: 'He has a daughter – from his first wife.'

'A son will be welcome then.'

Esmee knew he was probing, trying to get to the bottom of her relationship with Aeneas. Into the silence she said: 'I do not think I shall ever be rescued.'

Musa did not answer directly. He seemed cut off in a world of his own. At last he said: 'If your husband is a good man, he will still love you.'

She wondered just how much he had guessed.

Musa sat on the side of the bed, tying the cloth that covered his loins. He said: 'Nat Rouse thinks the wind and tide should be right in the next few days. I want you to take a message to Edrize. Tell him he must be brave. He must not let Captain Ortega suspect that anything is amiss. When I send word, he must be ready to slip away. We must all be ready. There will be no second chance.'

'Supposing they stop us?' Esmee asked the question without wanting to know the answer.

Musa drew in his breath. 'Then we will be punished. I doubt if many of us would survive. Ortega's men will take pleasure in inflicting the maximum amount of pain possible.' He hesitated. 'If my son cannot escape then I too shall stay behind. I will make it my business to release him.'

'How release him?'

Smoothing her hair with a gentle stroke that made her float with comfort, he said: 'If he cannot be liberated from Captain Ortega, then I shall kill him.'

'You cannot!' She pulled back from him, shocked by his words. The bleak message in his eyes drew her close again. Her face muffled against his chest, she said: 'And me? If I cannot escape, would you kill me too?'

He shook his head. 'I don't know. If Ortega gave you to his overseers to do with as they wish then . . .' He shrugged. 'You are a grown woman. You are in charge of your own destiny. You have a child. Like me, your responsibility is first and foremost to your son.'

Esmee thought of Gideon and what might happen to him if they were caught trying to escape. She glanced at the basket where he slept beside her cot, oblivious to the momentous events being planned. Would she, could she, kill him to save him from the barbarity of the Spaniards? She hoped she would find the courage to do so.

As she began to speak Musa stilled her words with his fingers. Gently she kissed the fingertips that rested against her lips.

He caught her hand. When he spoke his voice was low. 'None of us knows what will happen, what we are capable of. When it comes to my son, I have no doubt I will do whatever is necessary to protect him, even at the expense of my own life.' He cupped her face in his hands, forcing her to look at him. Slowly, he said: 'I don't yet know if I love you enough to do the same for you.'

'But you love your wife?'

He thought seriously about the question, eventually saying: 'I have two wives. For one I feel great affection. For the other . . .' He shrugged. 'They are both good wives.'

She felt a stab of jealousy, wanting his attention for herself. She asked: 'Do you think you will ever see them again?'

He did not answer immediately. When he did his voice was tinged with some far-off memory. 'I have to believe that I will, but I find it hard to imagine how I will ever do so.'

To distract him, Esmee said: 'Do you think it is possible to love two people?'

'It is possible to love many people.' Musa raised his eyebrows questioningly. 'I think you feel something very strong for some man. Not your husband.' When she did not deny it, he said: 'Do not fight your feelings. Do not spoil your life by feeling guilt. Only white men feel this guilt, I think.'

Outside the darkness descended fast as the snuffing out of a candle. She huddled closer to him. Almost imperceptibly he pulled away. When he spoke his voice was tinged with unease. He said: 'Esmee, perhaps it was wrong of me to take you as I did this evening. I did so for me, to prove to myself that even in these extreme times I can still play the man.'

'That does not matter.'

He looked down at her, gently shaking his head. 'It does. But I did it for you too, because you looked so forlorn, so – unloved. And you are so beautiful.'

'Musa –'

He kissed her forehead. 'There. We will say no more about it. Our fates are in the hands of the gods.'

She wanted to ask him which gods, what he believed in, but already it was dark and every minute he stayed put him at risk of discovery. If he was prevented from visiting her then they would be unable to plan their escape. She could not admit to herself how much she already needed him.

Trying to find comfort, she said: 'When will we leave here?'

'Soon.'

'How will we know when the time is right?'

Musa suddenly grinned and she had a glimpse of the man he must once have been – confident, fun-loving. He said: 'I have decided upon the signal.'

He did not enlighten her and Esmee had the sudden fearful thought that she might not get the message and would be the only one to be left behind. 'But how will I know?' she asked.

Again Musa grinned.

'Tell me!'

He shook his head. 'If I do so you will be forever listening out. Captain Ortega is no fool. He might notice and suspect that something is amiss.'

As he prepared to leave he bent forward and kissed her again. He was still smiling. He said: 'Do not fret, my dear. When the signal comes you will not mistake it.'

THIRTY-ONE

The last day of July marked Filipe Ortega's birthday. He planned to celebrate the event by inviting his overseers to dinner – not an ordinary dinner but a veritable banquet complete with entertainments.

Esmee awoke before dawn to the strange sensation of being dragged out of a tunnel. As she came to she realised that Gideon was crying, shattering her deep and exhausted sleep with his howls. She stumbled out of her cot and reached for him. Something brushed against her foot and she heard the rustling of cockroaches running for cover. Shuddering she scrambled back into her bed, screwing up her toes, holding Gideon close against her.

Her eyes felt gritty but she knew she would not sleep again. She was afraid that if she did she would miss the morning bell that called the slaves to work. She could not be late. With a sick feeling she remembered what had happened the day before.

She had been late taking Ortega's meal to the long, low room he called his studio. As she hurried in with it, he said: 'Where have you been?'

'I'm sorry, I mistook the time.'

He studied her with his cruel, condescending eyes. She could see that he was in an evil temper and as she put the dishes down, her hands began to tremble. Petulantly, he said: 'I suppose you have been wasting time feeding that *bastardo*?'

'No! I – '

Getting up, he called across to one of his black consorts who stood guard near the door. 'Adonis! Here!'

The man came silently over to him, skin shimmering with palm oil, his muscular body exuding a powerful sexual challenge.

'Master?'

'Go to the kitchen, quick quick. Take the bastard baby to the compound and leave him there.'

'No!' Esmee flew towards the door but Adonis was there before her.

Ortega said: 'You can have him back tonight, when you have finished your work.'

'But he'll be frightened . . . hungry!'

'He'll wait.'

All day Esmee heard Gideon's cries, at first angry, then panic-stricken, then increasingly forlorn and exhausted. She sobbed her way through an eternal afternoon, her tears dripping on to the maize floor, into the peccary fat that sizzled over the fire.

She knew she was helpless. Defy Ortega and he would heap some far worse punishment upon her, using Gideon as a weapon to make her suffer. Eventually Yinka, her eyes wide with fear, crept into the kitchen, saying: 'Adonis, he tell me. I go to compound and feed Gideon. Now he sleep.'

Somehow Esmee struggled through the rest of the day. As she was about to leave, Ortega came into the kitchen. For a long time he stood watching while she scrubbed the table and washed the floor, taking care not to splash his satin shoes.

As she worked he stood over her silently, his left shoe moving up and down as his toes twitched inside it. At any moment she thought that he might stamp on her hands, just for the pleasure of it.

Instead, as she emptied the last bucket of water and prepared to leave, he said: 'There are some plantains in the store house, nice and ripe and ready to make into wine. You can peel and boil them then set them up to drain.'

'But – '

His eyebrows raised the merest fraction and she bowed her head. 'Yes, master.' The only thing on her mind was escape.

As she thought back to the miseries of the day before, Gideon sucked noisily, his small fists working in agitated movements. She imagined he was remembering her desertion and her heart ached with love for him.

She longed to run to Musa for comfort but she knew that if he suspected what had happened to her then nothing would stop him from confronting Ortega. The consequences would be disastrous. Fortunately he had not managed to visit her the evening before or he would surely have suspected that something was wrong. His absence roused another worry, a fear that perhaps he was sick, yet she was powerless to find out. As Musa took a risk every time he visited the Captain's mansion, so Esmee would be breaking the rules in going to the negro houses. For Gideon's sake she could not risk getting into trouble. Please God, she thought, deliver us from this evil place.

Dressing quickly she secured the child to her back and climbed the slope up to Ortega's house, letting herself into the buttery. A steady wind blew from the east but it brought little relief for the air was hot as a kitchen. The wind merely fanned the heat, driving it into even the normally cool and shady places.

As the day wore on, Cesare, responsible for the evening's banquet, looked as if he might melt as he blustered around the hellish kitchen, chivvying his unwilling army of skivvies. More and more dishes were prepared for their master's delight. Staggering under the burden of pots and platters, Esmee thought that the Captain's tables would surely collapse beneath the weight. Red and green snappers, mullet, ling, pickled herring, shark and turtles were followed by plump hogs fattened on locust nuts and maize, turtle doves, Muscovia ducks and huge turkeys. Each dish was dressed and cooked to the highest standard.

In the centre of the table a huge calves' foot pie glowed to perfection. Before serving, the golden pastry lid was lifted, letting out the heady smell of cloves and mace and sweet herbs. A generous draw cup of kill-devil was then poured inside the pie to enrich it for their master's delight. Esmee only wished she had some poison handy to add to the heady sauce.

All day she worked, fighting the waves of exhaustion that swept over her. In the afternoon, she was transferred to the sweltering furnace of the laundry. There she placed an over-hot iron on the collar of one of Ortega's shirts. A dirty brown scorch marred the material. Esmee stared at it, numbed, unable to think what to do. Then, making sure that no one was near, she screwed up the shirt and poked it into the embers. Please let it burn! Please don't let him miss it!

By the time evening came she could only drag herself around. Ortega's guests began to arrive at about six o'clock. She saw that they had made an effort for the occasion, washing themselves, trimming hair and beards, wearing clean clothes. A fastidious man himself, Ortega would not accept slovenliness in others.

Esmee gave Gideon into Yinka's care and prepared to bring out the array of meats and pies and creams and fruit. She had not stopped to eat all day but she dare not take the merest crumb for fear of punishment.

The dining room was decked with flowers and along the polished oak of his table, the Captain's silver glistened in the candle glow. Besides Ortega and his guests, there was a handful of favoured negro servants, all handsome boys, young and immaculately turned out in red and gold livery. Esmee was reminded of the carriage horses she had seen in London, bedecked in rich tooled leather to reflect their master's wealth. A slave stood behind each chair, ready to refill the plates and glasses of the guests.

As the men ate and drank the noise grew more raucous. Ortega, holding court at the head of the table, wore a vivid blue taffeta jacket and white satin breeches. When his foot tapped in his habitual manner, the jewels on his shoe buckles danced in the flickering light.

A group of Africans were brought in to play music. Behind Ortega, Adonis and Edrize stood in attendance. The slave master turned and spoke to Adonis and the big man moved to the centre of the room where he began to dance. His movements were lithe, sinuous, his arms swaying with the elegance of grasses blowing in a breeze.

Esmee made journey after journey from kitchen to table. As she passed through for perhaps the twentieth time, Adonis was stripping the garments from his body, slowly, teasingly. Strutting, he paraded himself the length of the room but as he turned, his eyes were on Ortega. With a thrust of his pelvis he peeled away the final leather thong that fastened between his thighs then threw himself, naked, at Ortega's feet.

The gathering cheered. With the toe of his slipper, Filipe lifted his servant's chin, gazing into his eyes. Adonis rose to his feet and turned again to display his growing erection for all to see, then sank again at his master's feet.

The Captain looked about him, searching for more entertainment. To his right, two of his guests were discussing the merits of various horses they had bred.

As Esmee cleared away some of the remnants prior to bringing in yet another course, she was aware that someone was watching her. Glancing up she caught the eye of the man sitting to Ortega's left. He was a man perhaps in his thirties, blond, thin-faced with a mouth cruel as a man trap. She wanted only to run and hide from the lust in his eyes. Loud enough for her to hear, he said: 'Filipe, do you breed livestock too?'

'I don't breed horses.' Ortega followed the man's gaze and grinned, catching his meaning.

The man said: 'I wasn't thinking of horses.'

Esmee turned to leave the room but Ortega called out: 'Contessa, wait!' Her hands were shaking so badly she could barely hold the dishes.

Raising his voice so that the entire gathering was drawn into his sphere, Ortega said: 'I'm short of fillies, never felt the need of them, but there's no dearth of stallions.'

He patted young Edrize on the thigh and the overseers laughed, their eyes homing in on the lad's boyish body. Leaning back, Ortega said: 'How do you think I should go about selecting a good stud? Which of you gentlemen have any suggestions?'

To Esmee he said: 'Come here, my dear,' then to the gathering at large: 'A veritable beauty, don't you think? With excellent breeding, and what's more a proven brood mare.'

With mounting horror Esmee realised what they were planning. She went to make a dash for the door but at a signal from Ortega, two of the liveried slaves grasped her wrists and dragged her forward. They did not look at her and she knew they were ashamed of the role they played.

'Please, Capitano, let me go!'

The men began to discuss the various merits of the slaves that Ortega owned and which quality was the most important when selecting a sire.

'I say strength,' someone shouted.

'Good looks.'

'An obedient nature.'

Ortega looked around him then his eyes returned to Adonis, kneeling at his side. He patted the man's head as though he were a dog.

'Then I think this beauty has it all. Get up.' He prodded Adonis who stood and once more displayed his physique for all to see. Ortega reached out and fingered his servant's cock like a shopper testing the ripeness of fruit. Grinning round at his companions, he said: 'I think this will do.' The overseers cheered.

'Right then.' He turned towards Esmee, held fast by the slaves.

'Make yourself ready, my dear. Be nice and loving now.'

'No!' She struggled with a desperation born of utter terror. She kicked and bit, immune to the vice-like pain at her wrists and ankles, the blow aimed at her by one of the slaves as she tore at his hand with her teeth. Above the pounding of her brain and the bawdy yells of the planters, other sounds began to intrude. She suddenly realised that one by one the men at the table had stopped shouting, turning their heads to left and right in an effort to identify the direction of the disturbance. As the slaves loosened their hold, Esmee broke free and ran for the door.

Somewhere outside was the staccato of musket fire. At the same time she was aware of a strange orange hue showing through the window. The air seemed to be clogged with the sickly smell of boiling sugar.

As she dashed outside a black and orange carpet greeted her, hovering over the plantation. With disbelief she realised that the crackling sound came from exploding sugar cane. The fields were on fire!

With a burst of excitement, she thought: This is the signal. And lifting her skirts, she ran fast as she could for the slave quarters, stumbling in her haste. Ducking into her own cell she called: 'Come, Yinka, come! It is time to leave.'

Stopping only to gather up Gideon, she caught Yinka's arm and together they crept out, crouching low, scurrying to avoid detection. As she stole a glance back, men were staggering drunkenly from Ortega's house, staring at the inferno of the plantation. The whole colony seemed to be ablaze.

'Quick.' As they reached the beach Esmee had to fight the desire to run blindly, desperate to find safety among the group of men who waited impatiently at the water's edge. Some of them were too sick to walk and were being carried along by the able-bodied.

In the gloom she saw Musa, standing slightly apart, staring back up towards the plantation. His posture was stiff, anxious. She followed his line of sight and as she watched, a solitary boy detached himself from the frenzied mass outside Ortega's home and raced for the shore. Even at a distance she could feel Musa's relief. Now they were all present.

Esmee approached him. The terror of her ordeal and then the

miraculous escape seemed to have filled her with a bubbling sense of energy.

'What did you do?' she asked, barely able to contain her throbbing excitement.

'It wasn't just me. I worked with the rest of the slaves. We decided to leave our hosts a little present.' He grinned, looking back at the burning hills. 'All the others are fleeing to the other side of the island. They have their own plans. By the time Captain Ortega has the blaze under control, he won't have much of a plantation left.' He looked down at her and she saw something of the same excitement in his eyes.

'Is everything well with you?' he asked.

'It couldn't be better.'

'Then perhaps we should say goodbye to San Bernaldo.'

Those who could swim took charge of those who could not and like noiseless rafts they drifted their way out to the ship *Evangelina*, anchored some two hundred yards off the coast.

Esmee held tight to Thomas Warner, ignoring his protests, remembering how she and Yinka had struggled ashore an eternity ago. She had a sudden unreasoning terror that Gideon would become detached from her back and float away out of reach. 'Do you want to drown me?' Thomas complained.

Almost ghost-like they scrambled aboard, the strong pulling the women, the weak and sickly, up on to the deck. Their bare feet were silent and nobody seemed to be breathing.

Stepping back on to the deck of the *Evangelina* Esmee felt as if she was re-entering the past. This was the ship that had brought her to the Caribbean, the ship where she had been separated from Aeneas, where she – she re-arranged her thoughts – where Gideon had been conceived and her father had died. She looked round for Musa, remembering that it was here too that she had freed him from captivity, and in the process found a lover. Her heart filled.

For an eternity the main group huddled together while some of the men went to explore. Stealthily they toured the ship, looking out for a watch. To their joy, there was no one aboard.

Only two of Jeronimo Jackson's original crew remained alive. It therefore fell to Nathaniel Rouse and Thomas Warner, as the only able-bodied men with seafaring experience, to form a crew from those few remaining Africans who, far away on the Binny Coast, had once made their livings as fishermen.

246

Every man's physical weakness was such that it took a tremendous effort to weigh the ship's anchor. Men made faint by hard work and lack of food clung unsteadily to the spars as they fumbled with sails and rigging, clumsy in their haste, but at last the *Evangelina*, like a puppy longing for a walk, bounded away from the coast of San Bernaldo and towards the open sea.

Within minutes they made their first, unwelcome discovery. There was no food on board. No water. The elation that had followed their escape quickly began to evaporate.

'What shall we do?' The men looked to Esmee for an answer. As far as she knew they were several days' sailing from any other land. They had certainly not sighted any islands on their way to San Bernaldo. They would have to find some provisions before then. The best hope seemed to lie in continuing west – as long as the wind did not change course.

Her heart beginning to pound uncomfortably, she went below decks, making for her father's quarters. Her hand trembled as she lifted the latch of his cabin door and as she pushed it open, she half expected to find him there, to hear his voice saying: 'Come here, Chickadee.'

She looked at the neat desk and the narrow bunk. Both were bare. The cabin was empty. With sinking heart she saw that it had been cleared of all Jeronimo's belongings when the storm damage was repaired. None of his charts remained.

'Where are we going to aim for, Captain?'

Esmee was relieved to have company. She looked with affection at Nat Rouse who came awkwardly into the cabin. He too knew that there was little hope of finding food or water quickly.

She did not answer him immediately but stood deep in thought. Looking to the future, their best hope seemed to rest in finding a colony of cimarrons – escaped slaves who had managed to hold on to their freedom, or failing that a stronghold of boucanniers, men already outside the law who cared little whether those of their number were black or white. Whichever, Esmee knew that it would be dangerous. She had a mental image of walking through a herd of wild bulls. They might accept you, continue peacefully with their own preoccupations – or they might turn and trample you to death. She shook off the thought. Come what may, the biggest problem would be where to look, but that would have to be *after* they had found water.

Dismissing the problems, she reminded herself that they were in a fast ship and one in pristine condition. A plan was forming in her head.

She asked: 'Do we have any ammunition?'

Nat went to find out. He returned several minutes later looking glum. In response to Esmee's questioning look, he said: 'Eight cannons, two muskets, ten pistols – and no shot or powder.'

Her heart sank, but only for a moment. 'No matter. Set a course sou'-westerly.'

He looked at her in surprise. 'Won't that take us into the Spanish shipping lanes?'

She nodded and as he waited, she asked: 'And where else are we going to find the supplies we need?'

Reading her mind, a grin spread across his face. He gave a chuckle. As he went out of the door, he called out: 'Whatever you say, Captain. Whatever you say.'

Like a hare pursued by hounds the *Evangelina*, carrying maximum sail, set out on an uncertain course. As the ship sprinted across the waves Esmee strained to see what was happening ashore. Silhouetted against the black and gold of the blazing plantation, diminutive figures still raced madly in some bizarre parody of a game as they attempted to control the fire. Clearly they had little thought as to what might be happening at sea.

Above the *Evangelina*, a moon that was full and high cast a silver beam of light across the midnight waters, as if pointing the way to her unknown destination. Esmee took comfort in this sign that some higher destiny was guiding their journey.

She went below to feed Gideon. As he drew nourishment from her, so she drew strength from his closeness, the very fact of his existence. She felt suddenly emotional, overwhelmed by the mystery of life. Out of the evil that had taken place on this ship, a miracle had been born. When he was replete she settled him to sleep then returned to keep a lonely vigil.

'I will stay with you.' Musa came to stand at her side and she was possessed by a sudden hunger for him. Their newly found freedom seemed to be liberating her in every way.

Only Nat Rouse was above decks, standing at the wheel. The rest had bedded down how and where they could, hoping to find escape from their parched throats and hunger pangs in a few hours' sleep.

It would have been easy to slip away for half an hour down to Jeronimo's cabin. Esmee's thoughts came so fast she could not keep up with them. In the first place it was not her father's cabin but hers. She was the Captain now. Musa was standing so close that she leaned back just to feel the pleasure of his body against hers. Starbursts of longing enveloped her. With a supreme effort she drew away. Give in to the narcotic pleasure of love now and sleep would naturally follow. She needed to remain alert.

She was struck by the sudden crazy thought of Musa as a female dinah, there for her pleasure, and could not stop herself from laughing as she turned and rested her cheek momentarily against his shoulder.

'What makes you laugh?'

She shook her head, suddenly tender in the face of his curiosity. 'It is nothing. You go and rest. Later I will need you to keep watch.'

With a wry expression he bowed his head and left her alone. She turned her attention back to the empty sea and, to keep awake, indulged herself in imagining some paradise where they could truly be together.

At first light she scanned the horizon, looking for any sign that the Spaniards were in pursuit, but the sea was still empty. Several hours had passed since they had made their escape and as the gentle moon gave way to a merciless sun, Esmee's thirst grew increasingly tormenting. Her own suffering was intensified by the growing fear that without water her milk would soon dry up. The thought drove her back down below to her father's cabin where Gideon slept. She sighed with relief, absorbing again the wonder of his tiny face, peaceful in repose. Going back on to the deck she knew that they would have to find water soon.

'Ship to port!' Nat Rouse's cry had her racing to investigate. After a few seconds her keen eyes picked up the hazy outline of a vessel. It was too far away to see clearly but Esmee's heart leaped with hope. To Nat, she said: 'Right, let's make sure that it sees us.'

Quickly she issued her orders. Before long the weary men aboard the *Evangelina* were busy lowering all but the most essential sail. At the same time others went to find any objects they could and then bind them securely with ropes.

After about half an hour, with the aid of a spy glass, Esmee was able to identify the ship as a Spanish pink. To the assembled crew she called: 'Right, tip everything over the side.' There were a series of resounding splashes as the heavy objects, still secured by ropes and chains, quickly disappeared below the surface of the water. Before long the *Evangelina* had dramatically slowed her pace, dragging as she did a heavy and invisible burden of boxes, barrels, cables and mattresses.

'What are you doing?' Musa came to investigate.

Esmee's blood began to pound at the prospect ahead of them. She gave him an enigmatic grin. The distant vessel had changed course and was now sailing in their direction.

She said: 'All they can see is a slow, harmless merchantman. We will make a tempting prize.'

'But . . .'

Her grin widened. 'When they prepare to pounce, it will be a case of the biter bit.'

She ordered the cannon to be prepared, the guns to be handed out and every form of weaponry to be brought on deck. With the exception of the steersman, each man was ordered to take up position beneath the rail. There they crouched in silence.

The ship's approach seemed tormentingly slow but at last she was within hailing distance. On her deck stood the Captain, a portly figure, his hands crossed at the small of his back. Two or three men armed with muskets gazed across at the *Evangelina* with the confident air of those who know their own strength.

Esmee's heart thundered. Taking a deep breath she hissed at the crew: 'Now!'

From the quarter deck, she cupped her hands around her mouth and yelled until her lungs felt fit to burst: 'Strike your sail or we'll send you to the bottom!'

On cue her companions rose up, pointing their weapons in a ferocious line at the other ship.

The next moments seemed to last forever. To her men, Esmee rasped out: 'Pretend! Believe you are fully armed and loaded!' Carefully the crew took aim with their useless weapons. Likewise, the cannon pointed hungry, empty mouths across the diminishing divide.

Almost with disbelief she watched as one by one the sailors on the Spanish vessel dropped their guns. Forgetting their exhaustion, their hunger and thirst, the men from the *Evangelina* began to scramble across to the Spanish prize. As Esmee watched they rounded up the crew of the *Cordoba* and gathered their weapons. Now, fully armed, they found at last the succour they so desperately needed.

In the galley, fresh pork roasted over the ship's stove. Hogsheads of beer jostled with barrels of fine Spanish wine and next to those stood casks of good, fresh water. Sufficient supplies were transferred across to the *Evangelina* to satisfy her immediate needs and Esmee ordered the *Cordoba*'s Captain to be escorted aboard. Bowing his head in submission, he relinquished his command.

Cordially she escorted the Spaniard to Jeronimo's – no, to *her* cabin. He followed her down the ladder, along the narrow companionway, turning sideways to manoeuvre his bulk. Behind her she could hear his huffings and puffings. All the while she bubbled with a heady combination of exhilaration and disbelief.

Inside the cabin she offered the Captain the single stool and took her place beside her father's deck. Nothing was real, she was acting a part.

When at last one of the crew hobbled in with jugs of wine and beer, her thirst threatened to overwhelm her. She had to fight the desire to grab the jug of beer and drain it dry, but to show such a weakness would be to play into the Spanish Captain's hands. Although the *Cordoba* was now under her command, she knew only too well that their own lack of men, their poor physical condition and their inexperience, might still lead them to disaster.

Taking some restrained sips of the beer, she said: 'Captain, we mean you no harm. As soon as we have taken what we need, you will be free to go on your way.'

'And who is your *Capitaino*?' Manuel de Cantos drained his own cup of wine and put the vessel down with a resounding thud on the desk, but Esmee saw that his hand was shaking. His anxiety gave her confidence.

Bowing her head, she replied: 'I am Captain here. My father was killed, so the ship is under my command.'

His expression bore witness to his amazement but he merely said: 'You realise that everything aboard my ship is the property of the King of Spain? It is to him that you will be answerable. You fly no flag. Who is it you serve?'

After a moment's thought, she replied: 'We are under the protection of the King of England. Do not be fooled by our appearance, Captain. We are all free men here. We too can call upon the protection of a powerful nation.'

Could they? If they were captured by an English ship then the *Evangelina* would probably be confiscated for the King's navy. The crew could expect only imprisonment, slavery or hanging. She alone could call on the protection of a powerful husband, but in these unreal circumstances, she had no idea what his feelings towards her might be. Best not to think about it. Returning to her previous theme she repeated: 'We will take only sufficient supplies to take us to our destination.'

'And that is where, Senõra?'

She smiled at him and poured more wine. 'Who can say, Captain? Who can say?'

For safety, she ordered the Captain to be locked in the cabin she had once shared with Aeneas, the same cabin where her son had been conceived. After she and her men had taken their fill of food and drink, they set about exploring the *Cordoba*. Going aboard Esmee felt the same anticipation as when they started out on their voyage of discovery. Who knew what they might find?

The Africans searched the pink from stern to prow, the air alive with their cries of astonishment and pleasure. It was like entering a treasure house. Live ducks and goats mingled with sacks of maize and barrels of salt beef. Tubs of molasses were piled next to casks of kill-devil.

In the Captain's cabin a globe, log, charts and a sextant provided the navigational aids they needed. His wardrobe bulged with silks and taffetas, the best wools, stockings and shoes, hats and shirts. Before long Esmee's men were adorned with an odd assortment of finery, preening themselves like cockbirds.

It did not take long to discover that the ship was also loaded with every kind of wealth they could imagine. Caskets and boxes overflowed with precious stones, plate, jewels, gold doubloons and *escudos*, silver *reales* – all the property of the King of Spain. The Africans surveyed their finds with wonder, dipping into the chests and letting the coins trickle through their fingers. Laughter infected them, growing louder and louder until, in the echoing cavern that was the hold, Esmee's ears began to hurt.

'We don't need this,' she called out, turning to Musa. 'What we need is food and water, spare canvas and ropes and spars. We need a medicine chest, good tools. Take only what we can use. We do not wish to incur the wrath of Spain.'

The Africans listened to Musa, their eyes flickering towards

Esmee. She could feel the beginnings of resentment. He repeated her order and with one or two grumbles, the crew seemed to accept it. Soon they were diverted, chasing chickens and monkeys about the ship, dipping their fingers into every barrel to taste its contents.

Thomas Warner appeared on the deck of the *Cordoba*, grinning broadly. 'See what I have found!' He held up a fine carpenter's set, his eyes roving over the contents of the wooden box with an almost hungry pleasure. Behind him, men were edging barrels of powder and bags of shot to the rail of the *Cordoba*, ready for transfer to their own ship. It took several hours before they had all they needed and by then it was dark.

That night there was such a celebration aboard the *Evangelina*! As the crew of the *Cordoba* were locked in the hold along with their jewels, the Africans began to sing and dance. Wine flowed. Meats roasted on makeshift fires, crackled and spitted, adding their own music.

In the calm, windless evening, Esmee watched them, curiously at peace now that the task was complete. Below her on the deck, Yinka, with Sole strapped to her back, danced next to Musa's son. She too seemed to have found her own liberation.

Edrize wore one of Captain Cantos's jackets. The red of the fabric complemented the rich mahogany of his skin. Whatever had passed between himself and Captain Ortega, he seemed to have dismissed it. The boy did not take his eyes off Yinka and her own eyes flickered in response to his silent admiration. In his lithe movements, Esmee saw a youthful incarnation of his father and her own heart beat faster. The two young people moved to the rhythm of a makeshift drum, their bodies liquid in the flaring of the rush lights.

'For tonight all is well.' Musa came to join her and again she had the feeling that he knew her soul. She turned and met his eyes, not wanting to hide her desire for him.

Bowing his head slightly, he said: 'I have checked the guard. Nat Rouse is in charge. All is secure aboard the *Cordoba*.' He stood back, indicating that she should pass him, saying: 'I think it is time that the Captain took some rest.'

She nodded, her breast tight with happiness. In silence Musa followed her down to the cabin where Gideon lay dreamily, watching the gentle movement of a shadow reflecting through the tiny port hole and on to the cabin wall.

Esmee picked him up and bared her breast. The babe settled to feeding with earnest concentration and as she looked up, Musa was watching them. She reached out and took his hand, placing it against her other breast, where he stroked her with the tenderness of a child holding a dove. As soon as the babe was fed, Esmee laid him down to sleep and turned to the man for her own comfort.

Closing her eyes, she allowed him to lift her and place her on the narrow couch. There, passively, she gave herself up to the exquisite pleasure of his touch. As his lips brushed her throat, she threw back her head, revelling in each new sensation.

Briefly she opened her eyes to look at him. His own were closed as he kissed and caressed her. Here was a man not taking but giving pleasure, unhurried, sensitive to her needs, knowing by instinct what she wanted him to do. She could never have asked. When she was lifted to the very edge of ecstasy he climbed across her and moved with gentle movements inside her until at last his pace grew more urgent and with a gasp of release he bathed her in well-being.

She wanted to lie there forever, her arms about his shoulders, his head nestled against her breast. As he slid out of her she felt an almost immediate return of desire. Now it was her turn to give pleasure, to tour his body with her hands and lips until he was roused to take her again.

They slept. When Esmee awoke it was getting light. For a moment she panicked, thinking of the responsibilities that awaited her, then as Musa stirred she stole another moment to savour the joy of his body pressed close to hers.

After a moment he sat up, lowering his legs over the side of the bunk. Esmee studied his back and the joy of the night evaporated as she looked at the criss-cross scars from his shoulders to his thighs.

All her happiness seemed to be draining away. She tried to grasp it but it was like sand, slipping through the tiniest gaps, escaping no matter how she adjusted her precarious grasp. She said: 'What do we do next?'

Musa looked down at her and she saw the answering awareness in his eyes. He said: 'For today it will be enough to get away from here. Perhaps we will find the island we seek.' He stood up, and as he tied the cloth about him, observed: 'Perhaps next we will meet an English ship. They will carry you home.'

'No!'

He raised his eyebrows. 'Do you not wish to return to your friends, to your husband?'

She shook her head, desparate to recapture the magic they had shared. Not meeting his eyes, she said: 'It matters not whether I wish to go back.' Then, confessing to more than she should: 'My husband is a good man, but I do not love him.' She left her true meaning hanging in the air and Musa sighed.

He sat again on the edge of the bunk and took her hand. His own voice was troubled. 'Let us not look too far ahead. For today I cannot see into the future. There is only haziness, perhaps clouds. Who knows? We cannot tell what the future holds until we arrive. Be patient.'

He hugged her to him but it was the comfort of a parent, not of a lover, and as she dragged on her clothes Esmee felt only a pervasive chill.

Overnight the wind had freshened and as she came on to the deck, the *Cordoba* bobbed near at hand as if, like the dancers of the night before, she was performing her own ritual.

Thomas Warner greeted her. 'We are ready to sail, Captain. Do you wish the foreign Captain to be returned to his ship? Shall we release his men from the hold?'

Esmee nodded. There was nothing to delay them. They needed to get away from here and fast, find a hiding place before Captain Cantos reported his interception and others gave chase. She felt peculiarly impotent as if invisible chains bound her to the deck, unseen bands silenced her tongue.

Musa was now on deck, giving instructions to the Africans. Already the smell of smoke greeted them as a fire had been lit to roast more meat.

Throwing off her unease, Esmee gave the order to prepare to sail. Nat Rouse was sent to escort the Captain on deck. He came into the daylight brushing down his shirt and drawers as if they were contaminated by his presence on the *Evangelina*.

'Captain, we are pleased to release you now.' Esmee paused to give effect to her next words. 'We are faster than you and I fear we must keep your weapons so do not try to give chase.'

The Captain acquiesced, glancing across at his own ship, anxious to reach the safety of her deck. Meanwhile the billowing movement of the *Evangelina*'s sheets began to lift the ship, ready to pull away from her Spanish sister.

With surprising agility for someone of his build, Captain Cantos skipped across between the two vessels. He turned and waved a deprecating hand to his gaolers.

'Right, prepare to make sail.'

Esmee shouted the command. She turned towards the men at the foot of the main mast and in that same moment everything happened at once. A single blast cut through the air. Even as she swung round it was to see the smoking barrel of a musket aboard the *Cordoba*.

'In God's name – !'

Around her there was an answering gasp, a howl of anger. A wall of bodies stood between her and something on the deck. She did not have to ask. As the stunned men parted, drawing away, a pitiable object was revealed lying at the foot of the mast. His right leg was twisted at an obscene angle and from his thigh blood spurted scarlet on to the deck. Taller than any man aboard. A born leader. A natural target. Musa.

Esmee's head was filled with silent screaming, deafening her, shutting out everything but its own sound. Her legs seemed to buckle beneath her as she dropped to his side.

She was only vaguely aware of answering gunfire as Nat Rouse and Thomas Warner turned their pieces on the *Cordoba*. Those Africans who held muskets had no idea how to fire them. For the most part they stood silent, shocked by the injury to the man who had held them together. The *Cordoba* was already slipping away. In one corner of her mind where her role of Captain still reigned supreme, Esmee gave thanks that as well as the powder, they had had the foresight to take all the cannon balls. If not, the *Cordoba* would surely have launched a counter-attack.

Musa's breath was coming fast and shallow. Sweat beaded his brow but when Esmee touched him he was cold. In a sudden frenzy she tore off part of her calico shift and began to bind it tight around his upper leg, willing the blood to cease its flow.

'We need a surgeon!' She spoke knowing there was not one aboard. Feeling sick to the stomach, she examined the shattered leg where the musket ball had struck him just below the knee. Pieces of bone and gristle glared white through the mangled flesh. It was clear the leg could not be saved.

Esmee looked round to find Thomas Warner standing behind her. His face was ashen, tinged across the cheeks and around the mouth with green. Turning away he fetched the carpenter's box that he had taken from the *Cordoba* the day before and from its assortment of

256

tools, selected the largest saw. Mercifully it had been well cared for, greased to prevent it rusting. He said: 'I once saw someone do this.'

Esmee took Musa's hand and pressed it to her breast. She was mute, imploring him with her eyes to survive. His own eyes flickered in and out of awareness. Somebody pushed a beaker of kill-devil into her hand and she bent forward, slipping her arm under Musa's shoulders to raise his head. As he turned aside she trickled the fiery liquid into his mouth, making him gag. Fighting for breath, he grasped her arm, drawing her closer. His voice barely above a whisper, he said: 'My son!'

Edrize stood a few feet behind them, his face taut with shock. As Esmee moved aside, he too fell to his knees beside his father and Musa struggled to speak. 'Take care of . . .' But the effort was too great. Closing his eyes, he fell back against Esmee's shoulder. She looked round at Edrize and they gazed at each other, helpless, neither of them sure to whom the request had been addressed.

Esmee turned back to Musa, taking his hand. She had no good news to tell him, no comfort to offer. He was about to undergo an agony.

Thomas Warner stripped off his shirt. Taking a cutlass, he placed it in the fire so recently lit to make breakfast. When the limb was severed he would place the red hot blade against the bleeding flesh. It was the only way they had to cauterise the stump.

Several times Thomas picked up the saw, rearranged his knives.

'Do it!' Esmee snapped at him, sensing his indecision. All the while Musa's blood pumped, slower now but still draining his life away. Thomas took the saw one final time and glanced at the men who came to hold Musa by the wrists and ankles. He nodded to Esmee to pour more kill-devil down the injured man's throat. Her hand shook so much that the liquid splashed everywhere but between his parted lips. Taking a second measure, she tipped it over the injured limb to clean it.

Musa let out a roar of agony, twisting himself in a frenzy of burning pain. The men tightened their grip and Esmee smoothed his face. 'Hush, my dear. Hush now. Soon you will be well.'

'Edrize . . .'

'I promise to care for him.'

Musa arched his back, racked by pain, and the blood began to pump again, faster now, a red torrent gushing on to the deck. As Thomas bent to do his work, the African gave one violent jerk, a long, low gasp, and the tension left his body. Little by little his breath escaped in a bubbling whisper. His head tilted slowly to one side and he lay still.

No man moved or spoke. Scarcely a breath caused the lifting or falling of a chest. In the numbed silence Esmee knew that she was quite alone in some still, dark place. At last a muffled sob broke the tension. At her side Yinka turned to comfort Edrize. They clung together, two half children, old before their time. Esmee wanted to turn to Musa to find comfort of her own, comfort for the death that had just taken him from her.

'Come now.' Nat Rouse took her arm and led her away. She could not feel the deck beneath her feet. There was nothing, nothing but the memory of a man who had cared for her and made her feel safe, no matter what the danger.

She found herself in her cabin with no memory of having walked there. Gideon was awake and about to cry. She lifted him up and pulled down her gown, grateful for the hungry tug on her nipple. She realised that her shift, what was left of it, was soaked in blood. Gently she fingered it, raising her red-coated finger to study the source of Musa's life. She pressed the finger to her lips, tasting it, tasting him.

A growing anger began to consume her. He was free now, his spirit released to return to his home across the ocean, beyond her reach. That was where he would want to be, back with his ancestors, his kinsmen – his wives. Again a wave of raw jealousy lashed her. There was so much they had not done. Given time they might have found a new home, new roots, a place to be together where their own souls would return at the end of their life's journey.

They buried Musa that day, sewn into canvas brought from the *Cordoba*. Thomas Warner said a prayer. Edrize sent up his own plaintive anthem. The other slaves moaned and wept, releasing the misery, heralding the free man on his way.

As night fell, Esmee thought of all the deaths she had ever known – Matt Harbottle, Tolly Cross, Hosea King, her father, her mother, a hundred other sailors whose names she had forgotten, a thousand other slaves whose existence she had barely noticed – all men like Musa with loves and hopes and fears. From somewhere she found an inner strength. Her purpose now was clear: to find a place of safety for Edrize and Yinka, for Nat and Thomas and the rest of the crew. In this alone would she find the courage to carry on.

THIRTY-TWO

The committee selected to run the affairs of Eden Island met on the first Tuesday of each month. The natural choice of venue was the church and it was here, on the first Tuesday in July, that Samuel and his advisors faced a deputation of islanders.

Sam sat behind the table that at other times served as an altar. To his right Praisetogod Shergold, as shepherd of the community's souls, perched impatiently on a stool, long legs akimbo, leaning forward and nodding his head energetically in response to the speaker. To Samuel's left Thomas Axe, his military advisor, sat with eyes downcast, considering the wisdom – or not – of what was being said.

In front of Sam, a few feet from the table, his face scarlet with rage, James Redyard, planter and bigot, shouted his dissent.

'It is an affront to every Christian here to suggest that the slaves are capable of understanding the running of our island!' He turned to face the rows of men seated in the body of the church, and began to address them. 'It is we, brethren, who have given our money, our labour, and have followed God's good purpose in coming here. To suggest that a bunch of heathens, bought and paid for by us, housed and nourished as are all our livestock, should be asked their views, is outrageous!'

'Hear, hear!' Praisetogod nodded more vehemently and went to stand but Sam put out a hand to deter him and got to his own feet.

He knew that his was a lone voice, pleading for the future of the slaves, but still he hoped these men would listen to reason or at least consider what he was saying. If compassion and tolerance failed, then he would appeal to their greed.

Aloud, he said: 'First, gentlemen, it is not we ourselves who have

259

paid for these men, it is the shareholders back in England. Their primary concern is to make a profit. Can you not see that they will be well satisfied as long as they get their money back? After that, it is up to us.'

Already there were hands waving insistently, planters wanting to make their views known, but Sam raised his voice. 'If we keep these men in bondage, using the whip, controlling them with fear, then they will pay for themselves within eighteen months. If, on the other hand, they are given an incentive to be a part of this community, their contribution will be ten times what it would if we use them as animals.'

'Rubbish!' Redyard tossed his head, almost spitting with fury. Looking to the men behind him, he said: 'Within a week they will all have run away. How do you suggest we control them if they know no fear of punishment?'

Sam felt his blood pounding. Redyard's violence was almost legendary. Besides the slaves, he had two apprentices and three servants working his land and treated them like filth.

Praisetogod could no longer contain himself. Leaping to his feet, he shouted: 'A heathen cannot be a Christian! No slave can be baptised in the name of Jesus. The sole purpose of this mission is to form a Christian community. What you suggest is blasphemy!'

Such a hubbub broke out that Sam could not make himself heard. He sat back to let it burn itself out. As the noise died down, his uncle, seated in the front row, said: 'I believe the Governor to be right. God does not discriminate between slave and free man. What is it you want – to create a Christian community or to grow rich on other men's labour? Jesus was a poor man and chose to remain so.'

Several men snorted their disagreement while others looked thoughtful. Knowing he was burning his boats, Samuel said: 'We must vote on this issue. Either you are able to accept that the slaves work as bondsmen until such time as they have repaid their passage, by which time we will debate this issue again, *or*, we can take a vote on it now. I warn you, I cannot in all conscience agree to continue as Governor if there is no likelihood that the slaves will ever be entitled to their freedom.'

'Then resign!' It was Redyard who cried out, but behind him there was hesitation.

Isaiah Brentwood, a blacksmith, rose to his feet. He passed his hand over his mouth and shuffled his feet, uncomfortable in the role of spokesman, but his size alone brought him attention.

Drawing in his breath, he said: 'I think the Governor talks sense. We should wait and see how the Africans shape up. None of us has had dealings with black men before. Perhaps they are the same as us. Let's wait and see.'

'Yes!'

'No!'

The shouting continued. Wearily Sam banged on the table. He waited until the noise died down then said: 'As you know, gentlemen, in the running of this island I have the final say. It is not my wish to impose my will on you. I therefore contend that we vote on whether to reconsider this matter in one year's time. In the meantime, I decree that every African in our community be treated with respect. If you feel unable to accept this I shall tender my resignation to the company as soon as the next ship arrives. Now, those in agreement, please raise their hands.'

As the men muttered together, some half raising a hand and then looking round to see how their neighbours were voting, Sam wondered whether he wanted to win this vote or not. Part of him wanted to go home, to forget all about Eden Island, to find himself a less contentious way of living out his life. At the same time he had been handed a huge responsibility and to leave now would be to fail in it. Beyond all that was the knowledge that if he left the Caribbean then he would be leaving Esmeralda forever.

He wanted her with a sudden hungry yearning, a feeling so strong that it stopped his breath. He told himself that perhaps he was mistaken. Perhaps she had not been so different, so special, but the very thought of her still engendered emotions he had never experienced before they met – and he had let her down by not protecting her. Perhaps she hated him now. Perhaps she was dead! He had to believe, *had to*, that she still lived and that one day he would have her back.

He became aware of the murmurs around him and as he looked at the gathering at least half of the men had raised their hands. They might not share his views on slavery but they did not want him to resign. He felt suddenly jubilant.

Bowing his head in acknowledgement of the decision, he said: 'Right, gentlemen, now let us move on to the next item which is the need for us to find more crops to grow on Eden. As you know, a ship has been commissioned and when it arrives, it is my intention

261

to travel with it in search of anything that might prove marketable. I do not intend to be away more than two months, three at the most. In my absence, it is my wish that my uncle, Lord Craven, and Thomas Axe, jointly administer the island. Do I have your agreement?'

'Yes!' Redyard shouted his response, making his wish to be rid of Samuel crystal clear. Sam grinned sardonically as he bowed his head.

In his heart hope welled like a spring. As soon as the ship arrived he would leave, then they would comb every island, every inlet, looking for a new crop – and for Esmeralda. This time, surely, God would grant him success.

The assembled gathering was still waiting. Suddenly Sam could not wait to get out of the church and away from their company. Clearing his throat, he announced: 'If Minister Shergold will lead us in prayers, we will call this meeting to a close.'

Richard Jordan arrived at Eden on the seventeenth day of July. He did so in a frigate called the *Lapwing*. He was hardly ashore before Sam, unable to curb his impatience, was urging him to set sail again.

In the past months, Richard had spent little time ashore. He was glad to be away from the humid swamps of Barbados and in no great hurry to return.

'Whatever is the urgency?' he asked. 'A few more days will make no difference. Whether we find a new crop on a Thursday or a Saturday won't alter the course of history.'

Sam shrugged, embarrassed. 'I am just anxious to do what I can. Things really aren't going well here. That cotton which looked so promising seems to have been struck by some pest. The buds rot on the stalk.' He poured Richard a beaker of bonano wine.

As Richard thoughtfully sipped the liquid, Sam said: 'We are having poor success with our sugar too. The plants grow well but our refining is at fault. The crop we have is hardly worth shipping back to England. As for the tobacco, it is but poorly cured. It is really important that we find something more suitable to grow.' When Jordan remained silent, Sam casually asked: 'Do you have any other news? Of a more general matter?'

Richard eyed him shrewdly. 'If you mean news of your uncle's wife, then I fear I do not.'

Sam felt his cheeks redden. He let out his breath in a deep, confessional sigh, no longer denying his feelings for Esmeralda. He respected Dick Jordan, trusted him to understand. Besides, the burden of his feelings weighed him down. He longed to share his thoughts with someone.

As he narrated the sorry story, his friend nodded philosophically, but when Sam got to the part about the visit of Captain Tromp, the Captain raised a questioning eyebrow.

'Is this what your voyage is really about then – to go and seek for Lady Craven?'

'No!' In his own defence, Sam added: 'I don't see why we cannot combine the two.'

Richard drained his drink and his reply was non-committal. 'You are in charge, Samuel. It is for you to decide.'

The wind and tide being right, they prepared to leave Eden on the twenty-first day of July. Sam bade a courteous farewell to his wife and made an affectionate parting from his uncle. He did not tell him of Captain Tromp's story, or of his hopes of finding Esmeralda. Why raise the old man's hopes?

At the back of his mind he wondered what he intended to do if he found her – no, *when*, not if. He could not think past a romantic reunion: her running and clinging to him, he promising to take care of her forever. Aeneas, Serenity and his responsibilities were blotted out.

He fretted until the *Lapwing* was finally at sea, fearing that some outside force would stop him, even at the last minute. When they were finally away from Eden it was like getting out of gaol, or how he imagined that would be.

They paid a cursory visit to several of the smaller islands, threading their way towards the east. Although a whole jungle of plants greeted them wherever they landed, few seemed likely to fulfil their hopes of finding the perfect commodity. Neither was there any news of a beautiful, green-eyed captive. Meanwhile they collected specimens of madder and silk grass, indigo, and several different varieties of cotton in the hope that something would grow successfully on their return.

The further east they sailed the more anxious Samuel became. Apart from the need to find Esmeralda, that other business still tormented him. When Jordan was up on deck, he sneaked a look at the charts, hoping for some confirmation that they were on a true course for Fonseca. He needed to go back and check, make sure once and for all that the Carib girl had not borne him a son. If she had, then he would have to face up to his responsibilities and bring the child off with him. He tried not to imagine what it would be like. He thought of the Caribs with their bronze skins and sickle-shaped eyes, their lank hair and inscrutable expressions. Would a son of his be like that?

To his relief he found the island clearly marked but as the days passed he realised they had already reached that vast expanse of ocean and had not sighted land.

Dick Jordan kept silent on the subject but finally Samuel could bear it no longer.

'What is going on?' he asked. 'Where are we?'

Jordan shrugged. 'According to my calculations we are here, give or take a mile or so.' He circled the area that included Fonseca and shook his head. 'I don't understand it. We found the island before. I checked my bearings. I marked it on my chart and now – nothing!'

Sam felt a treacherous relief that he need not face up to the dilemma of the Carib girl after all, but immediately thoughts of Esmee's peril threatened to swamp him.

'I've got to find her, Dick. I've got to!' He poured out his agony, unable to face the thought of returning home again without her.

Gently, Jordan asked: 'If you do find her, what will you do?' We have no authority to go in and attack. If whoever holds her is unwilling to hand her over, how are you going to ger her away?'

Sam shook his head, not acknowledging the possibility of defeat.

Still probing, Jordan asked: 'And if we do find her, will you take her back to her husband?'

Angrily, Sam said: 'Find her!'

The days drifted into August then September and still there was nothing. Dick Jordan began to grow impatient. 'We are running out of time,' he insisted. 'If we travel any further east then there is another five hundred leagues before we reach more land. We must go back, Sam. Let's do what we always intended, go to the Moskito Coast and see what we can find there.'

Sam gave a reluctant shrug. Tromp's story had given him such hope. He knew it must be true. There was no reason for the Dutchman to make it up and there could not be two captive women with green eyes, married to an English lord.

Jordan had already given the order to return. Sam didn't know whether to continue with the struggle to find Fonseca against all the odds, or to give himself up to his destiny and let the elements decide his fate. As it was, the easterly wind they now depended upon did not materialise. For several days they made little progress and all the time he clung to the hope that some miracle would happen to bring him face to face with Captain Jackson and his daughter. By God, he'd give Jackson a thrashing when he caught up with him!

At last they picked up a prevailing wind that promised to carry them back across the Caribbean, and to Eden. Sam felt only despair.

'Ship ahoy!'

The call from the watch did not interest him. He felt unspeakably tired. When he got back to Eden he would resign his post, return to England. The climate there would suit him better and he could help to run his uncle's estates. He would take Serenity and the children and put thoughts of Esmeralda behind him.

He was distracted from his plans by a warning shot from the *Lapwing*'s cannon. He summoned the energy to go on deck and investigate.

'Samuel, you had better come. There's a Spanish ship to starboard.'

Richard Jordan ordered his bosun to alter course. The foreign ship was travelling at a tangent to them and Dick frowned. 'There is something amiss here.' He pointed at the inadequate sail the pinnace carried, the unlikely course she followed. To Sam, he said: 'We had better take care. Buccaneers have been known to lure men to their deaths by pretending to be in trouble.' He ordered cannon and musket to be primed.

'Ahoy!' He hailed them for by now they were within shouting distance. 'Ahoy there!' Dick repeated his call. 'We are fully armed but we do not wish you harm.' At last someone appeared on deck, gesticulating frantically. He was waving what looked like a white shirt, perhaps as a sign of surrender.

'There may be sickness aboard.' Dick looked uncertain. 'If she is truly crippled, we had best take her in tow.' His expression brightened. 'She will make a handsome prize.'

Cupping his hands, he shouted again: 'We are coming alongside. Do you understand?'

Another man then another appeared on deck. Some were black. Again Dick looked perplexed. 'They don't look like Spaniards. Perhaps they're runaways.' He grinned. 'I know you won't approve but we might have a good slave cargo to take back as well.'

265

By this time they were close enough to throw grappling hooks across. The white men on the ship were waving frantically. 'Hello there, we're English!'

'Good God!' Dick waited until the craft was secured alongside then went aboard. Sam followed behind. Now that they were close he had a strange feel about this ship, excited or perhaps plain scared.

He waited as Jordan introduced himself to the white men. 'What's happening here?' he asked.

'We were held captive on a sugar plantation and managed to get away. Since then we've been searching for somewhere to lie up but for the last week we've been becalmed. There are only fourteen of us left alive. Some of those are sick. We have women and children with us.'

Sam listened with mounting excitement. He knew the news was significant. Half a dozen crewmen from the *Lapwing* joined them, pistols at the ready. They were not needed. The men aboard the pinnace showed no inclination to resist. They were all exceedingly thin and hollow-eyed.

Jordan announced: 'I am taking charge of his vessel on behalf of His Majesty King Charles I of England.'

'What about us?' asked one of the white men.

'You are?'

'Rouse the navigator.'

'And your Captain?'

'She's resting.'

'She?' Jordan's expression was quizzical. Letting it pass, he added: 'You will be taken back with us and then shipped home.'

'And the others?' The man looked round at his black companions.

Dick Jordan surveyed them and Sam was about to intervene, but the Captain replied: 'I'll take charge of the slaves.'

'They are *not* slaves!'

A woman's voice was audible before she came into sight. When she did, Richard Jordan looked at her in surprise.

Standing just behind him, Samuel thought his heart would stop. Before him, bedraggled, her skirts in tatters, a small child clutched to her bosom, was the woman he was ready to die for: Esmeralda.

As the month of August had progressed, Esmee, like the *Evangelina*, felt herself to be becalmed. It was almost as if she had endured so much that her mind refused to tolerate more pain. She was closed down, numbed, only half alive.

She continued to go through the motions of commanding the ship, aware of her responsibility to the men aboard, but she did so without feeling. From now on she would experience neither hope nor fear.

Day after day the *Evangelina* bobbed in the water like a duck on a pond, barely drifting. Her sails hung limp as muslin. The air was stifling, the sun searing the ship until the paint bubbled and the decks blistered the crew's feet. The men flopped like dogs in the smallest shadows, panting out their discomfort. All the time the supplies taken from the *Cordoba* dwindled.

At long last the merest hint of a breeze began to whisper into the canvas. Sensing a change, the crew began to rouse themselves from their torpor. For the first time in weeks there was talk of finding an island and setting up camp.

The call of 'Ship ahoy' was the catalyst that finally stirred them into action. Only Esmee remained unmoved. She gave the approaching vessel a cursory glance.

'Shall we lower some sail?' asked Nat Rouse, intent on repeating the trick that had rewarded them with the capture of the *Cordoba*.

Esmee doubted if the deception would work twice. Rather, she thought they would be better served by making a run for it, only she hadn't the energy to explain her thoughts. Instinct as well as calculation told her that the island of Hispaniola could not be more than a day or two's sailing away. The men would be safe there – or as safe as they could ever be in this hostile climate.

She was about to open her mouth when Thomas Warner cried out: 'It's an Englisher!'

The news fired the remaining seamen like touch paper. Esmee felt a kindling of interest but her thoughts were not for herself. 'What about the Africans?' she asked, sensing the white men's desire to throw in their lot with their fellow countrymen.

'We'll see they're taken care of.' Nat Rouse avoided her eyes and she guessed that his desire to get home overrode every other consideration. She did not blame him but still her responsibility was to all the men.

Home. The thought stabbed her awake. Home. Jeronimo's cabin. Aeneas's house. London. Wind and rain. Cobbled streets. Gardens. Pictures flickered in her mind like the riffled pages of a book.

All the time the English ship drew nearer. Already it was too

267

late to challenge her, besides which Nat and Thomas were already gesticulating enthusiastically. 'Hello! We're English!'

Esmee left them to it. She went to find Yinka and the children. Yinka was curled up asleep in Jeronimo's old bunk. She at least seemed to have laid the ghost of his presence. Looking at her, fear descended on Esmee like a cold fog. What was to become of them next?

The violent bumping of the ship told her they were being boarded. Gathering Gideon to her, Esmee hurried back to the ladder leading to the deck, her heart beating wildly. She heard the English Captain say: 'I'll take care of the slaves.'

That was the spark that brought her back to life. Pushing her way up the ladder she stepped into the daylight, ready to challenge him, ready to draw on every ounce of courage she had to protect her friends.

The Captain looked at her in surprise, a youngish man, brown-haired and brown-eyed. His face was not unpleasant. It was several moments before a gasp from the man behind him drew Esmee's attention away and as it did so she too gasped, not believing what she saw.

For a moment she felt paralysed as her mind grappled with the impossible. She thought: I'm hexed! Bewitched! But even as her eyes played tricks on her, a long-remembered voice said: 'Hello, Esmee.'

She had no idea how long they stood there, staring at each other. Sam looked different. He was thinner, careworn, his skin darkened and his hair bleached by the sun. Perhaps it wasn't him. Perhaps he was not there at all, merely the spirit of the man she wanted to see and hear, but his own confusion confirmed that he was real.

In rising panic she knew that the Samuel who had sustained her dreams over the past year was different from the flesh and blood man who stood before her. She had no idea what to do.

The Captain was looking from one to the other and in that moment she remembered where they were and the danger they faced. Turning her attention to him, she blurted out: 'There are no slaves here. Everyone aboard this ship is free and equal.' Her voice wavered and she looked to Sam for his reaction. He inclined his head and she took courage from his presence.

'They are?' Dick Jordan gave a doubtful grin. 'And you are . . .?'

Esmee fixed him with a glare she had learned from Serenity:

disdainful, looking down her nose. In her best voice she said: 'I am Esmeralda Craven. My husband is Aeneas, Lord Craven. We are English.'

The Captain jerked round to stare at Sam, his eyes wide with disbelief.

He nodded, red-faced with embarrassement.

Dick Jordan looked back at her. 'Well, madam. What a surprise. We have been seeking you. This is most fortuitous.'

The news that Sam had still been searching for her gave her a sudden dangerous glow of comfort. She tried not to look at him but his very presence was bright as a full moon in a clear sky. There was so much she needed to know, so very much to explain.

Baby Gideon, aware of his mother's over-tight grip, began to protest. Lifting him, Esmee knew that Sam was watching her, watching her son, wondering. The glimmer of comfort quickly died.

Dick Jordan said: 'Madam, if you would like to return to your quarters, I am sure we will be able to come to some arrangement. Meanwhile, Mr Rushworth will surely escort you.'

In silence she descended the ladder, Sam following behind. Below decks they entered the tiny cabin where Yinka still slept in the bunk, Sole curled up against her. The girl's presence added to the awkwardness. Focusing on her, Sam whispered: 'Who is that?'

'Yinka, my . . . she was my father's . . .'

The silence was oppressive. Knowing what to say, where to start, was like picking a single cotton seed from a field of plants. Who could possibly choose?

'Esmeralda!' Sam spread his hands as if bemused. 'I thank God you are safe. Truly. I have searched everywhere for you. You have no idea what agony I have suffered, wondering what was happening to you.'

Esmee could not reply and he ground to a halt, asking instead: 'Why did your father take you away?'

The very mention of Jeronimo filled her with shame: shame that she was his daughter, shame that he had violated her and was the father of her son.

She shook her head, avoiding the question, saying instead: 'He is dead. My father died in a storm.' She willed him to ask no more questions, not to express any sorrow, or she might not be able to hold back her own pain and anger. When he did not speak, she said: 'We were taken prisoner, made to work.'

269

'On Fonseca?'

'The Spaniards call it San Bernaldo.'

Again there was silence, taut as bow strings. Dropping all pretence, Samuel said: 'Oh, Esmee, Esmee, forgive me. It is all my fault. I should never have sent you to England. I should have looked after you.'

'Yes, you should.' She could not at that moment offer any excuses. To lower her guard would be to release a maelstrom of tears and need. He had to know the extent of his failings, and yet at the same time, seeing him again, she was filled with a joy so sharp that it bordered on anguish.

Looking helplessly at her, he said: 'I was not to know that my uncle would marry you.'

She bowed her head in acknowledgement and he turned his attention to Gideon. His voice desceptively calm, he said: 'He did not tell us you were expecting a child – or perhaps he did not know?'

Again the panic gripped her. Looking away from him, she said: 'I must have conceived just before I was abducted.' This at least was true.

'On the island, you were – well treated?'

She knew what he was trying to ask. Again, sticking to the narrowest form of the truth, she said: 'The planter who kidnapped us was more interested in young boys than in women. My servant and I have been quite safe.' She suppressed the thought of that last evening.

Sam sought a new focus for his discomfort by looking at Sole. 'Your servant's daughter is a bonny child.'

'She is my half-sister.'

Esmee was aware of his shock. Despairingly she thought: Never, ever can I reveal to him that other truth. Trying to push her own feelings aside, she said: 'About the men on board this ship . . . I have given my solemn promise to ensure their freedom. Will you support me in this?'

'Of course, although Dick Jordan might be reluctant to lose a profit.'

'Then I shall ask Aeneas to compensate him.'

At her mention of his uncle, she saw Sam's face harden. He said: 'Your husband will be pleased to have you back.'

There was nothing to say. All the time her own unanswered question burned in her heart. At last, she asked: 'And Serenity?'

He looked at his feet. 'She and I are wed. We have twin babies.'

The hopelessness of her feelings dragged her down. She struggled not to show her jealousy, her growing despair.

With a supreme effort she managed to say: 'I congratulate you. You must be pleased.'

'My uncle will be even more pleased when he learns that he has a son of his own.'

They stared bleakly at each other. With a gasp of emotion, Samuel cried: 'Esmee! This is madness. You know I feel nothing for Serenity. You know I could never, ever have foreseen that my uncle would do what he did. Why did you not refuse?'

She felt angry that he understood so little. She could not hide her bitterness as she said: 'I only did what I thought was expected of me.'

'But I thought you loved me?'

'I knew that you were sorry for me.'

'Sorry? I was – I fell in love with you. I had a crazy hope that some day I could come home and marry you.'

'It is too late.'

'What are we going to do?'

All her tantalising daydreams were here to hand, waiting to be realised.

Taking her hand, he said: 'I could send Dick Jordan back to Eden and come with you on your ship. Together we could find somewhere safe, an island of our own.'

The thought was so beautiful that for a moment she let herself imagine what it would be like, but she knew he would not be able to do it. His sense of honour, his duty to Serenity, his loyalty to his uncle, would torture him. One day he would blame her for taking him away. With heavy heart she said: 'No. We must go back to the island. We both have responsibilities now.'

'Esmee! I – '

'Don't say it!' She could not bear to hear the words nor face the reality of what she was losing.

Drawing away from him, she said: 'For the time being my first thoughts must be for the well-being of my friends. After that I shall try to be a good wife to my husband.'

Even as she spoke she knew she was condemning herself to a life of loneliness and loss.

'Is that truly what you want?'

'You know that it isn't, but we could never be happy at the expense of everyone else.'

He inclined his head, accepting her decision. 'Then I had best leave you. I will go and plead the cause of your friends.'

She buried her own pain by concentrating on the Africans' needs. She said: 'Yinka has formed an affection for one of the young men. They must not be separated.'

'I have formed an affection for you, but you send me away.'

'Don't!' She turned from him, struggling to keep her mind on the Africans. She continued: 'As for the others, they are not to be sold into bondage.'

'I shall take them into my own service. If Dick will not see sense then I shall offer him payment.'

'Do you have money?'

'Enough.'

She could not express her thanks, not risk lowering her defences. For a moment Sam stood uncertainly, then when she did not speak, he turned and walked from the cabin. Her need for him was so powerful that even as she stood staring at the space he had occupied, it felt as if he had left part of himself behind.

From the bunk Yinka gave a grunt and stretched herself awake. She followed Esmee's gaze towards the door. 'Who was that?'

'Mr Rushworth, the Governor of Eden Island. We are going home.'

To her own ears her voice sounded quite matter-of-fact. At the same time the meaning of her words brought her face to face with the unthinkable. Captain Jordan would sail them swiftly back to Eden. Once there she could no longer pretend that Gideon was Aeneas's son. She could not begin to imagine what would happen next.

To Yinka, she said: 'You have nothing to fear now. You and Edrize will be cared for. From now on you will always be together.'

As she spelled out Yinka's bright future, her only thought was that by her own words she had closed the door on all that she held dear.

272

THIRTY-THREE

The noise of shouting was so great that Esmee longed to put her hands over her ears to shut it out, only she couldn't because her wrists were bound behind her back.

'Whore! Harlot!' The words formed themselves into a chorus, going on and on. They were hurled at her with such force that they stung as if they were stones.

At that same moment she saw that the people gathered around her were arming themselves with rocks and pebbles.

'No!' she whimpered.

In the crowd she saw Yinka, clutching Gideon. 'Please! Please take care of him . . .'. Yinka looked away from her, distancing herself from Esmee's ordeal. She thought she heard Gideon cry but the sound was swallowed by the hubbub.

At that moment Aeneas stepped forward and in a rush of relief she spoke his name. He too held a rock. His voice harsh with bitterness, he shouted: 'This woman has been taken in adultery. The punishment is death by stoning.'

'Help me!' Desperately she looked at the mob and there in the front row stood Samuel. She gazed at him, pleading with him to save her, and he smiled. In the next moment he raised his hand and the first stone was thrown.

Esmee awoke in such a fright that she was already on her feet. Sweat drenched her. Her heart thundered. From the hammock above the bunk in Dick Jordan's cabin, Yinka muttered a sleepy protest.

Trying to calm herself Esmee went outside on to the deck of the *Lapwing*. It was a fresh morning and the ship sped keenly across the waves. Relief at waking from the dream was tempered by the knowledge that that very day they would reach Eden. Was this how it would be? What would Aeneas do? She had no way of knowing, except that he could only be disappointed, or angry, or jealous, or a hundred other unhappy responses.

She should have told Samuel the truth so that he could pave the way for her. The knowledge would have horrified him, separated her from him forever, but he was bound to find out. You could not keep such an abomination hidden. Like a pus-infected wound, it would erupt, making its poison known.

Gideon – only he mattered. How would Aeneas respond to her son? A living nightmare began to overtake her.

From the shore Esmee heard the sound of the cannon, announcing their arrival to the whole of Eden Island. She couldn't face it, not Aeneas or Serenity, not Samuel's marriage or the lie she must live.

Trembling uncontrollably, she turned back towards her cabin, running straight into Samuel.

'Esmeralda? What is the matter?'

Fear made her incoherent. Turning her face from him, she said: 'I can't! I can't!'

He put his arm about her shoulders as a brother might have done. 'There now, you have nothing to fear.'

'You don't know.' She searched his face, tormented by such dispassionate concern. Since their painful reunion a week past, she had avoided him – and he had stayed away. It was what she had demanded and yet she was angry with him for accepting her wishes. She pulled her arm free, repeating: 'You don't know.'

'Tell me.'

'I cannot.'

He looked at her helplessly. 'Then take courage. Whatever happens it cannot be as bad as you imagine.'

She was too exhausted to argue, or to struggle. She allowed him to take her arm again as a gangplank was thrown across to the *Lapwing.*

Quietly he said: 'No matter what, I shall not desert you.'

Again she thought: You don't know.

Leaving Yinka and the children aboard the ship, Esmee allowed Samuel to escort her ashore. Round and about people called out greetings or turned to their neighbours to discuss this latest development. She heard somebody whisper: 'Truly, *that* is Lord Craven's wife!'

As they walked Samuel was half holding her upright, steering her up the steep path that led to New Bristol. Thoughts of a reunion with her husband shut everything else from her mind. She had no time to take in her surroundings. Her legs did not seem to belong to her. As she stumbled along she could not imagine what was going to happen.

For a wild moment she wondered if she could pretend that Gideon was Yinka's baby to save him from Aeneas's wrath, but Samuel knew otherwise. She could not prevent him from giving the news to his uncle – not unless she told him the truth.

'What are you afraid of?' he repeated, as they crossed the square that was bordered by about a dozen houses. 'Surely you don't fear my uncle?'

She shook her head.

'Then what?'

Already they were going up the path and he banged on the door, opening it a the same time. Bitterly, he said: 'You wanted to come here. Well, here you are.'

Esmee followed him inside, looking bleakly at the cool, shady room that would now be her home.

'Samuel, you are ...' Aeneas struggled out of his chair and started across the room. At the sight of Esmee he visibly staggered.

'See, Uncle, I have a surprise for you.' Determinedly Sam pushed her forward and she felt like a rabbit about to be pounced on by a ferret, frozen into submission.

'Esmeralda? Is it really you? Oh, my dear. My dear!' Aeneas wrung his hands together with emotion.

Esmee could not move. After a moment her husband came forward, his arms welcoming. He held her close.

'Oh, my dearest. Thank God you are safe!' She smelt that almost forgotten mustiness of him, felt the thinness of his chest. Her nightmare took on a bleak reality.

Esmee felt like a parcel, passed from Samuel to her husband and then back again as Aeneas felt so overcome he had to sit down. When he had recovered a little he ordered another seat to be brought close to him.

'Sit down, my dearest girl. Sit down. Your safe return brings me such joy!'

She remained silent, wishing that Sam would go so that she could confess all and get it over with, but he stood at a discreet distance, a tight smile on his face as he witnessed his uncle's joy.

Then he said it, the words that Esmee dreaded. 'There is more good news.' He looked at her to see if she wanted to be the bearer of the glad tidings but she turned her head away.

Sam said: 'When you left the *Destiny* that night in Barbados, you left behind not one but two people – your wife has borne you a son!'

Aeneas sat very still. His face seemed immobile. He was silent. Esmee risked a glance at him and her worst fears were confirmed. After an eternity he said: 'Well, this is indeed a miracle.'

Sam was looking from one to the other, a frown on his face. He knows, thought Esmee. Now he must know.

Running his fingers through his thick yellow hair, Sam said: 'Well, I will leave you alone and go back to the *Lapwing*. The babe is still aboard so I will go and fetch him.'

Esmee knew that he was looking at her but she could not meet his eyes. As soon as he was out of the room she looked up at Aeneas. He was still sitting like a statue.

'I am sorry,' she said. 'So very sorry.'

'For what?' He took a deep breath and sat upright. He turned a bright smile on her. 'On the contrary, what good news for any husband. A son, eh?'

'Aeneas – '

His look stopped the words on her lips. His eyes unwavering, he said: 'I am indeed to be congratulated, my wife and son returned to me on the same day.'

She lowered her eyes, confused, too exhausted to try to make sense of what he was saying.

As he continued, his voice was positively cheerful. 'And what is he called then, this son of mine?'

'Aeneas, please – '

'Hush, my dear. You have made me doubly happy. I have you back and now I have an heir to follow me.'

It was then that it dawned on her. He could not lose face, even with her, even though she knew the truth. With an heroic effort she joined in the pretence.

'His name is Gideon.'

'Gideon. A good name. I like it.' He rubbed his hands together with satisfaction and moments later Samuel came into the room, carrying the baby.

Turning to them, Esmee took her son and held him close. Sam looked at her then at his uncle, weighing up the situation.

276

Impatiently, Aeneas said: 'Quick, give him to me.'

In silence, Esmee handed the baby to her husband. He took him and looked him over, chucking him under the chin, speaking to him.

'Well, young fellow me lad, you're a fine boy.' Turning to Sam, he said: 'I do think that he favours me.'

'I think he does.' Sam did not look at Esmee. Shuffling his feet, he said: 'Well, I must leave you. It is time I called on my wife and bairns.'

'Of course. Thank you, Nephew. Thank you for bringing my dearest wife back to me.' As Aeneas spoke he reached out and pulled Esmee closer, forming the perfect family group, mother, father and child.

Giving herself up to this latest mystery, she thought: I wonder whatever will happen next?

When Samuel entered his house it was to find Serenity in the nursery with the babies. She looked up as he came in but paid him little more attention than if he had just returned from a visit to the church.

'Samuel.'

'Serenity, I trust that you are well?'

She snorted her discontent. 'These babes try me sorely. When one sleeps the other cries. It cannot be right to burden a woman with such torments.'

Sam came over and looked at the sleeping children, grateful for a focus other than his wife. In his absence the babes had grown. The boy, Zephaniah, was considerably bigger than his sister. He wriggled in his sleep, his mouth pursed in discomfort, and for a terrible moment Sam thought that he could see Serenity in him.

Salome, smaller, clenched her fists and gave an angry howl. His heart sank. These babes, flesh of his flesh, seemed like strangers.

Making the best of things, he said: 'We have momentous news. In our travels we intercepted a ship. On board was your – was Esmeralda.'

Serenity jerked to attention. 'Where is she now?'

'With your father.'

Her eyes opened wide as saucers. 'You have brought her back? Here?'

'Where else?'

She snorted again. 'Huh! I suppose my father is overjoyed?'

277

'Of course, but there is more. She had a child.'

Serenity simply stared at him. 'What are you saying?' she asked. 'How, a child?'

'What I say. She was pregnant when the *Destiny* was stolen away. She has a son.' Even as he spoke he felt the pain of jealousy. If ever Esmee was intended to bear a child then it should have been his. He could not believe in a God who would play such tricks on them.

Serenity leaped to her feet. Her face was white, her hands began to tremble. 'When? When did this happen? When was he born?'

'He is a few weeks older than the twins.'

She stared at him with increasing horror. 'Then you know what this means? Our boy will be dispossessed. She intends to steal away our inheritance. This cannot be!' She began to pace, her rage building like steam held in a kettle.

Sam gazed helplessly at her. In the end he simply said: 'This is how it is.'

'How it is? Don't you intend to fight for your son's right? Don't you care that a heathen savage whore has bewitched my father and stolen my birthright?'

'Serenity, be reasonable.'

'Reasonable? Reasonable?' She grabbed the pewter water jug that stood on a stool beside the babies' cribs and hurled it across the room. She began to scream. 'You are as besotted as that foolish old man. Go on, admit it!' She flew at him, pummelling him with her fists. He stood still, absorbing the punches, helpless to deny his feelings and at a loss as to how to counter her jealousy.

Finally she said: 'I am going to the church to pray. I am going to seek guidance.'

Now he shouted back. 'From that bag of hot air who calls himself a Minister? That man is more trouble than the rest of the colony put together.'

His wife gave him a disdainful look, her mouth twisted into an angry sneer. 'You're jealous!' she spat. 'You are jealous because he understands me and you – you have no idea what I think or feel! Well, I thank God I have met someone in this godforsaken island who cares about me. Someone who has courage and honour and – '

Sam slapped her. He could no longer bear the sight of her selfish, bitter face. The blow caught her across the cheek and she reeled back. As her hand went to her face he saw her lips tighten, then turn up triumphantly. With shock he thought: She is pleased. She wanted me to do that.

Moments before he had intended to forbid her to leave the room. Now he said: 'Go to him then. Go where you want. I want none of it – you, the children or the inheritance. Go and be damned.'

As he watched, helpless, already regretting his words, she gathered up both the babes and left the room.

That night Aeneas came to Esmee's bed. He entered silently and, throwing back the covers, began to unfasten the nightgown she wore, the one that had so long ago been prepared for her wedding night.

When she was naked he stepped out of his nightshirt and lay down beside her.

'You have no objection?' he asked.

'No.'

He did not look into her eyes. Esmee lay quite still, fighting an instinct to draw away from his touch.

For a while he explored her, caressing, then he turned his back, trying to rouse himself for the act of possession.

After a while, he said: 'Come along, my dear. You are no longer the innocent maid. Come and help your husband.'

Avoiding his eyes she sat up and began to caress him. 'Do what the old man wants, no matter what' – that was what her father had said. She had a terrible feeling that Jeronimo was back in the room with them. Now she was at the mercy of not one, but two men.

Aeneas had changed. He was courteous, gentle, but beneath his polite exterior she sensed his anger. As he finally took possession of her she thought of Gideon, banished to a room with Yinka and Sole. 'It will be best if he is reared by a wet nurse,' Aeneas had said. 'How fortunate that your maid should have so much milk.'

Dutifully Esmee made herself available to him, moving with his rhythm, holding his skinny shoulders. All the time she thought that now, because of Gideon, he had a new power over her, as once Ortega had done. She would never be free.

When he had finished he climbed from the bed and tucked the coverlet back over her. He deposited a kiss on her forehead. His actions were loving, considerate as those of a father. A father . . . Once again Esmee felt as if she had been raped. With despair she knew that from now on this was how it would be.

THIRTY-FOUR

In returning to Eden it soon became clear that Esmee had swapped one cage for another. True, this was a much better cage where there was sufficient food and drink, clothes and comfort, but the brief freedom she had known aboard the *Evangelina* was no longer hers.

Alone at sea, in command of the crew, she had forgotten the restrictions that faced English women – not that she was universally regarded as English. Indeed, Serenity, Shergold and many of his flock did not hide the fact that they viewed her with shock and displeasure, a dangerous hybrid, threatening the security of their godly community. Esmee could not fail to hear the whispers that she was some sort of siren, sent to tempt the virtuous Lord Craven and bring about his downfall. Bitterly she knew that many would have been pleased if Governor Rushworth had stuck to his search for new commodities and not rescued her at all. Sometimes she wished the same thing herself.

She did not know if Aeneas heard the rumours. Her first task on arriving in New Bristol was to persuade him to take Yinka and Edrize into his personal service. She sensed his doubts, although he did not voice them aloud.

Her concern for Yinka's safety was a real one. Esmee had often been the only woman on board her father's ships and there had been many occasions when she could not ignore the tension her presence created. Fortunately the sailors' fear of her father had offered her some crude protection, and when they could, the crew sought distraction in the services of the female slaves. On the island the slaves were all male. With the exception of herself, Serenity and Hannah Hardy, the planters too were all male. An underlying current of discontent lurked in the vast majority of the population.

'Please, Aeneas, they love each other. Think of Yinka's child. Sole needs a father.' She had not found a way to tell him that the babe who now toddled at Yinka's feet was her own half-sister. When she practised saying the words she had the terrible premonition of releasing a tornado which might overwhelm them all. She remained silent.

The union of one newly arrived slave couple when the rest of the men had to endure celibacy seemed to many to be unjust. Esmee feared that unless Yinka was safely united with the boy she loved, she might well be passed from man to man in order to keep some sort of peace.

In the face of her insistence, Aeneas acquiesced. An additional room was added to the slave hut so that Gideon too could pass his nights with Yinka, his wet nurse, and Esmee could then sleep undisturbed.

The two young people worked hard. Esmee, pampered and alone, envied them their simple pleasure in each other and the company of the children. In being separated from Gideon she felt as if she was being punished. There was nobody to whom she could turn for company or comfort. She was utterly alone.

During her absence Hannah Hardy, while still in Serenity's service, had formed an attachment to a very devout planter, and now, as a married woman, bore the unlikely name of Mistress Ezekial Smiles. It was difficult to imagine a more unsuitable title, for neither Hannah nor Ezekial appeared to view the world with either pleasure or amusement. Hard work and endurance seemed to be their chosen path in life, but they clearly found some comfort in being together. As Esmee overheard one discontented planter remark: 'At least Ezekial has something to smile about!' Clearly more women would have to be brought in soon.

Esmee had plenty of time to dwell on this and a hundred other issues, but above all her thoughts were dominated by the realisation that, having delivered her up to her husband, Samuel now pointedly stayed away. She could not blame him. It had been she who had made the decision to return to Eden. Even now they might have been together, aboard the *Evangelina* or perhaps in some uncharted paradise, living together as lovers, content in a perfect world. Miserably she taunted herself: Perhaps I was wrong in thinking that Sam would have regrets. She certainly did. Meanwhile she endured the knowledge that a few yards away, across the square, he was reunited with his wife.

In the meantime, Esmee had no way of knowing what her step-daughter's reaction was to her arrival though it was not difficult to guess. It was several days before they came face to face and the meeting was not a pleasant one.

Serenity visited early one morning with the express intention of speaking to her father. Esmee felt her pulse quicken as her rival came into the room. The acid pain of jealousy scorched through her at the thought of this woman, united with Sam for all the world to see, mistress of his bed chamber, mother of his children. She could hardly bear the thought of seeing Samuel's babies and finding the man she loved reflected in their image.

As it was, Serenity came alone. Ignoring Esmee, she went straight to Aeneas and proceeded to bend very close to him, speaking low and fast so that no one else should hear. Aeneas looked ill at ease. He kept nodding his head impatiently, trying to draw Esmee into their circle, but Serenity resolutely kept her back turned. It was clear that she had nothing of importance to say but was determined to claim her father for herself.

At last he managed to say: 'Serenity, my dear, will you not share my happiness in having my wife back with me?'

'If that is what you wish, Papa.'

'And my son – surely you would wish to meet you baby brother?'

It was just the sort of remark to provoke trouble. Even as Aeneas spoke, Esmee felt her cheeks grow hot.

Looking her up and down, Serenity said: 'My dear Papa, a grey-hound would not consider itself related to a mongrel. Neither, I fear, do I.' Before he could remonstrate she swept out of the room and was gone.

Aeneas eyed Esmee remorsefully. 'I am so sorry, my dear. I fear she has still not accepted our marriage. Please do not fret.'

'I won't.'

Esmee felt moved to place a kiss on her husband's forehead. In spite of all the difficulties he was consistently kind to her. She also realised with a sense of disbelief that over the past few weeks he appeared to have convinced himself that Gideon was truly his child. In a strange way she resented that fact. While they had been on San Bernaldo Gideon had belonged to her alone. Now he was young Master Craven, heir to a considerable property. It made her uneasy.

Meanwhile, as the wife of the only peer on the island and the only resident shareholder of the company, as well as being related to the Governor by marriage, Esmee herself, in spite of the petty jealousies, was a woman of importance. Perhaps one day this interesting phenomenon would come in useful.

As it was, the future stretched ahead with a narrow, unending promise of boredom. Planning meals, sewing garments, making medicines, overseeing the smooth running of her house, spending endless hours in prayer, became her life.

After the initial novelty of having her back, Aeneas took to coming to her bed chamber about twice a week. Always he came in quietly, as if afraid to disturb her.

'My dear, with your permission?'

Furtively he made love to her. Obligingly she turned this way and that, trailed her hands over his body, lifted herself, guided and stimulated him when his confidence seemed to wane. At such times she sought refuge in thinking about anything other than what was happening to her. Aeneas took pains not to hurt her, but like a starving woman offered a tit-bit, his love making served only to leave her increasingly hungry for the feast that was Samuel.

After he finished, Aeneas expressed his appreciation in the same way as he thanked her for the meal that appeared nightly on their table.

'I thank you, my dear. I am most obliged.'

She was relieved if he returned to his own bed, but some nights he fell asleep at her side. As she lay awake, feeling restless and dissatisfied, he appeared to sleep so heavily that a thunder clap would be hard pressed to rouse him.

One night she could bear the confines of the house no longer so she dressed and crept outside. By night New Bristol seemed ominous. The trees that in daylight offered shade and comfort now seemed to threaten her. The noises that by day were easily identifiable took on a sinister mystery. She nearly turned back but the thought of being cooped up in the house, and of Aeneas still in her bed, drove her on.

Deliberately she kept to the shadows to avoid drawing attention to herself. Who knew what monsters might be lurking in the dark?

Having tiptoed along two sides of the square she wandered round to the back of the church and there found a well-defined path leading up towards the summit of the island. Taking courage, she began to climb the slope. Finger-like twigs snatched at her hair and skirts. Spiders webs, sticky as honey, clung to her face but she would not be diverted.

Once or twice she came to junctions where other paths branched off but she stuck to the way ahead, hoping that on her return journey the track would be as easy to identify. She had a nasty feeling that once off the main route she might be lost forever.

When she finally reached the summit she was rewarded with a panoramic view of the island. Turning slowly she could see the ocean on all sides, the grey of the waters dazzled with moonlight, laced with white horses.

It was a beautiful sight. She was truly glad that she had come. Here it was like being on the very top of the world, an empress looking down on all that she ruled.

'Esmeralda.'

The soft voice made her jump so violently that for a moment she could not speak.

When she did, her own voice came out in a rush. 'Samuel! Whatever are you doing here?'

'I saw you cross the square. You shouldn't be out alone. Does Aeneas know where you are?'

'No. He – he sleeps well.' She blushed for the reason but in the dark he could not see.

For an age they were silent, both awkward in the knowledge that neither of them should be there. To break the tension, she said: 'What brings you abroad?'

'I wander out most nights, just to check on security.' He surveyed the bay below them as if expecting to see enemy craft approaching.

Esmee thought: At least he does not mind being away from his wife's side. It gave her a warm glow of pleasure. She said: 'It is a fair night.'

He brushed the pleasantry aside. 'I never see you. Do you avoid me?'

She shook her head. 'Of course not. Rather, you seem to avoid me. You never come to the house.' She didn't know what else to say. Whenever she had the chance she looked out for him, welcoming even the briefest glimpse as he went about his duties. Never had she been invited to visit his house. Not once had she seen the twins, except at a distance, so that it was impossible clearly to recognise them. Serenity had seen to that.

He said: 'I am much occupied.'

'Of course.' He was moving the conversation back to safer ground. She asked: 'How is your family?'

'Well. They are well. The children grow. And yours?'

'Gideon is in good health.'

'I am glad to hear it.'

For a moment they both stood in silence then Esmee said: 'I suppose I should go back.'

'I suppose you should.' Sam did not move.

She took a step forward and as she did so he reached out and caught her arm.

'Esmee, don't torment me like this. You can't know how the very sight of you drives me into a . . .'

'No, Sam. We musn't – ' Gently she tried to extricate herself from his hold but already his lips rested against her temple.

It was what she had waited for since that first moment she had seen him on the quay at Tilbury. She couldn't pull away from him now. She wanted the feel of his mouth, the pressure of his body, more than life itself.

It was she who loosened her bodice, unfastened the ties of his breeches, pressed herself to him until he moaned with ecstacy. For the first time ever she knew what love was about, what force drove the living creatures in the forest, the skies, the ocean, to risk everything for this fleeting moment of paradise.

'Samuel!'

'Oh, my love, my love.' He held her to him long after he was spent, smothering her face and neck with his kisses, staying inside her so that the hard reassurance of his presence filled her with delight.

Later, arm in arm they began the descent, stopping to hug and kiss, helpless to resist the pleasure of each other. As they emerged behind the church, Sam said: 'Will you come again?'

'Yes.'

'When?'

'When – ' She could not say when. It could only be when Aeneas was asleep. She could not equate his fumblings with this gift of magic, not spoil this perfection by referring to the perfunctory demands of her marriage bed.

In the end, she could only say: 'I'll come whenever I can.'

It was hard to let go of him but in the end her fingers slipped away from the palm of his hand, caressing him for a last brief moment before he turned and strode away. She waited until he was across the square then hastened back towards her own prison.

For the moment her joy was overlaid by fear lest Aeneas should be awake, but as she tiptoed into her chamber, he was still there in her bed, breathing deeply and regularly. Silently she slipped out of her clothes and climbed in beside him. He gave a tiny grunt and flung his arm across her, claiming her back into his possession, virtually imprisoning her. Closing her eyes she escaped again, to the joyful contemplation of Samuel's love.

The pattern was now set for a new way of living. Each night when Esmee retired to bed she lay in the dark, listening for the clues that would tell her what Aeneas was doing. In one way she was now more of a prisoner than ever, more dependent on his random actions. If he came to her she would endure the visit, impatient for him to sleep so that she could escape to that other world. When he did come, in a curious way she was disturbed by his intrusion to the point where she was already ripe and ready for Samuel to release her. They had so little time together.

On the nights when Aeneas did not come to her, she would lie rigid with frustration, listening through the panelling of the wall as he tossed and grunted. On those nights he was not a heavy sleeper. Once, throwing caution to the winds, she dressed and crept down the stairs, wanting Samuel too badly to care about the consequences, but as she was about to open the door she heard movements in the chamber above.

In all probability Aeneas had risen to use the chamber pot but she knew that he might, just might, decide to visit her. In abject panic she flew back up the stairway tearing off her clothes in a frenzy, flinging herself on to the bed and panting beneath the covers, listening for him above the rush of her blood. Once again there was the creak of his bed and then silence.

On those precious nights when Esmee could slip away, she scurried for the path, nearly floating in anticipation of what was to come. She knew that many nights Samuel watched for her in vain while she fretted at home, but sometimes when she did manage to escape, he was not there and she suffered an agony of jealousy and disappointment.

When he was there, the delight in each other was total. She seemed to be living on another plane of feeling, one that stayed with her for perhaps a day or two then drove her to distraction with the desire to taste again the rapture.

But as the weeks passed, another canker began to set in. All the while that Esmee lay in Samuel's arms, she was haunted by the knowledge that within the hour they would have to part. She found it increasingly difficult to enjoy the present for her knowledge of the empty future that would follow.

Sometimes Sam too seemed distracted. Sliding away from her one night, he said: 'When you were on San Bernaldo, did you see any other people?'

'What sort of people?' She was glad of a distraction.

'Natives? Indians?'

Esmee shook her head. 'I don't think the island was inhabited. Why do you ask?'

'I just wondered.' He looked anxious and she felt his heaviness begin to infect her. She did not say anything for fear of provoking him into admitting some dissatisfaction that might threaten their continued meetings.

He said: 'When you were on the island, were there many other women?'

'There were none.'

Carefully, he said: 'You must have made friends with the men?'

The tension increased. 'Friends, yes. Some were very kind to me.'

She did not want to think about Musa. She did not want to remember his wisdom, his tenderness. She said: 'You forget that I was alone. I gave birth to a child there, on a slave plantation.'

'Esmee, I am sorry, I didn't mean to . . .' He pulled her close and kissed her tenderly. 'It is just that I feel so . . .' He did not voice his pain.

'What are we going to do?' she asked, as they lay back in the hollow they had long since claimed as their marital bed.

'What should we do? We should never have returned here.' She felt him grow tense again. Easing himself away from her, he said: 'For myself I would be willing to abandon everything, to run from here if you came with me, but . . .' He sighed. 'I still cannot do that to my uncle. He has been goodness itself to me. If I desert Serenity that too would hurt him, and as for taking you away from him . . .'

'I know.' She held him close. 'We shall just have to be careful.' She searched for something to amuse him, saying: 'Do you realise there are only four women on this island and you are bedding two of them?' But as the words came out, scalding jealousy of his time spent with Serenity threatened to burn her up. She said: 'Oh, Samuel, I can't bear it!'

He rocked her in his arms. 'Don't think of it. In any case, I mostly sleep apart from my wife. She does not want me and I certainly do not want her.' He paused. 'Since the twins were born there have been a handful of times when the situation seemed to demand that I keep up the pretence of being a husband, otherwise . . .'

Esmee nestled against his shoulder. A grey pall of gloom continued to spread over their stolen joy.

Sam said: 'What of me? I have to live with the knowledge that my uncle has a claim on you every night.'

'Not every night, only when I . . .' She could not tell him that each time she gave herself to him, she had already been possessed by his uncle. Threatened by tears, she said: 'Samuel, don't. It has nothing to do with you and me. It does not touch me. If I do not play the dutiful wife then he will be suspicious.' She thought of Musa again and added: 'Nothing lasts forever.'

Hugging Samuel close, she sought consolation from the knowledge that she had kept her promise to Musa and taken care of Edrize. Even now Yinka's belly was swelling with a second child.

Sam sat up and began to put on his clothes. 'I must get back.' As he stood up she realised that her last words, meant to give him some hope, could just as easily apply to their stolen love affair.

The atmosphere between them was tense. At their parting place they were silent, not knowing how to separate without pain. Sam said: 'I will see you again?'

'Of course. Whenever I can.'

He kissed her on the temple, almost perfunctorily, and a mist of sadness settled over her as he walked away. What had started out as something wonderful was now spoiled by the need to have more and more of it.

Heavily she made her way back into the house, weighed down with regrets. As she went to mount the stairs she was mortified to see that a light burned beneath the parlour door. Creeping across and opening it, she found Aeneas sitting there.

'Esmeralda, where in the name of Our Lord have you been?'

'Aeneas, I – I could not sleep. I just went out for a breath of air.'

He shook his head, tutting to himself. 'How could you be so foolish? I have been beside myself with worry. It is more than an hour that I have waited. I almost went across to rouse Samuel and set a search party in progress.'

'No! There is nothing to be anxious about, truly. I sometimes feel the need for a little air.' She longed to escape upstairs and nurse her pain.

Aeneas rose from his chair and took her arm, searching her face. She smiled stiffly at him. He looked disturbed. 'Well, I forbid you to go out again alone. If you must venture outside, then call me and I will accompany you.'

'Thank you. You are kind.'

Relief that he did not seem suspicious was overridden by the dull ache of regret that already threatened her peace of mind. Never again would she be able to risk meeting Sam. For his sake as much as her own she must stay away from him. The thought of not seeing him, the knowledge that their love affair was over, was worse than anything she had ever endured. As she climbed the stairs with Aeneas holding her elbow, she thought: Please Lord, just let me die.

She managed to speak a few words to Samuel the next morning on the way into the church. 'Aeneas knows that I went out last night. He forbids it.'

In response he bowed as if she had merely passed the time of day. She could see that his face was tense. Throughout the service he sat stiffly, his eyes focused on some distant place behind Minister Shergold.

From the other side of the aisle, with Serenity seated in front of her in the place designated for the Governor's wife, Esmee asked herself: How am I going to survive? *However* am I going to survive? There was no answer.

THIRTY-FIVE

Sam was disturbed by the sound of voices, then he realised that they were inside his own head. He guessed it was about two o'clock in the morning. None of the clocks brought out from England worked any longer, their mechanisms having long since rusted in this humid purgatory. In response to the sultry heat, he lifted the damp hair away from his neck in the hope of finding some cool night air.

He was still sitting at his table, trying to complete a report to send back to England. He must have fallen asleep. With tired eyes he skimmed over it. Reading his own words only increased his frustration. Here he was, Governor in sole charge of Eden Island, and yet the company back in London still insisted on interfering.

In their latest instruction they had specifically overruled his decision to put James Redyard on trial for murder. The man was a bully, the worst sort of planter. He was mean with his servants, depriving them of all but the barest necessities for survival, and sometimes not even that. In addition he had a vicious streak that derived pleasure from inflicting pain.

Poor Edward Flood had become the focus for Redyard's violence. Twice Sam had officially warned the planter about his brutality, but he had paid little heed. Finally, perhaps inevitably, he had beaten Flood so severely that he had died of his wounds. Now the company insisted that Redyard be shipped back to England. The reason was clear. He had friends in high places. Once home he would escape the consequences of his crime. Sam fretted silently to himself.

He stretched his aching back, twisting his neck to ease the stiffness, then went over to the window. Somewhere a dog barked disconsolately, otherwise there was a brief silence before the emptiness of the night gave way to the bustle of the day.

He remembered what the square had looked like when they first cleared it, the half a dozen huts those early venturers had shared. Later he had watched the building of his own house, admired the construction of the church. Now the village consisted of at least fifty timber dwellings, two brick houses and a jumble of stores, boiling houses, curing sheds and slave huts. To his jaded eyes they looked like ugly scars on the green skin of the island. Neither he nor they belonged here.

His uncle's house was opposite and he could see that a light burned in the downstairs room. He knew instinctively that it was Esmeralda. As always, the thought of her gnawed at him like hunger pangs. These days he hardly saw her, only on those occasions when it would have looked suspicious not to do so, and then never alone. It was now eight months, two weeks and three days since they had last . . . In spite of himself he could not help counting off the days in his log, penned discreetly in the top right-hand corner of each day's entry. It was a foolishness, a weakness, and yet he could not help himself.

He knew that she was restless at night, suffering from cramps. He yearned to cross the few yards that separated them and massage her legs, offer her comfort. He felt the familiar tightening in his chest, as he thought: Her child is due very shortly.

With a heavy sigh he began to pace the room. The question was back in his mind, the one question that felt like the most important of his life – was he the father of Esmeralda's baby? He could not ask her. In any case, he guessed that she probably did not know. He shut out the vision of his uncle crawling over her, emptying his elderly seed into her.

Ever since the night Aeneas had discovered her gone from the house, they had conducted themselves with such restraint. Esmeralda had made it plain that she would not risk their affair coming to light. She was right, of course. There was too much to lose. Apart from hurting his uncle, he had his own position as Governor to consider. It was part of his role to set an example. But his burning thoughts gave the lie to everything he was supposed to be.

With a sigh that came from his boots, he returned to the table. Picking up his quill and dipping it in the ink, he wrote the word NEGROES and underlined it, then gazed into the distance. The slaves had become a nightmare. He had done everything he could to make their lot bearable but the company had brought in too many of them.

The rule of thumb was one slave per acre and they had a hundred acres under sugar. In fact at the most there had only ever been ninety slaves, but of those, thirty-seven had soon run away and formed their own community in the hinterland behind New Bristol.

The planters had organised slave hunts, bringing back six or seven at a time. By public consent, although not Sam's, the runaways had been punished. In his view punishment made no sense. Half of those chastised were no longer fit for work and two out of every seven hanged themselves rather than face the future. More had since run away. Sam's entreaties for the planters to try reward instead of punishment went unnoticed. Only those black men taken from the *Evangelina* and into Sam's personal service seemed at peace with the world.

The time was nigh for the committee to debate the issue of the slaves' freedom but he had little doubt that they would decide against it. All his best endeavours on the Africans' behalf had failed. The fact was the slaves were desperate men with nothing to lose. Many of the planters were afraid of them. Sam had made it clear that if they failed to set the black men free, then he would resign. That would mean returning to England with Serenity and leaving Esmee behind . . .

He found some diversion by preparing instead a report on the events of the day before. Yesterday, a sloop called the *Greyhound* had put into port with the first passengerload of women. Sam felt a curious mixture of amusement and pathos as he recalled the scene. Picking up his quill, he crossed out the word 'Negroes' and began to write.

Yesterday, thanks be to God, the sloop Greyhound *came safely into port. With the exception of those few wives whom we were expecting, we had no knowledge of how many other women might be aboard. This posed some difficulty as the majority of men on the island had expressed themselves anxious to marry. I was therefore left with the dilemma of how to decide in a just manner which men should marry – and to which women.*

As a result we set the sick to making up two sets of wooden balls, each bearing identical numbers. All of those planters wishing for a wife were instructed to take a ball. The identical numbers were placed into a sack to be picked out by however many women

292

happened to be on board. In the event we had ninety-one hopeful bridegrooms and only twenty-seven brides.

Sam put the quill down and began to walk around the room once more. He felt that the choosing ceremony had smacked of farce. One by one the women had been nominated to step forward and instructed to take a ball from the sack.

Sam had been called upon to act as an observer. Looking round at the men, he watched their faces. Their expressions depended greatly on the appearance of the women, at one moment hopeful then the next filled with trepidation in case they drew the corresponding number.

By and large the new arrivals did not look likely to inspire passion. The youngest was a girl of about seventeen and so scrawny she would have made an excellent billhook. The oldest was a bent creature in her fifties, toothless and nearly bald.

It had already been agreed that there would be no going back. Once a man's number was selected then he must accept that his chosen partner was decreed by God. No one was permitted to reject his divinely selected bride.

Some of the pairings looked bizarre to say the very least. Malachi Kent, the smith, found himself wed to a woman with one leg. Abel Stark, who was barely nineteen, won the services of the bald-headed hag. Those who had been unsuccessful in drawing a number were soon congratulating themselves on their lucky escape.

Stoically Sam completed his account, omitting the more ribald comments. He had little hope that the influx of the fairer sex would raise the morale of the islanders.

But none of this mattered in comparison with the bulk of his report. During the time they had been on Eden, things had changed out of all recognition. They had come here as planters, pilgrims, full of ideals and hopes. Year by year he had watched those early dreams abandoned. In spite of the fertile soil they could still barely grow enough to feed themselves. No matter what commercial crop they tried, it failed. The dye woods that had at first made the island so attractive had all been cut down. Where did they go from here?

The door opened and Serenity came in, her face grey from lack of sleep. 'What on earth are you doing?'

'I have to finish this report. Go back to bed.'

She hung around, ignoring his words. After a while she said:

293

'Zephaniah has a chill. I have only just got him settled. I myself am feeling feverish.'

He put down his quill and tried to give her his attention. The years on the island had quickly taken a toll on her looks. Her fair skin did not react kindly to the ravages of sun and heat. Her hair, once rich and corn-coloured, was now washed out, like overbaked straw. He felt a moment's pity for her.

'I'll come to bed,' he said.

Blowing out the candle, he followed her back up to their chamber. In the year since the twins' birth he had made love to her only two or three times, and then only when he was burning for Esmeralda. Afterwards he had realised how avidly she had responded to his demands.

Now he turned her to him and looked into her face, hoping to find something that he had missed before, some spark of love or sweetness. Her eyes, gold in the smoky light of the candle, regarded him provocatively. Her head tilted back, she loosened her robe and let it drop to the ground then fell to her knees and began to undress him, greedy in her need. It did not light a spark in him.

When he could bear her attentions no longer, he lifted her and carried her to the bed, kneeling over her and emptying himself. His heart was like stone.

Gasping and writhing, Serenity pleasured herself on his body. He waited until she had finished then cuddled her to him. Into the darkness he said: 'I think it is time we left here.' He felt her grow tense.

'We cannot abandon everything. The plantation, the colony – the church.'

Sam knew she was thinking about Shergold. He was almost certain that his wife and the Minister had denied themselves any physical contact, and he knew that this very denial only fanned the flames of their obsession with one another.

He wanted to be angry, but couldn't summon the energy. He felt sorry for Serenity with her sharp, spiteful nature. In the next room he heard Zephaniah cough. Immediately his wife jumped up as if tugged by some invisible string. Sam stretched and sighed. Her life, her obsession with religion, her overprotectiveness of the children, meant nothing to him. He feared that he was an unnatural father but the twins were strangers to him. He was kind to them but he did not love them.

His mind wandered back to his unfinished report. The Spanish

... that was the crux of the matter. Eden was no longer truly a colony but had become a harbourage for privateers. Ships came from England, France, Holland, and using New Bristol harbour as a base, preyed on the Spanish galleons that crossed the Main, packed to their gunwales with gold. Sam knew for certain that one day the wrath of Spain was bound to descend upon them. In preparation they had constructed thirteen more fortifications, employed master gunners, carried out weekly musters. Everyone was ready but in his heart Sam knew it was like a hare planning its flight from a pack of hounds: hopeless. Again, he did not know what to do.

When Serenity finally came back to bed there was a change in her. She slipped beneath the cotton cover but held herself aloof from him. Just as he was giving himself up to sleep, she said: 'I don't think I could ever go back to England. I am certain that God would always want me to stay here.'

He reached out and squeezed her arm, forgiving her. He would only leave if his uncle consented to come with him. If Serenity chose to stay, then she must do as she saw fit. He was not the sort of husband to force her to disobey her conscience. At the thought of such a parting, it was almost as if some light dawned in his darkness. He could feel the door of his own gaol begin to open.

Esmee felt that her pregnancy would last forever. The July heat was such that night or day it was impossible to rest. Going to the window, she looked out towards the church, remembering the path that rose behind it. She longed to walk there again.

'My dear, I hope you aren't thinking of wandering out after dark?' chided Aeneas. He regarded her with a furrowed brow. Since she had broken the news to him of her condition he had fussed over her like a hen with one chick.

She sat down in a cane chair and raised her feet on to a stool. The door of the house was flung wide, letting the merest whisper of a breeze across the low wooden verandah. A sun as big as a merry-go-round dived smoothly into a crimson-splashed sea. They lit no lamps for fear of attracting a thousand insects.

Esmee said: 'I am sorry if my restlessness disturbs you. It is just that sometimes I feel so – ' She shrugged. 'It is my condition,' she added quickly, in case he should misunderstand her remark.

He came to sit close beside her and she fought down her irritation. All she wanted was to sit and dream and his presence was intrusive.

How could she think about Samuel when Aeneas was breathing down her neck?

She said: 'I think the birth will be soon. I remember something of the same feeling before Gideon was born.'

Aeneas flinched, as if the subject of Gideon's birth were painful to him. Esmee feared that for him it was like accidentally biting on a bad tooth, a short, sharp pain that faded to a dull ache. This discomfort lingered in the air.

Finally he said: 'Well, I absolutely forbid it after dark, and even in daylight at least stay close to home. There are many dangers out there.'

'Nonsense.' She squeezed his hand which rested on the arm of her chair, adding: 'I always carry a stout stick. And besides, my cry would drown out a cannon.'

The birth was not due for a couple of weeks. In some ways she wanted it over but in others she wanted to stay in this limbo where she drifted through the days waited on by Yinka, pampered by her overindulgent husband. Above everything else she was relieved of the ordeal of his sexual forays.

She shifted position because the baby was pressing up under her ribs. 'He's kicking,' she said to break the silence. She always called the baby 'he' because that was what Aeneas wanted to hear. She could not blame him. Not once had he questioned her about Gideon's paternity although sometimes she caught him looking at her son with a puzzled frown, as if he might discern who the father was from the child's looks. Once he had learned that he was to have a child of his own, his interest in Gideon had waned. Esmee knew he had no real feeling for her boy and this only deepened her own maternal passion.

She fretted that Gideon still spent more time with Yinka than he did with herself but she said nothing, ever mindful that beneath his calm exterior Aeneas might yet nurse anger and resentment towards her son. If this other baby turned out to be a boy then surely her husband would want his true flesh and blood to be his heir?

She rested her hands on the hard bulge of her stomach and gently rocked him – or her. This time Aeneas had no reason to think that this was not his child, and Esmee had no reason to believe that it was. Everything told her that Samuel, beautiful virile Samuel, was the father of the baby that moved within her. It made the limbo of her existence bearable.

Getting up, Aeneas closed the verandah door. He hovered by her for a while then said: 'I'll just go and see if there is any news.'

For the past two days half a dozen Spanish ships had been anchored off the coastline, just outside the reefs and out of range of the cannon of the New Bristol fort. Earlier in the day an advance party had sent out a felucca and attempted to negotiate a passage through the rocks. Thomas Axe's musketeers had fired on them, driving them back to sea.

The island was on twenty-four-hour alert but everyone was confident that this was merely a Spanish show of force. They would surely not attempt to land amid the rocks and reefs that protected the coast. Fortunately there were no foreign ships tied up in New Bristol harbour that might serve to provoke an attack.

While Aeneas was out Esmee retired to bed but she could not sleep so she got up again. Ignoring his instructions, she put on her gown and slippers and went outside, seeking a breath of cool air.

She did not intend to do more than wander across the square, but soon she found herself behind the church, climbing the steep escarpment, scrambling up to the ridge, aware of the extra weight she carried in the form of her unborn child. Stopping to get her breath, she leaned back against the trunk of a maho tree, from which the sailors used the bark to make thongs for their oars. Slowly her heart stopped thumping quite so madly and she took stock of her surroundings.

Coming out of the summit, she welcomed the long-remembered view of the sea. Still panting, she tried to keep very still, regulating her breathing so she could hear above the whoosh of her heart. Gradually the continuous hiss of the waves reached her from far below. It was a somnolent, soothing sound.

Esmee let out her breath in a gasp of pleasure as she looked down on the fortifications of New Bristol. Figures paraded regularly along their perimeter. She wondered if Samuel was there – or was he at home in bed with his wife?

She stifled that particular pain before it started. Wherever he was, the Spanish presence would be his major preoccupation. Tonight his last thought would be of making love to his wife.

Serenity had still not accepted what she had been told of Gideon's birth. She had voiced all those questions that Aeneas had not asked: loudly, accusingly. In response her father had asserted: 'It is as you agreed, my dear. Gideon as the first-born boy is the Craven heir.'

'But Papa!'

Pushed to the limit Aeneas asked: 'Do you perhaps question my performance as a husband? My ability to father a child?'

'No, of course not, I – ' His directness had thrown her into confusion but still she nursed a silent, resentful malice.

Esmee began to feel tired. Here on the roof of the island the air was distinctly cooler. When she got home she would sleep.

She was about to begin the descent when something made her look back, down across the tumbling cliffs towards the south-east. She thought she saw a movement in the water, not one thing but a series of shadows. At first she thought it might be dolphins but the shapes were too regular and solid. She screwed up her eyes and gradually the outline of a shallop came into focus, then another and another. Smoothly, one by one, they slid on to the rocky shore and tiny figures waded across to the beach and started to climb the cliff.

With a gasp Esmee turned back and began to run, slipping and sliding in her haste. Her heart thundered and a sharp pain paralysed her momentarily but she did not let up in her descent. Breathless, almost incoherent, she ran home, pounding against the door, stumbling up the stairs and bursting into the parlour.

Aeneas had been about to remonstrate with her but at the sight of her face, he stopped. 'Esmeralda? Is it the baby?'

'No. No.' She took deep gulps of air. Grabbing his sleeve to stir him into action, she called: 'Quick, Aeneas, quick! Sound the alarm! The Spanish are coming. We are being attacked!'

Praisetogod Shergold was awakened by the sound of musket fire. He was out of bed before his eyes opened, trying to pinpoint what was happening. As he fumbled for his clothes every sense was assailed by gunfire, heat and smoke.

Stepping outside, the first thing he saw was an orange pattern of flickering lights down by the fort. He clutched his breast. The demon Spaniards had landed!

He began to race towards the church, ready to ring the bell, but as he did so he heard other musket reports – deeper, more coordinated. At the same time he saw the flash of sporadic musket fire away to the south.

By now other planters were emerging from their houses.

'Quick,' he called. 'We are being attacked from all sides!'

The able-bodied men dashed back for their weapons while the

women and children made for the security of the church.

Serenity! Praisetogod looked around but could not see her. Immediately he hastened across to the Governor's house. As he ran he found a certain satisfaction in the thought that at last Almighty God was making His displeasure known.

Without knocking, he barged into the house to find Serenity and the twins about to come out.

'Minister?'

He reached out and took one of the babies. 'Come, dear lady, come!' He bundled her outside, asking: 'Where is your husband?'

'He is organising the resistance. The Spaniards have landed.'

'And he left you alone?'

'I was to go straight to the church but first of all I stopped to pray.'

'My dear lady!' Praisetogod hesitated. The sounds of firing grew steadily more intense. Already a barrier of choking brown smoke blotted out their surroundings.

'This is a sign!' said the Minister. 'God's plague on the island. I have preached here in vain. You alone have paid heed to my words.'

'Praisetogod!' Serenity looked at him lovingly.

He said: 'Do you trust me, my dear? I know that God has plans for you and me. This is His signal. Now is the time to show our faith to Him.'

'How?'

He pulled her arm. 'We must leave here. I know where there is a boat – a canoe. It is laid up for when the men go fishing. We must travel north and take it across to the small island. There is a hut there that was erected when the island was surveyed. We shall be safe in God's hands. He will tell us what to do then.'

'But Samuel . . .'

Praisetogod bowed his head. 'Your husband is not an evil man, but he is misguided. He too has chosen to ignore my warnings. Now God is casting him down.' He turned Serenity towards him and the twins grumbled as their chubby legs were pressed one against the other. Shergold seemed unaware of them. To Serenity he said: 'And you – do you have the courage to put your faith in Our Lord and walk away from this Gomorrah?'

'But what of the twins?'

'They must come with us. They are God's innocents.'

Breathing in deeply, she gave a gasp of emotion. 'Then, yes! Yes!

If you think this is what God wants, I will go with you!'

Encircling her with his arm, placing his faith in his God, Praiseto-god Shergold led the woman he loved through the ruin of their blazing crops and on towards their destiny.

THIRTY-SIX

With her baby son strapped to her back and Sole slung across her hip, Yinka raced ahead towards the church. Carrying Gideon, Esmee followed behind, hampered by the bulk of her unborn child. As they passed through the doorway, she took one last look and was appalled by what she saw.

Plumes of smoke blotted out large tracts of the landscape. In other places flame raged over the fields. It seemed that all of their crops were on fire. Could it be that Filipe Ortega was on the island and seeking revenge for their parting act of retribution?

From New Bristol harbour itself a discordant hubbub of cries was punctuated by the whip crack of musket fire. Ice-cold with fear, Esmee knew that Samuel was somewhere down there. She could only guess where Aeneas might be.

An increasing terror hovered like a frosty haze over the rest of the women, huddled together in the well of the church. Watching them, Esmee asked herself: Can they really have come all this way just to die? Hannah Smiles was on her knees, praying.

Esmee looked around her thinking that someone should take control. She sought for Serenity who, as Governor's wife, might be expected to give some guidance. She was not there.

'Where's Serenity?' she asked. At her side Yinka hugged her baby son to her. She whimpered: 'Where can Edrize be?'

Patting her friend's arm, Esmee wondered whether she should go and search for Samuel's wife. There was a certain sense of self-laceration in the thought that she would be protecting the woman who stood between Esmee and the man she loved, but as she listened the sounds of the conflict grew even louder. She would not leave Gideon and could not take him with her. Serenity would have to find her own salvation.

'There is nothing to fear!' she called out to the panicking women. 'The Spaniards will respect a church as a place of refuge.' She did not know if this was true but the wives appeared to find some brief comfort in her words. She said: 'Take courage and pray for your men.' Her voice trembled as she thought of what was happening outside.

Stifling her own fears, she began to organise them, barricading the door with a stout pole that slotted across the centre of the archway. In her heart she knew it would not keep the Spaniards out for long but if offered some small sense of added security.

Inside the church it grew pitch black. No one had the means to make a light. The women moaned and sobbed and for a moment Esmee was reminded of the despairing cries aboard a slave ship. She called out: 'You must not give up hope!'

Her words did little to raise her own spirits. All the time she remembered stories she had heard of Spanish cruelty. Again she thought of Filipe Ortega and her courage threatened to fail her.

Raising her voice, she started to sing, a simple song that she had known all her life. It was called 'John, Come Kiss Me Now'. Why it came into her head she did not know but as she sang she felt herself to be back in those far-off days when she had sung it as a young girl, accompanied by a crewman on his pipe.

After a while other women began to join in. The sweet melody drew them together. They sang as if they were offering up a hymn of praise, sometimes a solo, then a duet, a quartet or all together, over and over. Everyone sought to make the song perfect. Nobody seemed to think it was strange that Esmee had chosen a secular, not a religious song to give them hope.

A hammering on the church door halted their performance. The women fell silent, staring at the archway. Nobody moved.

'Open!'

Esmee looked around her, wanting some sign that she should do so. Still nobody moved.

After a while the voice called: 'You come out now. We do you no bad. You stay inside and we burn church down.'

With despair Esmee realised that the Spaniards had been victorious. When no one else moved, she went forward and unbarred the door. As it swung open the extent of the disaster was revealed.

The square was thronged with people: one or perhaps even two thousand Spanish sailors. Their presence was overpowering. In growing panic Esmee searched the sea of jubilant faces, all strangers. She sought frantically for anyone whom she recognised, drowning in the knowledge that by now all the islanders might be slaughtered.

Then she saw them, a row of captives. 'Sweet Jesus!' She could hardly bring herself to look again in case . . .

Stealing herself for the ultimate pain, her eyes travelled along the line – and there he was, the defeated Governor. He stood very still, head held high, dignified in captivity. A trickle of blood had dried on his cheek.

'Samuel!' His name died on Esmee's lips. Almost as an afterthought she looked again and saw Aeneas. Old Ezra stood just by him, and farther down the line were Nat Rouse and Thomas Warner.

She did not remember going outside. All at once there was a volley of fire, demanding silence for the Spanish Captain.

He stepped forward, a short, thin, black-haired man, notable only for the quiet dignity of his bearing. Addressing the gathering, he said: 'I, Don Marco de Castillio, do today this seventeenth day of July in the year of Our Lord 1638, take possession of this island in the name of His Most Catholic Majesty, Filipe IV of Spain.' The Spaniards cheered, drowning out all other sounds.

As the hubbub died down, Samuel raised his voice. 'Captain, I ask you to show mercy to your prisoners. These are peaceful men and women. They have no quarrel with Spain.'

Don Marco said: 'I show mercy to women and children. They will be sent home to England.' With his head he indicated the harbour and the *Greyhound* tied up by the jetty. Addressing Sam, he said: 'Men will be prisoner. They go to Cartagena, then to Spain.'

Esmee swallowed back her fear. Memories of Filipe Ortega, of her father's dead crew members, crowded into her mind. She must not dwell on what might happen to her men.

Samuel asked: 'And the slaves?'

'Now they Spanish slaves.'

Esmee's first thought was for Edrize and her promise to Musa to keep him safe. Beside her Yinka set up the strange wailing noise that seemed to come naturally to African women in times of grief. Esmee turned to comfort her.

She was about to say something when two of Don Marco's men

moved away from the throng and came towards the women. For a moment Esmee did not realise what was happening then suddenly she was grabbed by the arms and the men began to drag her and Yinka away from the others. Memories of that last evening in Ortega's mansion crowded in upon her.

'Samuel!' She screamed his name, turning to him to protect her.

Sam pulled away from his captors and strode across, wrenching her free from the sailors, then holding her close and putting himself between her and the enemy.

'Leave her!' The authority in his voice halted the sailors in their tracks. He met Esmee's eyes, reassuring her. Her love for him was soured by impotent rage because the Spaniards had automatically assumed she was a slave. Even the fine clothes she wore did not matter in comparison with the colour of her skin.

The sailors looked towards their Captain then turned their attention to Yinka.

'No!' Esmee wailed again in panic. She would not let her friend be taken, she would never give up her small half-sister to these enemies.

Again Samuel intervened. To Don Marco, he said: 'This lady is the wife of my uncle, Lord Craven. She is near her time. She needs the presence of her body servant. Please, Captain, leave the girl, I pray you. If you wish I will compensate you for her loss.'

The Spaniard looked from Esmee to Yinka then to Samuel. 'There will be no need,' he said, then to his men: 'Leave the women together.'

Esmee sagged against him. She felt faint with exhaustion. All the time he held her close, soothing her, whispering words of reassurance against her hair. She managed to say: 'What of Edrize?'

'I'll do whatever I can for him.'

'What of you?' Her own fears intervened.

'We will have to wait and see.'

'Sam – '

He shook his head. 'Not a word now. You must look after your son – and the babe.' His hand moved towards her belly as if he wished to caress the unborn child, then he remembered himself and stepped away. As their eyes met they both knew the baby she carried was his.

'Samuel.'

'Be brave.'

Looking up, Esmee saw Aeneas watching them. His face was stark. Pain clouded his eyes. Esmee nodded towards him, offering reassurance, but her husband looked away. She knew he had read the truth in those few moments. But it was too late now.

Samuel was looking about him, searching for somebody in the crowd. Esmee said: 'Serenity has disappeared. It was before the attack. I – I'm sure she will have come to no harm.'

'Where's Shergold?'

For the first time Esmee realised that the Minister too was missing and as she looked at Sam they both acknowledged what the other was thinking.

'My children!'

'They will be with their mother. I am sure they are safe.'

She wanted to comfort him but the Spanish officers were already escorting the women away, back to their houses where they were to collect a minimum of goods for their journey. A few were given permission to seek out their dead or dying husbands.

Don Marco called out: 'Tonight there will be a celebration. Tomorrow the women will leave.'

That evening the victors celebrated a solemn mass in the square. Along with the other women Esmee was brought out to witness the ceremony. Nearby their men too were lined up in chains to observe the Spanish act of worship.

Esmee had not seen the like before. Inside the church the bell pealed with a jubilant note. Outside the square buzzed with human activity. In spite of their captivity, she was carried along by the magic of it all: the richness of the priest's robes, the hundreds of candles punctuating the darkened square, the deep resonance of the Spanish voices as they sang the *Te Deum*.

As she watched, a statue that was larger than life was wheeled into the square. It was the figure of a woman, very beautiful, hands clasped together in an act of prayer. In her rich blue robes, she seemed to bestow a blessing upon every man in the square. As one the sailors fell to their knees, murmuring: *'Madre Maria.'*

Esmee could not make sense of it all. It seemed that this woman, Mary, who was the mother of Christ, had the power to intercede for her followers. She wondered if the statue was actually a goddess. It was all very far removed from the plain speaking of Minister Shergold.

She shook her head, holding Gideon close. She could only marvel

at the splendour of this occasion which marked the defeat of everything Sam and his compatriots had tried to create. It was beyond
her understanding.

Next morning at first light the women were roused and escorted
to the ship. As an act of kindness Don Marco permitted them a few
moments to say farewell to their husbands.

Esmee had nothing to say. She faced Aeneas in the knowledge
that yesterday he had seen behind her pretence.

Taking her hands, he smiled sadly. 'Take great care, my dear girl.
Here, I have written a letter to my brother asking him to help you
in any way he can. There are other instructions too for Oliver St
James who looks after my legal affairs.' He pushed a packet into
her hands.

'Thank you. Aeneas – '

'And I would hope that when you reach England, you will plead
for my release in any way that you can.'

'But of course.'

'As for our child . . .'

'He will be well. Please don't fret yourself. It is you I worry
about.'

He raised a quizzical brow. 'And my nephew?'

She knew her cheeks were betraying her. In an effort to divert
him, she said: 'Serenity was seen making an escape with the children. I am certain that she will be safe.'

'What better safety than with a servant of the Lord?'

She was not sure what he was saying. Squeezing her hands, he
added: 'I may be old, my dear, but I am not blind. I know Serenity
does not love Samuel and neither does he love her.'

She could not meet his eyes and he sighed. 'It was foolish of me
to do as I did. I should have known that when my nephew sent you
to England, it was not just out of kindness.'

'Aeneas – '

'It is no matter. You have brought me much pleasure, and now
the greatest gift of all – a child.' He raised his eyebrows a fraction.
'It *is* my child, I know. Of that I am confident and I praise God for
your chastity.'

She hugged him to her to avoid meeting his eyes, drawing comfort from the knowledge that he would never have to admit the
ultimate hurt: that perhaps this child too was not his. 'About Gideon
. . .' she started.

Aeneas looked wryly at her. 'I have acknowledged him as my heir,' he said: 'I shall not disown him now.'

For a moment he appeared to be thinking. Then, making up his mind, he said: 'Esmeralda, I do not know when, or even if, I shall ever return, so I am going to entrust you with a secret of the utmost importance.'

She waited, wondering what he was going to say. When he spoke he did so slowly as if emphasising the seriousness of his words.

'There are certain objects of great value that my father passed on to me. No one else knew of their existence – not my mother, nor Endymion. I tell you this because I know there is growing conflict in England. One day you might find yourself caught up in it. You and the children could truly be in danger. Then, and only then, must you even consider using these objects to secure your safety.'

'What are they?'

He ignored the question, saying: 'You must be very careful to whom you show them for even now in England they would be viewed as heretical. But I feel sure that if the time comes, you will know what to do.'

'Aeneas, I – '

'I shall tell you where they are and you must remember, but unless you have no other choice you must forget their existence, and must never, ever tell anyone about them. Not my brother or my brother-in-law – no one.'

'I won't.'

He bent close and whispered instructions into her ear.

As he drew back she went to question him again but even as she opened her mouth, Spanish sailors came to drag her away. Twisting so that she could see him one last time, she called out: 'God go with you. I will remember what you say, but before the year is out I am sure we will all be back in London.'

He raised his hand and soon was obsured from her view. Bounded on each side by her captors, Esmee walked across the plank and on to the *Greyhound*.

As she went, she wondered if her prediction could be true, and if it was, what sort of future awaited her then.

THIRTY-SEVEN

The *Greyhound* was only three days from Eden Island when Esmee's labour pains began. They started as a dull ache, an undefined tightness around her belly. Before long there was a regular pattern as if her insides were being stretched like fingers forced into too small a glove.

In one way the pains were a relief for since they has set foot on the ship she had found no escape from the agony of wondering what would become of Samuel and his friends. Very soon the pains came faster. Although they were severe, there was none of the nightmarish terror that had preceded Gideon's birth. Yinka, mother of two children, sat beside her and pronounced that each time it got easier.

Within two hours of the first twinge, Esmee began to push her baby out into the world. As the *Greyhound* undulated over the open sea, a tiny girl was deposited on to her decks.

'Is a daughter!' Yinka cried out in delight.

Until this moment Esmee had not seriously considered that the babe would be a girl but as the infant lay across her, she felt a moment of supreme hope. This baby would not be a rival to Gideon for Aeneas's estates. There would be none of the animosity that might have developed between brothers.

It seemed appropriate that, like herself, her daughter should be born at sea. The very fact that it was a girl confirmed in her mind that this was not Aeneas's child. He had expected a son. Instead he had a great-niece.

'What you call?' Yinka busied herself with the afterbirth. Esmee knew that her friend too welcomed the distraction of the child. Of all those taken from Eden, Edrize would be among the most vulnerable. In a moment of reflection, she prayed: If there is a God, let

308

our men live. She remembered the huge statue the Spaniards had paraded around New Bristol. They had been victorious. Perhaps their Mary was more powerful than the hazy God she had just petitioned. In any case, a goddess would be more likely to understand. Revising her prayer, she said: Mary, God's mother, please bring our men safely back to us.

'What you call?' Yinka repeated her question, and Esmee studied her daughter. The little girl had dark waving hair, like her own. She searched the face, looking for signs of Samuel. Surely she could see him in the shape of her child's nose, the set of her mouth? Reluctantly she reminded herself that, like Aeneas, Samuel was a Craven. In spite of Sam's blond hair, Aeneas's brown locks, and even his brother Endymion's black curls, the three men had a certain similarity of feature. Anyway it was no matter. The babe was precious to her beyond words.

'Tamar. Her name is Tamar.'

'Why you call her that?'

'It was my grandmother's name.' Esmee said it with pride, for the first time ever talking of her family as other people did. Earlier she had looked in Aeneas's Bible and read about Tamar who had been deceived by her father-in-law.

To Yinka, she said: 'Tamar was twice married to brothers. When the second one died, her father-in-law did not keep his promise to wed her to his third son. Patient and virtuous, she waited in vain.'

In case some explanation was needed, she added: 'In those times a woman needed the protection of a man.' Was it so different now? It was not, she realised. Without Aeneas's protection Esmee knew she would be an outcast. The knowledge filled her with indignation but then, remembering her husband's standing and his wealth, she knew that some of that power would rub off on to her. With a sudden burst of pleasure she thought: While he is away I shall have my precious freedom back.

Returning to her story, she said: 'Tamar tricked her father-in-law into lying with her and she conceived twin boys. When he denounced her as a harlot, she revealed her identity and he knew that he alone had been her lover. Suitably humbled he allowed her to live the rest of her life in peace.'

Yinka frowned and Esmee added: 'I hope my daughter will have the same strength of spirit and find peace in her life.'

'What we do when we go to England?'

Looking at Yinka, Esmee realised that for her friend this was a step into the unknown. She said: 'There is nothing to fear. When we reach England I shall be an important lady. You shall be my personal maid. Together we will fight to get our men released, then all will be well.' In mentioning their men she had to remind herself that it was Aeneas, not Samuel, who was her husband.

They arrived in Plymouth on the last day of October 1638, to a grey day raked by razor-sharp winds. They carried nothing with them to guard against the biting cold. Esmee remembered the fur wraps and thick worsteds she had worn at Craven House, its huge fires and windproof rooms. At this moment she heartily wished herself there.

To her surprise, news of the disaster at Eden and the fate of its islanders had already reached England. As the ship tied up, a crowd had gathered to view the returning women. Such were the vagaries of fortune that many of those who had been transported to the colony as a means of punishment, now returned as free women. Representatives of the company were there to compensate them for the loss of home and husband and to see that they had all that they needed.

Surveying the waiting crowd, Esmee recognised the dark head of Endymion Craven. Her heartbeat quickened. She was both glad and afraid. She could not forget that Endymion had been foremost in opposing his brother's marriage. Would he help or hinder her now? In him she sensed the first hurdle she would need to overcome.

'Lady Craven.' The cynical twist of his mouth as he greeted her put her on her guard. She was aware that he in his turn was testing her out.

'Sir.' She gathered her children closer and he looked them over.

'I heard that my brother had been blessed with a new family.' He raised a questioning brow. 'I am delighted to learn he is still so potent.'

Esmee ignored him. She gave a momentary thought to Serenity, for once glad that she had had the opportunity to learn something from her reluctant step-daughter. In her most haughty voice, she said: 'I have here documents from my husband. It is his wish that I take up residence in London and he requests that you give me all the assistance I require. He expresses his hope that you will use all your influence to secure his early return.'

'But of course.' She sensed a change in his manner, a subtle reappraisal of her position.

The waiting carriage jolted and stuck as two sleek black horses strained to drag it through the mud-filled ruts. To Endymion's obvious chagrin Esmee insisted that Yinka ride inside with herself and the children.

'Sister, you risk bringing disrepute on yourself if you treat your servants as equals.'

'Then I must risk that disrepute. We are neither of us accustomed to this harsh climate.'

Again Endymion acquiesced, his expression non-committal. To make amends, he added: 'You will be an object of some envy in London, having a black girl of your own. Black boys are becoming quite the fashion these days.'

'Yinka is my friend.'

Thereafter they travelled in silence.

As Craven House came into view, Esmee remembered the months she had passed beneath its roof. Here she had been both servant and companion and eventually mistress of the house. Here she had endured Serenity's criticism, Aeneas's patronage, and learned the very skills that she would now need to help her survive.

As they went through the front door and into the dark vestibule, she was aware of the signs of Endymion's occupation. Discarded boots and cloaks littered the space. Going into the parlour, she saw the remains of a meal scattered over the table. Jugs and bottles of Aeneas's wine lined the mantel shelf and side cupboard.

Esmee said: 'Where have you been living while we have been away?'

She saw him flush, with both irritation and embarrassment. 'I thought it my duty to keep an eye on my brother's servants. I felt it necessary to be near at hand in case of trouble.'

Pointedly Esmee looked around her at the chaos. 'Well, I am sure my husband would thank you for that but now that I am back, it will no longer be necessary.'

As Endymion went to protest, she stopped him with a look, adding: 'And neither would it be fitting.' He had no need to ask if he had overstepped the mark.

Visibly smarting, he asked: 'Am I permitted to take refreshment before I leave?'

'But of course.'

He made her a curt bow.

Esmee ordered the fires to be lit and wine to be brought.

311

While they waited, she chose as her bed chamber the room once occupied by Serenity and Hannah Hardy. It was large and draught-proof and here she installed herself, Yinka and all four children. With delight she thought: Now I shall have the freedom to be with the babies both day and night.

Having found warm clothes, she realised it would be wise to soothe Endymion's ruffled feathers. Coxcomb and wastrel he might be, but she still remembered he had influence with the Queen of England.

She personally poured him a measure of brandy and as she handed it over, told him: 'I know I can rely on you to take every step necessary to secure the release of your brother and your nephew, but how will you go about it?'

Mellowing a little, he said: 'I have contacts who will speak to the Spanish Ambassador.' As his confidence returned, he bowed to her, suddenly gallant and flirtatious. 'Have no fear, dear lady. Your husband will soon be back at your side.' His lips twitched as if he found the idea that Esmee could want Aeneas back amusing.

She too bowed her head but ignored his insinuation. 'I know that I can rely upon you. How long do you think it will take?'

'We-ll.' He thought long and hard, finally saying: 'It will be delicate and costly, but if all goes well, there might be some news within six months.'

Esmee decided there and then that she would give him three.

THIRTY-EIGHT

'I think you should hear this.' Endymion Craven, coming into his brother's house, composed his features into an expression of concern.

As he approached, Esmee felt the familiar tightening in her chest. In the three months since she had been back in England, Endymion had been an almost daily visitor. It had not escaped her attention that when he could, he still ate freely at his brother's table and drank liberally from his cellar, ordered the household servants around as if they were his own and frequently borrowed Aeneas's horses.

He doesn't really care, she thought. It doesn't matter to him what becomes of Aeneas or Samuel. His only interest is the estate.

'It's not bad news?' She too composed her features, trying to be calm, not allowing him to see her agitation. She signalled to Yinka to pour him a glass of brandy. The girl did so then retired.

Taking the glass across to the fire, Endymion drained it as he went. The smoky grey of the glass flickered, reflecting the embers. He stood with his back to the glow, slapping his hands against his thighs to bring some warmth to them. Outside it was snowing.

'Shall I read it to you?' He produced a copy of the *Examiner*, unfolding it and then re-folding it to highlight an article.

'There's no need.' Esmee felt her hackles rise at the imputation that she could not read but he ignored her.

Bending the sheet to get the benefit of the light, he announced: ' "The latest Intelligence concerning those Prisoners held in Spain." '

He cleared his throat and glanced to see if she was listening before continuing.

' "Appeals by His Majesty's envoy to Madrid have again fallen on deaf ears. Until some settlement can be agreed over ownership

313

of various Caribbean islands, it seems unlikely that those unfortunate men held hostage by the Spanish have any chance of returning to the land of their birth. The envoy has not been permitted to visit them but unconfirmed reports suggest that the following Englishmen are still alive ...'' ' He skimmed down the list of names, finally saying: 'Aeneas, Lord Craven, owner of Craven House in the Stronde and of various estates in the counties of Berkshire and Buckinghamshire; Secretary of the Eden Company – and so on.'

He folded the news sheet and laid it aside. 'That's all,' he said. 'There is so much turmoil in England at this present time that there is little space for much foreign news.'

'Doesn't it say anything else?' Esmee wanted to snatch the paper away, avid to see the news in writing. Fear clawed at her as she added: 'Does it not mention his nephew?'

Endymion grinned sardonically. 'Yes, it mentions him. I thought you would be most interested in hearing about your husband.'

'I am.' She bent to put a log on the fire to hide her feelings. To divert him, she said: 'Are our own negotiations not continuing?'

'Of course. We have been trying to arrange for some sort of ransom. So far nothing has been settled.'

Esmee could hear the sound of her own heart thumping. She pictured Samuel in a filthy gaol, sick and without any form of comfort. Would he know that she had authorised one thousand pounds of Aeneas's money to be paid over if he and Samuel were released? She wondered what she would do if the Spaniards said they would only release one of them.

For a moment she thought of her husband, older, frailer, living with the knowledge that his wife loved another man. Her guilty thoughts tormented her, then she turned her anger towards Endymion. How did she know he was really doing anything to secure the captives' release? It suited him very well the way things were.

To calm herself, she asked: 'Have you no news of Serenity?'

Endymion grinned. 'The last I heard she had arrived in Barbados. It seems she is the disciple and hand maiden of the new Messiah – Sherwood or some such name. He is sorely pricking the sides of the planters there, trying to turn them all into saints.'

Dismissing the subject and tilting his head to one side, he said: 'But what of you, dear lady? I feel the greatest sympathy for your predicament. It must be difficult to be so young and full of life, yet consigned to an indefinite form of widowhood.' He stepped closer.

314

'You are like a beautiful butterfly condemned to be always in her chrysalis.'

'I have enough to occupy me with the children.' Esmee brushed his remarks aside.

She tried to think the best of him. Contrary to her fears when she had first returned home, he had been genuinely helpful, alerting the authorities as to what had happened in Eden, using his influence at court to get the matter raised at the highest levels, but still he made her feel uneasy. All the time she wondered about his motives. She knew about his reputation with women and would rather not be alone with him.

Picking up her sewing, she said: 'It is no worse for me than for Yinka – her husband too was captured.'

Endymion snorted. 'You mean the slave? You can hardly equate the two things.'

Esmee glared at him. 'No, you can't. Her situation is worse. But for me she has no one to plead for the man she loves.'

'Love.' Endymion bowed his handsome head with a dramatic sigh. Lines of dissipation were beginning to etch grooves from the corners of his mouth to his chin. He said: 'Is that what you feel for my uncle then, pretty sister-in-law?'

'Of course I do. I am his wife. He has been good to me.'

Endymion sighed again: 'Oh, Esmee, you torment me with your ways. You were never meant to live the life of a nun. What is a poor, lonely man to do?'

'You are neither lonely nor poor.' Getting up, she crossed to the door and opened it pointedly.

'I thank you for coming, but now perhaps you should leave.'

With a gesture of assent he walked to the door but as he drew level with her, turned and said: 'Such a pity a man cannot marry his brother's wife. If your husband does not return, then one day you will be desired by every man in England.'

'Even with my brown skin?'

'A rich, beautiful woman of whatever hue would win the heart of any red-blooded Englishman. And one as beautiful as you . . .'

'Endymion, please!' She opened the door wider and with an exaggerated bow he walked out.

With a sigh Esmee closed the door behind him and leaned back against it to gather her wits, then she scurried across and picked up the copy of the *Examiner* which he had left on the settle. Taking it to the window, she spread it out and began to read.

With her fingers she followed down the line of names until she came to the one that mattered most: 'Samuel Rushworth – former Governor of Eden Island, step-son and heir to Lord Silchester of Mountford'.

The sight of his name seemed to summon him from the very page. Esmee sank on to the settle and screwed up the paper, clutching it to her chest. Praise God, he was still alive, but for how long? She could not conceive of the time when he would return. In the meantime she was alone in this cold, bleak city, pointed at when she went to church, whispered about when she dared to take the air. She felt as much of a prisoner as Samuel.

'Piccannin is hungry.'

Yinka's voice jerked Esmee out of her reverie. Wiping her hands over her skirts, she reached out to take her baby.

'And how are you then, my little pet?' She pulled back the bonnet that threatened to obscure the infant's face and looked into the brown eyes that beamed up at her. 'How is mother's dearest little girl?' As she spoke she unfastened her bodice and placed the baby to her breast.

'She grow fast,' Yinka observed.

'Very fast.'

As the child fed, Esmee teased the dark curls away from her damp temples. Little Tamar was the sweetest thing imaginable.

'Tamar? Why on earth do you call her that?' Endymion had expressed disbelief when she had announced what her daughter was named.

'It was my grandmother's name.' Again she said it with pride, enjoying the pleasure of talking about her family as other people did.

The door opened and Gideon came toddling in.

'Mama.' He held out his arms, scrabbling to climb on to her lap, and she lifted him, caressing the crown of his head with her cheek. As always she felt a tightening in her belly as she remembered again the dark moment of his conception, but immediately it was swept away by exquisite tenderness at the sight of his small sturdy body, still covered with soft baby flesh.

'And how is Mother's boy?'

He took her thumb and put it into his mouth, imitating the guzzling noise that Tamar made. Esmee laughed and held him close.

No one, not even Endymion, had questioned that her son might not be legitimate. So closely did he resemble her that no one looked for his father's stamp. For the moment at least her children seemed secure.

As Gideon's eyelids grew heavy and Tamar dozed over her feed, Esmee gazed at the flickering logs in the grate. The colours and heat reminded her of Eden. For all its troubles, she longed to be back there. When both the children slept she carried them upstairs and curled them up together in the crib that for generations had held the Craven heirs then tiptoed back downstairs. Again she picked up the *Examiner* and searched through it for the other news, but it was full of the troubles between the King and his Ministers which did not interest her.

She returned to the report of the prisoners, smoothing out the sheet, tracing Samuel's name with her finger. She checked the date of the journal and found it was a week old. Something might well have happened since then. They could even be on their way home. She rocked herself, drawing comfort from that possibility.

Outside the world was lit with a cold mantle of snow and frost. The houses opposite were touched with white. A horse and carriage formed a fleeting black silhouette as they passed the window, hooves and wheels muffled by the dusting of snow. She sighed. Never had she seen snow before, but although from the window it looked soft and comforting she knew it to be cold and harsh – like this country, she thought.

She looked again at the list of names almost as if it was the print itself that determined whether they lived or died. Edrize of course would not be there, neither would lowly sailors like Ezra or Nat or Thomas. The knowledge made her angry. How could their lives be less important than those of other men like Aeneas?

At that moment Yinka came in with her supper on a tray and Esmee chided herself for her laziness. In comparison with the black girl's her life was easy. She tried to imagine what it must be like to be stolen away from a hot, light place like Africa, to lose your family, suffer at the hands of someone like Jeronimo, then find a brief glimmer of hope in the love of a young man – only to lose him again, perhaps forever. Getting up, she gave Yinka a hug.

'Don't lose heart,' she said. 'I am going to sort things out.'

As the weeks passed, Esmee continued to derive comfort from

317

having her children close by both night and day. Curled up nightly in her large bed, she revelled in the fact that for the present there was no man to dictate how and when she might spend time with her babies. Yinka's presence in the room gave her a sense of safety, as once long ago she had drawn comfort from Accubah's closeness.

Tonight, however, she regretted not sleeping alone for she had business of a very private nature to conduct.

In spite of the temptation to do otherwise, she had kept her promise to Aeneas and not sought out the treasure he kept hidden in his house. Sometimes she passed near the place it was secreted and had to fight not to let her eyes be drawn in that direction. She had no idea what it might be. Aeneas had implied it could be dangerous. How? The instructions for finding it were engraved on her mind and this afternoon she had decided the time had come to act. Until she knew what the treasure was, she had no idea what its usefulness might be.

By the time that Yinka and all four children were sleeping soundly it must have been well after midnight. Only then did Esmee risk creeping from her bed and down to the parlour.

Aeneas's daily sitting room was a low-ceilinged oblong, lit on two sides by windows and insulated by rich panelling on all four walls. As Esmee crept into the room her eyes were drawn immediately in the direction of the wall to the left of the fireplace.

The fire itself was little more than a glow the size of an apple. Bending down, she teased it into life with a handful of dried grass and a few pieces of kindling. Taking a smoking stick from the fire, she reached up and lit a candle in the sconce just to her left. It unveiled the delicate intricacy of the wooden panelling around it, alternating squares of deeply pleated linen-fold with smooth plain quadrates.

Taking a deep breath, Esmee began to count the panels. Five along and two down from the ceiling . . . With trembling fingers she felt her way around the appropriate square, stopping at every knot and indentation until suddenly she found it: a peg so small it was barely visible. Her heart thumping with excitement, she pushed it hard. Silently the panel swung back to reveal a hidden cupboard.

Nervously she reached into the dark space, fighting an unreasoning terror that some long immured monster might grab her and drag her into the hidden depths. Her hands closed over some sort of box.

Carefully she lifted it out and carried it across to the fire. It was

318

not very big, perhaps ten or eleven inches long and five or six deep. Setting it down on the woven rug that Aeneas prized so much, she fiddled with the clasp until at last the lid lifted.

Inside there was a squarish object wrapped in cloth. She lifted it out and unfolded the covering. With amazement she gazed at a painting small enough to hold in her hands. Esmee knew little about art but one glance told her that here was a work of great beauty. As she looked at it she was drawn simultaneously back to Filipe Ortega's house, where a portrait of a woman stood above an altar in his own private chamber, then to the square in New Bristol where the victorious Spaniards had paraded a statue of their goddess on the night of the town's capture. Here again was the same likeness of Mary the mother of Christ, but painted in the richest golds and blues she had ever seen. The face had a serene quality as if some inner light shone through from her very soul.

Esmee found it hard to put the painting aside but eventually did so, looking again into the box and drawing out a second smaller package. As she carefully unwrapped it she felt her heartbeat increase. There, in the folds of the linen, lay a crucifix. It was just about the same length and breadth as the palm of her hand. In the now flickering firelight it glowed richly, its gold liberally embedded with white and red and green stones which she guessed to be pearls and rubies and emeralds.

For an age she simply sat on the rug, looking from one object to the other, then a distant creaking of a floorboard or door reminded her that at any moment somebody could walk in. Hastily she wrapped up the treasures, replaced them in the box then slipped it into the hole behind the panelling.

With a sigh of wonder she sat down and tried to absorb what she had found and what it all meant. These were clearly Catholic icons. In this lay their danger. While at court the Queen and her closest friends openly practised their Popish religion, in theory such worship was outlawed. Those not protected by the Queen and in her wake, the King, could expect short shrift.

Aeneas was certainly not a Catholic, but he loved beauty. In possessing these objects he had something of great artistic and monetary value. No wonder he had been loath to let them go.

Esmee searched her mind, trying to think what she could do. Surely somebody, some wealthy Catholic would pay highly for them? Only she did not want money. What she needed was the right

319

contacts, a lifeline to those Spanish noblemen who negotiated with the King's ministers and had the power to make decisions.

Elated by her discovery, and knowing that she needed a clear head for the morrow, she returned pensively to her bed.

'I have been thinking . . .' Esmee said to Endymion, who had called round to borrow Aeneas's carriage. He did not spell out exactly why he needed it but Esmee suspected he had an assignation with a woman and needed somewhere weatherproof and discreet in which to entertain her.

'I miss being able to speak Spanish. I was wondering about giving a dinner and perhaps inviting you and some of your Spanish friends.'

Endymion shrugged. Clearly he had more pressing things on his mind.

'Perhaps you know somebody who might have news of what is happening in Spain?' she persisted.

He gave a little laugh. 'Are you thinking of charming them with your beauty, my dear?' His grin broadened and he turned his attention full on her. 'You might do well at that. Perhaps you could sell your virtue in return for your husband's release – what greater sacrifice could a faithful wife make?'

She snorted impatiently at him. 'I am merely saying I would like an opportunity to meet whoever it is with whom you are negotiating.' To make her intentions clearer, she added: 'Perhaps he could bring his wife?'

Ignoring her last remark, he said: 'And what would be in it for me? I should prefer to dine with you alone.'

'The knowledge that you are doing everything you can to rescue your brother!'

'Ah, that, of course.' He smiled teasingly at her.

Esmee flashed him a warning look. 'Whether my husband comes back or not,' she reminded him, 'it is my – *his* son that is heir to this estate and I am his guardian. Really, Endymion, there is nothing in it for you except the knowledge of doing your duty.'

'Not even the tiniest kiss?'

'Invite your Spanish friends round first.'

To her amazement, when next he called round, her brother-in-law said: 'I have taken the liberty of inviting Don Alfonso de Carreras to call on you on Thursday next. I have promised him a splendid meal and the best wine from your husband's cellar.'

'Will you be staying?' Esmee had the feeling of setting in motion something she would not be able to stop. She needed to see this man alone but was afraid of what might happen.

How would she find a way of introducing the subject of the treasures? Once he had seen them, how could she rely on his discretion? Supposing he told Endymion? Supposing he threatened to blackmail her with the knowledge? Supposing he took them and then failed to keep his promise?

'You wish me to stay – or are you planning an intimate dinner for two?'

'I – I should like an opportunity to talk to him alone.'

Endymion looked at her sulkily. 'Does that mean you are going to allow him certain privileges that you deny me?'

'Certainly not!'

'Well, dear sister, pretty as you are, I think it will take more than a few smiles to persuade him to intercede on your behalf.' He came closer. 'I hope you aren't going to embarrass me? I've gone to some trouble to persuade him to come here – he isn't the sort of man who does anything for nothing.'

She raised her shoulders philosophically. 'We shall see.'

Endymion reached out and lifted her chin. 'How about that little kiss?'

'After the visit.'

Esmee thought about it night and day, going over and over it in her head. By the time the day arrived she was in a state of panic. Only by concentrating on the arrangements for the meal could she control her anxiety.

'You make big fuss,' observed Yinka.

'This Spaniard might help to rescue our men.'

'Ah. What you give him?'

'Whatever he wants.'

Don Alfonso de Carreras was a man who had seen the best and the worst that the world could offer. In his forties, short, with a rounded belly and black wavy hair that hung to his shoulders, his eyes would have looked at home on a vulture: watchful, ready to pounce at the first sign of weakness. As Esmee met his gaze it was totally devoid of compassion.

'Don Alfonso, it is a great honour to have someone from your country at my table.' She curtseyed low, knowing that the neckline of her gown allowed the curve of her breasts to be glimpsed before she stood up again. All the time she had the terrible feeling that Don Alfonso was waiting to eat her. His hunger appeared to be more for the delights of her body than for the dishes she was about to serve to him.

He kissed her hand. 'Senõra Craven, the honour is mine. Alone in a foreign country, I miss the comforts of home.'

She remained silent, busying herself by pouring him the best French wine the cellar held.

He sipped appreciatively, leaning back in his chair and giving himself up to the taste. Esmee feared that he viewed her as the main course.

As they ate, he talked widely of art and literature, music and hunting. Esmee struggled to reply wittily.

The bream was cooked to perfection and the lamb tender, tantalising the air with the succulent tang of rosemary. Her guest ate noisily and with gusto.

'Tell me about yourself,' Esmee asked, getting him on to his favourite topic. He talked at length about his family, its pedigree, their estates and interests. Finally he said: 'And what of yourself? How does such a tropical jewel come to be in the Arctic wastes of London?'

Esmee told him honestly of her life, taking care to emphasise that now she was rich and well-connected. If he expected something from her he must realise that there was a price to pay. He must not believe she was available for the asking.

At last she got round to the subject of Eden and the events that had resulted in her husband's capture.

'So as you can imagine, I would give anything to secure the release of those friends and relations still in Spain,' she finished.

'Perhaps there is some way in which I can help.' He put down his glass and wiped his mouth with his fingers.

'Perhaps there is.' Esmee rose from the table, a little unsteadily because in her nervousness she had imbibed several glasses of the wine. She poured Don Alfonso a generous measure of brandy and said: 'I do appreciate your giving me this opportunity to speak Spanish.'

'And I appreciate the opportunity to sit opposite a lady of such infinite beauty.'

She smiled deprecatingly.

As she returned to her seat, he observed: 'It is such a filthy night. Perhaps I should stretch the kindness of your hospitality further . . .'

Now was the time to act. The wine had dulled her anxieties but she knew she was walking a fine line – decline his suggestion of bed now and he would lose interest in her; let him hope for her sexual favours and she might not be able to withdraw them later. She said: 'To be frank, Don Alfonso, I invited you here to discuss something of great delicacy.'

'Of course, dear Donna Esmeralda.'

'I – I need to be certain that I can rely on your discretion.'

'But naturally.'

'Then I have something to show you.'

Knowing that there was no going back, she invited him to take a seat near the fire then retired to her room where she had earlier secreted the treasures.

When she returned he was standing near the hearth, admiring a tapestry that hung on the opposite wall.

'How charming. Your husband has good taste, I think.'

This was the opening she needed. Seating herself so that Don Alfonso was bound to draw nearer, she said: 'Am I right in believing you may be able to help in securing the release of Aeneas and his friends?'

He made a doubtful noise in his throat as if the difficulties were almost too large to contemplate.

'I realise that you would not do so without some form of reward.' As she spoke, she unwrapped the portrait of the Madonna and handed it to him in silence.

Don Alfonso took it and moved closer to the fire again. He let out a whistle of surprise. 'But this is exquisite – quite beautiful.'

As he turned to look at her she held out the crucifix. Again he studied it by firelight, weighing it in his hand, turning it this way and that.

'I have never seen anything so perfect. Where did you get it?'

'I cannot say. I can only tell you that it is mine to dispose of as I see fit.' She paused, giving weight to her next words. 'Let us just say that I would be willing to give it to anyone who could secure the return of my husband – and a few other valued friends.'

'I see.' He looked thoughtful. 'Well now, if it turned out that I could arrange such a thing, how would I know you would not change your mind – after the event as it were?'

'You would have to trust me.' She met his gaze.

'How many men are we talking about?' he countered.

Quickly she did a calculation. 'Six. My uncle and his nephew, three seamen to whom I owe a certain loyalty, and an African slave.'

His eyebrows shot up. 'You owe him loyalty too?'

'I do.' Knowing that she was taking a risk, she added: 'I have to stipulate that the bargain would only apply if all of these men were returned.' She feared he might otherwise not bother himself about Edrize and the seamen.

Don Alfonso thought, then let out a short laugh. 'Does your brother-in-law know what you plan?'

'No. That is another condition of the agreement. He must know nothing of this at all.'

He pulled a rueful face. 'Then he was wrong when he led me to believe that perhaps you were hoping to offer your body in exchange for your husband's return?'

Esmee blinked fast. 'That is not my intention. I imagine the other items have a far more lasting value.'

Don Alfonso gave a laugh. 'I have to say, I am relieved to hear it. Nothing is more tedious than for a lady to offer herself and then expect a huge recompense. I have to say, dear lady, that beautiful as you are, I no longer set the same value on possessing a woman as I might have done twenty years ago. Forgive me for saying so, but the delights of one night in your bed chamber would not be worth the time and energy needed to arrange your husband's release.'

She felt her spirits rise. 'Then you are saying you could arrange it?'

He nodded his head slowly.

Esmee flopped back in her chair, her cheeks burning.

'Then, Don Alfonso, I pledge to you that I will give the treasures to you the moment the men set foot on England.' Heady with triumph, she added: 'And now, if you wish, I will arrange for my carriage to take you home.'

THIRTY-NINE

'Was your evening successful?' Endymion asked the question with a superior smirk, regarding Esmee as if she was a naive child with no idea what she was about.

'I thank you, yes.' She inclined her head and turned away so he should not see her expression.

When she did not enlighten him further he continued: 'So, when do you expect your husband to arrive then – next week . . . tomorrow?'

She detected an edge of jealousy in his voice and declined to reply. Suitably provoked, he added: 'You think now he has had what he wants, Don Alfonso will keep his side of the bargain?'

'Ah, but he hasn't had what he wants yet.' She smiled sweetly at him and before he could question her further, left the room.

Although she was pleased with the prospect of tormenting her brother-in-law, in the cold light of day she was beginning to have innumerable doubts. The conversation of the previous evening suddenly seemed unreal. There was no guarantee that Don Alfonso would carry out his promise. They had made no arrangement to meet again, no provision to report on the progress of his mission – assuming that it ever took place. In reality she could do no more than continue as before and hope that her efforts bore fruit. She would have to wait and see.

But as the days became weeks, Esmee became increasingly demoralised. The more she tried to visualise it, the more that fateful evening seemed like a hazy dream. Endymion made no reference to it and her pride would not allow her to ask him if he had news of Don Alfonso's whereabouts. She had to keep imagining that the Spaniard had gone straightaway to Spain and was even now escorting the English party back home.

Then one afternoon about six weeks later, when Esmee was preparing to go with the children into the garden to pick dandelions to make into wine, Yinka came to find her.

'Spaniard. He here to see you.'

For a dreadful moment she thought the girl meant Filipe Ortega, then with rising hope and fear she realised who Yinka was talking about. Leaving the children in the garden she ran for the house, wiping her discoloured fingers on the skirt of her gown.

'Don Alfonso.' She bowed, striving to appear calm.

'Donna Esmeralda. You look charming.'

She acknowledged his compliment, aware of her stained skirts and ruffled hair. Struggling to appear unconcerned, she encouraged him to take a seat. 'May I offer you some sack or a glass of brandy?'

'I thank you but no. I am on my way to visit Lord Conway but thought I should acquaint you with the latest news.'

'She drew in her breath, trying to read his expression. It was carefully non-committal. Her mind whirled with exhilaration because something was happening, yet she dreaded the prospect of bad news.

Don Alfonso said: 'I face something of a dilemma. On the evening of our little talk you implied that unless all the gentlemen you named returned safely to these shores, you would not be prepared to part with those certain items that we mentioned.'

It was clear that the news was bad. He continued: 'Unfortunately it seems that not all of the men are still alive. As far as I can gather they have all been accounted for, but at least three of their number have died.'

'Which three?' Esmee felt behind her for the support of the table so that she could lean against it. Her breath came in anguished bursts, no longer able to sustain her against the pain of what was to come.

Don Alfonso sat forward in his seat. 'Ah, well, therein lies the difficulty. The communication I received does not say. It merely reports that only three of the six men are still living.' He eyed her shrewdly. 'This leaves me with a problem. Do I proceed with this matter, at great inconvenience to myself and with the prospect of no reward – or do I abandon the exercise?'

Esmee tried not to think of Samuel dead in some faraway place, or Aeneas dying alone or despairing, or of Edrize, wiped out before he reached the full maturity of his years.

She looked into Don Alfonso's eyes and whispered: 'Wait there.'

Head bowed she walked from the room and across to Aeneas's parlour. Once inside she felt her way along the panel with trembling fingers, clumsy in her attempt to open it. Catching her breath, she lifted out the box and withdrew one of the packages. She opened it to take one last look at the crucifix, crushing it into her palm until the sharp edges left white ridges across her hand. After replacing the casket she then hurried back across the hall and to the ante-chamber where Don Alfonso waited.

Holding out the parcel, she said: 'Here, take this as a proof of my intention. When the business is completed, I will give you the other item.' She searched his face but again the cold eyes regarded her only with greed. Glancing down at the crucifix he licked his lips like a hungry man offered a meal. He bowed his head in thanks, eyes suddenly alight with triumph.

Her voice near to breaking with despair, she said: 'No matter who lives or dies, I appeal to you, rescue them!'

'Then certainly, my dear lady. It will be an honour.'

'Don Alfonso.' She caught his sleeve as he stood up. 'You have no idea about any of the men?'

'None at all, I regret to say.' He stood back to let her precede him from the room. As she reached the front door, she asked: 'How long? How long before they return?'

He spread his hands in an expansive gesture. 'Not long.' He looked slightly discomfited, adding: 'They are already on their way but before they arrived I felt the need to confirm our bargain.' With a parting bow, he said: 'If all goes well they should be here before the week is out.'

Until that moment the days of waiting had become a way of life, a time for dreaming of what might be, of living through reunions, romantic liaisons and endless other possibilities that the mind conjured up. Now Esmee faced the stark reality. Soon, very soon, her entire future would be altered by the arrival of three men.

She almost wished for the days of uncertainty to be back. At least she had been able to imagine her own happiness. Very shortly that priceless gem of hope might be dashed forever.

Trying to steer her mind away from her own anguish she wondered whether to tell Yinka, prepare her for what might happen. The more she thought of it the more likely it seemed that Edrize, as a slave, would have succumbed to disease or starvation or just plain inhuman treatment. What should she say? What would Yinka do when she too was denied the elixir of hope? At that moment Esmee did not feel strong enough to face her friend's despair. Give her one more day of comparative peace. Once more she returned to the lottery of who lived and who died. It seemed logical that Ezra, already old and bent, would be likely to succumb. Edrize and Ezra, was that how it would be? But the third man . . . Who was the third man?

Nat and Thomas were both mature men but strong, inured to hardship. Aeneas, on the other hand, was older, softer – surely more likely to die – and yet by the very fact that he was a lord, would he not receive better treatment? Of Samuel she dared not think.

Having to face up to the world, Esmee wandered back into the garden, into the indecently cheerful spring-time. The children were plucking at the grass, filling their baskets with snatches of greenery.

'You have news?' Yinka separated herself from the little ones and came over to her. As Esmee looked at her friend she could see the barely concealed anguish. With the merest hesitation, she said: 'No news. Nothing definite yet.'

The next few days became a living hell. Esmee tried to conduct some sort of normal routine but all the time her eyes were drawn to the windows at the back of the house, staring along the wide expanse of garden that led down to the river, or craning her neck to see out over the wall and into the busy thoroughfare at the front that led from the City.

The slightest noise made her jump, imagining that somehow the three men had crept up to the house and were about to come in, three men out of six, a one in two chance of happiness or hell.

'Whatever ails you?' Endymion, making his daily visit, looked offended as she snapped at him. She had not told him of Don Alfonso's visit. To put it into words was to make it real. Best to pretend that everything was as it was before: uncertain. She jumped as the door opened and Yinka came in with wood to store by the fire.

Knowing that Endymion was watching her, Esmee stood up. The dandelions that she had picked three days ago lay withering in a basket on the table. Catching sight of them, she said: 'Well, you had better go. I have a lot of work to do.'

He pulled a face and followed her to the door. As she gave him a curt nod, he said: 'I hope that the next time I call, you will be in a better humour.'

Esmee turned her back on him and climbed the stairs. In the gallery above she stopped to look at the portrait a Mr Van Dyke had painted of Aeneas when he was about ten years younger. He was seated in a chair with a white satin covering. His legs were stretched out in front of him, encased in silk stockings and fine white leather boots. In his hand he held soft buckskin gloves.

Esmee glanced up into his eyes as if he was actually in the room with her. His face was framed with rich brown hair, darker than when she had first met him, but his kind brown eyes were as she remembered them and looked down tenderly at her. His mouth was creased in a gentle familiar smile.

'Aeneas, I'm so sorry,' she said. 'I cannot help wishing it is Samuel who lives.'

Her thoughts were disturbed by a noise that was impossible to identify. For a moment she thought some wild creature had come into the house. The loud animal wail froze her to the spot. There was a brief silence then the sound was repeated, over and over.

Yinka! Esmee fled for the stairs, tripping in her haste. As she tumbled down the last steps she looked up to see Yinka standing by the door and beyond her the silhouettes of three figures. One of them was young and black-skinned. He hugged Yinka to him, rocking her, murmuring words of love. She continued to keen in a state of high emotion.

Esmee grabbed the banister for support. She was immediately back in the square at New Bristol when the victorious Spaniards had lined up the surviving prisoners. On that day she could not bear to look. Now she could not raise her eyes to take in the two remaining figures who stood in the doorway.

'A waggon load o' horses won't drag me outta this country again.' She heard Ezra's voice and with quaking heart her eyes strayed towards his companion.

He was looking over Ezra's shoulder, into the gloom of the hall, his eyes resting upon her, sad and serious.

'Esmee, I'm so sorry . . .'

'Samuel!' She flew to him, oblivious to everything but the knowledge that he lived.

'My dearest.' He gathered her close, enveloping her in his

329

strength. 'Hush now, hush.' Separating himself enough to look into her eyes, he said: 'I am truly sorry. Aeneas died peacefully. He had some sort of seizure. He – he talked of you and his new baby son until the end.'

Esmee wiped the tears with the back of her hand and tried to smile. 'It's a girl,' she said shakily. 'A daughter.'

Sam hugged her again. 'Well, will you not let me inside? We are travel-weary and sorely in need of refreshment.'

'Samuel, is it really you or am I dreaming?' She tucked her arm through his, her entire being light with joy. The others following behind, they made their way to Aeneas's parlour. As Esmee went, the tears began to fall again for her poor, kind, dead husband and for Nat and Thomas who had shared so much with her on the *Evangelina*. 'I'm so sorry, so very sorry,' she kept repeating.

Sam hugged her. 'You have nothing to be sorry for. You did everything you could to make my uncle happy.'

She nodded. It was true. She had never set out to hurt Aeneas. In her own way she had loved him.

Separating herself from the three men, she went with Yinka to find them food. Before long the table groaned with everything the kitchens could provide.

As they were finishing their meal, Yinka returned with the children. Esmee watched with moist eyes as Edrize gathered his son to him. At the same time he picked up Sole and kissed her soft cheek. It was a moment of pure tenderness. Looking across the room at Samuel, Esmee held her own baby close and said: 'This is Tamar, my daughter.'

'Tamar.' Sam looked at the little girl then met Esmee's eyes. With more unshed tears that threatened to spill over, she nodded to him, too moved to speak, acknowledging that he was looking for the first time on his daughter.

Late into the evening, when Ezra had been found a room of his own and Yinka and Edrize had retired with the children to the room Yinka normally shared with her mistress, Esmee found herself alone with the man she loved.

Sitting over a dying fire, sipping wine, they talked quietly of the past months and all that had come to pass.

'So, my dear, you are now a widow.' Samuel looked ruefully at her.

'I am.' Knowing what he was thinking, she added: 'I hear Serenity is in Barbados – with Minister Shergold.'

Sam nodded his head, gazing at the embers. 'So you are free but I am not.'

'That is how it seems.'

For an eternity neither of them spoke. Eventually Esmee said: 'As your uncle's nephew, it would be quite natural for you to stay here.'

He shook his head. 'I would not choose to live off his estate – or more properly, off your son's as I believe.'

'Aeneas left everything in trust for Gideon when he comes of age. I am to be his guardian.'

There was a moment of silence, then Sam asked: 'Who is Gideon's father?'

Esmee looked across at him. There was no longer room for lies. She said: 'It happened only once, the night we reached Barbados – it was my father.'

She waited for his abhorrence but it was not forthcoming. He merely shook his head as if at the mystery of life.

He said: 'I went to Fonseca once – to San Bernaldo.' He told her about the Caribs and the girl.

Esmee moved across to him and put her arms around his shoulders. 'What shall we do?'

'I don't know.' He pulled her on to his knees and kissed her hair. 'There is nothing that we can do. I have a wife. At best I can only be your lover.'

'At best? That *is* the best!' She bent forward and kissed him again.

Reaching up, he smoothed her hair, thinking it was sleek as the wing of a raven. He had a sudden fanciful thought that as the Tower of London would surely fall if the ravens left, then so would his life collapse without the presence of Esmeralda. Aloud, he said: 'You might wish to remarry.'

'To whom?' She gave a laugh. 'Why should I choose to be a wife when I can be a mistress? Don't you see? For the first time in my life I am free. I want for nothing. I have health, wealth, and now . . . Where would I find another man like you?'

She stopped, serious for a moment, resting her lips against his hair. She murmured: 'We truly have a chance of happiness.'

She saw with tenderness that his eyes were heavy with sleep.

'Come.' She grasped his hand and pulled him up.

'Where should I sleep?' He followed her up the stairs.

331

She said: 'Normally I share a chamber with Yinka but tonight she has better company.' She led him to the room that had once been hers, the room where so long ago Aeneas had attempted and failed to make his bride into his wife. She said: 'This is my chamber. If you wish you can have my uncle's room, otherwise . . .' In spite of herself she knew she was pulling him through the door. He did not resist.

They undressed in silence and lay down side by side. The hazards of the journey, the days of anxiety, the final lifting of their fears had left them both heavy with exhaustion. Sam held her close but did not try to make love to her.

'Samuel.' She pressed her lips to his shoulder.

'Esmee.' He expelled his breath with an exquisite surge of relief. 'Let us sleep a little. We have the rest of our lives to . . .' He did not finish the sentence. Moments later he was sleeping deeply, his head heavy on her breast.

Esmee stretched and it felt as if in that moment all her pain and torment fell away. In the darkness she held him close, marvelling at the upturn in her fortunes.

With some pain she remembered the last time she had seen her husband, the sadness of their parting and his admission that in marrying her he had made a mistake. It was his own folly that had led them all along the path their lives had followed. But Aeneas had truly loved her and he would not wish her to be unhappy. She had no need to feel guilty.

She thought about the painting of the Madonna that she now owed to Don Alfonso. It was quite beautiful and she regretted having to part with it, but a promise was a promise. In any case, she had something of far greater value in return.

At that moment Sam turned in his sleep and she turned with him, nuzzling his broad back with her cheek. She had no way of knowing what the future might hold, not for Samuel or herself, not for her children; not for Yinka and Edrize – or even for Serenity over in Barbados. Some day they might face hardship or danger, but her mind rebelled at thinking of anything unpleasant in the face of this perfect happiness.

'Good night, Samuel.' Pressing her lips against his shoulder, she expelled her breath with a long, luxurious release of tension. For tonight she had everyone she cared about safe under the same roof. The knowledge brought its own perfect sense of peace. Snuggling closer to Samuel, she prepared for the sweetest sleep of her life.

THE ISLAND OF FONSECA/SAN BERNALDO

Throughout the sixteenth and seventeenth centuries, the island of Fonseca was widely believed to exist. It was thought to lie to the north-east of Tobago and exact compass bearings were recorded. Sebastian Cabot marked it on his map of 1544.

In the 1630s, Spanish corsairs frequently claimed to have sought refuge on its shores. At the same time a dispute arose between the Earls of Pembroke and Carlisle, both of whom had some claim to trading rights, while the Providence Company planned a voyage of discovery but abandoned it as being too great a financial risk.

In the nineteenth century, Fonseca still appeared on certain maps, on one occasion being marked as a rock. Finally in 1852, the United States navy sent a brig, the *Dolphin*, to investigate the claims. At the site where the island was reputed to lie, ocean soundings were taken. They went down to 2,570 fathoms. The island has never been found.